Aileen Armita[...] [...]
by birth. She [...]
sight forced [...]
outside world and in 1988 she was winner
of the Woman of the Year award. She is
also the author of *Hawksmoor*, *A Dark Moon
Raging*, *Touchstone* and *Hawkrise* and the
'Chapters' series of novels, *Chapter of Innocence*, *Chapter of Echoes* and *Chapter of
Shadows*. She is married to Deric Longden,
journalist, broadcaster and author of *Diana's
Story*, *Lost for Words*, *The Cat Who Came In
From the Cold* and *I'm a Stranger Here Myself*.

THE JERICHO YEARS

Aileen Armitage

CORGI BOOKS

THE JERICHO YEARS
A CORGI BOOK : 0 552 14049 X

Originally published in Great Britain by Bantam Press,
a division of Transworld Publishers Ltd

PRINTING HISTORY
Bantam Press edition published 1994
Corgi edition published 1995

Copyright © Aileen Armitage 1994

The right of Aileen Armitage to be identified as the author of
this work has been asserted in accordance with sections 77
and 78 of the Copyright Designs and Patents Act 1988.

All the characters in this book are fictitious
and any resemblance to actual persons, living or dead,
is purely coincidental.

Conditions of Sale
1. This book is sold subject to the condition that it shall not,
by way of trade or otherwise, be lent, re-sold, hired out or
otherwise circulated in any form of binding or cover other than
that in which it is published and without a similar condition
including this condition being imposed on the subsequent
purchaser.
2. This book is sold subject to the Standard Conditions of Sale
of Net Books and may not be re-sold in the UK below the net
price fixed by the publishers for the book.

Set in 10/11pt Century Old Style by Kestrel Data, Exeter

Corgi Books are published by Transworld Publishers Ltd,
61–63 Uxbridge Road, Ealing, London W5 5SA,
in Australia by Transworld Publishers (Australia) Pty Ltd,
15–25 Helles Avenue, Moorebank, NSW 2170,
and in New Zealand by Transworld Publishers (NZ) Ltd,
3 William Pickering Drive, Albany, Auckland.

Reproduced, printed and bound in Great Britain by
Cox & Wyman Ltd, Reading, Berks.

My sincere and grateful thanks
for their expert guidance to:

David Dyson
Canon M. Haynes
Hervey Andrew Knott
and Lieutenant-Colonel Frederick Orr

and for his care and loving patience
to my husband
Deric Longden

Love snatched away, like autumn leaves,
The heart must shiver in a wintry chill,
Shrouded in diamond ice, forever still
Until
The unexpected child of spring, warm-fingered,
Brings
A new-born glow to melt
The frozen tears of sorrow.

Aileen Armitage: *Frozen Tears*

THE JERICHO YEARS

ONE

1965

The mists had rolled away from the hillside, leaving the moor exposed to the warmth of the autumn sun. A foam of purple heather amid browning bracken spread for miles ahead. Lisa's heels sank into the springy heather as she tried to keep pace with James's stride.

He glanced down. 'Cold?' he asked. 'Shall we go back to the house?'

'I wouldn't mind a cup of tea before I go.'

'Bart, here boy.' The sheepdog raised its head as James swung around to where the farm lay nestling in the hollow. 'It's a hard land is this,' he muttered. 'Kind to neither man nor beast.'

'But beautiful,' Lisa countered. 'Just look at those hills.'

He looked up at the far dark blur. 'Beautiful right enough,' he agreed, 'but harsh. Generations of my folk have found that out.'

Lisa said nothing, watching the dog frisking ahead of them. For her Yorkshire was all that a homeland should be, strong and protective, the undulating hills of the Pennine chain enclosing Jericho Farm in a maternal embrace. There was reassurance in their enduring strength.

James seemed to sense her disagreement. He dug his hands deeper into the pockets of his duffle coat as he strode down the rough track towards the road.

'Too many Hemingways have given up their lives to this place,' he growled, 'struggling to wrest a living out of the land. I've spent all my life here, but I'm lucky, I've only to play at it nowadays. And I'm glad David went away.'

She glanced up at him, his dark hair blown back in the breeze, eyes half-closed against the wind. 'You got away in the war, didn't you?' she asked. 'When you were in the army?'

He chuckled, and she could see the gleam of his teeth in the sunlight. 'Know how far afield I got? All the way to Catterick, that's where. Not forty miles away.'

The road wound down ahead of them towards the farm. A man wearing a trilby and a tweed jacket was striding uphill towards them, swinging his walking stick in measured rhythm with his step. Bart bounded up to him, wagging his tail. The man greeted James with a cheery wave of the stick and James gave a curt nod in reply.

'Neighbour of yours?' asked Lisa when he had passed.

James shrugged. 'Comer-in. One of those rich folk who bought up property round here as weekend homes just after the war. He took over Thaxton Manor but we never see him for months on end.'

'Hardly a comer-in, surely,' said Lisa. 'The war's been over twenty years.'

James looked down at her with a grin. 'Not round here, it hasn't.'

On the blustering breeze came the sound of a sharp crack, and then another. Bart stopped snuffling in the hedgerow and Lisa looked back. 'What was that?'

James jerked a thumb towards the western skyline. 'Shotgun – it'll be the brigadier and his friends out shooting grouse again.'

They reached the farm gate. Lisa could see a row of pigeons squatting along the ridge of the roof. James paused, his hand on the latch.

'I'm thinking of selling up,' he said quietly.

Involuntarily she laid a hand over his, felt his palm turn up to meet hers. 'James, you can't! Not after centuries of Hemingways . . .'

He squeezed her hand. 'That's just it. It sucks you up, dries you out, clinging on to tradition. I wouldn't have that happen to David.'

She understood him now. Whatever his feelings for Jericho, he was determined to free his son to live his own life. She touched his arm.

'I'll have that cup of tea now,' she said softly, 'and then I must be on my way or I'll be late.'

She surveyed his tall, broad figure as he led the way across the straw-strewn cobbles of the farmyard, the dog scampering after him. He opened the door then stood back to let her enter. The warmth of an open fire greeted her in the old stone-flagged scullery with its rows of open shelves loaded with dishes and gleaming brass pans.

She sat down at the deal table littered with papers and watched him pour tea carefully into a china cup, its delicate fragility oddly at variance with the ruggedness of the man and his broad, capable hands. He nudged the papers aside and set the cup and saucer before her.

'How is my son?' he asked. 'Still painting?'

Lisa hesitated. 'He's fine. Busy on a new collection of posters – you should see them. He's so original.'

'He was always that,' James agreed with a slow smile, 'but still not earning much, is he?'

Lisa spread her hands. 'We earn enough between us to get by. We're fine.'

She could see he wasn't taken in. He shook his head as he picked up the teapot to fill his cup. 'He never did give a damn about money. But London's a dear place to live. Not like St Ives.'

Lisa sipped thoughtfully for a moment. 'David loved the light there. I thought he'd enjoy the stimulation of other artists around. But he couldn't sell much and

13

it seemed to make sense to go back to London. At least I could get work.'

James leaned his fists on the table, 'Listen, if ever you need a hand . . .' he said, the awkwardness of his tone belying the directness of his violet-blue eyes.

'Thanks, James. We're fine, honestly.'

He pulled back a chair with one foot and sat down. Bart rested his muzzle on his master's thigh. 'You weren't either of you really cut out for the hippy scene,' James remarked. 'All that living in communes.'

She knew what he was thinking. It was difficult for him to come to terms with the permissive age, free love. She could anticipate his next question.

'Have you two talked about – you know?' He tilted his cup, his eyes on the liquid as it poured into the saucer. Bart licked his lips expectantly.

Lisa shook her head. 'There's no hurry. If ever we decide to have children . . .'

She saw the sudden light in his clear eyes. 'Children? You'd need a proper home, with a garden . . .'

'In time, James, not yet.'

He put the saucer of tea on the floor, then stirred a spoonful of sugar into his cup. 'You know, Jericho'll fetch a fair price with all the improvements . . .'

She could hear Bart lapping noisily as she put her cup down. 'I wouldn't part with it in a hurry if I were you – so much of your life, your memories . . .'

James ran his fingers along Bart's back and the dog stopped drinking just long enough to enjoy it. 'That's just it, love. I'm beginning to think there comes a time to part with the past, let it go.'

He leaned back with a sigh. 'I'm only glad David found you,' he went on. 'You believe in him. You're good for my boy.'

She smiled and stood up. 'We're both good for him. Look, I'd better go now. The interview's at twelve.'

He led the way along the carpeted corridor through the newer part of the house, the wing which had once been barns and byres but was now divided on different levels into finely-furnished bedrooms, sitting rooms and a lavish kitchen.

'It's a lovely old house,' Lisa murmured.

He smiled back over his shoulder. 'Anna's doing. She was the one with the artist's eye. David gets it from her. You'd have loved Anna.'

She followed him out of the door and down to the roadside where her battered Mini lay wearily on the verge, the sunlight betraying the flecks of rust. She lifted the door to jerk it open then turned to James.

'Do you have to sell Jericho? I'd hate to see it go. You could always sell off another pocket of land if you need the money.'

He shook his head. 'It's not that. I've money enough – I haven't touched Anna's yet. I just don't want you two feeling you've got a duty to the place. It's time to let go.'

'We love it, James. Me just as much as David.'

A sudden smile chased away the frown from his weather-tanned face. 'Be off with you now, or you'll be late. I'd like you to get that job – maybe I'll see more of you then.'

'I'll have a damn good stab at it. You'll know just as soon as I hear.'

As she reached up to kiss him her lips felt his cheek crease into a smile. She was turning to get into the car when she felt his hand cup her elbow. 'Give the lad a hug from me when you get home – tell him I wish him all the best.'

Lisa switched on the engine. A sputtering noise ebbed and died. She tried again. 'Shit!'

And then silently the car began to move. James was pushing her downhill, his dark head bent between broad shoulders. As the old car gathered speed Lisa slammed it into gear and heard with relief the engine cough and splutter into life.

She could see through the mirror James's tall

figure waving to her all the way down to the bottom of the hill.

He watched the old car snaking away down the lane towards the village. She drove with all the carefree confidence of youth, he thought, with the sure touch of a woman who knew what she was doing. If only Ellen were more like her . . .

Lisa was good for David, just as Anna had been good for him. A man needed a woman with drive and determination, a woman who truly believed in him. A woman with a smile lighting her face and trust in the depths of innocent eyes could melt away all the doubts and fears which beset a man in his darker moments.

More shots rang out. With a sigh he turned back to the house. He must sweep the leaves from Anna's terrace before they drifted against the walls. Mouldering leaves, decay and death . . . He hated the melancholy of autumn and the memories it evoked.

TWO

1938

But spring was flooding the whole of the Garthdale valley with glorious sunlight the day he first set eyes on Anna. It was May Day, and Father had laid all the hands off for the occasion.

'Get yourselves off down to the fair,' he'd ordered. 'Have a good time and come back fresh for work in the morning.'

So it was that James was lolling on the grass under one of the elms bordering the village green, watching the passers-by until it was time for the tug-of-war. Chatter and laughter filled the air, mingled with the sound of tinny music from a barrel-organ, and over by the church a gaggle of children were being marshalled into order to begin the maypole dancing.

Two girls strolled by, arm in arm, and his breath caught in his throat. The fair one was the most beautiful creature he had ever seen in her pink cotton frock and with such happiness sparkling in her eyes that she brought a smile to his lips. He leaned on his elbow to watch where she went. She stopped by the maypole, pointing and smiling at the dark girl whose arm was threaded through hers. James found himself sauntering across to stand close behind her in the crowd which was beginning to gather.

He could smell the scent of her skin, fresh and clean as a hayloft of newly picked apples. He could hear the lilt of her voice, excited as a child's yet at the same time musical and inviting.

'Just look, Dorothy, that girl, the little one in pink – isn't she beautiful?'

17

Ay, she's beautiful, James agreed inwardly, unable to take his eyes from her. She spoke differently from people hereabouts; she must come from away somewhere.

The tiny girl was having trouble lifting her ribbon clear of the head of a big boy as they wove in and out in the dance. The blonde girl threw back her head and laughed. Sunlight rippled down the flaxen curls and his heart thumped. The dark girl glanced back and he looked away, embarrassed, when she caught his eye.

A couple of lads flung themselves on the grass, their gaze firmly fixed on the girls.

'Cor, look at the arse on her,' one of them said in a loud stage whisper. The other youth put his fingers to his lips and James heard his piercing wolf-whistle. He could have hit them. The girls moved away.

'You coming, Jim? We're all about ready to start.'

It was Eddie, the team's anchorman. James turned back to the tug-of-war circle, reluctant to lose sight of her, but this year's match was critical. They couldn't let Otterley take the prize for the third year running.

It was going to be a tough one, the teams evenly balanced for weight and strength. James bent all his energy and concentration to the task, jamming his heels into the earth and feeling the pain of every sinew strained to bursting point, sweat running down his forehead into his eyes. It was only when the Otterley men were showing signs of weakening at last that he glimpsed the pink frock out of the corner of his eye and his spirits soared.

The rope moved slowly back and forth, its blue ribbon inching towards the Thaxton edge of the circle. One mighty heave . . . and the Otterley men cracked. As the ribbon slid over the line he heard the cheer go up.

'Well done!' she cried, clapping her hands and

jigging up and down. 'That was magnificent!'

He couldn't take his eyes off her. She looked like the china fairy his mother used to put on top of the Christmas tree, all pink and white and fragile.

'Right,' said Eddie, 'pints of ale all round.'

By the time James had sluiced himself down at the village pump and supped his ale with his team-mates, she was nowhere to be seen. He excused himself from the jubilant Thaxton men and hurried across the green to where the stalls and booths were doing a roaring trade. Maybe, with luck . . .

Pink, pink. It was extraordinary how many women had chosen to wear pink today. His gaze flitted anxiously from one to another, desperately searching for pink with flaxen curls. Then suddenly his heart stood still – she was over there, standing with the dark girl by the shooting gallery.

He tried hard to appear nonchalant as he strolled over to the stall and picked up the rifle, conscious that she had seen him and was watching.

'Tuppence a go,' the chubby man behind the stall sang out. 'Six ducks get you any prize on the stall.'

James handed over the coins and found his fingers were trembling as he curled them around the trigger. He was conscious of her moving closer as he took aim at the battered duck as it juddered across the sight-screen.

'That's not the way to hold a gun.'

Startled, James lowered the rifle and looked round. She was smiling at him. 'Pardon?' he said.

'I said that's not the way to hold a gun. You won't hit anything if you don't cradle it along your forearm and rest your cheek against it.'

'Won't I?' He was bewildered by her confidence, and at the same time his heart was fluttering. She was alone.

'Of course not. How can you take aim if you don't look along the sights?'

Her voice was sheer magic, golden and glistening as buttercup syrup. Overwhelmed, he turned away and took aim the way he always did, ignoring the bent sights, then fired. One, two, three . . . All six ducks fell back.

The chubby man took the rifle from him. 'Any prize you want,' he muttered, then turned to the next customer. The girl in pink came close.

'I didn't think you'd do it,' she breathed softly. 'You hold a rifle like a cowboy, no style at all.'

'It's the way I've always done it,' James replied.

She shrugged. 'Well, it seems to work. What are you going to have as your prize?'

'You choose.'

She put a finger to her mouth, cocked her head to one side and thought for a moment. There was a pink rabbit tucked under her arm. 'The blue rabbit, I think. Dorothy would like that.'

'Dorothy?'

'My sister – she's gone to the tea-tent.'

Of course – the dark girl. The vision before him seemed to have scattered his wits. He must pull himself together or he'd lose her again. 'Would you like some tea?' he asked as she tucked the blue rabbit under her arm alongside the pink one, then cursed himself. The sister would be there. 'Or maybe some ice-cream?' he suggested.

'Ice-cream would be lovely, thanks.'

She turned, tossing her hair back as she fell into step beside him. He was aware of the envious eyes as they walked together towards the ice-cream cart, and his heart swelled with pride. The most beautiful girl at the fair had chosen to be at his side.

She picked the strawberry flavour. He watched the little pink tongue flicking in and out, scooping the pink ice-cream into the moist little mouth, and felt his stomach turn topsy-turvy. None of the village girls he'd dated had ever made him feel like this.

'What's your name?' she asked. Her head was cocked to one side again. 'Mine's Anna.'

The vanilla trickled cool down his throat. 'James Hemingway.'

She nodded approval. 'That has a good solid ring to it. What do you do?'

'Work on my father's farm.' He nodded uphill. 'Jericho.'

'Is it a big farm?'

'Biggest for miles. You don't live hereabouts then?'

She swung the mass of golden hair from side to side. 'Harrogate. We're staying with cousins in Barnbeck. Are you going to the barn dance tonight?'

'Are you?'

She tucked the last piece of the cornet into her mouth. 'We thought we might.'

'Then I'll be there.' This was no time to tell her he hadn't meant to go, couldn't make his boots keep time to the music. All that mattered was that he must see her again . . .

He was becoming fretful by the time the church clock struck half-past nine and she hadn't turned up. The fiddlers were still playing vigorously and the dancers clearly having a whale of a time but for James the night was hollow. He sat on a bundle of hay, kicking his heels and yearning for his vision in pink to arrive.

'Hey James,' one of the lads called out. 'Your lass is here.'

He looked up. She was standing framed in the doorway just as he remembered, only now she was wearing a green flowered dress. He stood up and she came straight over to him, her lips parted in a wide smile. Instantly he forgave her the impatient hours he'd waited.

She gave no explanation as they took the floor to dance. It seemed presumptuous to take her in his arms, lay his rough palm against the small of her

21

back. He prayed his hands weren't sweaty. She felt as firm as a young calf, and once more he savoured the apple-fresh smell of her. If his feet mistimed the music she didn't appear to notice. Nor did he, intent only on holding that slender little body close to his own and gazing deep into her lovely, impish eyes.

He felt her fingers tighten on his arm and a tremor ran through him. 'You've got quite a muscle there,' she murmured. 'Is it hard work, pulling a plough or whatever you do?'

He laughed. 'It's the horses who pull the plough. It's heaving sheep and that.'

She looked up sharply. 'Whatever for?'

'Branding, shearing – it gives you a hell of a backache after you've dragged a couple of hundred sheep between your knees and turned them over on their backs.'

The little pink tongue flicked along her lips, then she smiled. 'I bet you're awfully good at it,' she murmured.

He flushed. She surely couldn't mean what he thought. No of course not – she was a lady.

She listened, her blue eyes never leaving his face. She was clearly a city girl to know so little about farming, and it afforded him pleasure to tell her everyday things which astonished her. She was fascinated by raddle-bags.

'You mean you can tell which sheep will have their babies first? By the colour of the paint on their backs?' she said in wonder. 'Whatever will they think of next?'

No-one else existed for James. It took him by surprise when her sister broke the magic spell. Dorothy appeared out of the gloom and touched Anna's arm.

'It's time, Anna – the car's waiting.'

James tried not to let go of her hand as she turned to leave. 'You have a car?' he said in surprise.

'My uncle's actually. Ours is in Harrogate.'

He stumbled after her and caught up with her

22

outside the door. The night breeze shivered a curl on her temple and he ached to touch it. 'Shall I see you again?' he asked, angered by the unintentional sharpness in his tone. He couldn't just let her disappear out of his life . . .

'Church – on Sunday,' she called back over her shoulder.

He stood outside in the darkness under the porch where he could see the gleam of the car's bodywork under the street lamp. Dorothy was waiting by the open door. He saw them both scramble in, and then the car moved off.

The window slid down. 'Late service,' he heard the golden voice call. 'I'm never up in time for the early one.'

He heard a low chuckle behind him. It was Eddie. 'So you'll be going to church this week then, eh Jim?'

James felt elated as he climbed the rutted lane towards Jericho. A tapestry of stars was shimmering above him, and ahead he could see Venus, the evening star, glowing like a lantern. Sundays had always been a dreary routine, when he was a lad, having to clean his shoes, scrub his nails and brylcreem his hair ready for church. Only this he'd be preparing with eagerness . . .

THREE

1965

The image of James outlined against the purple slope of the moor remained in Lisa's mind as she drove on towards York. She should be concentrating on the coming interview but David and his father filled her thoughts.

There was no doubt that James loved this desolate countryside despite what he said. He was as much part of the rugged landscape as that rock over there. So why should he want to leave now? And where on earth would he go after he'd spent all his forty-seven years here? It was unthinkable.

She too had grown to love the place as deeply as David. Maybe it was having no roots of her own, moving all her life from school to boarding school and then to college while Mother and Dad were abroad. Maybe it was because it had given birth to David and nurtured his childhood years.

Whatever the reason, it was odd, since the moorland around Jericho had little to recommend it to those accustomed to the feminine charms of the south. This was a visually assertive landscape, understated in comparison with the Lake District, yet somehow wonderfully impressive.

She wound down the window to feel the breeze on her face. After the dust and litter of London the air smelled refreshingly wholesome. Starkly pure and unyielding, like the area's heritage of Nonconformity. She could understand James's observation that it was cruel – it certainly held an implacable air despite its grandeur. Beautiful now in September, but in bleak midwinter it could be unforgiving when the snow fell. She thought of being stranded on this desolate stretch of Scarthwaite Moor alone in a driving blizzard, and shivered.

It was hard to gauge how the interview went. The questions over lunch, though apparently sociable, were clearly part of the assessment but Lisa didn't like the feel of the young Mr Lewis. There was an air of complacency about him as he sat behind his vast desk to conduct the afternoon interview.

His questioning was slow and deliberate. 'You've come a long way for this interview?'

If you mean why have I come so far, then why the devil don't you ask me? 'That's right. I wanted this job.'

She saw his grey eyes travel the length of her crossed legs. She uncrossed them and pulled her skirt an inch lower.

He leaned back in his chair and arched his finger-tips together. 'You know we're expanding fast – that's why we're looking for a representative in London. You've had considerable experience with one of the best advertising agencies there is.'

'Ever since Harris and Powers opened two years ago.'

That's my biggest asset – it should mean quite a lot to a provincial firm anxious to grow rapidly.

Mr Lewis gave her a shrewd look. 'And why do you want to leave them?'

Cunning. A negative question invited a negative answer. I can't say I want the higher salary they're offering. 'I don't really want to leave – I just feel it's time I broadened my experience.'

He nodded. 'So in a couple of years you may feel it time to broaden your horizons again?'

Implying I'm a butterfly? How do I get out of that? I'm not going down on my knees to this pompous young man. 'Who can say, Mr Lewis? We none of us know

25

what may happen in the next six months, let alone two years.'

It was impossible to tell from his controlled expression whether the answer satisfied him or not.

'How well do you think you related to your clients?'

He's inviting me to pay myself compliments now. 'Very well.'

'So you think you may be able to bring some of them with you?'

She picked her words with care. 'Given time I might be able to persuade one or two. Might.'

He leaned forward and she saw the gleam of curiosity in his grey eyes. 'What about your boyfriend?'

Lisa groaned inwardly. *Here we go – married or going steady, it was all the same. They always wanted unattached women. I could say I have a friend . . .*

She took a deep breath. 'He's an artist. He can work wherever he chooses. As a matter of fact, he's done quite a bit of work for Harris and Powers.' *Don't ask how much,* she prayed inwardly, *or how he got the commissions.*

Mr Lewis stood up in a smooth, unhurried movement and turned away to the window, examined well-manicured fingernails in the sunlight. 'The post we are offering would mean coming up here often, probably staying for several days at a time – would that be a problem?'

Quick thoughts flitted through Lisa's mind. David wouldn't object – it was inevitable they'd want her to attend meetings and consultations. They'd agreed from the beginning that they both needed space, she just as much as he did to paint. Nothing could damage the relationship they had . . .

'I have my own car.' *Such as she is, dear old Gladys. Game old bird – she managed to get me here but God knows if she can get me back to London in one piece . . .*

'I see.' Mr Lewis sat down again at his desk, opened

26

a drawer and pushed a pile of papers inside. 'Well, we'll let you know in a day or two.'

Don't call us, we'll call you. She emerged from the studio into the teatime rush hour. Ah well, she thought as she drove through the narrow streets out of the city, there's probably a better job waiting somewhere that I don't even know about yet.

Lisa picked a careful, barefoot way between scattered brushes and pots of paint to the window. The curtain rings clattered along the wooden pole, leaving pools of overlong velvet trailing on the floor in their wake.

Early sunlight lay flat across the grey roofscape of London's skyline. Below she could hear the rattle of milk crates and a cat yowling hungrily for breakfast.

A moan behind her made her turn. David was nearly awake.

'Shut the curtains, for God's sake.'

'Headache again?' she asked, suddenly filled with concern. He'd had so many lately.

'The light's too bright. And it's Monday.'

'So? I'm the one who has to catch the tube to work.'

The mound of bedclothes heaved and he struggled upright. She watched the slow smile spread across his sleepy face, his dark hair all awry, and felt tenderness. That vulnerable, little-boy air still stirred her as deeply as it did that day three years ago . . .

'I remember you telling me last night you made a mess of the interview,' he murmured. 'What else did you tell me?'

'I might still get it,' she replied. 'Don't you remember anything?'

'I was drinking with the cast after the play ended.'

She half turned and paused, aware that her body was silhouetted against the window in her flimsy nightdress. After all, it had been two weeks now . . .

27

'You look cute,' he murmured, 'just like a kid.'

'Your father sends his love,' she said quietly. 'He's thinking of selling the farm.'

David stopped rubbing his eyes. 'Is he now? And what does Ellen think about it?'

'I didn't see her – she must have been at work. James didn't mention her and, to be honest, I never even thought about her.'

He yawned. 'That's always been her problem – no-one ever does. Poor little non-event Ellen.'

She saw the smile fade quickly, the shadow which crossed his face. 'You all right?' she asked.

'Too much cheap wine last night, I guess.'

'You didn't use to get headaches from drinking.'

'I think this must have been paraffin.'

Long legs swung out of bed and he padded, naked, around the kettle drum into the bathroom. Lisa could hear water running.

'Was she always like that?' she called out.

'What? Who?' a muffled voice replied.

'Your sister. Was she always so withdrawn?'

'I remember she used to boss me around when I was a kid. She just seemed to go quiet when she grew up.'

'When your mother died?' Lisa looked around for the breadbin. It wasn't next to the kettle where it usually lay. Come to that, the kettle wasn't there either.

'I guess so. She just seemed to change. Stopped going out, going to church, everything.'

'I can understand that. I felt furious with God when my parents were killed.'

David emerged from the bathroom, rubbing his face with a purple towel. 'Sorry, I couldn't hear what you said. You know, I hope Dad doesn't sell up. I always fancied I'd like to go back there one day.'

'Where's the bread, David?'

The smile spread across his handsome face once

28

more. 'I forgot to tell you – they needed a breadbin for the play.'

'And the kettle?'

'They took the fridge too.'

'With all our stuff in it? You mean I have to go down to get our milk off the stage?'

David went back into the bathroom. 'Don't worry,' he called out, 'it's plugged in, and it's only for tonight – we can have fish and chips for supper and we'll have everything back in the morning.'

Lisa shrugged. It wasn't the first time. Sharing the furniture for props was part of the agreement for living rent-free in the flat – that and acting as care-takers for the little theatre.

She was crossing to the door to go downstairs when she caught sight of David through the cracked mirror on the wall. He was standing, still naked, at the bathroom sink and as she watched he tossed something into his mouth and washed it down with a glass of water.

FOUR

1965

Autumn, despite the beauty of its rich colours, always filled James with melancholy. He pressed his cheek against the cow's rump, feeling the creamy milk spurt from under his fingertips into the bucket and welcomed the creature comfort of the warm flank against his face.

Anna's flesh had been comforting. His fingers paused as he remembered the hours they'd lain in the long grass that summer before the war, his cheek against her naked breast. He could still recall the smell of her skin, feel her fingers caressing his hair.

'We shouldn't be doing this, James. My father would have a fit if he knew.'

'He's done it himself or you wouldn't be here.'

'Not before he was married.'

'That's what he says. You like it, don't you?'

Each time she made gentle protest his lips sought out her nipple again. Soft moans, a sigh, and then she melted. Their need for each other was desperate, the hunger to be one. By the time summer was beginning to fade into autumn and she was due to go home they could no longer tolerate being apart.

He remembered how she clung to him that dew-damp night. 'I can't bear to leave you, James,' she cried. 'I want to stay with you, for always.'

'We don't have to part, love. We could stay together, get married.'

Her face fell. 'My father will never agree to me marrying a farmer. He wants me to marry a rich man, like Dorothy – she's engaged to an Honourable.'

He made no answer. Hemingways worked hard but never made the kind of money she was used to. It was presumptuous of him even to think it.

Her silken voice whispered in the gloom. 'But it's you I want, James – not money or position. I'd give up anything for you.' In the darkness he thought she touched his cheek, but it was only a leaf fluttering down from the oak . . .

With a shiver James picked up the pail of milk. The fall of the year, they called it. The earth gradually dying into winter – maybe that was what saddened his soul. Anna had slipped away with the first fluttering leaves of autumn . . .

He took a look at the two pigs snuffling in the trough. Bart sniffed through the gate then lost interest and raced away up to the copse to hunt for rabbits. James headed back into the scullery. Ellen would be coming down now for breakfast.

He was refilling the kettle when she came in, still wearing a bathrobe, her hair falling loose over her shoulders. Of course, it was Saturday – she didn't need to pin it up for work today.

Lovely hair she had, the rich brown colour of hazelnuts, but straight as a yard of tap water. She pulled out a chair and sat down.

'Morning, love. Sleep well?' he enquired. 'Have a cup of tea with me?'

'If you're making one.'

He gave her a bright smile. 'What are you going to do with your day off? Bit of shopping, perhaps?'

She shrugged thin shoulders. 'I haven't decided yet. I've a new book I might read.'

Books. He sighed. As if working in the library all week wasn't enough she spent all her spare time reading books. She'd rather read than talk any time.

He touched her hair as he passed behind her. It felt silky and fine like a kitten's. 'Ever thought of putting

31

a few curlers in?' he murmured. 'Your mother used to.'

She reached across the table to pick up his still unopened newspaper. 'No point,' she said briefly. 'I always wear it up.'

He busied himself with the teapot. Ellen spread out the paper and bent over it, her hair spilling about her cheeks so that he could barely see her face. Did all fathers find it this hard to talk to their daughters, he wondered? It wasn't that she ever rebuffed him, only that she somehow signalled that for her conversation was unimportant. It was far easier talking to Lisa than to his daughter.

'Anything in the news?' he asked as he placed a cup of tea before her. She shook the veil of hair.

'Nothing special.'

He poured his own tea. She never showed much interest in world events, not the war in Vietnam, nor had she shared his concern about the Bay of Pigs and the Cuban missile crisis. John Kennedy's defiance of the Russians had almost brought them to the brink of a third World War yet Ellen had shown no emotion. She hadn't been like that as a child, so sunny and full of eager curiosity. It was almost as though with Anna's death she had opted out of life.

Maybe it wasn't good for the girl to be cut off in this remote place. Maybe he ought to persuade her out of a country library into the hurly-burly of the real world. He tried to see her face under the screen of hair. She was a pretty girl, though a bit pale. City life might liven her up, give her the chance to meet people of her own age, a young man even . . .

'How would you feel about leaving Jericho, Ellen? If I were to sell the place. What would you do?'

She didn't look up from the paper. 'I could always get a flat somewhere, share it with another girl perhaps.'

He glanced at her sharply. 'You mean you wouldn't mind?'

She swept the hair away from her face and looked up. 'More to the point, Dad, what about you – what would you do?'

He waved a deprecatory arm. 'Oh, I'm young enough – I'm not fifty yet – I could set up in business with my guns, anything.'

She bent back over the paper. 'Why bother? You don't need the money. You're all right as you are.'

He leaned across the table, wanting to touch her hand but she sat upright and began folding the newspaper. 'It's you I'm concerned about, love,' he said softly. 'You need to get away, get about a bit.'

He saw the curl of her lip. 'Like David?' she said crisply. 'No thanks. Look where it's got him.'

'He does get work from time to time.'

'It's not that.'

'What then?'

She sighed. 'Oh, don't let's talk about it.'

He could guess. It was because David was living with Lisa. And it was supposed to be his generation which tut-tutted about the morals of today's youth . . .

He held out the teapot to refill her cup but she covered it with her hand. 'Fancy going for a ride with me?' he suggested tentatively. 'The horses could do with more exercise.'

She stood up, pulling the robe close about her slim body. 'No thanks. I'm going to have a bath and then read.' She glanced out of the window. 'In the garden, if the rain holds off. Oh damn!'

The cup stopped halfway to James's lips. 'What is it?'

'It's him, the vicar – he's coming round the back. I'm off.'

James smiled. 'He probably only wants something for the harvest festival.'

'I don't care what he wants – I'm going.'

33

He watched the swing of her nut-brown hair as she turned and hurried from the room. She really was an enigma to him. There was a time before Anna died when she used to welcome Reverend Bax, hurry down to church to help with whatever project he embarked upon. Until Anna died. Maybe it was too painful for the girl to see the man who had officiated at the funeral. James knew only too well how much sudden, unexpected reminders could hurt . . .

He rather liked the Reverend Clifford Bax despite his being a public school southerner. He was a big man, in voice as well as body, as impressive a preacher in the pulpit as any country church could boast. Now, in his fifties, his hair was silvering, though his black eyebrows and the arrowhead of black hairs pointing down towards the nape of his neck indicated he'd once been gypsy-dark.

He declined James's invitation to go through into the sitting room overlooking the pond. 'This'll do fine in here,' he said, seating himself and planting thick hands over plump knees and gazing around at the long, low-raftered kitchen.

'I like Jericho,' he remarked. 'You can sense history in the place. I can just see half a dozen farmhands in the old days, sitting at this old table eating their dinnertime bread and cheese. During branding and harvest time.'

James smiled. 'Those days are long gone, Vicar. I raise nothing but a couple of pigs and a cow nowadays and I might even give that up.'

Reverend Bax raised his eyebrows. 'How do you mean, give up?'

James crossed to the window and gazed out across the yard. Rainclouds were beginning to gather over Scarp Fell and Bart was scrambling back over the yard wall. The rabbits had made a fool of him again.

'It might do Ellen good to get away from here,' James said slowly.

The vicar thought for a moment. 'She should have gone to college – she seemed cut out for the academic life.'

James gave a shake of the head. 'I was thinking of maybe selling up, moving into town. Somewhere where there's something she can get involved in. She used to be so alive.'

He could hear the vicar's slow breathing as he absorbed the news. He too must remember how she used to be when she was sixteen, when she was his right-hand man teaching the little ones at Sunday School, whipping up their enthusiasm for the more vivid Bible stories to the fervour of a football crowd. Their Nativity play had to be seen to be believed.

The vicar cleared his throat. 'Well, we'll miss you both, of course, but if you think it best . . .'

'I've not settled on it yet. It's just that she's changed so much.'

The Reverend Bax sighed. 'Her mother's death couldn't have come at a worse time. Adolescence can be hell.'

James squared his shoulders and turned back to face him. 'Still, it was the Festival you came about, was it?'

'No, the central heating actually,' the vicar replied. 'We desperately need a new boiler. The old one must be as old as Methuselah.'

James reached into his inside pocket for his cheque book. 'How much?' he asked.

The vicar spread his hands. 'I leave it to you, James. The Brigadier has been very generous but we're still a long way short.'

James completed the cheque, tore it out and handed it over. The vicar glanced at it and smiled. 'Very handsome, James. It more than matches the Brigadier.'

35

As James accompanied his guest to the gate the first drops of rain were starting to fall.

'Mrs Bax home from Nottingham yet?' he asked.

Reverend Bax's gaze flitted away from his. 'Ah no, not yet.'

'Poorly is she, your sister-in-law?'

The vicar pulled up his coat collar against the rain. 'No, no. It's more of a break for Sarah, you know – all that charitable work can become a trifle tiring.'

'She's a worker all right,' agreed James. 'You must miss her.'

'I wonder you haven't thought of marrying again,' the vicar replied. 'It's been a good few years now.' He lifted the latch of the farm gate. 'You know,' he added brightly, 'there's more than one woman around these parts who'd jump at the chance. You'd be surprised how often your name crops up amongst the ladies, and not only the single ones either.'

James smiled. 'I think I'd better start packing my bags now then.'

He watched the vicar stride away downhill towards the village. It was hard to visualize the plump, energetic Mrs Bax feeling in need of a break. She could always be relied upon to mastermind every village event from the jumble sale to the bingo. She was always there, organizing and wresting control with the frenetic drive of a woman who wouldn't know what to do if she stopped.

Maybe if she'd had children of her own . . . As he turned back to the house a movement at an upstairs window caught his eye. As he looked up Ellen let the curtain fall.

FIVE

1965

Lisa ran upstairs to the flat and flung her briefcase on the bed. David wasn't in the room. 'Hi, I'm home,' she called.

As she slipped off her coat and tossed it alongside the briefcase she heard the sound of the toilet flushing. On the far side of the room she could see a long, half-painted flat depicting trees and a few shrubs.

The door of the bathroom opened and David came out. He looked decidedly pale. He really ought to get out more into the fresh air.

'Has anyone telephoned?' she asked.

He shook his head. 'Not a sound. God knows how many bookings they get.'

She sat disconsolately on the edge of the bed and kicked off her shoes. 'It's three days. They must have rung someone by now and told them they've got the job. It's obviously not me. What's that piece of scenery you're painting?'

'View from the window in next week's play. Not too good, is it?'

'You're supposed to be working on those posters. How can you get on with them if you keep doing flats?'

'It makes a change. I don't mind.'

'It's not part of the agreement. You're just too darn soft for your own good. Just like your father.'

She would have kissed him as she passed him to go into the bathroom but he bent to pick up a brush from the palette. In the doorway she paused and sniffed. There was an unpleasant smell in here.

It was a sharply bitter smell. Vomit. She hurried out

37

into the bedroom again. He was sweeping long, slow strokes of blue wash over the canvas flat.

'You've been sick,' she said quietly. 'I'm worried about you. Is it another headache?'

'It's nothing much,' he answered without turning around. 'It's probably because I was concentrating so hard on the detail in the coffee poster. It's gone now.'

'If it's making you sick it sounds like migraine to me. David, you've got to see a doctor – you've been putting it off too long. They can give you something—'

'OK, OK, if it makes you happy. Now, what do you fancy for supper tonight?'

They had just finished eating and were pillow-fighting to settle who was to do the washing up when a distant telephone bell shrilled. Lisa stopped belting David over the head and knelt upright on the bed.

'Listen – box office. I wonder . . .'

A moment later Lazarus called up the stairs. 'Lisa, darling – call for you.'

Lazarus was the theatre's dresser, costumier and everyone's dogsbody and he relished mothering them all. Lisa could see his tall, rangy frame leaning against the wall at the foot of the stairs as she ran down barefoot.

'Gentleman on the line for you, sweetie,' he said mischievously. 'Lovely voice – sort of deep treacly brown.'

It was Mr Lewis's voice. 'Miss Drew?' Lisa could barely whisper.

'Yes.'

'Martin Lewis here. I'm sorry to keep you waiting so long. I'm afraid I have some disappointing news for you . . .'

So forget it and make fresh plans, my girl, she thought as he went on. 'But there is something else if you wish to consider it.'

'What's that?'

'We do have another vacancy which we feel might suit you better. Client liaison officer. The job is to consolidate goodwill with our clients. The salary's slightly lower but there is a company car.'

She listened, only half taking it in as he told her what the post would entail, picking up clients from railway station or airport, driving them to meetings, helping to entertain them. Organizing meals in restaurants, arranging theatre tickets and a private box at the races – it sounded too tempting to resist.

'So the Board have authorized me to offer you the post,' he concluded. 'Would you like time to think it over?'

'There's no need. I'll take it.'

David was delighted for her. 'There you are, I told you those rusty curls and long legs would get you noticed. They can't go wrong offering an escort service like you.'

'I was offered it because I've got brains and poise.'

'And because you're a very luscious lady – one look at you and the clients will agree to anything.'

She hugged him. 'Just think – free meals!'

'No more of my cooking – lucky devil. It's the high life for you now.' David eased her back to arm's length. 'You're sure this is OK – I mean, how far do they expect you to entertain these fellows?'

She laughed as she replaced the bolster and crawled over the bed, curling up and hugging a pillow close to her cheek. 'Don't be daft – but it will mean being away a lot.'

He sprawled beside her and curved his body around hers. 'Then I shall have to look to my laurels – make a real fuss of you so you won't desert me for one of your millionaire clients.'

She turned and wriggled close to him. 'Silly, there's only one man who turns me on.'

'Tell me who he is and I'll wring his neck.'

He began unbuttoning her blouse. 'Remember the time', she said softly, 'when they took our bed and we had to go down and sleep on the stage?'

She heard his low chuckle as his fingers slithered inside. 'The audience went wild, didn't they?' he murmured. 'Did wonders for our sex life. I just hope they don't want the chandelier till I get the hang of it.'

A distant clock struck three. David knelt by the bed and looked down at her sleeping face. She lay curled like a child, her hair streaming out on the pillow, its redness drained by the moonlight. He couldn't resist touching a finger gently to the contour of her cheek.

Lisa stirred and smiled, eyes still closed. 'Oh no, not again,' she murmured.

She gave a dreamy sigh and rolled over. She looked just as vulnerable, just as delectable as she had done the first time he caught sight of her three years ago in the coffee bar, surrounded by her student friends.

Only three years? Somehow it seemed as if she had always been in his life. Before Lisa came into his world he hadn't realized that he had been waiting for her – to give focus, to give meaning to his existence.

He slithered down carefully into bed beside her. She mustn't know that the pain in his head had been driving him mad. Nor must she learn about the way his eyes kept playing him up – the way the slats of the venetian blind in the bathroom had gone all wavy today. They weren't really dipping in the middle – he'd run his fingers along them and they were straight as a die.

It was his eyes all right. He'd looked out at the long flat roofline of the factory opposite and it too had a big dent in the middle, and the sight had made his stomach turn cold.

To lose his sight was the nightmare of any artist. His living depended on his visual acuity. To go blind

. . . It was the last thing in the world he wanted Lisa to know.

She stirred again. He held his breath. 'What's the matter?' she whispered. 'Can't you sleep?'

'I've just been to the toilet.'

'Hmm. Now I'll have to go too.'

Moments later she came back, holding out something in the moonlight. He recognized the empty aspirin bottle.

'I found this in the waste bin,' she said quietly. 'It wasn't there when I went to bed.'

'I just had the last two.'

'It was full on Monday.'

As she climbed back into bed he turned away. Across the room he could see the canvas flat leaning against the wall. It was dipping in the middle . . .

He felt the sheet pulled taut and then heard Lisa's voice, small and tight. 'You're going to the doctor first thing in the morning.'

The coffee bar was crowded. David found a table for two in the corner and set the plastic cups down.

Lisa sat in silence. It was hard to make conversation above the noise of the juke box belting out pop music and in any event David seemed disinclined to talk.

'You don't have to come over the road with me,' he muttered at last.

Behind them the Beatles wailed. Lisa leaned across the table.

'I'd like to know what's causing it, David. I want to help in any way I can.'

'I'd be happier on my own. I'll tell you everything, I promise.'

She could see a flake of yellow ochre on his chin. Her finger reached out to scratch it gently away before she recalled how she hated to see a woman fussing proprietorially over her man. She smiled an apology.

41

'OK, I'll wait here for you. But be sure you tell him about the sickness, everything.'

'I will.'

Through the window she watched his tall figure as he zigzagged with easy grace between the cars to get across the busy road. She wondered what James would make of his son in green flares and pink shirt and with his wild, dark hair curling round his collar. He hadn't seen his son for some months now but, knowing James, she guessed he'd probably approve – after all, his son was an artist, entitled to be just a little bohemian. For a father James was remarkably with-it, even if he wouldn't know the meaning of the phrase.

David was lost to sight now. Lisa turned her attention to the couple sitting by the window, their fingers intertwined in a string of coloured love-beads. His fair hair hung lankly to his shirt collar and he wore Jesus sandals on his dusty feet. The girl's flimsy caftan streamed about her knees to the floor and, outlined as she was against the sunlight, it was clear she wore nothing else but the strand of psychedelic plastic flowers about her neck. They were obviously in love, for their looks were as intertwined as their fingers in the beads and the two cups of coffee remained untouched.

Lisa toyed with the tomato-shaped sauce bottle. Funny thing love, she thought. The miracle of it was that out of all the world someone should find the one person who would make life complete. Just look at that middle-aged couple over there, each sipping coffee and looking around without ever speaking to the other. Somehow you could tell they didn't need words to know they belonged.

Just as David and I belong together. We both knew it the moment we met. Life without each other would be unthinkable. She shivered.

Another coffee. Nothing to worry about. Migraine could be dealt with, and David was in the right hands now.

An hour later he came back. As he reached the table Lisa could see his lips were tight and his cheeks pale. 'What is it?' she asked. 'What did he say?'

He sat down opposite her. 'He wants me to go to the hospital to see a neurologist friend of his.'

'A neurologist?' The very word was alarming.

'Don't worry – it's the routine thing for migraine. He rang his friend and he's agreed to see me today.'

'Is that what he said it is? Migraine?'

'He says it's best to get it checked out, just to make certain. I'll get the bus – you go on to the office now. You know what hospitals are like – they can keep you hanging around for hours.'

She shook her head firmly. 'I'll ring the office and then I'll drive you. I'm not quitting till this thing's sorted out.'

The waiting room was close, not a breath of air to dispel the scent of bodies and disinfectant. It seemed like hours since David had disappeared into the consultant's room.

A trolley loaded with cups and a tea urn clattered past the row of patients still seated in the corridor. Behind it a flushed woman in a grey cardigan smiled. 'Tea, anyone?'

A man with his arm in a sling juggled with the change in his pocket. Lisa watched the woman extract the right coins from the collection in his outstretched palm and then hand him a cup of tea. A small boy whimpered to his mother for chocolate and she gave an embarrassed smile to her neighbours before going up to the trolley.

The consultant's door opened and David came out. Lisa scrambled to her feet.

'I've got to have some tests and X-rays,' David said in a bright voice which wasn't David. 'It would be best if you went, really. This could take ages.'

Apprehension leapt in her. This was more than migraine. 'Forget it – I'm staying,' she said firmly. 'Where first?'

It was late in the afternoon before the tests were finished and they sat together in Mr Casey's office. Lisa knew before the consultant laid his papers aside that her shivers of misgiving had not been unfounded.

'I'm sorry, Mr Hemingway, but the news is not good,' Mr Casey began.

'What is it?' David asked quietly. 'I can take it.'

The consultant took a breath before answering. 'It's a tumour, I'm afraid. In the back of the brain, and judging from its size it must have been developing for some time.'

She swayed in her seat, stunned. She heard David's murmured comment. 'Brain tumour. I might have guessed. All those funny images . . .' His head swung up to face the consultant. 'Is that it? Is that what's affecting my eyes?'

Lisa stared. He hadn't told her he'd been having trouble with his eyes. Brain tumour – people died from those, didn't they?

'It can be treated, can't it?' she asked. 'There was that actor – he had an operation and he's fine now.'

Mr Casey looked down at his notes. 'I'm afraid that because of its size and position it's impossible to operate, more's the pity.'

'So my sight could get worse?' David said. 'Could I go blind?'

'It would be gradual, the outer field of vision first.'

Lisa sat aghast, feeling the panic rising. She had a sudden vision of David with a white stick, groping his way along a busy street while passers-by knocked into

44

him. Then angry determination replaced the panic. She'd be there to help him, be his eyes . . .

She found her voice, small yet defiant. 'He can't go blind – he's an artist. There must be something – chemotherapy or something – that can get rid of the tumour, can't it?'

Mr Casey shook his head. 'I'm afraid not. Matters have gone too far for treatment now.'

David looked straight into the consultant's eye. 'And if I can't have treatment – what then?'

'The outlook is poor, Mr Hemingway. The tumour will progress and matters will grow worse, I'm afraid.'

'Worse?' echoed Lisa. 'What could possibly be worse for an artist than not being able to see?'

Mr Casey coughed before he answered. 'I'm afraid it will endanger your life.'

Lisa leapt to her feet. 'You're saying he could die? Oh no! He can't – he's too young, he's got so much talent—'

David laid a hand on her arm. 'No, Mr Casey,' he said quietly, 'I'm not going to die. I've only just started to live.'

Days passed and they spoke little of what had occurred. Lisa was still finding it hard to believe. David seemed so absolutely normal. The headaches had gone, he was working on the posters again and, but for last week's visit to the hospital, she could have sworn the whole thing had been a terrible dream.

'How long have you had those headaches?' she asked him one night.

'Oh – a year or so, I guess. Seeing things all wobbly only started recently.'

'And you never told me.' She spoke the words with wonder, not accusation. She'd always thought she knew him inside out, his every thought. Total honesty, they'd agreed, no matter what. And yet he'd kept this thing from her . . .

*   *   *

On her last day at Harris and Powers the office girls brought out an iced cake and bottles of wine. Farewells over, she hurried back to the flat.

David took her in his arms and kissed her tenderly before he caught sight of the bottle on the table. 'What's that? Leaving present?'

'Bottle I stole from the party – I hid it in the filing cabinet so you'd get your share. Now, what do you want to do tonight?'

'Nothing special. Why?'

'We've got to make plans.'

We've got to make plans just as if we have the rest of our lives together, many years of it. If we make concessions to this thing . . .

'OK then,' he said brightly. 'Pictures?'

She pulled a face. 'There's nothing on worth seeing.'

'You're always worth seeing.' He pulled her close again. Her fingers entwined in the hair at the back of his neck. It was hard to believe that just there, only centimetres beneath her fingertips, lurked the evil thing which was robbing him of life. Harder still to give the name to it. Cancer.

It was so bloody unjust. Cancer was for old people, those who had already enjoyed a life, not for the young.

'Oh – I forgot,' he said suddenly, letting go of her to dive under a canvas. 'Letter for you. From York.'

She scanned the contents quickly. 'It's a schedule of engagements for the new job,' she told him. 'Starting with a Mr Braithwaite next week.'

He looked over her shoulder at the sheet of paper. 'Bloody hell! You're taking him to *South Pacific* – we couldn't afford the tickets.'

She smiled. 'I might find room for an assistant one day if you play your cards right.' She put the letter down. 'Maybe I shouldn't go.'

'Why not? It's your job.'

'You know damn well why not. When I took this work on we didn't know about – you know, your illness.'

'There's every reason to go – you can't be with me every minute of the day and anyway, I'm fine. No headaches, nothing. You'll be here when I need you.'

She sighed and turned away. David grabbed her hand. 'I do need you, Lisa, but not next week. Promise me you'll go.'

She understood. He didn't want to stand in her way, any more than he'd wanted to worry her. Tears filled her eyes. 'Your father perhaps—' she began.

'No!' David exploded. 'Dad mustn't know! No-one but you and me. I couldn't bear it . . .'

She nodded mutely. He was gazing out of the window now, where dusk was creeping over the flat grey factory roof. 'There's only one reason he should ever know,' he said softly, 'and that's if the time comes . . . In that case . . .'

'Don't,' Lisa said vehemently. 'I can't bear it.'

'I should have asked the doctor how long.'

She could find no words. She too had wondered the same thing, debated whether to put the question, and held back . . .

'Only I didn't want to hear what he'd say,' David murmured.

For a moment silence hung heavy in the dusty room. Then she heard him take a deep breath.

'If and when it comes to the worst,' he said quietly, 'I want to go home to Jericho.'

SIX

1938

The river Garth, diminished now to a narrow thread after the long summer drought, trickled steadily downstream through Thaxton village. Jericho Farm slumbered under the evening mist, unaware that the rainclouds gathering over the fell would soon be replaced by the clouds of war.

The last of the milking done, young James Hemingway sat by the hearth with his father, who had kicked off his boots and now lay, half-dozing, with the newspaper over his face. James had only one thought in his head and now was as good a time as any. He cleared his throat.

'I'm thinking of getting married,' he said quietly.

'Oh ay?' came his father's voice from under the paper. 'Bit early, isn't it? You're nobbut twenty yet.'

'I love her, Dad.'

'Do you now? Anyone I know?'

'No, she's not from round here.'

Father removed the newspaper from his weather-beaten face and rubbed his eyes. 'Oh? I somehow fancied it might be that young lass of Boothroyd's. She's a bonny little thing.'

'She's from Harrogate, Dad. They're very well off.'

'Are they now? Does she know owt about farming?'

'She's a lady.'

The newspaper slid to the floor. Father reached for his pipe. 'And does she have a name, this lady?'

'Anna. Anna Harcourt.' It gave James pleasure to roll the words around his tongue.

'The Harcourts of Harrogate,' mused Father. 'Ay, it

48

sounds posh, does that. How come you met her –
you've never been to Harrogate?'

'She's staying in Barnbeck for the summer. I met
her at the May Day fair.'

James watched his father's stubby fingers pull
shreds of tobacco from the leather pouch and
stuff them slowly into the bowl of his pipe. He
reached for the matches. 'A couple of months,' said
Father. 'That's no time at all for courting. How old is
the lass?'

James swallowed. 'She's nineteen, but she's very
mature – she'll learn fast. You'll be proud of her, Dad.
Mother would have been too.'

The match hissed and spluttered into life and James
smelt its acrid odour. Blue eyes searched his. 'But
will her folks be proud of you, lad? If she's from a
rich family like you say . . .'

'She doesn't care for all that. She wants me.'

Smoke swirled above his father's head as he puffed
on the pipe. James watched it drift towards the
chimney. 'Wise lass,' Father murmured, 'but how
well does she know you? If she's not been here that
long . . .'

'We've met at church every Sunday. And most
evenings.'

Father nodded. 'So that's what accounts for all this
sudden church-going. And where you're off to of a
night. And I thought it were the Boothroyd lass.'

He rubbed his chin thoughtfully for a moment. 'But
don't you think you could hold your horses a bit?
You're nobbut a lad yet when all's said and done.'

'She's due to go back to Harrogate this week. I'm
not going to lose her.'

'Then why haven't you brought her home?'

'Just look at the place.' James nodded towards the
table, taking in the half-cut loaf standing next to
the lading-can of milk, the unwashed dishes piled
in the stone sink, the heap of shirts lying on the floor

by the set-pot waiting to be boiled. 'Just look at it.'

His father smiled. 'She'll have to get used to it if she's to be a farmer's wife. Still, it's your life, lad. You'll have to make your own mistakes same as I did. You've no mother to advise you now, more's the pity.' He leaned back in his chair, stretching out his feet towards the hearth. 'Be nice to have a woman around the house again,' he said.

James nodded. 'Thanks, Dad.'

'Only bring her back here and let her see what she's letting herself in for. She might want to change her mind.'

James laughed. 'No fear of that. She loves me.'

'Ah, well.' His father glanced up at the mantel clock. 'Hey up – it's nearly news time. Switch on and let's hear what Mr Chamberlain's up to now.'

As the wireless set warmed up sounds began to crackle through into the stone-flagged kitchen. The sounds resolved at last into music and to the strains of a Lehar waltz Richard Tauber's rich voice rang through the evening air with *'Girls were made to love and kiss.'*

Suddenly James wanted to take Anna in his arms . . .

The bedroom glowed pink and luxurious by lamplight. Dorothy frowned, struggling to drag the silver-backed hairbrush through her sister's tangled curls as she sat at the dressing table. Anna watched her through the mirror.

'Ouch! You're pulling!' she complained.

'I've got to get all the straw out before we go down to dinner,' Dorothy retorted. 'It's an absolute give-away. Are you sure you're doing the right thing? I mean, he's terribly good-looking and all that, but if Father finds out you're seeing someone of his sort . . .'

'He won't, unless you tell him. And don't be such a

50

tiresome snob. I know you'd give your eye teeth for
a chance to go out with him.'

Dorothy put down the brush. 'For a fling, perhaps,
but not for keeps.'

She squeezed the perfume spray liberally over her
shoulders. Anna wrinkled her nose. 'Attar of roses
again?' she said.

'It's Myles's favourite, he bought it for me. I shan't
wear it after we're married.'

Anna surveyed her thoughtfully. 'I can't think why
you're marrying him, really I can't. He doesn't sweep
you off your feet with passion.'

'He's solid and reliable,' Dorothy replied crisply.
'He'll keep me in the style I want, which is more than
your farmer friend can do.'

Anna took the lid off the silver-topped powder
bowl. 'That's where we differ, you and I. You
want respectability, and I crave excitement.' She
cradled the swansdown puff against her cheek. 'That's
what devastated me about James – he's wonderful
and exciting and romantic, everything a girl dreams
of.'

'He's hardly a Beau Geste,' murmured Dorothy.
'More a sort of Heathcliff.'

Anna swung round to look at her. 'Which is far
better than being a pompous old stuffed shirt like the
Honourable Myles. He hasn't an ounce of romance in
him. You haven't even read the letter he sent you
today.'

'I will, after dinner.' Dorothy sat down to roll on
her stockings.

Anna smiled. 'Let me tell you a secret – James wants
me to be Mrs Heathcliff, and I fancy I'd be far happier
with him than you with your precious Myles.'

Dorothy stopped rolling and stared for a moment.
'But you won't, will you?'

'Why not?'

'It'll be so different – I'll be going to Ascot and

51

Henley. I'll be shopping at Fortnum and Mason's and holidaying in Deauville, but what about you? You'd be scrubbing floors and milking cows and things. Oh Anna, think carefully – I know which style of living I prefer.' She snapped the suspenders into place.

Anna stood up. 'But I'm the one in love with the most wonderful man in the country – you should feel those strong brown arms around you, all hard from working. He's just incredible.'

She stepped out of her skirt and opened the wardrobe. 'He's mine, and I wouldn't swap him for the world,' she murmured as she took a pale blue frock from a rail then turned to her sister. 'So will you promise to cover for me tonight? After dinner, when they're all playing bridge?'

Dorothy's eyebrows rose. 'Again? For heaven's sake, you're incorrigible. You're playing with fire.'

Anna pulled the frock over her head. 'Tell them I've gone for a ride if they notice, though I doubt if they will.'

Dorothy sighed. 'Oh well, I suppose since we're going home on Saturday – only make sure you're back by ten when they stop for supper.'

Anna kissed her cheek, then gave her a mischievous smile. 'I wouldn't bank on Saturday if I were you. You could just find you're going home alone.'

Dorothy shook her head firmly. 'Leaving me to explain to Father? Oh no, my girl.' She wagged a stern finger. 'I've told you already, have your fling with your village Romeo but don't try and make a career of it. You could regret it for the rest of your days.'

Anna gave her nose a final dab with the powder puff. As the dinner bell rang she flicked a lipstick across her lips and made for the door. Dorothy took her elbow.

'And just you take care you don't get carried away – I know how impetuous you can be.'

'Don't worry,' Anna replied with a smile. 'I can take care of myself.'

James could see the gleam of her bicycle between the bushes as she rode down the lane towards him, the eager smile as she leapt off and propped it against the fence alongside his rusty old Raleigh. He couldn't wait to hold her. Her grip was fierce, her lips hard against his.

At last they stood apart, for the moment satiated. 'Where shall we go tonight?' she demanded. 'Up to the pool again for a swim?'

That had been the most intoxicating night; he could still smell the scent of hawthorn blossom on the evening air; he could still see her in the moonlight, hair plastered darkly around her face, the silk cami-knickers clinging wetly to her slim body, her nipples standing impudently proud. He could still feel her wet skin and moist lips pressed against his as their bodies entwined on the reedy bank.

'I want to take you home,' he said.

She stared. 'Now? At this time of night?'

'So you can see Jericho. It'll be your home.'

She sighed and leaned against him. 'I wanted us to be alone, James,' she murmured. 'Just the two of us.'

'There'll still be time, after.'

She straightened, and he could see the expression of resignation on her face. 'Well, if your father won't mind . . .'

They rode single file along the rutted lane. James watched the slim legs rise and fall as she pedalled, and felt anxious each time her wheels juddered into a furrow and she wobbled, but Anna only laughed.

The last stretch was a steep incline and they could freewheel. Anna took her feet from the pedals and stretched out her legs.

'Wheeeee!' she sang as the bicycle wavered and bounced downhill. 'Isn't it wonderful to be young and in love with the most perfect person in the world?'

'Yes,' James called back. 'It is.'

She raised her arm and pointed ahead. 'Is that Jericho?'

The farm lay fat and sleepy in the moonlight, its shadows stretching clawlike across the cobbles of the yard.

'That's it,' he said, and waited for her reaction.

'Mmm. Big place,' she remarked as they dismounted at the gate. He felt a glow of pride.

'Told you – biggest for miles.' He lifted the latch.

'Have you got horses?' she asked.

'Two, for the ploughing.'

'I meant for riding. I love riding.'

James's warm feeling of pride faded. He led her across the yard towards the door. He had nothing to offer her to compare with what she was used to. She wasn't going to like Jericho . . .

Father did his best. Knowing better than to offer a lady a tankard of home-brewed ale he fetched out the bottle of elderberry wine Mrs Kelsey, the schoolmaster's wife, had brought round last Christmas.

Anna declined it with thanks. 'I'm always wary of home-brewed wines,' she explained sunnily. 'They can be awfully heady even if they taste mild. I got terribly squiffy once with some plum stuff – it was so potent . . .'

James saw his father's smile. He was evidently warming to her. She settled for a cup of tea, and then James showed her round the house. Until this moment he hadn't noticed how shabby the curtains looked, how dusty and neglected the whole house appeared. Finally they reached Mother's old sewing room.

'Pretty,' said Anna. 'Is that it? I thought the house looked bigger from the outside. What about the other wing?'

He tried hard to fight back the disappointment; he wanted so desperately to please her; he loved this place and wanted so much for her to love it too. 'That's all barns and byres,' he said quietly. 'The milking shed and that. I'm afraid it's not what you're used to.'

'I don't want what I'm used to.'

Anna moved to the window and looked out into the darkness. As she turned back to him he saw her nod. 'Hmm. I think I could do things with this place. It's nice.'

Relief surged in him. He had no need to feel ashamed or to apologize for what he was offering her after all. He slid his arm about her waist as they returned to the scullery. As they passed the steps down to the basement she pointed.

'What's down there? Is it your wine cellar?'

James laughed and shook his head. 'I'll show you.'

He took a candle from a shelf, lit it with a match, and led the way. At the foot of the stairs he opened a door and stood back so that she could see the long, low-ceilinged area running under the whole house. She stared, puzzled.

'The roof isn't high enough for you to stand up,' she said.

'It only needs to be cow-height. It's where we bring the cattle and sheep in during a bad winter. With them all packed in down here you'd be surprised how warm it makes the house. And it saves going out into the fields to feed them in the snow.'

She looked back at the steps. 'But how on earth do they get in here?'

'Look, there's a door at the far end, straight in from the fields.'

She hugged him close. 'How clever! And with all that straw, we could come in and be all private without anyone knowing—' Her fingers were sidling up the buttons of his jacket.

James laid a hand over hers. 'All in good time, love,' he murmured, 'not yet.'

Back in the kitchen Father was waiting. 'Well?' he said as they came in, 'what do you reckon to it then?'

Anna sat down at the table, cupping her chin in her hands. 'It's sweet – it's got a wonderful atmosphere,' she said thoughtfully, 'but I'd like to see a bit of colour – flowered curtains perhaps, and some matching cushions. It would bring it to life again.'

She broke off suddenly, touching her fingers to her lips. 'Oh, I'm sorry – that was stupid of me – I do apologize, Mr Hemingway.'

James's father shook his head. 'Nay, don't fret. It's three years now since my Dolly passed away. It'll be up to the next Mrs Hemingway to do as she pleases.'

She smiled at him. He busied himself reaching down the knitted kettle-holder and pulling the kettle back on the hob, avoiding her gaze. 'Ay, making a home is a woman's job,' he murmured. 'A home's not the same without a woman.'

'I like your father,' she confided in James as he rode home with her. 'He's a good man.'

James laughed. 'Even though he went to great pains to let you know you'll be marrying a grammar school boy?'

'He's proud of you, James, and that's nice. My parents aren't proud of me because I don't want to be presented at Court and I don't like the pompous prigs they keep inviting to dinner for my benefit. Dorothy's OK – she does what they want but I'm a hopeless case.'

At the lane end distant lights glimmered in Barnbeck cottages. Anna dismounted. 'Don't come any further, love – someone might see you.'

James felt a sinking feeling. 'What are your folks going to think about me when they learn? They'll hate it. What if they refuse to listen, you being under age and all?'

'Your father didn't object.'

'He liked you.'

'My lot can't help liking you either when they get to know you. They'll get used to it.'

'And if your father doesn't agree? What then?'

Anna tossed her head. 'Then bugger him,' she said firmly. 'I love you.'

James stared. 'Don't you love him?'

She frowned. 'How do you mean?'

'Your father – don't you love him too?'

'What kind of question is that? Of course I do, I suppose. I never really thought about it.'

'You wouldn't want to upset him, would you?'

She chuckled. 'Daddy's always been used to getting his own way. He'll be shocked, angry even, but he'll give in in the end. And if he doesn't, then hard luck. I'm going to marry you.' She took hold of James's hand and laid it on her breast. 'Now, there's just enough time left before ten, so how about a quick swim and a cuddle?'

SEVEN

1938

For days after Anna returned to Harrogate James could settle to nothing. Whether he was milking or mucking out the stable, she was always distracting his thoughts. One after the other he kept pulling out memories of her, like snapshots in his head, reliving their sublime moments together. His favourite was of the wet, clinging camiknickers . . .

His father shook his head gravely. 'The sooner you get yourself wed, the better. We can't be doing with lovesick lads leaving one udder unmilked.'

'It can't be too soon for me,' James replied. 'I wish she'd write.'

Every morning he was out waiting at the farm gate for Eddie to bring the post. At last the letter came; Eddie waved it over his head as he trudged up the lane.

'This the one you been waiting for, is it?' he said as he leaned on the barred gate to catch his breath. 'Postmarked Harrogate. Love-letter, is it? I like delivering them.'

James sat on the edge of the horse-trough to tear it open, eager to read her words, to know she was missing him as desperately as he ached for her. A photograph lay inside the folded sheet.

'This is my house,' Anna wrote, 'and if you look hard you can see two small white specks under the oak – that's Dorothy and me.'

He read on, savouring the words that told him how much she longed for his arms around her, how she was counting the moments until he came to her.

'I've persuaded Daddy to let you come to dinner with us on the twelfth, so you can talk to him then. There will be others there too, but don't worry, I'll make sure you get the chance to be alone with him. Just remember to compliment him on his Purdeys and the Meissen bowl in the hall and you'll be on the right side of him.'

James heard his father's heavy boots on the cobblestones behind him.

'You heard from that lass of yours at last?' Father asked.

'Yes, and she sent a picture.' James looked down at the photograph. It was impossible to recognize which of the two diminutive figures under the tree was Anna. Behind them, at the top of a long drive, stood an imposing mansion surrounded by magnificent shrubs and lawns. It must take an army of gardeners to maintain them. He felt a shiver of apprehension. He knew she came from a rich family, but this was palatial enough for an aristocrat . . .

His father looked over his shoulder. 'That her house?' he asked. 'By heck but it's a whopper. I never thought she lived in a castle. Come on in for your breakfast or Boothroyd'll be here with his bloody tractor to do that hayfield before we've eaten.'

For a time they ate their porridge in silence. 'Never mind,' said James philosophically as they heard the rumble of the tractor out in the lane, 'maybe the Harcourts'll accept me for what I am. Once they realize how much I love her.'

His father clearly had reservations. 'Ay,' he snorted, 'and pigs might fly.'

'I'm going anyway,' said James as he got up, pulling on his jacket.

His father wiped his mouth and stood up. 'Ay, well just you take care on that bloody tractor thing else you'll not be here to go. I hate them damned machines.'

James opened the door. 'Why are you borrowing it then?'

'I'm not borrowing – Boothroyd's lending. His way of paying off a favour.'

'You didn't have to accept.'

His father shrugged as he walked out into the sunlit yard. 'I did. I can't abide folks feeling indebted.'

The train ride to Harrogate followed by a tram ride out to the suburbs seemed to take ages. Very soon now he would see Anna again. James was elated as he walked along the tree-lined avenue in the evening dusk until he found the stone pillars at the end announcing Thirlbeck Manor.

He could see lights in the house at the end of a long gravel drive sweeping around rhododendron bushes up to the impressive door. For a moment he felt daunted; the place looked even bigger and grander than in the photograph. He took a deep breath and stepped out.

It felt unnatural to be wearing his best suit on a Thursday, with his shoes brilliantly polished and his hair greased and brushed, just like setting out for Church on Sunday. There was a crunching sound behind him, the headlamps of a car approaching. He stepped aside to let it pass and caught a glimpse of glossy paintwork as it overtook him.

He rounded the last bush. The occupants of the car were already alighting outside the front door, a distinguished-looking man with a grey beard helping a heavily-bejewelled lady to climb out. As James approached a maidservant opened the door to let them enter, then closed it again.

As he came nearer he could see people in a brightly lit room, glasses in hand, faces smiling, heads thrown back in laughter. They all looked considerably older than him, carefree and completely at ease. These were wealthy people, sophisticated men and women of the world, accustomed to recognition of their status and privilege, and suddenly he felt at a loss. This was no place for him. If it wasn't for Anna . . .

He climbed the steps and rang the bell, then waited. The maid who opened the door eyed him curiously. 'Your card, sir?'

James lifted his chin. 'I don't have any. My name is James Hemingway.'

'Come this way, sir.'

In the oak-panelled vestibule he looked around, hoping to see her. The maid opened a panelled door. From inside James could hear a babble of conversation.

'Mr James Hemingway, sir,' the maid announced, and stood back. James took a slow breath and walked in. The conversation died, and a dozen faces turned to him.

Anna wasn't one of them. He tried to pin a smile on his face as a tall, balding man approached, holding out his hand.

'Ah James, I'm Anna's father. So kind of you to come so far. I hope the journey wasn't too tedious?'

'Not at all.' How could he add that any journey, however long, however arduous, would be worth it for a glimpse of Anna?

'Drive down, did you?' Harcourt asked, signalling to a maid to bring a glass of sherry for his guest.

'No, sir. I came by train.'

'I see. Excuse me a moment, will you? Anna will be down directly.' Harcourt left him to go across to rejoin the group by the fireplace. James stood awkwardly by the door, the untasted glass of sherry in hand, waiting, trying to ignore the covert glances being cast his way.

Then suddenly she was there, swathed in pink satin in the doorway, beaming and holding out her hands to him. His hand trembled as he put down the glass on a nearby table. It was all he could do not to snatch her up in his arms and cover her with kisses.

'I've missed you, James,' she murmured, holding his hand tightly between hers, gazing up at him with a look which melted his heart. 'Ever so much.'

He squeezed her hand gently. 'And I've missed you – more than you'll ever know.'

'Three weeks is eternity without you. Talk to Daddy later, when most of the others have gone. Did you look at the Meissen?'

'The what?'

'The big bowl in the hall – apart from the Purdeys it's his prize possession. Tell him you know it's Meissen before you turn it over and see the crossed swords on the base. He'll be awfully impressed.'

Harcourt was suddenly at their side. 'Anna, darling, I want you to come over and meet Mr and Mrs Radcliffe – he's the new Chief Constable, you know – and their son Gerald who's putting up for Parliament. He's taking you in to dinner.'

The meal was a trial for James. No-one told him he was supposed to take the elderly Mrs Byrne in to dinner until she took his arm. She smiled as he settled her in her seat and retrieved her bag which had fallen to the floor.

'Thank you, young man. What's your name?'

'James Hemingway, ma'am.'

'You're a gentleman, James. I'm very lucky to have such a handsome young man sitting next to me.'

He smiled. She was a bright, birdlike little woman with bright, birdlike eyes which observed everything. James felt distinctly ill at ease. Even in his Sunday best he was aware that he was no match for the company; they were so glittering and self-possessed. Never before had he sat down to a table like this with a row of glasses and a baffling array of cutlery before him. A silver candelabra obscured his view of Anna further along the table, and as his eyes grew accustomed to the dazzle of the light he could make out the red-gold halo of her hair as she leaned in lively conversation towards a young man he took to be Gerald.

During the soup course he became aware that the old lady next to him was following his gaze.

'She's lovely, isn't she?' said Mrs Byrne. 'I can quite appreciate your interest.'

'I want to marry her,' said James.

'Oh dear. Are you very wealthy?'

'No. But I know she loves me.'

A maidservant reached between them to take the soup bowls. James leaned away. Another pair of hands holding a platter of fish appeared on his other side and he leaned back. He saw Anna watching him, unsmiling. Mr Harcourt was watching too while nodding to his neighbour's words.

When the maid retreated and another hovered, Mrs Byrne whispered under her breath. 'Don't move, Mr Hemingway, let them work round you – they're used to it.'

He flashed her a grateful smile. For the remainder of the meal he tried to keep his eyes off Anna while he talked with Mrs Byrne.

'What do you do, James?' she wanted to know.

'I'm a farmer, in Garthdale.'

She looked him up and down. 'Well I must say, you've got a great deal more about you than many of the young men Mr Harcourt has brought here to meet his daughters. Rich and spoilt, most of them.'

Harcourt's daughters – he had forgotten she had a sister. He looked along the table. 'Where is Dorothy?' he enquired.

'In Switzerland, I believe,' Mrs Byrne replied, 'on holiday with her fiancé's family.'

Anna and her father alone in this vast house, thought James. He felt proud, thinking of her playing hostess to these people.

'It's a pity about Anna's mother,' he remarked, 'dying so young, I mean.'

Mrs Byrne chuckled. 'Is that what she told you? Anna's mother ran away to India years ago with a tea-planter. They've never heard from her since.' She shrugged thin shoulders. 'I suppose that's as good as dead.'

'What do you think, Mr Hemingway?' Harcourt's voice called down the table. 'Are you interested in the market?'

James declined the wine the maid was offering with a smile. 'I can quote you the going price for sheep and cattle, sir,' he replied. 'Pigs too, if you're interested.'

'Ah, yes.' Harcourt turned his attention back to his neighbour. James had the distinct feeling that he'd said something inadmissible in polite society. Mrs Byrne smiled at him.

'I think they're talking about the financial markets,' she murmured.

'James is a farmer, you know,' Anna's clear voice rang out. 'He owns thousands of acres up on the moors, don't you? Lots of pheasant and grouse.'

'Do you now?' asked Gerald, his eyebrows arched in surprise. 'Organize shoots, do you? How much a gun?'

James laid his fork down. 'What kind of gun?'

The eyebrows arched higher. 'It depends on the make, does it? Well, I've got a Churchill at the moment but I'm hoping to get a Purdey.'

'I can't tell you what they cost, only I believe it's a fortune,' James replied. He heard the titter and looked around. Harcourt was frowning.

'Gerald was asking the rent for shooting on your land,' he growled. 'Evidently you don't shoot. You're not a sportsman.'

'Oh I shoot,' James replied calmly, 'but not for sport.'

There was an awkward silence, just for a second, then another woman spoke. 'You hunt though, don't you, Mr Hemingway? What's the difference?'

'I don't hunt,' he said quietly. 'I shoot and fish, but only for food or to keep down the vermin.'

The maids reappeared carrying dishes of sherry trifle and profiteroles. Harcourt threw up his hands. 'And speaking of food, here comes the dessert.'

Mrs Byrne nudged James's elbow. 'Pity you haven't got your gun with you now – there's a lot of vermin round this table.'

James shook his head. 'I think I've shot myself in the foot,' he murmured.

She gave him an impish smile. 'You could kidnap her,' she suggested, 'and if that doesn't work you could always come back for me.'

Harcourt was seeing the last guests off from the doorstep. James sat with Anna in the drawing room.

'Now's your chance,' Anna whispered.

Her father reappeared in the doorway. 'Anna, I'd like to talk to James alone,' he said mildly. 'Come along to my study.'

James felt the pressure of her hand on his as he rose to follow. In the hallway he noticed the big blue bowl on the centre table.

'Ah, Meissen, isn't it?' he said, touching a finger to its smooth surface.'

'You know it is,' said Harcourt. 'My daughter told you so, didn't she? I know my daughter – that's why I want to talk to you. Come in.'

He led the way into a large, booklined room where a fire still burned in the hearth. He stood with his back to it, his feet astride. 'Please sit,' he said, but the words were not so much an invitation as an order. James seated himself reluctantly on the low leather settee. From this angle Harcourt appeared even taller.

Harcourt lifted the back of his jacket to warm his backside. 'I want you to know that I am fully aware of what has been going on. My family in Barnbeck are not stupid.'

James stared. How could he know? And how much?

'Let me tell you it has got to stop,' Harcourt went on.

James found his voice. 'But I love her. I'm going to marry her.'

'Do you realize how ridiculous you sound? She spends more on clothes than you earn in a year.'

James felt ridiculous. He looked at Harcourt's suit, moulded to his body like a glove, and felt acutely aware of the rough cloth of his own Burton suit jutting awkwardly between the buttons.

He spoke quietly. 'I'm not rich, I know, but I have a good farm—'

'Three-quarters of it only fit for grazing. Oh yes, I know exactly how many sheep and pigs you own and how many acres including the quarry. You can't possibly keep my daughter in the manner to which she's accustomed. Marriage is out of the question.'

'She wants to marry me,' said James.

'Rubbish. At her age she doesn't know what she wants. But I have her interests at heart – she will make a good match like her sister.' Harcourt turned and rang the bell. 'Now if I have made myself clear there is an end to the matter. You will not have any further contact with my daughter. Now I would be obliged if you would leave. Good night.'

He reached the door just as the maid arrived. Harcourt swept past her. 'Please show Mr Hemingway to the door,' James heard him say, and he was gone.

Anna came out of the drawing room as he was following the maid across the hall. She waved a hand.

'It's all right, Betty, I'll see to Mr Hemingway.'

The moment the maid had gone she turned to James. 'Well?' she said eagerly. 'What did he say?'

James shook his head. 'He won't hear of it.'

She jutted her chin. 'We're not going to let it end there, are we?'

He put his hands on her shoulders, warm and satin-smooth under the pink gown. 'No, darling, we won't.'

'We'll elope,' she said defiantly, 'we'll run away like Mummy did.' She flushed. 'I'm sorry. I never told you. We all pretend she's dead. But we could, couldn't we? We could run off to Scotland tonight. That'll teach him a lesson.'

He started. 'Tonight? We can't—'

'Why not?' she demanded. 'The sooner the better. I can pack a few things—'

He gave a rueful smile. 'I've got seventeen-and-sixpence in my pocket. That won't get us very far.'

'I've got twenty pounds up in my room, a birthday present from Aunt Phyllis. That's plenty.'

He held her close. 'We'll go when I say. With my money – I won't take a penny from you. I'll be back very soon, I promise.'

She couldn't argue, his lips pressed hard on hers. Before he knew it James found himself outside the front door and large drops of rain were beginning to splash spider-shapes on the stone steps. There'd be no more trams, no more trains at this hour. He'd have to find a room for the night.

Turning up his collar he set off down the gravel drive . . .

EIGHT

1965

Lisa was enjoying her new job and especially entertaining the Braithwaites. She told David about them over supper.

'Honestly,' she said enthusiastically, 'you wouldn't believe they were a couple, he's so big and she's so tiny. He must weigh three times as much as her, but they think the world of one another.'

'Do you feel you're winning him over?' David asked.

Lisa pulled a face. 'It's hard to say. He's no fool – he's got his wits about him.'

David smiled as he refilled her glass. 'You always fancied older men,' he remarked.

She laughed. 'Not this one. At least you don't have to worry about him making a pass at me.' She picked up her fork and played with the remaining strands of spaghetti on her plate. 'And how have you been today?' she asked casually.

He was aware that she was trying, for his sake, not to appear unduly concerned. 'Fine,' he answered. 'I made a start on the new poster.'

He jerked his fork towards the canvas.

'It's nice,' she said without looking round. 'Look, I've got to go tonight – the tickets are booked and everything.'

He held up his hands. 'Who's stopping you?' he said brightly. 'Of course you've got to go.'

She laid the fork down and gave him that candidly direct look he'd always found so lovable. 'You're doing it again,' she said in that same restrained tone.

'Putting on an act. I used to think I could sense your every change of mood, but now . . .'

'And now I'm not covering up anything. I'm fine, I said so.' He leaned back, draping one arm casually over the back of the chair.

'No more headaches?' she asked.

'Not a glimmer since we went to the hospital.'

'And your eyes?'

He hesitated only a fraction of a second. 'No change. Nothing to worry about, honestly – would I lie to you?'

'You lied to me once, David. I know it was to try and spare me but now I don't know what to believe. You never kept anything from me before.'

He looked away from the probing eyes. 'No, I'm sorry. But it was the one and only time, I swear. I'll never do it again.'

As they entered the brilliantly lit hotel foyer Harold Braithwaite rubbed his hands together, his chubby face aglow. 'That was one hell of a good night out, Lisa lass,' he enthused. 'Cynthia and me have had a right good time and no mistake.'

His petite wife took his arm. 'We have that, and we shall make sure to tell Mr Lewis what a grand job you've made of showing us the sights. I don't know why we don't come to London more often, Harold.'

'From now on I'll make time, business or no business,' he replied warmly. 'Just so long as it's Lisa here who's in charge. I didn't think I'd like going to the theatre but that musical were fair grand. Now, what's on for us last day tomorrow?'

'Your choice,' said Lisa. 'I've left it clear for you to do whatever you'd like.'

Harold looked down at his wife. 'What do you fancy, love? A bit of shopping while you've chance of them big shops?'

She looked up at him in surprise. 'You hate

shopping, love. All that traipsing round – your feet, remember.'

'Ah well, I were thinking of you ladies going on your own. Make the most of having a smart young lady to advise you – have a nice cream tea after, happen. I could meet you there.'

'Fortnum and Mason's,' Lisa suggested. 'You'd like that.'

'Fortnum and Mason,' repeated Cynthia dreamily, 'I've only ever read their lovely catalogue. Oh yes! But what about you, Harold – what will you do?'

He smiled. 'I'll think of summat, if it's only having a snooze in the sun on the hotel terrace.' He saw her gaze darting about the foyer. 'What are you looking for?'

She pointed. 'Is that the Ladies over there?'

'And you can buy yourself a pretty frock or two,' Harold called after her. He turned back to Lisa. 'Well that's settled then, she's happy. Now, there's summat I want to ask you, but I don't know quite how to put it.'

Lisa smiled. 'Coming out with it is usually the easiest way.'

'Ay. I've always prided myself on being blunt. Well you see, it's like this . . .'

She heard the hesitation, saw the anxiety dulling his eyes. 'I want to grab the chance while I'm on me own, without Cynthia, to go somewhere I've only ever heard tell about, do you see?'

'I'll see to it,' said Lisa. 'Where?'

'Only there'd need to be a telephone call for me, urgent business and that . . . Cynthia would never question that. And I know I'll need a ticket.'

'Leave it to me – I'll see to all that. Just tell me what it is.'

David left the old car behind the pub and took his restless thoughts to the park, hoping the warm

70

evening air and the sight of other people would help to dispel them. Being alone in a hot, airless flat did little to lift the oppression.

It wasn't that he felt ill any more; on the contrary he felt so alive and filled with vigour these days that he could be forgiven for thinking that the specialist's words had all been a dream. He felt so charged with energy he imagined he could live for ever. Only the eyes kept playing him up . . .

Suppose he had to face it. Maybe he ought to practise, in readiness for when the time came. He closed his eyes and groped his way along the railings.

The park gate was further than he'd thought. He could have sworn it was nearer than this. He opened one cautious eye; there it was, another twenty yards away. He closed the eye and carried on.

The stone pillar met his fingertips and at the same time he caught the heady scent of roses. He turned in, and gasped. Damn – he'd forgotten the concrete bollards they'd put up to keep cars out. Eyes still closed, he rubbed his shin and went on. Footsteps were approaching, the light, clicking step of a woman in high heels. He'd have to learn the art of deducing facts from hearing. He opened his eyes to check as the footsteps passed, just in time to avoid falling over the leather lead strained between the woman and her bounding boxer dog.

There must be a knack to this. He looked at the war memorial at the far end of the path. Fifty yards, he guessed, and no-one in his way. Closing his eyes again he began to walk, a measured step of approximately one yard. Forty-eight, forty-nine, fifty. He opened his eyes again. The steps of the memorial were only five yards away.

So he could do a blind return journey to the gate by counting fifty paces back. Counting – that was it. If counting off the number of railings back along the road to the crossing was too slow and arduous, he could count the lamp posts instead. Count everything from now on. Count the steps up the memorial while you're here.

Suddenly overcome by the hopelessness of it all, he sank down on the bottom step. Over the far trees the sun was setting, a molten red-gold spilling along the horizon, and he felt he could weep at the sheer beauty of it. This was what he would miss soon. This was beauty which enraptured and enriched the soul; he must savour it now, soak it up against the future's darkness.

If only he could talk about it, try to explain, but words were inadequate. Lisa was too busy right now, much as she loved him. She'd changed, ever so slightly but it was there, a kind of restraint which had never existed between them. And he'd brought it upon himself by deceiving her.

Not for the first time. He sat dejectedly, elbows on knees, watching the dying sun. He'd never meant to keep anything from her, but how could you tell the girl you adored that they'd only come by a reasonable flat with the help of another woman?

Melanie had been the first woman in his life, back in his student days before he met Lisa. He couldn't take his eyes off her at the college cocktail party, so elegant and poised, so warm-eyed and beautiful. She'd made no secret of the fact that she was contentedly married to a flourishing accountant, worshipped her two small children, and would never dream of shattering her peaceful life. But she craved the excitement of an occasional illicit fling, and what could be more dashing than an artist?

He felt ashamed of how readily he'd given in, overcoming without much difficulty his initial reluctance to betray a man he didn't know, but having an affair with a woman who was older and much more sophisticated was heady wine for a young man. She'd been wonderful. She never questioned him, never pried. Just so long as he was available.

And she always understood. When he told her about Lisa she'd been happy for him. And when they decided to live together it had been Melanie who suggested the flat over the theatre where she sometimes performed, Melanie who arranged the peppercorn rent . . . And Lisa had never learned of her existence.

Melanie. He shouldn't. He'd sworn he never would again. But then she'd always been a ready listener, and right now he needed a receptive ear. The pattern seemed to repeat itself, a month to fight off the self-disgust and a month to fight the rising need for her. It had been two months since they last met . . .

The sun had sunk out of sight now and the park was dimming into gloom. He stood up, dug into his pocket and pulled out some coppers, then set off purposefully down the path towards the gate. Nearby stood a telephone box.

He heard the dialling tone. Please let her be alone.

'Hello?'

'Melanie – it's me. Can you talk?'

'Yes – what is it?'

'Can I come over? I need to see you.'

'Now?'

'If I can. Just for an hour.'

There was a second's hesitation. 'Not here – Geoffrey could be back early tonight.'

He closed his eyes to shut Geoffrey out. 'The Red Lion then,' he said urgently. 'There's something I want to tell you.'

The moment he put the phone down he felt ashamed. You're a weak bastard, he told himself as he walked back towards the Mini. Lisa had refused to sell Gladys when she took delivery of her new car. It would give him more freedom, she said.

73

It must be growing late. He could hear cars revving up outside. David pulled back the curtain, letting the light of the streetlamp flow into the shabby room, showing up the antiquated dressing table with its bloomed mirror, the leaning wardrobe whose door hung open, unable to shut properly, and the tumble of sheets strewn over the bed.

He sat down on the edge of the bed and began pulling on his trousers. The heat was gone now; once again he was filled only with shame and self-disgust. They had never got round to talking.

'I've got to go,' he said abruptly. The sheets moved. A woman's dark head appeared, smiled, and vanished under the sheets again.

That's it, he thought angrily as he pulled on his jacket, never again. This time was once too often. I'll never see her again, never.

He was already in bed by the time Lisa arrived home. She undressed quickly and slipped in beside him.

'You awake, darling?'

'Mmm.'

'You've been OK on your own? What did you do?'

'Oh, took Gladys for an airing, had a walk in the park.'

'You'll never guess what Mr Braithwaite wanted me to do – only arrange for him to go to Raymond's Revue Bar without his wife knowing.'

She heard David's mumble under the bedcovers. 'So there's life in the old dog yet.'

'He's never seen a strip show before. He isn't a dirty old man at all, but he just wants to have been to one, man of the world and all that. I'm to take his wife shopping while he goes. I don't like lying to her, but it's quite sweet, isn't it?'

'What's sweet about it? He's going to gawp at naked women.'

'Yes, but that's all he'll do. He might be as un-scrupulous as hell in business, but he's really quite a faithful old soul. You can always tell.'

'Can you?'

'Always.'

NINE

1965

Alex Seifer was clearly doing very well out of promoting his rock artists, thought David as he entered the smart offices in London's West End. The spacious reception area boasted an abundance of smoked glass and chrome and potted plants, and along the terracotta walls hung photographs of all the best known rock and skiffle artists. Several more rooms led off the area; they reminded David of piglets around a sow at Jericho. With rents at some astronomical figure per square foot in town, Seifer must be making a packet.

The snub-nosed girl at the reception desk barely looked up from her typewriter. 'Mr Seifer is terribly busy but he shouldn't be long.'

'My name is Hemingway. I have a two o'clock appointment with him.'

She shrugged pretty shoulders. 'Like I said, he's dreadfully busy. Please take a seat.'

He sat on one of the low space-age units which he assumed was supposed to be a chair, hugging his canvases between his knees. The gentle voice of Mary Hopkin drifted through the air, singing about the days she thought would never end.

At twenty to three he heard a deep voice buzz through to say he was ready. The girl led David to a smaller room and pointed to a long table. 'If you would lay your work out there ready, or prop them up – Mr Seifer hasn't much time.'

He uncovered his canvases and leaned them carefully against the wall, then stood back. Under the office lighting they looked every bit as good as they did back at the flat, and he felt pleased with himself. Lisa had liked them too. He'd got something here, he knew it. They reflected his own feeling of optimism, vibrant, lively, capturing the spirit of the new age. And they had a touch of wit, his own personal stamp. It was what the college tutor had called finding your own voice, and he'd got it here.

The door opened and a small man with a glistening bald head bounced in, vitality oozing from every pore. From his voice on the telephone David had somehow visualized a much bigger man. He was about to offer his hand when the little man spoke.

'Well, where are they? I've no time to waste?'

David pointed behind him to where the posters stood. Seifer swung round, as if on a pivot, and his eyeballs bulged. 'Jesus, what's that?' he demanded. 'Those the posters I commissioned for The Swamp?'

'Yes, sir.'

'Christ almighty!' The little man peered closer. 'Well they're different, I'll give you that, but who the hell ever saw a purple alligator flying? And what's all this scribble down here?'

David's self-confidence swayed. 'You wanted something eye-catching, something which reflected the spirit of the group. What do you think?'

The little man straightened. 'I think I want my ten per cent advance back. Eye-catching, I said, not screw your fucking eyeballs out. They're too damn strident, all of them, too aggressive. I wanted something more tasteful.'

David tried to control his voice. 'Of course they're aggressive – it's The Swamp we're talking about, not Mantovani.'

'You've never heard them play, have you? You're wasting my time, Hathaway, this is rubbish.'

'Hemingway. And I have heard them play – doing a gig in Hyde Park when they were nobodies. I'll give

77

you a poster to reflect them, Mr Seifer – how about a huge pile of crap with this bald-headed dwarf sitting on top?'

Snatching up the canvases David marched out of the office.

Outside in the crowded street a thin drizzle was starting to fall.

He was still fuming when he reached the stage door and let himself in. Lazarus was waltzing down the corridor with a pile of costumes over his arm.

There was concern in his dark eyes as he came close. 'Oh David, my dear,' he said softly, 'I'm so sorry to hear your bad news. I just want you to know if there's anything, anything at all I can do . . .'

David stared. 'Bad news?' he echoed faintly.

'I know I probably shouldn't upset you by talking like this, but I want you to know that if I can help, now or later, with Lisa, you understand . . .'

David felt his gentle touch on his arm and brushed it away. 'Oh for God's sake, you old queen,' he snapped, and ran up the stairs.

Lisa was stirring something in a pan over the gas ring and a warm, spicy smell filled the air. She turned with a welcoming smile as he flung the canvases down.

'Why the devil did you have to go and tell Lazarus about me?' he demanded, throwing the canvases on to the bed. 'I thought we'd agreed we'd tell no-one. Now the old poofter will leak it round to everybody. Why the hell couldn't you keep it to yourself?'

He saw the smile slip, the frown corrugate her forehead. 'Well?' he repeated. 'Why did you tell him?'

Lisa shook her head. 'I don't know how he found out, David. It wasn't me.'

For a second the world juddered. If it wasn't Lisa, then who? Melanie. Oh God – she'd said something about reading for a part in the next play . . .

He took Lisa's arm and drew her to him. 'I'm sorry, maybe I misunderstood him. I've had a lousy day. Seifer turned down my posters and wants the advance back.'

She looked up into his eyes. 'David, I'm so sorry.'

'Doesn't matter. It's made me decide something. I am going to live, Lisa.'

'Of course you are.'

'And I'm going to paint something really worthwhile.'

She glanced at the posters on the bed. 'You have done – I think they're terrific.'

'I've got to do it before my sight gets any worse.'

She touched a finger to his temple. 'And it is getting worse, isn't it? There's no need to pretend with me. You nearly fell over that toddler in the shop yesterday, and that waitress – you didn't see her, did you?'

He smiled. 'Not till I clopped her with my elbow, poor kid.'

'Why did we have to leave in such a hurry? I hadn't finished my coffee.'

He looked down. 'The music – it was too loud. It hurt.'

For a moment she was silent. 'Listen,' she said at last, 'I've been thinking.' She put down the spoon and reached for a bottle of wine standing on the kettle drum, then poured red liquid into two glasses. 'There's no point in doing commissions that give you no satisfaction. Why don't I pack in my job and we'll go away where you can paint what you really want?'

He hesitated. To get away from the noise of London; peace to paint while he could still define shape and colour – to get away from the lure of Melanie . . .

'You love the job,' he said as he took the glass from her. 'What would you do? What would we live on?'

'I can always get some sort of job – I'll find something. I just want us to be happy together.'

For the time I have left. She won't say that. He

79

smiled. 'Just when you're becoming a woman about town – what about your new car?'

She shook her head and sipped the wine. 'I couldn't care less about all that and we've still got Gladys. What matters is that I see you fulfilling yourself.'

He saw the pleading in her eyes and felt moved to aching tenderness. Lovely, loving Lisa. How would she cope without him? There would be no-one to ease the pain . . .

'Where could we go?' he asked.

She brightened at once. 'Well, as it happens, Frank Mason told me he has his holiday cottage in Staithes – he won't be using it now the season's over.'

'Staithes?'

'Near Whitby – it's beautiful. Lots of artists go there. He's willing to let us have it rent-free until the season starts again.'

Till the season starts again, he thought. I wonder if I will be able to see it.

Lisa raised her glass. 'Let's drink to it, darling – Staithes, and the most wonderful painting of your life.'

Lazarus was standing on the doorstep, tearing up a stale crust and throwing morsels to the dozen or so pigeons strutting and squabbling at his feet when Lisa set off for work. Five minutes to catch the train. She glanced over her shoulder. David had gone back into the flat.

'Lazarus, how did you know about David?' she asked. He turned anxious blue eyes on her.

'So it is true? Oh, Lisa!'

'But who told you? How did you find out?'

He looked down at the remnant of bread in his hand. 'I've said too much already. My mother always used to say I had this naughty habit of poking my nose in where it wasn't wanted. He was very cross with me.'

'Lazarus – I've got a tube to catch.'

'Don't let me keep you – just tell him I'm sorry. I promise I won't tell another soul. He was dreadfully rude to me.'

She could see his eyes glistening and touched his arm gently. 'He can't help it – he's under a great deal of strain right now. You understand.'

'Oh, of course. And listen, my sweet, if ever you need me, now or after—'

'I know. Thanks, Lazarus.'

She glanced at her watch. Three minutes to go. She raced off down the street.

Mr Lewis's usual composure was clearly shattered when Lisa telephoned.

'You want to hand in your resignation?' he repeated. 'Already? Well really! You've only been with us for a couple of months – yet I clearly remember warning you at your interview that I wanted no job-hoppers who would leave us in the lurch after a couple of years—'

'And I recall saying that none of us could see what the future might hold,' Lisa said quietly.

'I thought you had the makings of a good member of the team. Now it seems I was wrong. You clearly have no sense of corporate loyalty, leaving us high and dry without a word of warning.'

Lisa gritted her teeth. 'I'm willing to work out a reasonable notice, Mr Lewis – a couple of weeks.'

'Reasonable? How would you know what is reasonable? I find the whole business totally unreasonable. You will of course work the normal month's notice—'

'I haven't got time,' she cut in. 'Time is running out.'

Mr Lewis swept on. 'And I think in the circumstances, although your work has been perfectly satisfactory in the short time you've been with us, I am not prepared to give you a reference. I'm sure you'll agree that that is reasonable. One month's notice.'

Lisa closed her eyes. 'You haven't asked why I'm leaving, Mr Lewis.'

His voice sounded starched. 'The reason does not concern me. My concern is for the company and its smooth running. I am most disappointed in you, Miss Drew.'

'My boyfriend is dying. I want to spend the last months – or weeks – with him.'

There was a long silence. When Mr Lewis's voice came back it sounded small. 'I'm sorry. Of course you must go. No question.'

'You'll manage if I leave at once?' she asked.

'I'll find a way. And Miss Drew – instead of your resignation, just give me a memo for the board asking for extended leave. Your job will be waiting when you're ready.'

Ellen was clearing away the supper dishes. James switched on the television and settled himself in the chair. Voices cheered, a little man looked bewildered while Michael Miles offered him a handful of banknotes.

'Open the box!' the audience screamed, and the little man shook his head at the outstretched wad of notes.

'Oh no,' said Ellen. 'Not that programme, please. It makes people look so greedy.'

James switched off the set. 'I think I'll ring and see how David and Lisa are getting on,' he said.

Ellen slapped the dishes noisily into the sink. 'Why bother? If they can't take the trouble to put pen to paper . . .'

He went out into the hall. A man's voice answered, the same man who always answered. 'Hello?'

'Could I speak to David or Lisa please?'

'Hold on a sec – Lisa's just come in.'

She sounded uncertain when she picked up the phone. 'Hello – Lisa here.'

'It's me – James. You two OK? We haven't heard for a bit.'

'Oh, yes, we're fine.' The doubtful note was still there. 'Actually, we've got some news for you. We're moving – we're going to stay in Staithes for the winter.'

'Stay for the winter? What about your job?'

The voice was small now. 'I haven't got a job any more.'

'What? You haven't got the sack, surely?'

'No. I've given it up. It's important for David to have the chance to show what he can really do, and he can do that up in Staithes.' Her voice changed to a lighter note, but there was an artificial ring to it. 'You never know, you could find you've got another Constable on your hands.'

James was puzzled; it didn't sound like Lisa. And he felt angry. 'You don't mean he's let you throw up everything so he can go off and paint? How on earth will you manage?'

'It's rent-free. We don't have to pay a cent.'

'But you've got to live. Oh for heaven's sake, how irresponsible can he get?'

'He's not,' she said quietly. 'It's not like that. You've got it all wrong.'

'How is it then? You're the only one who's been earning, yet he lets you pack it all in so he can indulge himself. It's time he grew up.'

From the kitchen he heard the clatter of a saucepan, then Ellen switched on the radio. Country and Western music flooded out into the hall. James covered one ear. 'What's that? I couldn't hear you.'

'I'm sorry if you don't approve, James. Can't you just trust us? It's really for the best.'

He gave a deep sigh. 'Let me send you a cheque,' he said. 'At least there's one good thing – Staithes isn't too far away. Perhaps you'll be able to make it over here.'

Dimly he made out the distant voice telling him that they could manage, but it was almost drowned out by Tammy Wynette as she stood bravely by her man.

Ellen was contemptuous. 'He's selfish to the core,' she said. 'Isn't that just typical, living off a woman? We're all exploited by men.'

James looked up in surprise. 'Who ever exploited you?'

She snatched up her book from the chair and made for the door. 'He's selfish,' she muttered, 'and he won't change till the day he dies.'

It was late when James took out the little box of mementoes he only ever savoured when he was alone. He fingered the lock of bright hair Anna had laughingly cut off with his penknife to give him in the woods, feeling once again its silky texture and re-calling the sunlit afternoon.

He replaced it at last next to her favourite butterfly brooch and took out one of the thin bundle of letters. Even now the sight of her spidery writing made his throat clench. It was hard to read through misting eyes.

My beloved James, I'm afraid I have bad news for you . . .

TEN

1938

The lads were all waiting in the field behind the Rose and Crown when James arrived with the bucket of resin. Eddie gave him a brief nod.

'About time – I've had the devil's own job keeping this lot off the ale while you got here.'

'Sorry – I did my best.' James set the bucket down on the grass.

Eddie scowled. 'Training's important – we haven't won the Olympics tug-of-war every time by turning up late for training.'

Fred came to pick up the bucket. 'Who's won Olympics every time?' he asked.

'We have – England. Now get a move on else the light'll be gone.'

Eddie turned away. Towering above him James could see the tripod of telegraph poles and on the ground below the huge steel drum filled with rocks attached to the pulley. Eddie stopped and dug a hand into his trousers pocket.

'And while I think on, I've a letter for you, Jim. Save me traipsing up the hill, that will, but put it away for now.'

James took the pink envelope, feeling the thud in his chest as he recognized Anna's handwriting. He tucked it away casually in his pocket, trying not to smile as he followed Eddie.

The acrid smell of smoke from the day's stubble-burning still lingered over the river meadow as the men ran one lap backwards around the field to limber up. Eddie barked an order. Will, the lightest man of the team, dipped his hands in the resin bucket and took up his position alongside the rope stretched taut from the tripod.

James watched the drill, awaiting his turn. Will stood facing the rope, a yard or so from the tripod, one hand on his hip.

'Now Bob,' Eddie called.

The second man approached, dipped his hands, measured an arm's length from Will's elbow, and stood similarly akimbo.

'Fred. Then James.'

James spread the tacky resin mixture reeking of petrol on his hands and took up his place. By the time Bert, the heaviest man, had taken up the anchor position, threading the rope around his body and down, the light was fading fast. Eddie glanced up at the darkening sky.

'We'll make it three pulls and call it a day,' he said. 'Rope no more than six inches high – ready?'

Right leg braced, heels dug hard into the turf, lean back, pull . . . pull . . . The new rope felt thick and awkward to grip, its raw bulk not yet thinned and stretched by years of contests. Arms screamed in their sockets and James felt as if his back muscles would tear apart. At last, slowly, the steel drum began to tilt and waver clear of the ground. The rope gave a whiplike crack, and James heard Bob curse under his breath.

'Harder, harder,' Eddie cried. 'I want that drum ten feet high before you've done.'

Darkness had fallen by the time Eddie was satisfied. The lads crowded into the bar, desperate for ale to soothe their parched throats.

'But no boozing tomorrow night, lads, think on,' Eddie warned. 'Not unless you want to throw up in front of the Agley Bridge team on Saturday.'

'Are we using our rope?' Bob wanted to know. 'It's

still cracking like blazes – we'd be better off with the old one of theirs.'

'It's got to be used else it'll never be an old one,' said Will.

'Me back's playing me up again,' muttered Bert. 'Let's hope it'll be OK for Saturday.'

Eddie smiled. 'There's always the vicar there – he's heavy enough to be anchor man if you drop out.'

Bert looked across to the corner of the bar where the Reverend Culley sat, knees spread wide, sipping a light sherry and chatting to Molly, the barmaid. 'Would he thump,' he muttered. 'It's all flab, is that, not muscle. You don't get muscles standing preaching.'

James was no longer listening. He sat with his pint in front of him, fingering the letter in his pocket and wondering how soon he could excuse himself and slip away . . .

Father was already in bed. James sat by the fire, his fingers trembling as he tore the letter open, releasing a whiff of her scent.

My darling James, (she wrote) *It seems so long since I held you. I miss you terribly . . .*

He felt delirious with joy. She loved him still, as passionately as he loved her. He read on eagerly.

I shall ask Dorothy to post this for me. You see, my beloved, I'm afraid I have some bad news for you . . .

There was a sudden lurch in his chest. The words wavered in front of him as his hand trembled.

Daddy is furious with me and refuses to listen to a word I say. He won't let me out of the house either.

He says he is sending me away today. I don't know where, but I'll write just as soon as I can . . . I love you, my precious James, and always will . . .

He leapt up from the chair, shaking with anger. His first impulse was to rush out of the house and fly to her. But what was the use? By now she had already gone – but where? Tears were pricking his eyes. It was no use – he'd just have to wait, try to be patient until she could let him know where she was and then, by God, he'd find her and fetch her home . . .

His father's weathered face expressed no emotion as he listened. He nodded as James finished.

'Aye well, she's nobbut a lass after all's said and done, is she? I reckon I'd feel the same if she were mine, not knowing you and all.'

'I'm not rich enough for her in his eyes,' said James bitterly. 'Now if I owned Thaxton Manor instead of Jericho—'

'You'll not own that neither for some time yet, I hope,' his father cut in. 'So just you bide your time – she'll write. In the meantime, put your mind to what matters – there's the cattle cake to order and there's the match tomorrow. Agley Bridge are a pretty fair team.'

James smiled at his father's attempt to make him feel better. 'Not as good as they were in your day, eh Dad?'

'Now there was a team.' Hemingway sighed and rubbed his shin. 'Eh, if it wasn't for me war wound I could still show you how to pull, that I could.'

Day after day James waited for the letter from Anna. Day after day Eddie shook his head as he neared the gate where James stood waiting.

'Sorry, Jim. Nowt for you today but a bill. I reckon that lass of yours must have found somebody else.'

James shook his head firmly. 'She'll not do that. She'll write.'

It was weeks later when he saw Eddie hurry uphill, beaming. 'I reckon this is it, Jim. Smells lovely.'

James sat alone in the cowshed to read it. The moment he tore it open he knew the scent was not hers.

Dear James, (he read in small, neat handwriting) *Please forgive my delay in writing as I have been in London for several weeks. I know Anna would want me to let you know . . .*

His eyes slid to the name at the bottom of the sheet. Dorothy.

. . . that my father sent her to stay with relatives in Boston. He will not say how long she will remain there, only that she must stay until she has forgotten you. Please accept my kind regards . . .

He laid the letter down. How far away was Boston? If only he could discover her address . . . He looked down at the sheet of paper again.

P.S. I forgot to say, Boston, Massachusetts.

A hoarse cry rattled in his throat. America! The whole Atlantic lay between them! How on earth would he find her now? If only he could do something, confront her father, demand to know Anna's whereabouts, but he knew it would be futile.

James gritted his teeth as he went back to the house. Harcourt might be a relentlessly determined man, but James could be equally tenacious . . .

Christmas came and went, and in the deep snows of the new year James went joylessly about his work.

He'd written back to Dorothy, thanking her for her kindness and begging her to reveal her sister's address, but there had been no answer. Harcourt's doing, without doubt.

Bitterness filled him as he immersed himself in the battle to keep the farm animals alive through the merciless winter. Daily he hauled bales of hay for the sheep now in the lower fields, their blank, bewildered faces reflecting his own desolate dejection.

Survival, and thoughts of Anna, filled his mind. He sometimes caught sight of his father struggling gamely after him through the snow, and felt a stab of affectionate admiration. Dad would never let on just how old he was but he must be forty-six or sevenish now, and yet he never uttered a word of complaint about the pain he endured in his leg where the shrapnel had got him back in 'seventeen. The cold always brought the pain on, and James would see him wince but he only followed it with a wry smile and a muttered remark about his rheumatics and went on to talk of other fears.

'Mark my words, there'll be trouble,' he'd say, poring over the newspaper with a gloomy shake of the head. 'That Hitler's gone and invaded Prague now. He won't stop there, I know. I've seen it all before. Them noisy little bastards always spell trouble.'

The last of the snow was melting, leaving only grey streaks on the hillside. James was rounding up the ewes to bring them down to the pens ready for lambing when he suddenly sensed the first flickers of hope beginning to rekindle. There might have been months of silence now but somehow he knew she hadn't forgotten. She still thought of him daily, spoke his name in her prayers. Hope blossomed into excitement. He stood on the high ridge, looking down towards Jericho. As far as the eye could see nothing moved but grazing sheep. He could be the only human being for miles, and suddenly he felt alive and eager. Stretching his arms high in the air, he threw back his head and shouted.

'Anna! I love you!'

From across the valley the echo sang back to him, muted and hollow. 'Anna – I love you.' And he turned and strode back down the track, revelling in the warm glow which flooded his body. It was going to be all right, he knew it; somehow he would find his Anna again and the world would be whole once more.

Hemingway was standing gloomily by the sideboard, one hand resting on the wireless set as he listened to a crackling voice. He switched off as James came into the kitchen and sat down to pull off his boots.

'He's done it now,' Hemingway muttered.

'Who has?'

'Chamberlain. He's recalled our ambassador from Berlin. I tell you, lad, there'll be another war. He's going to double the Territorials now.'

'They won't call you up anyway, not with your leg.'

'Happen not, but what about you? I wouldn't want a son of mine going through owt like the last lot, God help us.'

James stretched frozen toes towards the fire. 'Don't fret so much, Dad, it'll never happen. Everything is going to be great, I can feel it in my bones.'

ELEVEN

1965

A cold November wind was driving in off the North Sea as Lisa parked the car and they climbed the steep steps to the cottage. David dumped the battered suitcases on the floor and went across to the window. Lisa eased the haversack from her shoulder and lowered it on to the table.

David was leaning on the windowsill, gazing out over the sea. 'Just look at that sunset,' he breathed. 'All those colours – there's ultramarine and sage, there's purple and black in the shadows of the waves, white breakers, and vermilion where the sun's rays reflect on the water. God, but it's beautiful.'

She smiled. 'Glad we came?'

He turned, holding out his arms to her. 'Too damn right I am. Do you know, I'm feeling great already – much better than I did in London. I feel so full of energy – I can't wait to get started.'

'Not tonight, you aren't. I've locked Gladys up so you can get your easel and stuff in the morning.'

He turned from the window, his eyes glowing. 'You're going to see the best of Hemingway now, I promise you.'

His enthusiasm was infectious. It was true, he did appear much better these last few days, charged with eagerness and vitality, just like the old days. No sign of a headache and his sight seemed no worse. No-one would guess that under that bright face lurked the evil thing which was draining him of life.

Or was it? He looked so fit and healthy she could almost allow herself, cautiously, to begin to hope.

'It's cold in here,' she said. 'You get a fire going and I'll get some soup on.'

David looked around. 'There's coal here but no wood. I'll go down to the beach and look for driftwood.'

'Don't be silly, it's miles away. Frank said there should be some logs somewhere.'

David glanced around the room. 'Quite cosy here, isn't it? Lazarus would really enjoy prinking it up, like one of his stage sets. You know, I'm quite going to miss the old rogue.'

They found the logs in the lean-to in the little back yard. By the time dusk fell a fire blazed in the hearth and the soup was bubbling on the gas stove, filling the room with a tantalizing aroma of onions.

When Lisa came down the narrow staircase from the upstairs room David was lying on the hearth before the fire.

'At least there are plenty of blankets and I've put hot water bottles in the bed to air it,' she said.

'Come here.' David held out his arms to her. She sank on her knees beside him. 'Have I ever told you,' he said softly, 'how bloody lucky I am to have found you?'

'Often. Do you want toast with your soup?'

He laughed, trying to draw her close. 'I know what I'd like for starters.'

'For afters. The soup will burn if I don't take it off now.'

There was a glow in his eyes. 'Do you know what I'd like to do after supper? Go down to the beach, take all my clothes off and run in the water. Will you come?'

'In the dark? At this time of year? It's freezing.'

'We'll keep our clothes on then.'

She tugged at his hands, pulling him to his feet. 'Eat first, and we'll play games later. OK?'

* * *

93

During the next days they were blissfully happy, playing on the beach like children while the sun cast its thin rays until chill November rain sent them running back up the steep hill to the cottage. David painted with frenetic energy. Lisa surveyed the growing row of canvases propped against the wall to dry and was astounded by their wild spontaneity.

'Well, what do you think?' David asked, standing back, brush in hand. She answered cautiously.

'They're certainly different,' she said. 'Exuberant – you could almost say undisciplined.'

He jabbed the brush at a cliff. 'Break the rules,' he muttered. 'Break out of the mould – it's the only way to discover your own voice.'

'You're doing that all right. I've never seen a cliff look so fierce.'

'I've got so many pictures burning in my head,' he muttered. 'So many images, and so little time . . .'

He painted far into the night, with a savage intensity she found frightening, oblivious to the clock and to Lisa lying awake in the double bed waiting for him to come up. From below she could hear Stevie Wonder's voice drifting up the stairs.

When at last he clambered up the stairs David looked hollow-eyed with fatigue. He stepped out of his clothes and left them lying in a heap on the floor as he slithered into bed. Lisa held out her arms and felt his icy skin as she drew him close and folded her warm body around his back. He lay tense in the darkness. She slid her fingers across his stomach and felt his hand cover hers.

'Not tonight, love. I'm shattered.'

She hesitated, uncertain what to do. She might have tried again but tonight she could sense that he would not welcome it. It wasn't rejection; she knew beyond all doubt that he loved her. For the first time she felt lost.

94

She spoke softly into the back of his neck. 'You've been working too much,' she said.

His voice came low and hard in the darkness. 'I've no choice. Colours are starting to blur and I can tell my field of vision is getting worse.'

She felt a stab of alarm. This was what the specialist had warned.

'All these pictures in my head – what the hell am I going to do if I can't see to paint? I'm finished.'

She swallowed and spoke softly. 'There are other ways – writing for instance. You could paint with words instead, couldn't you?'

'I don't have your knack with words,' he muttered. 'I didn't go to university.'

She tried to soothe. 'My kind of education only gets in the way. You have a natural directness, like your father. Expressive simplicity has a lot to recommend it.'

She heard his smile. 'He's a lovely man, my father.'

'Yes he is,' she agreed. 'Like you.'

'You'd have liked my mother too.'

'I'm sure I would.'

'She was a wonderful woman. So kind, and yet . . .'

'Yet what?'

'I don't know – there was something about her, as if she lived in two worlds at once. It was hell when she died. We loved her very much.'

Lisa thought of James and felt sure they did. When he learned about David it would break his heart . . . She drove the thought from her mind and cuddled closer to David's back.

'You know, Lisa,' he murmured, 'if I had my life all over again I wouldn't change a thing – my childhood, my parents, you . . . I can't get over how bloody lucky I was to find you.'

She smiled. 'What I was trying to say before is that all is not lost. There are other ways, like painting with words instead of oils. Will you think about it?'

He flung himself over to face her. 'For Christ's sake, who are we fooling? We both know I'm finished, as an artist and as a lover. What have I got left to offer anybody?'

There was anguish in the cry, and fierce pain stabbed her. She was helpless to console, to soothe away the fears. Tears of frustration began to prick. He reached out a hand to touch her face.

'I'm sorry, love.' She could hear the contrition in his tone. 'I have no right to do this to you. I love you so much.'

'I know. And don't worry, there's more to love than sex. We can lie and cuddle.'

His voice was gentle. 'Listen, before it's too late I'm going to do one last picture, just for you. It'll be the best thing I ever did and every time you look at it you'll see the real me.'

She couldn't speak. She buried her face in his neck and heard his voice deep in his throat. 'Just remember this, darling – whatever happens I'll never leave you. Wherever I am you'll always feel my spirit near you, I swear.'

It was the first time he'd said it, acknowledged that death might claim him after all. Lisa felt as though she would choke.

They clung close together in apprehensive silence, like children afraid of the dark . . .

Lisa sat on the damp grass on the cliff top, arms hunched around her knees. Far below she could see him standing on a ledge, steadying his easel with one hand against the blustering wind while he painted.

The hood of his duffle coat was flung back and his hair fanned out around his head like a dark sunburst. He was still unaware that she was squatting there, watching him.

He'd been down there for hours, ever since first light.

'I want to catch the dawn light,' he'd said. 'It's got a sort of metallic quality you don't get the rest of the day.'

She soaked up every line of his slim young body, the widespread feet, the proud tilt of his head. She loved him so much she could burst. He was so honest, so open and loyal – qualities James and the mother she never knew must have bred in him. His son would have been a wonderful child. Maybe still . . . A boy with his tough resilience – even now he wasn't going to give in, despite his fear. She felt so proud of him . . .

The waves were crashing angrily against the rocks just below him, sending up sprays of spume, and David felt exhilarated. It was as though the elements felt at one with his own turbulent anger.

And almost at once the exhilaration gave way to sweeping sadness. Time was running out. He knew it for a certainty even if Lisa refused to recognize it yet. He knew by the way his eyes were playing up now, allowing him only brief glimpses of the world out there.

He was probably seeing all this beauty around him with heightened perception for that very reason, and the thought dismayed him. So much beauty in the world, and he was probably seeing it for the last time. He watched the great breakers rolling in, hurling themselves against the rocks, then receding to recoup energy before attacking again. He watched, mesmerized by their rhythm. He could feel the fibres of his body straining to soak it all up, savour it, extract every particle of pleasure from it before it was too late . . . His senses reeled at the onslaught.

It hurt, like hell it hurt. And what hurt most was the thought that all this would go on just the same when he was gone, not even noticing his absence. Those waves would still be crashing against those rocks when he lay cold in the ground; those boys down on the jetty would grow up and have children of their own. The whole world would continue its unending routine, uncaring . . .

What was the point of going on? Ahead lay only pain and disintegration. Pain for others too, watching him helplessly. He couldn't bear to think of Lisa's anguish in the final days. Lovely, trusting Lisa. For the thousandth time he despised himself for his weakness over Melanie. Lisa didn't deserve to be betrayed like that. He wanted to pour it all out to her, beg her forgiveness, but he couldn't. To ease his own conscience would only bring her more pain . . .

He put down the brush and peered over the ledge of rock, searching for the edge with his foot. It would be so easy to jump – let himself sink into those murky, seething depths . . . They'd think it was an accident. A huge wave which swept him off the ledge . . . Lisa would tell them of his bad sight – 'He must have missed his footing . . .'

He closed his eyes and lifted his head, feeling the wind whip his face. His tongue flicked along his lips, tasting the salt. It would be so easy – one step, plunging down through the breakers, sinking into that silent, black infinity . . . a few moments trying to resist the urge to surface and breathe . . . strength of will, that's all it would take . . .

Lisa saw him put down the brush and look out over the water. By his stance she knew he must be feeling pleased with what he had done, and she was glad she had left him undisturbed all day. It was vital for him to do that special picture before his sight went. James would be proud of him, despite his sadness.

She stretched out her legs, chafing her cold shins. Any moment now he would be packing up to come home . . .

* * *

Gulls screeched overhead and he opened his eyes for
one last look. He watched the sweep and dive of their
beautiful sleek bodies, and saw again the crows
scavenging over the fields of Jericho.

Suddenly it came to him: home and Dad, the pain
his unforeseen death would cause him and Lisa. There
must be time to say goodbye. He loved them so much.
The beauty in his life was too great to leave behind.
Not yet . . . He looked down once again at the waters
seething below . . .

She saw him bend to pick up his brushes and paints,
and was relieved. He'd been standing perilously close
to the edge. She stood up and waved.

'Hi, David,' she called. He looked around him, then
turned back to lift the canvas down from the easel.
He couldn't have heard her in this wind. He'd be
thinking already about the number of steps he'd
counted on the way down . . .

He held the canvas in his hand and stared at it
moodily. At arm's length or held up close, it was no
good. A child's slapdash attempt at a seascape, and
he'd failed to capture the metallic quality he'd wanted.
He felt leaden. Nothing he could paint would ever
match up to nature's work.

He stepped close to the edge and swung his arm in
a huge arc. The canvas slipped at once out of reach
of his sight as it soared, but he thought he heard
above the scream of the wind the crash as it hit the
rocks below. The incoming tide would soon sweep it
away. He picked up the easel and bag of brushes and
paints and began the climb to the top.

'Why did you do that?'

Lisa's voice startled him as he reached the cliff
path. He looked at her blankly. 'Do what?'

99

'Throw your painting away – you've spent all day on it.'

He shrugged as they fell into step. 'It wasn't any good. I can't paint what I can't see.' He turned a quizzical look on her. 'How long have you been here?'

'Oh, twenty minutes or so. I thought it was going well.'

Twenty minutes. What a mercy he hadn't jumped. She linked her arm through his and looked up at him. 'What is it, David? You've never done that before.'

He hadn't meant to, but he found himself telling her. 'I felt like ending it all,' he muttered. 'I very nearly did.'

She said nothing for a moment, but as she laid her head on his shoulder he could make out her face, tight and pale. 'I think it's time to tell your father,' she said quietly. 'You can't go on putting it off.'

'I know. In fact, I've decided. I want to go home to Jericho.'

She nodded. 'There's a phone box in the village. I'll ring him if you like.'

'Only don't tell him I'm dying, Lisa. Not yet. Just let him think we're coming home for Christmas.'

'He'll have to know sooner or later. It's only fair.'

'I'll tell him in my own time, I promise. Only don't let's spoil Christmas for them.'

TWELVE

1965

James felt too restless to carry on cleaning his guns. Much as he loved the intricacies of making his miniature reproductions, it wasn't the same without Bart's wet nose prying into everything. The old chap seemed decidedly off colour – he'd been listless yesterday and today he wouldn't touch his food. He was old, he had a touch of arthritis in his back legs, but it couldn't be anything serious . . .

He replaced the cap on the bottle of machine oil and put the Holland and Holland back in the gun cabinet alongside the Purdey. Before he closed the door of his workshop he looked around to check that everything was safely locked away.

'Just think on, lad,' his father used to say, *'never leave owt to chance. Lock up, then you can sleep easy.'*

Father had been the scrupulous one in the family. Ellen had taken after him. Mother, on the other hand, was easygoing and more inclined to bend rules when it suited her.

'Go on then, seeing as it's nearly Christmas you can open your Christmas box. Only now I'll have to think of summat else to surprise you when everybody else opens theirs.'

What was now his gun room and workshop in the original part of the farmhouse had once been Mother's little sitting room in the old days, where she did all the family sewing and mending. A Myford lathe now gleamed where once her trusty old Singer sewing machine had stood. Many a childhood secret had been confided to her in that room, in the certain knowledge that she would listen intently and repeat nothing. Dear Mother. It was sad she had not lived to meet his beloved Anna.

He locked the door and walked on down the narrow corridor, past the bedroom he and Anna had shared when he first brought her home to Jericho. He couldn't settle to anything today. No matter what the vet said, it wasn't like Bart to lie listlessly all day in his basket by the fire. James fidgeted first with the grandfather clock in the hall which was in need of no adjustment, then watered Anna's aspidistra for the third time this week.

She had loved having the house filled with plants. After her death he'd felt guilty every time one of them drooped and died. He just didn't have her green-fingered touch, but somehow the aspidistra had survived.

Every part of this house brought its memories, he thought as he neared the new wing. Walking through it was like a journey through his life. At the foot of the stairs he paused to finger the polished wood of the balustrade, then walked into the erstwhile barn.

Anna had had her way here, turning the single high area into rooms on staggered levels, each one surrounded by wooden railings so that it was possible to look down from the sitting area to the music and dining areas below.

He still could not bring himself to touch her piano. David was the one who, as a young boy, had first lifted the lid again and tried to make music. He'd been so anxious it had been only fair to let the child have lessons. According to Lisa he still played and sang folk-songs in London.

David. He was partly the cause of James's disquiet. The boy must never feel obliged to come back to Jericho.

'What are you doing, Dad?'

Ellen's voice made him start. He turned and saw her leaning against the doorframe. There was curiosity in her dark eyes.

'Just thinking,' he replied.

'What about?'

'Oh, this and that. About Aunt Dorothy for one thing.'

Ellen pulled a lip. 'It's a long time since she got in touch. What else?'

'About David.'

She straightened up, flicking her hair back out of her eyes. 'I wouldn't worry about him. He'll always do his own thing, whatever others might think.'

'I don't want him coming back home, that's all,' said James.

'No more do I,' Ellen said crisply. 'I'm going to do the ironing.' She turned away and left him.

She had already pulled the ironing board out of the cupboard by the time he retraced his steps to the kitchen. It stood in the middle of the room, piled high with creased washing. Ellen was bending over Bart's basket, and James could see the dog's head lolling over the edge.

'He's not well, Dad,' Ellen said, running her fingers gently over the dog's nose. 'Don't you think we ought to call the vet again?'

Bart's eyes surveyed him dully as James moved closer. His tail made a feeble attempt to wag, and then fell motionless. The mournful look followed James as he headed out to the telephone in the hall.

Eric Trotter wasted no time in coming. He shrugged off his overcoat as he entered the kitchen and dumped his bag on the table.

'Now what have we here?' he said, running his fingers through sparse red hair. 'Not feeling your usual lively self, old boy?' he addressed the dog. Again the tail tried to flick a welcome as the vet knelt beside him. James stood anxiously behind while the vet examined him.

At last he straightened up. 'Well?' said James.

The vet shook his head. 'He's not a youngster any more, James. How old is he now?'

'He'll be twelve come Christmas.'

Trotter's eyes didn't meet his. 'That's not a bad age for a sheepdog. He's had a good run.'

James felt sick. It was what he had feared. 'He's only been off colour a couple of days,' he heard himself saying, trying to argue away what he didn't want to hear. 'I know he's been arthriticky for a bit – he only followed me halfway up to the moor when I rode up on Monday, he seemed off it yesterday then he wouldn't eat today . . .'

'His kidneys have packed up, James. He's burnt out.'

James swallowed hard. 'Is he dying?' he asked quietly. 'Can you do anything for him?'

The vet bent to scratch the dog's head. 'I can give him something to ease the pain. I don't think he'll see the morning. Or I can take him away with me—'

'No,' James cut in quickly. He knelt beside the basket. 'He'd hate it. He was born here. He belongs here.'

'Very well.' The vet took a syringe from his bag. James turned his head away, unable to bear the pitiful look in the dog's eyes. For the first time he became aware of Ellen standing by the table, her hands clasped and her eyes wide.

The vet replaced the syringe in his bag and reached for his coat. 'I'm afraid that's all I can do, James. He'll feel nothing now.'

Ellen showed him to the door. When she came back she plugged the iron in again in silence. James picked up the basket carefully and carried it to the sofa, then sat down beside it. Bart's eyes never left his face.

James felt his heart would break. Anna was still alive when Bart was born; she too had loved him frisking at their heels when they rode together on the moor; she had hugged and kissed him in joyful gratitude the day he rescued James from the snow-drift.

'My faithful friend,' James muttered, tears pricking his eyes. Ellen put down the iron and crossed to switch on the radio. The room was flooded with the haunting beauty of Elgar. Bart uttered a deep sigh and closed his eyes.

James leaned over and put his cheek to the dog's head. He was still breathing. Ellen folded the last shirt.

'You should have let Eric put him down, Dad. It would have been kinder.'

James buried his face in the dog's shaggy fur. 'He's not in pain. I want to be with him.'

'You'll only upset yourself.'

'I'm a farmer for God's sake.'

Ellen had been in bed for a couple of hours when Bart moved. He struggled across to lay his head on James's lap, nuzzling a hot, dry nose between his thighs. James cradled his arms about him. The dog opened his eyes, gave a deep sigh, and closed them again. He was no longer breathing. For a long time James sat hugging him close, then wiped away the teardrop glistening on the shaggy head . . .

It was still early in the morning when he dug a grave in the frozen earth. Bart had always loved the paddock.

He turned on his knees to lift the blanket-shrouded bundle tenderly. A bare foot caught his eye and he looked up. Ellen stood there, a robe flung over her nightdress and her hair streaming loose. Her face looked drained of colour in the wintry light. He blinked a tear away.

'What on earth are you doing out here like that?' he demanded gruffly. 'Get back inside before you catch your death.'

She knelt beside him and touched the bundle in his arms. 'I just wanted to say goodbye,' she said quietly. 'I'm going to miss him.'

He nodded. 'You used to be good mates, the two of you.'

'We still were, only he was able to show it.'

Her hand lay still on the bundle and for long seconds they knelt in silence. James could see the dirt on the soles of her bare feet, and he felt moved.

She stood up, and he could see the shimmer in her eyes. 'I'm so sorry, Dad,' she whispered. 'I know how you must be feeling—'

'Go on now,' he cut in gently. 'It's freezing out here.'

She gave a thin smile and touched his shoulder, then walked quickly back to the house.

James leaned on the spade. He'd buried dogs in the past but never one like Bart. There would never again be one like Bart.

The earth lay flattened now, only a black rectangle marking the dog's resting place. Come the spring, the new grass would soon obliterate all sign of it. Rabbits would chase here and horses graze again; life would go on.

He would erect no marker – he wanted no reminder of the pain of parting. He'd had enough of death.

Ellen had just left for work when the telephone rang. James heard the beep-beep of a coin box before the voice came through.

'James? It's me – Lisa.'

His spirits lifted. The warmth and vitality of her young voice was just what he needed to drive the gloom away.

'Lisa, love – how are you both? Enjoying the seaside, are you?'

There was a tentative tone in her reply. 'Yes, it's lovely.'

'Has David been able to get some work done?'

'Yes, quite a bit. But listen, James, how would you feel about us coming over to Jericho to stay for a while?'

Delight surged in him. 'I'd love it – when?'

'As soon as possible – tomorrow? Would that be too soon?'

'Today wouldn't be too soon for me, love. Sling your stuff in the car and get on over.' A thought struck him. 'You could stay over Christmas if you like.'

'You're sure now?'

'Lisa, love, I can't tell you how much it means to me – we could do with a spot of young blood around here.'

'Tomorrow then.' He was puzzled by her quiet matter-of-factness. Usually she bubbled.

'Lisa – is everything OK?' he asked.

'Fine. We'll fill you in on the news when we see you.'

He felt a prick of misgiving. 'News?' he repeated. 'Is there something you haven't told me?'

'Nothing that can't wait.' He was sure of it now; there was a hint of reticence in her tone. Anxiety flickered.

'Are you all right? And David?'

There was a brief pause and he heard her take a breath before she answered.

'David's had a bit of bother with his eyes but we'll sort it out.'

'Yes of course – we can arrange for the optician while he's here.'

'We'll see you tomorrow then, some time after lunch.'

* * *

Ellen was not pleased when she learned the news that evening.

'Why do they want to be coming here?' she muttered as she peeled the potatoes for supper. 'And how long for? I don't like it – them living together like that. What will everybody think?'

'It's almost Christmas, love,' James replied gently. 'Christmas is the time for family.'

'She's not family – she's not married to him.'

'Maybe she will, some day.'

Ellen dropped the potato peeler in the sink and turned, wiping her hands. 'Then why hasn't she done it by now? They've been living together all this time, I reckon she never will. Slut.'

'Ellen!' he snapped. A moment passed. 'She's a nice girl,' he went on in a calmer tone. 'She's done a lot for him. She really cares. He's very lucky if you ask me.'

Ellen grunted and turned back to the sink, giving the potatoes in the colander a violent shake. 'Maybe, but I'm damned if I want them living here under the same roof.'

He surveyed her back, stiff with indignation, as she arranged vegetables around lamb chops, and couldn't help wondering what she would have thought if she'd known about Anna and Catterick . . .

THIRTEEN

1939

Throughout the summer James worked and saved and waited for word from Anna, but nothing came. Not even a postcard. Her relatives in Boston must be under orders from Harcourt to keep a strict eye on her or she would have found some way to contact him, he was sure.

Weeks dragged into months and still he ached for her. Around him others were talking of war, but it all seemed unreal until the day Hitler marched into Poland.

'That's done it,' his father muttered moodily as he switched off the wireless. 'We're going to have the whole bloody caboodle all over again now, God help us.'

The hay harvest was safely in and September lay warm over the Garthdale valley the day Chamberlain declared war against Germany. The men had more than the next darts contest to grow excited about down at the Rose and Crown. Darts and dominoes lay neglected while they clustered about the bar.

'You mean you've joined up of your own accord, Eddie?'

'Merchant Navy. Can't wait to get going.'

'I wonder how soon they'll start conscripting?'

'Bugger that, any man worth his salt'll be off to enlist like Eddie, without waiting.'

'Not you, Bert – your missus won't let you go as far as Agley Bridge on your own.'

'Well, somebody'll have to captain the tug-of-war

team once Eddie's gone. Any road, we can't all go and leave the women undefended.'

'Go on, who's going to attack Thaxton? We've nowt here but sheep. What about you, Jim? Are you going to volunteer?'

James looked up from his pint. 'Might not be a bad idea. I've nothing to keep me here.'

He found his father in the yard outside the pigsty. Hemingway set the bin of pig swill down and straightened, spreading his hands helplessly.

'We need you here, lad. I can't run the place alone with my gammy leg.'

James stared fixedly down at the cobbles. 'I've had a word with Fred – he's willing to fill in till I get back.'

'And what if he wants to bugger off too?'

'He won't – he failed the medical on account of his asthma. He promised he'd stay till this lot's over.'

Hemingway grunted. 'And how long's that likely to be? We all thought the last do would be over by Christmas. Four lousy years, it took. Blood and muck and stink.' He wiped his hands down the side of his trousers and sighed. 'Think it over a bit – you might see things different in the morning.'

James looked up. 'I've already decided, Dad.'

'Decided what?'

'I'm signing on – in the army, like you. I'm off to the recruiting office first thing tomorrow.'

Several letters lay on the hall table. Dorothy picked them up and flicked through them. Mostly they were for Myles but one was addressed to herself and bore an American postage stamp and her sister's neat handwriting. She carried it through into the breakfast room.

The maid lifted the silver teapot. 'Shall I pour the master's tea, ma'am?' she enquired as Dorothy took her seat.

'No, just mine.' Myles was still fussing in front of the shaving mirror. It was an incredibly tedious business and always took ages, stropping the razor, lathering, scraping, rinsing . . . And often dabbing with that horrid little styptic pencil where he'd nicked the skin.

Once the maid had gone she slit the letter open.

I don't know whether Daddy will have told you he's decided I should stay here now there's a war on. But I'm not having that. I've booked my passage and I'm due to arrive in Liverpool on the fourteenth – could you meet me? Don't tell a soul . . . I've so much to tell you . . .

Dorothy frowned. It wasn't going to be easy to get away without Myles questioning her. On the other hand, Anna seemed to have been leading quite a dashing life over there; she'd dearly like to hear more. Good gossip was, like everything else these days, in short supply.

There were two tiny pieces of paper adhering to Myles's chin when he finally came down. Dorothy sighed. As always, he would glance through *The Times* before inspecting his mail. How could anyone be so incurious?

The maid cleared away the plate after he had finished the kedgeree and he spread marmalade thickly on a slice of toast and refolded his paper before tearing open the first letter. She saw his frown of irritation before he spoke.

'Damn tailor – thinks he can charge the earth now there's a war on. We'll see about that.'

He tossed the bill aside and opened the second letter. 'Oh, I say – old Nigel's invited me to a weekend shoot with some of the chaps. Says most of them may be off to the front before long. Maybe a last chance for a get-together . . . What do

111

you say, old girl? Mind spending a few days on your own?'

He flashed that breezy smile which already, after only a year, was beginning to irritate her. 'When?' she asked.

'The twelfth to the fifteenth. Plus a day either side travelling up to Scotland, of course.'

She smiled and gave an indifferent shrug. 'Of course you must go. I'll take the chance to go on a shopping trip.'

'Good idea,' he agreed, laying the letter aside to take a bite of toast. 'Buy yourself a pretty frock or two.' He swallowed the mouthful, then added thoughtfully, 'I'd better get the old Churchill out for a good clean. I wish I'd had myself measured for a Purdey like your grandfather . . .'

For James the world seemed suddenly to have taken on the unearthly quality of a dream, from the crowded darkened railway platform with its mingled smells of gas lamps and soot and oily engines, to this dim, smoky compartment where he sat waiting for the train to start.

Under the blue light of the single bulb his fellow travellers took on a strangely ghost-like appearance; the pale blue woman in the corner knitting a pale blue fluffy thing; the lean man frowning at his crumpled blue newspaper; the chubby-faced young man opposite dragging on a blue cigarette and blowing streamers of blue smoke down his nostrils.

Even the railway platform had an unnatural air. He stared through his reflection in the dirty window at the dim figures on the wet concrete, moving in and out of the pools of light from the blacked-out shades, looking like shadowy characters in some macabre play.

The young man opposite stood up and peeled off his jacket, revealing a shapeless grey cardigan. He

112

grinned at James as he pulled a packet of squashed cigarettes out of his pocket.

'What time are we due out?' he asked, offering James the packet.

'Any minute now. No thanks.'

The young man lit up, then shook out the match. 'How far are you going?'

'Richmond. On my way to Catterick.'

He saw the young man's face brighten. 'Me too – shake.' James held out his hand and felt the other's firm grip. 'My name's Arthur Binns,' the young man went on cheerfully, 'but the kids at my school call me Dusty. What's yours?'

'James Hemingway. Call me Jim.' He heard a tea trolley clatter away along the platform and the hiss of the engine. 'I think we're off.'

The lights of the station slid away behind them to the slow chuff-chuff of the engine. As it gathered speed Dusty leaned forward, elbows on knees. 'What's your line of business, Jim? In civvy street, I mean.'

'I'm a farmer.'

Dusty's eyebrows rose. 'I thought that was a reserved occupation?'

'I thought teaching was too.'

Dusty shook his head. 'Ah well, blighted love life and all that. What's your story?'

'Something like that,' said James. 'Seems we've got more than just the army in common.'

As the train rattled on through the night they fell silent again. James stared out at the black tree-skeletons flashing by, trying not to think of the old, ordered world he knew, trying not to think how every second was taking him further away from Anna . . .

This was an alien world he was entering now.

It was late when they arrived at Richmond. A thick moor-mist overhung the station, making the cobbles slippery underfoot. A biting wind swept in from the

113

moor, stinging James's cheeks. Torches flickered like fireflies among the huddle of men standing miserably in groups. Uniformed figures barked orders. Alphabetical groups, they said. James lost sight of Dusty as they separated and the figures shuffled into ragged lines.

It took time before they were led outside to where a line of trucks waited. James found himself standing, hanging on to the roof bar, between two long benches where shivering men sat clutching their suitcases. Someone slammed the tailboard shut, rammed the bolts home, dragged down the tarpaulin cover and the truck began its shuddering journey through the night.

The men sat silent. The tarpaulin was no match for the misty rain as the truck rumbled along twisting lanes. After what seemed an eternity it came to a halt and someone unbolted the tailboard.

'Welcome to Catterick holiday camp,' a cheery voice called out.

All James could see was a jagged huddle of hut roofs against the night sky, wire fences and sentry boxes at a gate where torchlights flashed. Voices challenged, voices called back.

'New intake for Kemmel lines.'

Marshalled into groups, they were marched along gleaming wet gravel to their huts, blundering into each other in the dark. The whole thing still had the bizarre sensation of a dream.

At last a hut door opened, and the world grew light again. A corporal led the way in.

It was a bleak and bitterly cold room, brick walls surmounted by a tin roof where two oil lamps swung in the draught, casting leaping shadows along the walls. Not even the pigsty at Jericho could be more cheerless . . .

'Choose your mattress from the pile over there,' the corporal said. 'Three blankets apiece, and if you want extra there's straw out in the yard.'

The men didn't talk much as they stowed their cases away on top of the two-door metal cabinet which stood alongside each bed and which put James in mind of the meat safe back at home. Meat. For the first time he realized he was desperately hungry.

The mess hall was as unwelcoming as the billet, a long, raftered shed with three iron stoves smouldering moodily down the centre among rows of scrubbed tables and benches.

The men moved along the counter at the far end where huge urns gleamed alongside cardboard boxes of cutlery. James watched the fried sausages and boiled potatoes and carrots being dolloped on his plate and drowned in thin gravy. It looked highly unappetizing, nothing like the juicy chops and steaks he was accustomed to at home. The salt and pepper at the end of the counter were chained to the wall. Somehow his appetite seemed to have vanished.

He took his seat at one of the tables, watching the others eating in silence. He stared at the bottle of Daddy's Sauce in the middle of the table, chewing on one of his two slices of bread and marge and sipping the scalding pint pot of well-stewed tea. What was he doing here, among all these unfamiliar glazed faces?

Trying to forget, that's what. Trying to forge a new life without her. That night, as he lay in a strange, hard bed and buried his face in the harshness of the striped bolster, searching for sleep, he became aware of embarrassed coughs and sniffles around him in the darkness. He wasn't the only one feeling lost and just a little apprehensive . . .

Jericho seemed suddenly empty without James. He'd gone because of that girl as much as anything, thought Hemingway. If only she'd written. Such a pretty little thing; no wonder James was smitten. He

115

hadn't spoken of her for months, but he knew his son. He wouldn't forget in a hurry. Enlisting in the army was his way of trying to bury the hurt . . . like joining the Foreign Legion . . .

Hemingway sat on the yard wall. He'd been standing here when he'd watched his son trudge off down the lane with his suitcase, striding out with those long legs of his and a jaunty smile on his handsome young face. Hemingway couldn't help feeling anxious. So many young men of his own generation had set off just as cheerily twenty-five years ago. He'd been one of the few who came home . . .

'Pot of tea just brewed, Mr Hemingway. Shall I pour?'

Doris Brook stood in the kitchen doorway, the old brown earthenware teapot in her hand. He nodded and stood up wearily.

'Aye, might as well.'

'No point brooding,' she murmured as she poured tea into two cups. 'He's only gone for basic training any road.'

'Aye, you're right.'

'I know you'll miss him. It took me years to get over my Harold and that's nigh on fifteen years now.' She added milk to the tea. 'I could pop in more often if you like.'

He smiled as he spooned sugar into his cup. She was a good woman. She got on with life, never making a fuss about being on her own. And always a cheerful smile on her ruddy face, no matter what. A sudden thought occurred to him; as well as coming in for the cleaning she might make good company of an evening. Just now and again.

'You ever go down the Rose and Crown?' he asked, trying his best to sound casual.

She raised shocked eyebrows and put her cup down with a clatter. 'A lady in the pub alone? I should think not indeed. I was brought up better than that.'

'I just wondered if you might fancy a drink with me one evening, that's all,' he muttered.

The frown vanished and she beamed. 'Oh, with a gentleman escort – that's a different kettle of fish. I'd be delighted, Mr Hemingway.'

Dorothy had spotted Anna waving even before she disembarked. She was trying to push past the others on the gangway to reach her, waving and calling her name. They sat together now in the Kardomah café with tea and fancy cakes.

'You've no idea how much fun I've had,' Anna was saying enthusiastically. 'The Americans really know how to enjoy themselves. They took me to all the balls and soirées in town. Aunt Eleanor gave the most wonderful party for my twenty-first. I met the most exciting people – you'd have loved Dwight.'

She spoke with a faintly American accent now, Dorothy noted, and it sounded just a teeny bit common. Father would not like it at all. And that hat – Myles would consider it in execrable taste. It was an audacious little number with a swish of eye-veiling which she had now thrown back.

'Dwight?' she repeated.

'He's a gorgeous man cousin Verity brought to the house. He got quite a thing about me – I had a few dates with him.'

'Rich?'

'Filthy rich.'

Dorothy nibbled a meringue. 'Daddy would approve of him, I'm sure. He might even forgive the Dwight bit.'

'He was just a fling. Listen, I don't want Daddy to know I am back – he doesn't know, does he?'

'Not from me.'

'And you haven't told Myles or anyone about meeting me today?'

'No-one. But why?'

117

'Because I don't want anyone stopping me from going to Jericho to see James. I've got to find out why he never answered my letters.'

Dorothy stopped nibbling. 'Surely you're not still hung up on him? After all this time?'

Anna selected a vanilla slice. 'I've never stopped being hung up, as you so quaintly put it. I've missed him terribly. I just can't understand why he never wrote to me.'

Dorothy brushed a crumb from her lapel. 'Do you really think that's wise? Daddy would be furious to know you're chasing him.'

Anna jutted her chin. 'There's nothing Daddy can do to stop me. I'm of age now and mistress of my own destiny.' She took a bite of the cake. 'Mmm – you must try one of these.'

'What if he's found somebody else – he could be married even.'

'He promised he'd wait for me. I'm going to see if he has.'

Dorothy reached over and clasped her hand. 'Hold on a minute – what are you going to tell Daddy? He's bound to find out sooner or later. You're not counting on me to tell fibs again, are you? I've had enough of that in the past.'

'Only one – that you know nothing about where I am. You haven't seen or heard from me.'

'He'll go hairless when he finds out – he's bound to telephone Auntie. He'll get the police in to find you.'

Anna finished her cake and wiped her fingers on the napkin. 'Let him. I've got to find out if James still wants me.'

She gathered up her gloves and handbag. Dorothy gave a slight cough.

'Anna—'

'Yes?'

Her sister looked down at her plate. 'I'm sorry.'

Anna frowned. 'What for?'

A flush suffused Dorothy's face. 'There's something I've got to tell you . . .'

Hemingway was just leaving the cobbler's little shop at the end of the village high street. Alfred, bending over his last, took a nail out of his mouth.

'Reckon it'll be a while yet before you're bringing in them boots of Jim's for steel heels again,' he commented. 'I hear they've had to disband the tug-of-war team now most of the lads have gone off.'

'Ay, and there's only us old 'uns left for the darts now.'

'Old? Nay, they'll call you up and all before this lot's done.'

'Not with my leg they won't. Any road, farming's a restricted occupation – which is more than you can say for cobbling.'

He could hear the train chugging along the valley as he climbed the steep lane towards Jericho. Fred would already have started the evening milking but the pigs still had to be fed. Doris wouldn't be there now but she'd have left something ready for supper.

His leg was playing him up by the time he reached the gate. He paused to lean on it and look back down the hill. To his surprise he saw a woman, a small case in her hand, hurrying uphill towards him.

She wasn't a local, not with a hat like that. She walked with the easy grace of a young woman and as she came closer he saw her wave. He screwed up his eyes against the evening sun to see her better.

'Hi,' she called. 'It's me – remember me?'

He knew her now and was startled. 'It's Anna – I thought you'd gone to America,' he said.

'I did. I've just come back.' She had that wide, warm smile he remembered that night James brought her home. She dropped the case, pulled off the ridiculous little hat and leaned on the gate beside him.

119

She glanced around. 'Is James in? Or is he still out working?' she asked.

'If you'd written, you'd know,' he said stiffly.

She looked up at him with wide eyes. 'What do you mean? Know what? Where is he?'

Hemingway straightened up. He couldn't help recalling the pain she had caused his son. 'You walk out of his life nigh on a year ago, he hears not a word from you in all that time, then you walk back in as if it was yesterday. A lot can happen in that time.'

She turned pale. 'Why – what's happened? For God's sake, tell me – he's all right, isn't he?'

'As all right as anyone can be – in the ruddy army. He's enlisted.'

He saw her swallow hard. 'He didn't find anyone else after me, did he?'

'After what you did to him? Nay, he went off to Catterick to do his basic training.'

'Catterick?' she echoed.

'Where he'll be posted to after that God only knows.'

She bent to pick up her case. Hemingway caught her arm. 'Hang on – you're not off again without a cup of tea at least. Come on into the house.'

She smiled and prised his fingers off gently. 'I've got to go,' she said, pinning the hat back on her head. 'I must get to Catterick tonight. But I'll be back to explain, I promise.'

'Don't be daft – you can't . . .'

But she had already set off back down the lane. He watched her until she disappeared out of sight, except for the absurd little hat bobbing over the hedgerow.

FOURTEEN

1939

'My Yiddisher momma . . .'

The duty sergeant groaned. The drunken soldier lying in the cell was no Al Jolson. That was the trouble with drunks – they never could sing in tune. He rapped his stick on the cell bars.

'Knock it off, private. Get some sleep and sober up, for Christ's sake – you don't want to make things worse for yourself.'

The soldier gave a sickly smile and lay back on the bunk, closing his eyes. Please God he wouldn't throw up, thought the sergeant. He prided himself on rigorous attention to detail and cleanliness in his guardhouse. The orderly would soon clean up the mess but the smell would linger for hours.

As he turned back to his desk he caught sight of the corporals. They were both staring out of the window in silence. 'Well?' he demanded. 'What is it? The King in his golden coach?'

The younger one shook his head. 'I think it's Mata Hari, sarge. She could wheedle any secrets she liked out of me.'

The older corporal chuckled. 'Ay, and me too. She's a corker and no mistake.'

The sergeant clicked his tongue. 'Women, that's all you young lads ever think about. There's more to life than getting your leg over.'

He was unwilling to show curiosity about the latest camp follower to hang about the barrack gates. At least the local girls couldn't get their hands on the

121

new recruits until they'd finished their basic training. Once they'd completed it they would have to fend for themselves.

He came across to stand beside the corporals at the window.

'Jesus!'

The most stunningly beautiful blonde was turning in at the gate, and he could tell at a glance she was no village hussy; even without that hat and the expensive leather suitcase it was clear that this one had class.

He opened the hatch as she drew close. She gave him a brilliant smile. 'Good evening, Sergeant,' she said amiably. 'Could I have a word with you?'

Everything about her spoke of money and poise. She was no camp follower, this one – not unless she was the C.O.'s bit on the side, and knowing his wife it seemed highly unlikely.

He cleared his throat. 'I must point out this is an army camp, Miss,' he said cautiously. 'We don't have no women here.'

She gave him another of those dazzling smiles. 'Don't be silly, Sergeant, this is most desperately important. Would I trouble you otherwise?'

He glanced back over his shoulder. The corporals were staring, open-mouthed. 'Get about your business,' he snapped. 'The lady and I will be in the interview room.'

Seated on the far side of the desk she still looked like a film star. Those were undoubtedly silk stockings clinging to her elegantly-crossed legs, and that damn silly hat must have cost more than a month's army pay.

'I've travelled all the way from America, Sergeant,' she was saying in that low, husky voice which put him in mind of Tallulah Bankhead. 'I must see one of your officers.'

'Which one?' he said warily. She could just be a German spy.

She shrugged, and gave a pout just like Scarlett O'Hara. 'I don't know – Michael Gardiner perhaps, if he's still stationed here? Or Nigel Rayne-Smith.'

The sergeant brightened. 'Lieutenant Rayne-Smith – yes, he's here. If you hold on a moment, I'll give him a ring.'

He picked up the telephone. 'Guardhouse here, Lieutenant. There's a Miss Anna Harcourt asking for you . . . Yes sir, I'll bring her over right away.'

At least now he could hand the whole thing over to a higher authority. As he escorted her out through the general office he was aware of the corporals' envious glances and the feeble voice still wailing from the cell. If only his Yiddisher momma would come and take him away.

Nigel Rayne-Smith sat on the edge of his desk watching her as she stood at the window sipping a glass of his best sherry. She was even more a delight to the eye than he remembered and no mistake. It would do his reputation no harm at all if the other chaps should catch sight of her in his window. He was quite looking forward to the ribbing he'd get in the mess later . . .

'So you haven't seen any of the others?' he enquired.

She shook her head and the blonde hair shimmered in the evening light. 'I told you – I haven't even been back to Harrogate yet. I came straight here.'

'Have you somewhere to stay? I can recommend a decent hotel. I could perhaps join you for dinner.'

'I've got to find James. I know he's here.'

'Is this fellow Hemingway important to you? It doesn't sound as if he's one of us.'

She swung round and gave him an impish smile. 'He's important to me, anyway – I'm going to marry him.'

Nigel swallowed. It was disappointing news; he'd

123

have cheerfully stopped seeing Clarice for her. Fancy throwing herself away on a small-time farmer. Old Harcourt would surely have a heart attack. Still, from what he knew of Anna, if her mind was made up . . .

'Oh, well, in that case,' he said amiably, yielding to the inevitable, 'I could arrange for you to have a brief interview with him.'

She came closer. 'And a night out?' she said softly.

He hesitated. 'Recruits still on basic training are not allowed – once he's given a posting—'

'But his training's almost ended,' she murmured persuasively. 'He could be posted away anywhere – abroad even. Just one night – please?'

James lay exhausted on his bed. Around him the others too lay prostrate, groaning and cursing.

'If I have to march around that bloody parade ground once more I'll go nuts.'

'That bastard corporal – if he tells me once more to pick my bleeding feet up I'll stick the ruddy bayonet down his throat, I swear I will . . .'

The soldier on the next bed rolled over on his elbow and grinned at James. 'What about you then, Jim – you're saying nowt.'

James folded his hands behind his head. 'I was thinking – we'll be getting our postings soon. I wonder where we'll be sent.'

The soldier curled his lip. 'Straight into the front line for you, never fear. Best bloody marksman they've had, like you was born to it.'

'I was brought up with guns. I've shot since I was a nipper.'

The private in the opposite bed nursed his feet between coarse hands and growled. 'I wish you'd shoot that ruddy corporal. Can't you miss for once and get him – accidental like?'

'Shoot his balls off – ruin his bloody love life – that'd serve the bugger right.'

Ribald laughter was echoing round the bare room when the door opened. The corporal glared and the laughter suddenly died.

'Still have energy left for merriment, do we?' he barked. 'We'll see about that in the morning. Hemingway – get over to the main block and report to the duty officer at once. At the double!'

James pulled on his boots, wondering what the devil he could have done wrong. The corporal's face gave nothing away as he stood at the door and let James pass. As he trotted across the drill square he could still hear raucous laughter in the billet behind him.

James sat in the dining room of the small hotel, still unable to believe what was happening. He couldn't take his eyes from Anna's face as she leaned across the table, smiling at him.

'Happy, darling?' she murmured.

'I can't believe it. You look even lovelier than ever – are you really here or am I dreaming?'

Her fingers slithered across the tablecloth to touch his hand. 'I'm here, I'm real, as you'll find out,' she said, a mischievous twinkle in her eyes, then seeing the glances from the next table she withdrew her hand.

James shook his head. 'I thought I was going to be put on a charge. You were the last person I expected to see when I walked into that office. After all this time . . .'

'I was afraid you'd forgotten me.'

He trembled, unable to speak for the lump in his throat. She looked unbearably beautiful, her glorious hair transmuted into a golden halo by the wall lights behind her.

'Never. Had you forgotten me?'

'Oh James! How could you think it? Every day I kept looking in the post, dying to hear from you.'

He stared in amazement. 'Write? How could I? I had no idea where you were.'

She pulled a face. 'I know. I really believed you'd got all my letters but then Dorothy confessed to me today. Daddy put my aunt up to it.'

'Up to what?'

'Making sure I didn't get in touch with you. I used to put my letters with all the others in a silver tray, then their secretary saw to stamping and posting them. I had no idea mine were being sifted out.'

So that was it – the old bastard Harcourt up to his tricks again. He should have guessed.

Her fingers sidled across the table to touch his. 'Still, I'm here now – I'll make up for everything, I promise.' She gave him an arch smile. 'I haven't been able to touch you yet,' she said softly. 'Not in the office or the taxi. We'll go to our room soon.'

He felt uncomfortable. He glanced at the next table; did they know he'd signed the register as Mr and Mrs Hemingway as she suggested? Surely his guilty face would give him away.

'You know, you look different,' she said, resting her chin in her cupped hand. 'You look funny.'

'Funny?'

'Where's all your lovely thick hair gone? You're almost bald.'

He smiled. 'Army style make-over. Don't you like it?'

'I'll get used to it.'

He cupped his hands around hers. 'You won't have much time. I'll be posted soon.'

'Where to?'

'God alone knows.'

She drew away, her back straightening. 'Then I'd better arrange to have the banns called right away. We'll be married in the register office. You're not going to escape until I'm Mrs Hemingway.'

The fingers were sidling across again. He seized

them and cradled her hand between his. 'Do it then. I'm not going to let you get away again.'

The fingers tickled the inside of his palm. 'Do you really want pudding?' She glanced at her wrist watch. 'We've got ten hours before you have to report back. Let's just settle for a quick coffee.'

He thought he'd known passion, lying with her in the scented woods or among the reeds by the pool last summer, but it had been nothing like this. Women, he'd always been told, were the passive partners, being done to rather than doing, but Anna had clearly never learned of it.

From the moment she helped him out of his battle-dress jacket she filled every second with delight. 'Heavens! How can you bear to wear such a nasty, itchy thing?' She came close, her body gleaming in the light of the bedside lamp. 'You should wear silk next to your skin,' she murmured, 'like this.' And he lay back with closed eyes, savouring the silken caress of her body against his.

Throughout the night the surprising joy of her never dimmed, enchantment piling upon ecstasy until he felt he could bear no more. Rapture exploded in every pore. He had reached nirvana.

At last, as dawn was creeping through the gap in the curtains, he lay in the crook of her arm, his cheek against her breast.

'There,' she murmured dreamily, 'we've begun our honeymoon. It's going to be like this for the rest of our days.'

He couldn't believe he'd got her back. She was every man's fantasy, the woman with the class and poise of a lady, but lurking just beneath that glamorous veneer lay the consummate whore. And she loved him . . .

* * *

Doris Brook shook out the tablecloth and draped it over the kitchen table. Hemingway watched in amazement.

'We never put a cloth on there,' he muttered. 'Why bother, getting stains on and having to be washed all the time?'

'Since it's me doing the washing you've no need to worry, Mr Hemingway. It looks more civilized, specially if you have company coming.'

'Company? When?'

She dimpled her plump cheeks. 'Well there's me, from time to time. Like last Thursday before we went down to the pub. And if your Jim—'

'James.'

'—has a young lady he'll no doubt want to bring her home when he's on leave, won't he?'

Hemingway's eyes turned to the mantelpiece where the letter stood propped behind the clock. 'Ay, I reckon,' he admitted.

Doris picked up a cushion from the settee and pummelled it into shape. 'Do you know there's a hole in that settee cover?' she asked. 'I could stay on this evening and darn it for you. Get things nice for when he does come.'

He didn't want to discourage her; it would be nice to have company but – 'Haven't you things to see to? Your own supper, like?'

She gave a triumphant smile. 'There's plenty enough for two in that casserole I brought. Right then, I've got a bit of green wool . . .'

His eyes followed the deft movements of her needle, threading in and out in rhythmic sweeps, but his thoughts were on the letter behind the clock.

Two bits of news for you, Dad. My posting came through at last and would you believe it? I'm posted to Catterick as an armourer, mending and maintaining guns . . .

128

But it was the line in the last paragraph which had pulled him up short. All that time the lad had been breaking his heart over a girl on the other side of the Atlantic, and now . . .

Anna and I were married this morning in the register office. One day soon I'll bring her home to Jericho . . .

Many years had passed since Jericho last welcomed a new bride and Hemingway was looking forward to his son's home-coming. Three days' leave he had, so they'd have to make the most of it.

The day's work done he bade Fred a curt goodnight and turned to come in out of the yard. He stopped short in the kitchen doorway.

It didn't look like his kitchen; the stone-flagged floor gleamed almost white and the old range had been blackleaded till it shone. It hadn't looked like that for years. Doris Brook stood proudly, arms akimbo, by the sink.

'Boots,' she said crisply.

Hemingway's head jerked up in surprise. 'You what?'

'Best get them boots off before you come across here. I haven't scrubbed my fingers raw for nothing.'

'I've to go out again yet for the milking.'

She gave a sad shake of her grey head 'You said you wanted the place nice for them two coming home tomorrow, didn't you? Just look at the state of them boots.'

He leaned against the doorjamb and pulled off the mud-caked boots. Doris emptied suds into the sink and placed the bucket on the floor.

'I've put nice clean sheets on James's bed,' she told him, 'the best ones you never use, though goodness knows why. No point leaving 'em to get mildewed in the cupboard.'

She turned and busied herself in the sink again. 'She's a real lady, isn't she?' she murmured without turning round. 'That young lady of James's – she's one of them two who stayed in Barnbeck last summer, I hear.'

'Ay, she did.'

'Pretty little thing, as I recall. I heard tell the other one – her sister – has got married to a title.'

'Has she now?'

Hemingway picked his way in stockinged feet between bucket and mop to the chair. 'I been thinking,' he said as he sat down, 'it'd be nice to give 'em something special for their Christmas dinner, them being newly-weds and all.'

'Ay,' agreed Doris. 'They'll not have been feeding him proper in the army.'

'And I'm no great shakes at cooking. So I was wondering – if it wouldn't be too much trouble, it being Christmas and all . . .'

Doris's plump face broke into a broad smile. 'I'd be delighted, Mr Hemingway. It's many a year since I had chance to do a proper Christmas – it's just not worth the bother for one. Roast duck, all the trimmings and everything – oh yes, it'd be a real treat for me.'

Hemingway cleared his throat. 'And you might as well come and eat with us too,' he said gruffly. 'Save a lot of bother all round.'

Doris folded her floorcloth into two, and then four. 'Well, if you're sure it's all right, Mr Hemingway. I'm not one to intrude . . .'

It was with great pride that James brought his bride home to Jericho on Christmas Eve. Her face glowed with happiness despite the torrential rain which had been sweeping down the length of the hillside as they climbed the lane, plastering her fair hair to her face in dark fronds.

He was looking forward to seeing his father. Hemingway opened the door.

'Come on in,' he said, standing back to let them enter. 'You look fair drenched, the pair of you – get your coats off and come and get warm by the fire.'

The kitchen was cosy, the atmosphere full of genial affection as the three of them sat together in the glow of the firelight.

'Just listen to that wind out there,' said Hemingway. 'There's been nowt like it since them gales last February – brought down the big old oak and blocked the road out of Thaxton, that did.'

James felt proud of his father. As far as he was concerned his son was a good catch for any woman. James was content. It was clear from the way his father smiled at Anna that, whatever misunderstanding there might have been, he thought fondly of the girl who made his son so happy.

'How was the wedding then?' he asked. 'Register office, did you say?'

'Short and sweet,' said Anna, 'but very moving.'

'Funny place,' said James. 'Like going in a Co-op.'

Anna looked up at him in surprise. 'Was it? I've never been in a Co-op.'

When she went upstairs Hemingway watched her go then turned to his son. 'I'm only glad you've found yourself the right lass,' he murmured. 'I just hope she'll get used to our ways, that's all.'

James stretched his legs. 'She will – give her time.'

Hemingway swung his head slowly from side to side. 'It won't be easy, her being used to servants and all. Her folks'll not like it neither when they hear. They'll have wanted her to marry money, I'll be bound. Somebody grand, like her sister did.'

'She didn't want that kind of life, Dad. She wants to be with me.'

'Is she going to stop here when you go back? There's room enough.'

'She wants to stay nearby so we can be together. We'll be fine, don't worry.'

'In a hotel? They cost money – can you afford it?'

'Anna has money,' James said quietly.

'I see.' He couldn't tell whether his father's words implied accusation or not, and felt embarrassed.

'Ay well,' Hemingway went on, 'I'd like to see you well settled, lad. I only wish this blooming lot was over. Jericho needs a secure hand running it if it's to prosper.'

'That's a long way off. By the time I take over this war'll be ancient history.'

Christmas Day dawned bright and clear, only the channels of mud in the lane giving evidence of the rains which had lashed the valley for days.

Doris came in early to get the bird into the oven. She stopped in the doorway to pull off her shoes and fetch a sheet of newspaper, set it down by the fire and placed her shoes on it. Hemingway watched her in silence.

'There,' she said, 'they'll dry in no time then I can clean the mud off easier.'

'Why bother?' he asked. 'You'll only get 'em mucked up again when you go home.'

She turned her round eyes on him. 'Go out in mucky shoes? Never. I'll chip 'em clean just as soon as they've dried.'

As she set about preparing the vegetables, bustling around the kitchen, Anna came down.

'Can I help?' she asked.

Doris shook her head. 'I'm best off on me own – I know where everything is in this kitchen. Any road,' she added with a smile, 'I'm used to cooking.'

'But I'd like to do something,' said Anna. 'Lay the table, perhaps? Or I could make cranberry sauce – I learned how on Thanksgiving Day.'

'With duck? Nay, I'll make my sage and onion same

132

as always – you just go and make yourself pretty, sit and talk with the men. I'll call when it's ready.'

Hemingway stayed hidden behind yesterday's newspaper, clearly unwilling to become involved.

Anna retreated to the bedroom where James was shaving. 'Is your housekeeper always so bossy?' she enquired, coming up close behind him and sliding her arms about his waist. 'Daddy would soon give her the sack.'

The razor paused while he detached her arms from his chest. 'She's not a housekeeper, just a neighbour doing us a favour. She comes in now and again to oblige.'

Anna's fingertip gathered a scoop of lather from his chin. 'Really? She's extremely proprietorial,' she said, and blobbed the lather on the tip of his nose. 'Do you think your father will ever marry again?'

He wiped the blob away. 'Knowing how he felt about Mother, I doubt it. But you never can tell.'

'No,' said Anna thoughtfully. 'He's been on his own a long time. I wonder – do you think she's trying to be the next Mrs Hemingway?'

James smiled and pulled her close. 'One Mrs Hemingway is enough for any family.'

Through the shaving mirror as he dried his face he caught sight of her thoughtful expression. 'I meant to order a hamper from Fortnum and Mason,' she murmured. 'I wanted to be a proper housewife, order some York ham and things—'

'Ham?' he echoed. 'We have our own home-cured ham.'

She turned him about and stroked his chin. 'I know, but I thought it might be nice, since it's Christmas, if you had the proper stuff for once, not home-made.'

He tried hard to control the twitch at the corner of his lips and turned away quickly to open a drawer in the dressing table. 'I have a little gift for you,' he said quietly. 'Not as grand as I'd like to give you . . .'

'You didn't need to get anything – you've just bought me this.' She twisted the thick gold band on her finger.

He placed a small parcel in her hand. 'Happy Christmas, darling,' he murmured.

She flung her arms about his neck and kissed him before unwrapping a small tortoiseshell box. 'It's lovely – and I have a gift for you. Merry Christmas, James.'

He stared down at the silver tie-pin with a pearl head. 'It's beautiful,' he said.

'I noticed you never wore one,' she explained. 'And when I was here before I noticed your father picked his teeth with a length of cotton so I got a little toothpick for him while I was in Boston. That's silver too – I hope he likes it.'

James couldn't resist smiling. 'I'm sure he will.'

'And I didn't know Mrs Brook would be here – do you think it would be all right if I give her a silk hanky with Nottingham lace round the edge? It's brand new – I haven't used it. I don't think I've got anything else . . .'

James hugged her to him. 'I think she'll be delighted. Come on, let's go down to them. This is going to be the best Christmas ever.'

FIFTEEN

Christmas 1965

Lisa put the old car into bottom gear. Gladys laboured gallantly on up the steep gradient of the lane, grinding every sinew, determined to reach Jericho.

David was staring out of the window over the darkening moor. 'Looks like we could have a white Christmas,' he murmured. 'Either snow or rain.'

Lisa glanced up at the threatening clouds. Miserable weather to match his gloom, she thought, but the subject couldn't be sidestepped for long. 'A white Christmas would be nice,' she said. 'Listen, David, what are we going to do about James? Are you going to tell him?'

He strained forward as he caught sight of the farm, winding the window down. 'I wonder why Bart isn't at the gate?' he muttered. 'He must be out somewhere with Dad.'

He was still avoiding the issue. Lisa tried to keep her voice level. 'David – what are you going to do?'

She heard him draw a deep breath before he spoke. 'I'm going to tell him straight away, I've decided. Get it over with. I wasn't going to – I didn't want to spoil Christmas for them, but I couldn't stand all the pretence of Yuletide fun knowing I still had to come out with it in the end. I'll tell him tonight.'

She nodded. At last he was facing it head-on. 'Good for you. I think that's only fair. All right if I park here?'

She drew the car up on the grass verge alongside the drystone wall, leaving the track clear. Beyond the farm gate no light shone in the kitchen. David climbed out, unfolding his long body as he stood up and stretched his arms above his head. 'Home again,' he said, peering into the mist. 'Just look at the view down there.'

In the valley lights glimmered between the trees. Above their branches soared the tower of the church, ethereally pale in the half-light. David took hold of Lisa's arm.

'Thaxton – been there for centuries,' he murmured. 'And it'll still be there long after I've gone.'

She jerked his arm, pulling him towards the gate. 'Come on,' she said brightly, 'if he's in he'll have heard the car and be wondering where we've got to.'

David snapped on the kitchen light and led the way in. Lisa watched him cross to the far door and open it.

'Dad – are you in?' he called out.

A distant voice answered, and seconds later James appeared, his eyes glowing with pleasure. 'David – Lisa – I wasn't expecting you yet.' He advanced on his son, holding out his arms, and Lisa watched the two men embrace. They were of a height, she noticed, both dark-haired though one had flecks of grey on the temples. The same man in two time-scales, she thought, one the older version which the other was destined never to become . . .

James was smiling at her over David's shoulder. He broke away from his son and held out his arms to her. 'And how is my lovely Lisa?' he asked, and the affection in his gentle voice matched the warmth in his eyes. She let herself lean against his chest as he folded his arms about her, welcoming their strength.

James turned back to where David stood by the fire. He was looking down at the empty corner where the dog slept.

'Where's Bart?' he asked. 'And where's his basket?'

The smile fell away from James's lips. 'Ah – I shouldn't have kept it from you. I meant it for the best. The old boy died a couple of weeks ago.'

David stared. 'Poor old Bart. I suppose he had a good innings, but all the same . . .'

'I know – I miss him. I should have told you,' James murmured. 'I'm sorry – only I didn't want to spoil your holiday.'

He turned away from the empty space where the basket had been and the smile crept back into place. 'But tell me about you – how are you, son?'

Over James's shoulder Lisa saw David's expression, bewildered for a moment, casting around for the words, then the bewilderment was suddenly replaced by decision.

'I'm fine, Dad, absolutely fine.'

Ellen arrived home shortly afterwards. She blinked behind her spectacles as she came into the light of the kitchen and dumped her bag on the table. 'Oh – you've arrived,' she said to David. It seemed to Lisa that she made a point of not looking at her.

'It's starting to snow,' Ellen remarked as she pulled books out of the bag. Lisa couldn't help thinking how like a stage schoolteacher she looked, with her spectacles and screwed-up knot of limp hair, her brown tweed jacket and no-nonsense grey linen skirt.

'It won't last,' said James. 'It'll turn to rain directly.'

Ellen pulled off her jacket and draped it over the back of a chair. 'I just made it to the shops in time. I got fish for supper – anyone who doesn't like fish, too bad.'

Lisa stood up. 'Let me help you,' she said. 'Would you like me to do the vegetables?'

Ellen remained stiff-lipped and silent while the two women worked. The men were talking quietly by the fire. After a time Ellen spoke.

'Men – sitting doing nothing while the women slave for them,' she muttered. 'I don't suppose David ever lifts a finger.'

137

'No, that's not true. He often does the hoovering, and he's been known to wash up on occasion.'

'Really? Perhaps he'll prove it later on.'

Despite the irritation which prickled in her, Lisa tried to keep the conversation pleasant. 'Your sauce looks good – I'm looking forward to supper. We can't often afford the more expensive fish.'

Ellen gave her a quick glance. 'No, I don't suppose you can. Why on earth did you give up your job?'

Lisa looked away. 'To give David a chance to paint.'

Ellen grunted. 'Doesn't he have any pride, living off you like that? He never did give a thought to money.'

Lisa felt angry and it was with great effort that she bit back the words of denial. She longed to grab hold of the girl by the shoulders and shake her, cry out 'For God's sake, your brother is dying!', but she couldn't.

Ellen lifted a dish of potatoes out of the oven. 'Supper's ready,' she called out to the men.

James swung round with a smile and stood up. 'I was just saying to David, this reminds me of the time I first brought your mother home for Christmas.'

'Oh yes?' said Ellen. 'Well if my brother would like to make himself useful and pour the wine . . .'

Though David and James appeared not to notice anything amiss, Lisa was conscious that Ellen seemed to resent their presence. Throughout the following days she seemed to take every opportunity to disagree with anything David said.

One evening Frankie Vaughan was filling the kitchen with his cheerful voice.

'I like him,' David remarked. 'He does a lot of work for boys' clubs.'

'Jewish boys' clubs,' sniffed Ellen.

'So? You can admire him for doing charitable work, whoever it's for.'

Ellen drew herself up. 'I'd admire him more if it

was for all boys, regardless of religion. Sectarianism only leads to trouble. Half the world's wars have been caused by religion. I've got no time for it.'

David smiled. 'There used to be no more ardent church worker than you once upon a time.'

'That was before I saw the error of my ways. We're all idealists in our youth till we learn better.'

James gave her a sidelong glance. 'And some of us remain idealists unless something happens to sour us.'

'And even then,' said Lisa quietly.

Ellen rounded on her. 'And what would you know about it? Have you ever had your faith put to the test?'

'Yes – when my parents were killed in Kenya.' The words fell singly into the quiet room, like pebbles in a pool. Lisa was aware of the ripple spreading around her.

James gave his daughter a sharp glance and then turned to Lisa. 'David told me – I'm sorry.'

She touched his hand. 'It's all right – it was a long time ago, when I was still at boarding school. I hadn't seen them for a year. It was during the Mau Mau uprising, they were murdered one night in their own bungalow. Hacked to pieces.'

For long seconds there was silence in the kitchen, only the sound of the clock ticking slowly on the mantelpiece. James patted her hand. Ellen hung her head.

'That's different,' she said at last. 'I was merely talking about hypocrisy when it parades itself as a virtue. That can also destroy your faith.' She glanced up at the clock. 'Well, I'm for bed,' she said, rising from her chair.

Lisa could see James searching his daughter's face as she crossed the room. David sat hunched forward, his head in his hands, and she felt anxious.

'You ready for bed too, darling?' she asked.

His hands fell away and she could see his face was

pale. 'I think so,' he said quietly. 'No need for you to come up yet though if you want to stay.'

'OK, I'll be up shortly.'

James sat silent for a while after David had gone. Lisa lay back on the settee and watched his thoughtful face.

His fingers slid down the crack between his seat and the arm of the chair.

'I don't know,' he said quietly, 'I think I must have failed somehow as a father. My children don't talk to me.'

'Nonsense,' said Lisa. 'They both adore you.'

'But they don't trust me enough to tell me what's on their minds. I've never been able to make Ellen out, not since her mother died. And now David . . .'

Lisa sat up. 'What about him?'

She saw him draw his hand out of the gap. Between his fingers lay a leather dog-lead. He stared down at it, running its length between his fingertips.

'There's something bothering him,' he murmured. 'Didn't you say he was having trouble with his eyes? Is that it?'

She answered guardedly. 'Perhaps it is.'

He sat with his elbows on his knees, the lead drooping between his thighs. 'What kind of trouble? He hasn't even mentioned it.'

Lisa slithered off the settee and curled herself at his feet. 'Oh – odd disturbances in his vision. He'll tell you.'

'He's seen a specialist, hasn't he?'

She leaned her forehead against his knee. She could smell the tangy scent of the frayed leather only inches from her nose. 'I think you'd best ask him about it, James. It's for him to say, not me.'

The leather slid up out of sight as he coiled it slowly around his hand. 'I don't know,' he sighed, 'when they're little they run to you with every bruise, and when they grow up they keep all their troubles to themselves. Have they grown away from me, I wonder, or are they just trying to spare me? I'd rather know, but if they don't trust me . . .'

She looked up sharply and put a hand on his knee. 'They do trust you, James. And I can't speak for Ellen but I do know David loves and respects you more than anyone else. You must believe that.'

He smiled, covering her hand with his. 'Bless you, you're a wonderful girl, Lisa, and I hope my son recognizes how lucky he is.' He leaned forward and kissed her cheek. 'Now go on up to him and give him a hug from me.'

When she left the room James slumped back in his chair, staring at the embers of the fire. There was something wrong, he could sense it. The boy was definitely keeping something to himself.

The telephone in the hall shrilled. He dropped the lead and hurried to answer it before it might wake the others. A woman's voice spoke.

'Is David Hemingway there, please?'

'I'm sorry,' said James. 'He's gone to bed.'

'Oh.' She sounded surprised. It was only just after half-past ten.

'Would you like to speak to Lisa? I think she's still up.'

'Oh no.' The answer came quickly, too quickly, he thought, and then she added hesitantly, 'Are you David's father, may I ask?'

'That's right.'

'I thought so. I looked you up in the directory as a last resort. I just wanted to know how David was – is he OK?'

'Fine – why do you ask?'

'Oh, no reason. I hadn't heard from him for a while, that's all. I just wanted to make sure everything was all right. Thanks anyway.'

141

'Just a minute – who shall I tell him called?'

'It's not important. I'm just a friend.'

A close friend, he thought. 'I can't tell him that,' he said, 'he'll ask your name.'

There was a brief pause, and then she said, 'Tell him Melanie was asking for him, and sends him all the best. Sorry to trouble you. Goodnight, Mr Hemingway – oh, and Happy New Year.'

James felt uneasy as he locked up and put out the lights. There was something wrong and everybody seemed to know about it except him. He only hoped to God it wasn't serious . . .

Ellen lay curled up in bed, cuddling the velvet-covered hot water bottle close to her chest. She heard the light footsteps as Lisa came upstairs and went into the next room, heard the muffled voices of her brother and the girl, talking privately together . . .

It was disgusting, the two of them not yet married and with no apparent intention of marrying. There was only one reason for it, of course. Sex. What was it in the novel she was reading the other day? *'Sex will drive a man further than gunpowder can blast him.'*

What kind of malicious God could there be who would burden man with such a degrading, primeval instinct? One which allowed for no reasoning or decency? Any minute now they'd probably start up in the room next door and she didn't want to hear their sordid animal sounds, conjuring up images which would bring on nightmares.

Beyond the wall a bedspring creaked. Ellen felt sick. She curled into a ball, her knees up against her chest. She heard the girl's long-drawn sigh and she shuddered. Any second now . . . It would be crude, dirty, nauseating . . . She buried her face in the pillow and wrenched the bedcovers up tightly around her ears.

142

'Are you asleep, darling?'

A grunt came from under the bedclothes. Lisa sat on the edge of the bed. 'How are you feeling? Headache?'

David's rumpled face appeared. 'No. Just a sort of tight feeling in my head, that's all,' he said wearily. 'I just had to come up.'

She smoothed back the hair from his forehead. It felt hot and sticky. 'I know,' she murmured. 'It was a bit tense down there. Your sister's not the easiest person in the world to get on with.'

He shook his head. 'Don't blame her – it was more than that. Dad knows I'm holding out on him – I can tell by his face, the way he looks at me.'

Lisa withdrew her hand. 'You're right – he's worried stiff. He's trying to wheedle it out of me.'

David looked up anxiously. 'You didn't tell him?'

'I said it was up to you.' She stood up and began peeling off her shirt. As she pulled down the zip she was aware of him watching, but the look in his eyes was far away.

'Tomorrow,' he muttered as she slithered into bed beside him, 'I've got to tell him tomorrow.'

She draped her arm across his chest and gazed up into his face. His body felt muscular and strong; it still seemed a terrible mistake that anything could be wrong.

'How are you feeling now?' she whispered.

'I'll be all right. Look, I'll get him alone in the morning, when he goes down to his gun room. Oh hell! It's going to kill him.'

'He's distressed enough right now. He thinks you don't trust him.'

David groaned and turned over. Lisa rolled on to her back and lay staring up at the old blackened beams above the bed.

'David.'

'What?' His voice sounded drained, exhausted. She sighed.

'Nothing. Go to sleep.'

This was no time to tell him. She'd have to speak soon, however; there wasn't much time left, and it was what she wanted more than anything.

In her mind's eye she played the scene over again, the scene which had been flickering in and out of her head for days, ever since she'd seen him and James embracing . . .

SIXTEEN

1966

Lisa had almost finished washing up the breakfast dishes when Ellen set off for work in the morning. James pushed back his chair from the table.

'Right, well I'd better make a start on the stock of my new gun,' he murmured. 'Why don't you two get a breath of fresh air, go for a ride? The weather's cleared up now and the horses could do with the exercise. You'll find the tack on the wall in the stable.'

He went out towards the gun room. David folded the newspaper and stood up. Lisa dried her hands and came to him.

'Now?' she said, searching his face. There was no light behind his dull eyes and she could sense the pain he was feeling for his father.

He squared his shoulders. 'Leave us to it, love. See you later.'

She watched him walk slowly out down the corridor, and her heart ached for them both. Letting the tea towel fall she sank on to the chair, still warm from David's body, leaned across the table and buried her face in her forearms.

She could visualize them now in James's little room, hear David's softly-spoken words trying to speak the evil with as little hurt as he could; she could see James grow pale, turn away to the window to hide the anguish . . .

She beat her fists on the table in fury and frustration. Oh God! How could You do this to the two most gentle, loving men I know? How could You be so downright uncaring and malevolent?

There was no justice in this cruel world . . .

James sat head bowed, unmoving, at the bench. Out of the corner of his eye he could see his son's leg dangling where he sat on the corner of the bench. He was only inches away from him, and James longed to touch him.

'Did you hear me, Dad?' David asked quietly. 'It's inoperable so there's no possible room for hope.'

'Yes,' he replied, and the word came out in a croak. He'd expected bad news, but this . . . He found himself pulling the length of leather out of his pocket. There was comfort in the familiar feel of the worn handle. Bart had never been on the lead for years, but he'd dragged it from under the chair every night as a sign he was ready to go out.

Oh God, why did one's mind always think of other things when the enormity of the present was too much to bear? David stood up and crossed to the window.

'You will take care of Lisa for me, won't you?' he said without looking round. 'She's a wonderful girl.'

'Of course I will.'

He wound the lead around either hand, and tugged. He used every ounce of energy, pulling until he could feel the veins pulsating in his temples. Suddenly the leather cracked, and he stared down at the ragged piece in either hand. David turned around.

'I'm going out,' James said abruptly. 'We'll talk later.'

David stood alone by his father's workbench, toying with the half-formed length of steel. It lay cold in his hand. Ironic, he thought; when Dad picked this up a quarter of an hour ago he had no idea of what was about to hit him. He would need time on his own to absorb the news.

David touched the miniature gun lying on the shelf

above the bench, a reproduction of an antique rifle. He lifted it down, cradling it gently to admire its delicate intricacy. He held it close so that he could see the detailed working. Only an artist would have an eye for such careful, painstaking precision. Making this was a labour of love, and he could almost see his father crouched over this bench, hour after hour, perfecting it. He turned it over in his hand. Dad was every inch an artist, though you would never get him to admit it.

Funny, thought David, he'd never recognized it before. It seemed as though he needed the terrible finality of death to be able to see things which had been under his nose all this time.

Perhaps he'd be able to tell them before the end how much they meant to him, Dad and Lisa and even poor, misguided Ellen. With this new-found clarity of mind he knew she too was still searching for real meaning and purpose to her life, and the bitter, thoughtless words were born only out of frustration. If he couldn't tell them, he could try to show them all how much he loved them . . .

He laid the gun back in place and, glancing up out of the window, he saw his father cantering up the hill towards Scarthwaite Moor.

Lisa stood up quickly as the door opened and David came into the kitchen.

'Well?' she said breathlessly. 'How did he take it?'

David shook his head. 'Not too well, I'm afraid. What could you expect?'

She looked across his shoulder. 'Where is he now? Still in the gun room?'

'No. He took one of the horses – I think he's gone up on the moor.'

'And you?'

'I'm all right. I'm getting used to this – it isn't the first time.'

She smiled. 'I'd like to go after him – would you mind?'

He hesitated. 'He wants to be on his own – but that's only because he hasn't got Mother. Yes, I'd like you to go.'

James rode hard, regardless of the glancing sleet whipping his cheeks. He rode like a man pursued by the hounds of hell, but it was impossible to outpace them.

Demons crouched on his saddle, torrents of love mingled with rage and anguish, and a wild refusal to believe this horror. But he knew it was in vain; some relentless, merciless force was going to rob him once again of someone he loved.

Guilt leapt up to join the other demons – what awful sin could he have committed that those he loved should be punished like this? Or was it some gene unwittingly transmitted in his blood which had doomed his hapless son?

David was young and strong and clever, loving and kind – it was unnatural for a son to die out of his turn while the father still lived. The world had gone crazy; there was nothing stable to believe in and hang on to any more.

The sleet was easing off now. On the crest of the hill he reined in and looked down over the valley. Thaxton lay half-veiled in the mist, as unreal as a fantasy which might fade from view at any moment. Like David.

Will there be pain? Again James suffered the tormenting pangs of helplessness. He slid down out of the saddle, leaving the horse cropping the wiry grass.

Tears burned on his eyelids as he stumbled over the rough ground to the outcrop of rocks. It came to him with another stab of pain that it was here he'd yearned for Anna all those years ago, here he'd cried her name aloud to the wind . . .

Anna, I need you now, I need your soft arms about my neck, your gentle voice to murmur words of comfort. But there is no comfort . . .

Torn apart with grief he flung his arms around a jutting spur of the crag and lifted his tear-soaked face towards the sky, his cry howling on the wind like an animal in pain.

'For God's sake, give me back my son – take me and spare my son . . .'

Lisa slowed the horse to a trot. She'd been convinced it would be easy to find him on this exposed stretch of moor, but there was nothing to be seen for miles, only the heather and the crags and trickling rivulets after the rain.

She felt damp and cold. Maybe she should give up and turn back. And then suddenly the horse pricked its ears as a strange cry rang out, like that of a trapped animal.

It came from the high ground, up by the crags. She strained her eyes to see – yes, there was something moving – a chestnut horse, alone . . .

Alarmed, she urged her horse up the slope and it was with a surge of relief that she caught sight of him, squatting on the ground between the rocks. He sat slumped, his head sunk on his folded arms.

He didn't hear her until she dismounted and came to him. When he looked up she could see his eyes were puffy and reddened. She spoke no word, simply knelt beside him and put her arms about his shoulders.

He leaned his forehead against her breast. 'It's all wrong,' he muttered. 'All wrong.'

'Yes.' She stroked his hair. Dampened by the sleet it sprang defiantly away from her fingertips.

'I can't bear to think what he's going through.' She could barely make out the choked words.

149

'He's being very courageous, James. We have to be strong for his sake.'

'And he might have to suffer a lot of pain. Oh Christ!' He broke away and clutched her arm. 'Tell me they won't let him suffer – please!'

She shook her head gently. 'They won't, I promise. The specialist told me so.'

'Thank God.' He squeezed her arm. 'I'm sorry, I'm being very selfish – you're going through hell too.'

She clung to him wordlessly. For long minutes they held one another close, each lost in thought, each drawing strength from the other . . .

At last she stood up. James scrambled to his feet and drew his sleeve across his face. 'We'd better be getting back – he'll be worrying.'

He put his arm about her shoulders and led her towards the grazing horses. As he helped her to mount he smiled up at her and scooped up the reins. 'Thank you for coming, Lisa,' he murmured. 'I felt so bereft I was out of my head. You came when I needed you.'

She took the reins from his hand. 'We're going to need each other to get through this thing. Almost as much as David needs us.'

It was James's idea to move into the dining room in the new wing for a change. 'Time we got out of this old kitchen and used the rest of the house,' he'd said. The conversation around the table was unnaturally bright but Ellen, overwhelmed by the news, could hardly bring herself to join in.

It was growing late when James went off to the kitchen to help Lisa with the washing up and Ellen finally had the chance to speak to her brother alone.

She watched him nervously as he patted his stomach and rose from the table. 'Great meal,' he said. 'I think I'll go and have a tune on Mum's piano before bed.'

She followed him out to the music room, wondering where to begin. No-one would guess from his appearance. He looked as healthy as always – a shade on the thin side perhaps, but then they'd probably lived on little more than baked beans for months.

He sat down at the piano and lifted the lid. She watched his long fingers caress the keys in a series of chords, his expression dreamy and far-away. After a moment she moved close to him.

'Dad told me,' she said quietly, her eyes downcast. 'I want to say I'm sorry.'

It seemed so inadequate; for God's sake, she read so many books, thousands of words every week – why couldn't she lay tongue to just the few that would tell how she felt, to let him know that she loved him and that her heart was breaking?

David reached out a hand and touched her waist. Involuntarily she moved a step away. 'It's just one of those things,' he said. 'Funny how you come to terms with it after a while.'

She felt ashamed, as if she'd let him down. 'I'm sorry,' she murmured.

'What for?'

'I just don't like touching.'

He leaned back and smiled up at her. 'You used to – I remember catching you and Kenny Baxter up in the copse playing doctors and nurses.'

She smiled. 'Ah well, I play nuns and librarians now.'

He turned back to the piano and played a few notes. 'You know,' he said quietly, 'at times I can hardly see the keys.'

She could hardly see them for the tears in her eyes. 'It didn't stop Ray Charles,' she said lightly. 'And he can't see them at all.'

'That's a thought.' He closed his eyes and, roughening up his voice a little, strummed the opening bars of *'Take these chains from my heart'*.

151

He stopped and smiled at her. 'I could have a future yet.'

She looked at the nape of his neck, vulnerable as a child's, and felt a lump in her throat. 'I feel so rotten,' she muttered in a small voice. 'After all the unkind things I've said—'

'Forget it. Brothers and sisters always do. It doesn't mean a thing.'

'I'm talking of all the things I've said about you. I guess I was jealous. I'm sorry, truly I am. And I'm glad you came home.'

He smiled as he closed the piano lid. 'So am I.'

She longed to lean down and hug him, show him how she loved him, but to take his body in her arms, touch him even, her own brother – she couldn't bear it.

'If there's anything I can do . . .'

He swung round on the stool, his eyes darkly solemn, and took her hands in his. 'I'd like you to do one thing for me, Ellen – I know what you said about religion but this is important to me – I'd like you to pray for me, that I'll have the strength to get through this. I'm so afraid I might weaken if there's pain—'

'You won't,' she cut in sharply. 'You've been strong enough up to now, keeping all this to yourself—'

'Lisa's been a tower of strength.'

'—and asking favours of no-one. I'm very proud of you.'

'Please, Ellen, say you'll pray for me. It'll mean so much.'

She swallowed hard before she answered. 'OK. I don't need a church to kneel down in. Of course I'll pray for you – all the way.'

SEVENTEEN

1940

Hemingway was trudging down the lane from the top field, his boots squelching in the fast-melting slush, when he caught sight of the car coming uphill towards him, and he frowned. A big blue car, such as those he sometimes saw turning into the drive of Thaxton Manor – what the devil could it be doing way up here? The driver was slowing to a halt outside Jericho.

He must have got lost, whoever he was. Hemingway dug his hands deeper into his pockets and trudged on. He could make out a man's face behind the steamed-up windscreen.

As he reached his gate and lifted the latch the car window slid down. 'Pardon me,' he heard the deep voice say, 'but is this Jericho Farm?'

He turned to face the voice. It was a man of distinguished appearance, broad shoulders covered in the best tweed. 'Ay, it is.'

'I'm looking for James Hemingway,' the man said.

Hemingway raised his eyebrows. 'Are you now?' he said.

The man frowned. 'Can you tell me where I can find him?'

The coolly imperious tone irritated Hemingway. 'Depends. Who is it wants to know?'

He saw the man's lips compress into an impatient line. 'I do. Please don't waste my time – is he here?'

'No.'

'Then can you tell me where I can find him?'

'I can – but I won't. I'm his father, and you haven't told me what for.'

The man glared for a moment, then swung the car door open and stepped out. He was about Hemingway's height and though fuller in the body, he looked pasty. Too much soft living by the look of him, and his fine leather shoes were no match for the Thaxton slush brimming over the laces. 'I'd like a word with you,' he said crisply.

'You're having one,' said Hemingway, 'though much good it's doing you.'

The man heaved a deep sigh. 'My name's Harcourt – I'm Anna's father,' he said quietly.

'You should have said,' muttered Hemingway. 'You'd best come indoors before we both freeze to death.'

Harcourt refused to sit down. He peeled off his gloves, tossed them on the kitchen table alongside the remains of Hemingway's lunchtime bread and cheese, and stood with his back to the fire.

'There's no denying it,' he said angrily, 'I know they got together as soon as she returned from America and she never came home.'

Hemingway, seated in one of the armchairs, rubbed his chin. 'The lass is of age now,' he said quietly. 'Happen she didn't want.'

He heard the other man's impatient click of the tongue. 'Nonsense, of course she did. She was prevented.'

Hemingway felt irritated; Harcourt was a cheeky bugger, talking to a man in his own home like that, and standing on the hearth like he owned the place. 'How do you know she wanted to?' he demanded crisply.

Harcourt's face reddened. 'She's my daughter. She wouldn't just disappear for weeks on end without getting in touch. Your son kidnapped her.'

'Kidnapped?' echoed Hemingway in surprise. 'Them's strong words, Mr Harcourt. I should take a care to what I say if I were you.'

Harcourt ignored the warning. 'And if you won't tell me where they are I am prepared to go to the police to get her back.'

Hemingway smiled. 'You'll make a right fool of yourself if you do. I'd leave matters as they are if I were you.'

'I'm not asking your advice, only her whereabouts, Mr Hemingway.' His tone was icy. Hemingway couldn't resist a smile.

'That's for her to say. The lass knows full well what she's doing.'

'Oh no she doesn't – she's a child still in the ways of the world. She needs a father's care.'

Hemingway rose from his chair and, picking up the soft kid gloves from the table, offered them to his guest. 'She has it, Mr Harcourt, you've no need to fret. You see, I'm her father as well now. I'll see she's well looked to, have no fear.'

Harcourt stared as he took the gloves. 'What the devil are you talking about, man?'

'They got wed three weeks ago – she's my daughter-in-law now. You've no need to worry over your lass – they're very happy.'

Harcourt's mouth dropped open. 'Married? They can't be . . . Where is she?'

Hemingway ushered him towards the door. 'I'm sure she'll let you know when she's ready. Good day to you, Mr Harcourt.'

He watched Harcourt's slow, careful steps as he picked his way across the muddy yard to the waiting car. At the gate he paused and looked back.

'You're lucky, Hemingway,' he said soberly. 'I was never blessed with a son.'

'Ay,' said Hemingway dryly, 'if I get him back. He's in the army.'

Harcourt's eyes widened. 'Army? She can't be with him then – not if he's in camp?'

'She's near enough.'

Harcourt let go of the latch and walked back across the yard. 'She's here, isn't she?'

'No,' said Hemingway, filling the doorway with his body.

'I'm going to look,' said Harcourt. 'Let me pass.'

'I wouldn't,' Hemingway murmured. 'It might be more than your nice city shoes that gets spoilt.'

He saw the other man's gaze travel up and down his body, saw the eyes flicker as he considered, then he stood back. 'I'll be in touch with my solicitors,' Harcourt muttered. 'You'll hear more about this. It's not over yet.'

'I think it is,' Hemingway said mildly. 'Just mind that pig-shit by the gate as you go out.'

In the darkness of the country lane Anna's face was only a pale oval, but James could see she was smiling at him. He'd been looking forward all day to the feel of her small hand in his, the gold band encircling her finger. He wouldn't be here now but for Dusty. He'd made friends with Devlin, a muscular hunk of an Irishman who was on guard duty that night and who'd turned a convenient blind eye.

'Only for the love of Christ, Jim, be back in an hour or I'll be strung up.'

But still it irked him that Anna had to hang around outside the barracks, waiting, hoping, like one of the local tarts.

'I ought to be with you, caring for you,' he muttered. 'This isn't right.'

She squeezed his hand. 'You will be, once the war's over – it won't be long.'

He wished he could share her optimism; the way Hitler was threatening the Netherlands now things looked ominous. She stopped and turned to him.

'Don't worry so much – I can take care of myself, honestly. I've found a wonderful boarding house – I'm checking out of the hotel at the end of the week and moving in. The landlady is very accommodating – she says she'll let me have you in whenever you get a pass.'

He said nothing. The savings he'd given her and her own money should have lasted for months. She put a finger under his chin.

'We'll be fine,' she said coaxingly. 'I could always look for a job if things get really bad.'

'A job? What on earth could you do?'

She smiled. 'I'll find something. At least we're together, aren't we?' she murmured, 'and we need that. That's worth any sacrifice. Come on now,' she said soothingly, drawing him into the bushes, 'we've got so little time – let's make the most of it.'

James saved the letter to read in private on his bunk after breakfast. He could hear his father's voice behind the words as he read:

> 'Mr Harcourt has been here looking for his lass. I didn't tell him where she was, only that you and her got wed. I reckon he was none too happy about it. He said he was going to get his solc . . . solicc . . .'

The last two words were crossed out, and the letter went on,

> 'lawyers in on it. There's nowt much he can do, as I see it, but you'd best take care. Give my love to our bonny Anna . . .'

Harcourt stood tapping his pencil impatiently on the telephone table while he waited to be connected. At last a voice answered.

'Is that Lieutenant Rayne-Smith's office? . . . Ah Nigel, at last. Look, I'm trying to trace a chap called Hemingway and army records tell me he's in

Catterick. I want you to arrange for me to see the fellow. Can you do that? . . . No, not strictly a military matter, more a personal one. I want to find out what he's done with my daughter . . . Yes, Anna . . . What? You've seen her? When? Where?'

He listened intently as Nigel recounted the meeting. 'Yes, I know she's of age,' he snapped, 'but it's important I see her. Tell me the name of this hotel you say she's staying at . . .'

As he turned away from the table, the pencilled address in his hand, he saw Dorothy leaning on the handle of his mother's wheelchair. The old lady lay back, eyes closed, but his daughter's eyes showed her disapproval.

'You're not going after her, are you?' she asked. 'What are you planning to do?'

'Fetch her back, of course,' he replied. 'She must be running out of money by now. It's my duty to rescue her.'

'And what if she doesn't want rescuing, as you put it?'

'Nonsense. How would you like to live in destitution with a poor farmer who's an even poorer soldier for the duration? It doesn't bear thinking about.'

Dorothy straightened the rug over her grandmother's knees. 'You've got her future mapped out for her, have you? Doesn't Anna have a say in it?' she asked.

'I know what's best for her. She's a child. She'll thank me one day.'

'I think you'll have your work cut out persuading her of that.'

Harcourt folded the sheet of paper and tucked it into his inside pocket. 'If young Hemingway is anything like his father he could put up quite a fight,' he mused.

'This is one battle you might not win,' said his daughter.

He smiled. 'Maybe not, but I usually win the war.'

As Dorothy turned to push the wheelchair on to the drawing room the old lady opened her eyes. 'Sometimes it pays to let nature run its course,' she wheezed in a thin, reedy voice. 'Sometimes it's a mistake to interfere.'

Mrs Woodcock was a gaunt-faced woman with scraped-back thinning grey hair from which the hairpins kept falling out, but she was kindlier than she appeared.

'It'll be grand having a young lady in the house,' she said affably, leading Anna into the little room upstairs at the back. 'I've got a fire going and the bed's all aired and ready. There's plenty of hangers in the wardrobe too, so you put all your stuff away and make yourself right at home.'

She bustled about the room, rearranging the clock on the mantelpiece and the vase of dried flowers. 'Tell you what,' she said, turning to Anna, 'there's the gramophone doing nothing in the attic – would you like it in here so you and your husband can have a bit of music when he comes? There's some records there – they haven't been played since my boy went off to war.'

Anna was excited. Here she could make a love-nest, warm and cosy for James whenever he got a pass. Even a twelve-hour pass – it would be far more romantic than the quick embraces in the icy darkness they'd had to make do with up to now.

A quick trip into Richmond, she thought, to buy a few knick-knacks to put her stamp on the little room. That dear little red Venetian glass vase she'd seen, and some new gramophone needles. And maybe some more records – Mrs Woodcock's collection, ranging from Gilbert and Sullivan to Bob Crosby and the Bobcats and 'Keep the Home Fires Burning', was not likely to provide the intimate atmosphere she wanted.

'I've got to go back to the hotel and fetch the rest of my things,' she told Mrs Woodcock. 'I'll be back by teatime.'

'That's right, love,' said the landlady, 'you be back by black-out and then I won't be worrying about you.'

She'd caught the bus into town but as dusk began to fall and she found herself with a heavy shopping bag near the taxi rank it had been a natural instinct to hail a cab.

Just as it had seemed perfectly natural to buy the delicious little silk camisole for James's delight. Now she sat in the cab, the bag on the seat beside her, counting the money in her purse. With luck there would be just enough in change for the fare to the hotel and then on to Mrs Woodcock's. The notes she must save for the rent.

It had seemed such a vast sum, the gift Daddy had sent for her twenty-first birthday, but now he no longer provided a monthly allowance the windfall was vanishing all too fast.

It's no good, my girl, she told herself firmly, you'll have to put your old habits behind you. No more impulse buying; from now on you'll have to have more self-control and learn to be thrifty.

The taxi drew to a halt outside the hotel. Anna jumped out. 'Wait here – I'll only be a moment,' she called to the driver as she headed for the door.

They had her suitcase ready waiting at reception and it took only moments to settle the bill. The porter carried her case out to the taxi and she smiled and gave him a sixpence.

It was just as he was closing the taxi door behind her that she saw the big blue car pulling up at the gate, and she felt her stomach turn over. There were few big blue cars like this one, and surely not one in Catterick. It had to be Daddy's. Instinctively she ducked as the car glided past.

160

When she straightened again she saw the taxi-driver's curious face in the mirror. He slid the glass window back. 'Lost summat, miss?' he asked.

'I dropped one of my earrings – I've got it now.'

She turned to look back. In the distance she could see the car parked outside the hotel gate. Daddy would be in the foyer now, asking questions. It would take only moments for him to discover that she'd left, and he might be told that it was only minutes ago. Thank heaven she hadn't left a forwarding address.

But he would come looking for her. Having come thus far he wouldn't turn back without a determined effort. She leaned forward and tapped the driver on the shoulder.

'Go as fast as you can, please,' she said urgently. 'It's terribly important to get there before dark.'

She told James about it as they lay in the firelight on the big double bed. On the gramophone a record turned, hissing a scratchy version of '*Somewhere over the rainbow*'.

Anna rolled over to look up into James's face. 'I'm so happy with you, darling. I don't want him to find us and spoil things. I don't know how he traced me to the hotel – Dorothy wouldn't breathe a word even if she'd known where I was.'

'Hush,' said James without opening his eyes. 'He won't find us, and even if he does I won't ever let you go. You're my wife now, till death us do part.'

'Yes,' she agreed dreamily, letting her head fall on his chest. 'Daddy can go to blazes.'

EIGHTEEN

1966

James knelt on the floor by the sink, mopping up the spilt water and replacing the brushes in the jar.

'I'm sorry,' said David. 'I didn't see it.'

'Don't worry about it,' said James, scrambling to his feet.

There had been many accidents like this – a wine-glass knocked flying, a cup not quite reaching the table . . . He felt proud of his son. He was behaving as though nothing was out of the ordinary, taking it all in his stride. In fact they'd both been wonderful; Lisa had been so calm, so practical and full of loving concern yet at the same time not making any undue fuss, so that David should not feel like an invalid. Her serenity had spread itself round amongst them all.

During these past weeks he'd sat here often, watching David paint. Occasionally they'd gone off to ride together on the moors when the weather was good, but most of the time David painted in the little attic room James had set aside for him.

He enjoyed watching his son at work as he applied paint to canvas, wearing an expression of dreamy abstraction. For the moment at least he seemed content. If only it could go on like this . . .

James bit his lip. 'Just how much can you see now, son?'

'It's like looking through a porthole. Just a little bit right in the middle – anything outside that doesn't exist.'

James stood at the sink, refilling the jar with water. 'You know,' David confided, his nose close to the canvas, 'I used to think I needed exotic surroundings to do my best work – it's only now I realize that everything I hold dear is here.'

James glanced up out of the window. Lisa was leading the chestnut across the frost-whitened cobblestones towards the stable. He wondered if David saw her as a blur, or whether he saw her at all.

'I wanted so much to do a portrait of Lisa,' David murmured, 'but she won't stay still long enough. No,' he went on quietly, turning to face his father, 'the truth of it is, I can't see her features clearly any more.'

He was trying to sound normal but James could detect the tremor in his voice and struggled to find words of comfort. 'You could do it from memory. You must know every detail of her face by now – I know I do.'

'I suppose I do.' David fell silent. James still stood at the window. Lisa was out of sight now, lost in the stable's gloom. He heard his son take a deep breath.

'There's something weighing on my mind, Dad, something I feel I ought to tell her before it's too late.'

James felt a prickle of apprehension. From the boy's tone he could guess. 'Are you sure?' he muttered.

David turned to him. 'I won't feel easy till I do. I promised I'd never lie to her.'

'And have you?' He looked up at his son and saw his head sink.

'As good as. I've been unfaithful to her.'

James grunted. 'I guessed as much.'

'Guessed? How?' James heard a crash and looked round. The jar of brushes lay on the floor again, water spreading around it. He picked up the cloth from the sink and knelt.

'A girl rang asking after you. I'm afraid I forgot to tell you with all this going on. I somehow felt she was more than just a friend.'

David came a step closer. 'Did she say who she was?'

163

'She said her name was Melanie.'

David groaned. 'Oh Christ!' Tears were glistening in his eyes. 'It meant nothing, honestly it didn't. A moment of desperation, that's all it was.'

As James straightened he saw David's expression change, his lips tighten. 'No, that's not true either,' he muttered. 'It happened more than once, but it didn't mean anything. It had nothing to do with the way I love Lisa.'

James nodded. 'I understand.'

'I feel rotten about the whole thing, and keeping it from her makes it worse.'

'It's the heart that matters, not the body,' said James.

'Exactly – that's why I ought to tell her.' He looked up at his father curiously. 'You were never unfaithful, were you?'

'No, but there's not much in the way of temptation in Thaxton.'

David sank on to a chair. James could only just make out his softly-spoken words. 'Do you think Lisa will understand? She's so loyal herself . . .'

James shook his head. 'Why tell her? It might make you feel better but what would it do to her? It would only cause her more pain.'

'You'd keep quiet then?'

James crossed to the window. Lisa was lifting the latch of the five-barred gate. 'There's no two ways about it,' he muttered. 'I wouldn't for the world see that girl hurt any more than she's suffering already. For her sake, I'd hold your tongue if I were you.'

The cold air stung Lisa's cheeks as she walked into Thaxton. She'd only ever come here with David occasionally in the past to fetch bread from the baker's or stamps from the post office, but once again she admired the slate-roofed cottages clustered around the church and the low stone bridge. The river

164

Garth was no more than a stream at this point but today it was swollen with melting snow from the high ground.

The post office lay nearest to the bridge. The doorbell clanged loudly as she entered, but the two women waiting by the counter didn't look round. They were deep in conversation and in no hurry to conclude their business.

The postmistress flicked back an escaping strand of grey hair and stamped the pension book.

'And has your niece gone home now?' she asked.

'Oh ay, thank the Lord,' the woman replied, tucking the notes away in her purse. 'I couldn't have stood much more of that blooming awful racket she calls music. Morning, noon and night that transistor thing were on, no matter what.'

The second woman nodded, a pretty, faded woman in her forties. 'Our Kelly's just the same,' she said. 'Seems as though they can't think without that pop stuff.' She turned to Lisa with a smile. 'Oh hello – I know you, don't I? You're the young lady as stays up at Jericho – young David's fiancée?'

'That's right,' said Lisa. 'My name's Lisa Drew.'

'Pleased to meet you, I'm sure. I'm Thelma Dent – my husband Fred works up at Jericho, he's worked there for years.'

The other woman and the postmistress were listening and Lisa was aware that they were scrutinizing her closely. 'Of course,' she said. 'I know Fred well. You'd know David when he was a baby, wouldn't you?'

'Oh yes,' said Thelma enthusiastically, 'and his mother. Lovely lady she was, Mrs Hemingway. Ever so kind.'

Lisa heard the other woman's grunt before she spoke. 'Speak as you find,' she said tersely. 'There's some would say she were toffee-nosed, cut you dead if she'd a mind to.'

'Nay,' said Thelma. 'Bit short-sighted I reckon,

165

that's all. Should have worn specs but I reckon she left them off because she were that pretty.'

The second woman grunted again. 'Handsome is as handsome does. I don't think she were that pretty at all.'

'Sour grapes,' laughed Thelma. 'Just because you fancied Jim Hemingway yourself once.'

The woman hunched her shoulders. 'What if I did? He were a good-looking fellow.'

'Still is,' said the postmistress with a smile. 'He's worn better than the rest of us. Now what is it you were wanting, Thelma?'

Despite the cold wind Thelma Dent hung around outside, staring in the window at the collection of yellowing postcards spattered with the dead flies of last summer, the views of Thaxton Manor and the bridge and the fattest berry ever to take the prize at the Barnbeck annual Gooseberry Fair. Mrs Tattersall's window display had not changed in years, but it served to fill the time until the young lady came out.

Miss Drew was a very pretty young lady and she had a touch of class about her. It was a pity Kelly wasn't here to see her – maybe a real lady in a stylish little suit and wearing stockings would give her some idea how to smarten herself up a bit. A sixteen-year-old needed to have someone like her to model themselves on, not those outrageous-looking pop singers she was so dotty about.

She did so want Kelly to grow up nice, find herself a nice job when she left school next summer and a nice husband. With her looks and figure she could easily be a model like them in the fashion pages of the magazines. She'd done her best for the girl – given her a name with a touch of class to it. There was nobody else in the village called Kelly. Fred hadn't liked it at all.

'Kelly Dent?' he'd said scornfully. 'What kind of name is that for a baby? Sounds like a bloody toothpaste.'

But Thelma had stuck to her guns. The pity of it was that she hadn't been able to give the girl the right kind of playmates and as she grew up she'd been influenced by the other kids in Thaxton. Clothes and make-up, records and boys – that's all she ever thought about. Just like all the others. Now if this nice Miss Drew was to be the new Mrs Hemingway, and if she was going to live up at Jericho Farm . . .

The doorbell clanged and she turned as the young woman came out and dropped a letter into the post box. Thelma gave her a broad smile.

'Take no notice of Mrs Thewlis,' she said. 'She never has a good word to say about anybody, but she means no harm.'

'It doesn't matter,' said Miss Drew. 'I never knew David's mother anyway.'

'Bitter weather,' Thelma remarked. 'Was you staying here long?'

Miss Drew seemed uncertain. 'For a time, yes. I'm not sure how long.'

'Only I was thinking,' Thelma went on, 'if you should be needing any help up there – I do for the vicar, you know, been doing his place ever since Mrs Bax went off to see to her sister.'

Miss Drew smiled. 'Thanks, I don't think so, but in any case it's not for me to say.'

Thelma hugged her shopping basket closer. 'Ah well, happen not yet, but one day.' An afterthought struck her. 'And if you should be looking for a younger person, there's always our Kelly. She'll be leaving school soon. Grand little worker she is – she often helps me out. She can polish and clean with the best of them. Best little scrubber in the village is our Kelly.'

'I'm sure she is,' said Miss Drew.

Thelma gave up. 'Ah well, can't stay here gossiping – I'm due at the vicar's twenty minutes ago. Nice talking to you.'

What a nice way Miss Drew spoke, she thought admiringly as she headed down the lane alongside the church towards the vicarage. Now maybe if she could get elocution lessons for Kelly . . .

The Reverend Bax sighed and put down his book as he heard the back door open and close with a slam. Thelma Dent was back.

'It's only me, Vicar,' she called out from the kitchen. 'Don't mind me – you carry on working and I'll start on the hallway.'

Working? Fat chance there was of that, he thought, with the hoover buzzing away outside his study door and Thelma singing at the top of her shrill voice.

It was no good. Not even the most dedicated saint could concentrate with that racket going on. And it wasn't as if it was even worth it in the end.

The noise of the hoover stopped and Thelma poked her head round the door. 'Any news from Mrs Bax yet, Vicar?'

'No, Thelma, nothing to speak of.'

She shrugged her thin shoulders. 'She's been gone a long time now – her sister must be proper poorly.'

Humming, she began shifting the papers on his desk, dusting around them in small, perfunctory dabs. Bax bent to retrieve the sheet of notes for Sunday's sermon which she'd dusted on to the floor.

She didn't look up as she carried on flicking. 'I met that Miss Drew today – you know, that young lady who's staying up at Jericho,' she told him. 'Very nice young lady.'

'I'm sure she is,' he said wearily.

'We had a nice chat, her and me. Seems like her and David might be staying for a bit longer yet.'

'Perhaps I should call to see them.' Bax stood up.

168

'Thelma – I've been meaning to mention to you – there's a funny smell in the bathroom.'

Her scanty eyebrows shot up. 'Funny smell? It's not that dratted cat from next door again, is it? I've made sure not to leave the back door open.'

'No, it isn't the cat.'

'Only you could have left it open yourself, you being so wrapped in your books and all. You know how absent-minded you can be at times, Vicar.'

Dear heaven, she sounded more and more like Sarah every day. 'It's not the cat,' he repeated patiently, 'it's the toilet. I think it needs something putting down it. Regularly,' he added firmly.

For a moment she looked mystified, and then suddenly her face cleared. 'Harpic – I think there's some left in an old bottle under the sink. Don't worry, I'll see to it.'

She was spitting on her duster now and dabbing at the coffee ring on his polished desk.

'Has anyone been round to see you about calling the banns, Vicar?' she asked casually.

He was on his guard at once. 'Why do you ask?'

She shrugged. 'No reason.' Then after a pause and another rub at the coffee ring she added, 'I saw that young Maggie Bryant doing the altar flowers yesterday. She's been courting Jim Wood a long while now, hasn't she? Seems to me she's put on quite a bit of weight lately.'

He wandered out into the hall like a refugee. Wherever he went she would pursue him, relentless as Nemesis, anxious to acquire and to disgorge every scrap of village gossip.

The bathroom – she wouldn't hound him in there. The bathroom seemed to be her least favourite place. He was standing at the foot of the staircase when her voice caught up with him from the study.

'Our Kelly's coming for me when she comes out of school. She'll be here directly.'

So she'd be off again soon. Spasmodic, that just about summed up her cleaning efforts. Thank the Lord he hadn't taken her up on her offer to cook for him as well. He'd rather survive the way he did, on burned chops and half-cooked potatoes.

He sat down on the closed lid of the toilet and leaned across to run a finger along the inside of the bath. Once again she'd replaced the grey ring with a gritty coating of white powder. Sarah never left it like that. Nor did she leave a crust around the taps and smelly wet floorcloths mouldering in the cupboard. Oh Sarah, if only you would come home . . .

He wasn't aware that anyone had arrived until he came downstairs and saw a tight little bottom in blue jeans bent over the hearth. Kelly turned round as he came into the room.

'Hello, Vicar,' she said brightly. 'I thought I'd give Mum a hand so she's got time to go down the shops with me before they close. It's my birthday on Sunday.'

He wasn't listening. He was captivated by the liveliness of her blue eyes, the translucent skin of her pretty face surrounded by a froth of dark curls, the slim little body. He had often wondered how on earth Thelma and Fred Dent could have produced a child like this.

She was bending over the hearth again, her little bottom wiggling as she rubbed. Thelma bustled in, unfastening her print overall. 'You ready, lovey?' she asked her daughter. 'We'll just make it if we hurry.'

The Reverend Bax pushed the blackened sausage miserably around his plate. Even buried under a heap of mashed potato it still tasted like charcoal. What he wouldn't give for a helping of Sarah's shepherd's pie or Lancashire hot-pot right now!

Pushing back his chair he left the table and headed

for the telephone. Mercifully it was Sarah who answered and not her thin-lipped sister. He spoke in his
smoothest, most persuasive tones.

'It's no use,' Sarah said at last. 'I thought I'd already
made it plain to you, Clifford, I have no intention of
coming back. Not now or any time.'

'Sarah dear, I wouldn't insist . . .'

Her voice sounded stern. 'If you think I'm coming
back into that big bed—'

'We could have separate rooms. I never really knew
you weren't keen on it.'

'Keen? I loathed it.'

'I promise I'll leave you alone. All I want is to have
you near, your dear presence by my side. My friend,
my helpmeet.'

He could swear she gave a quiet chuckle before she
answered. 'Frankly, my dear, I don't give a damn.'

And then the line went dead. With a sigh he put
the receiver down and turned to stare out of the
window at the night-black sky. What the devil was he
going to do?

His fingers trailed across the little table under the
window, finding the china figurine of a young girl
which had caught his eye long ago in a curio shop in
York. His fingertips traced the slender body arched
backwards in its flowing robe. They caressed the tiny
breasts and lingered there . . .

NINETEEN

1966

'Where's David?' Lisa asked.

Ellen had her legs draped over the arm of the easy chair. 'Maybe he's with Dad in the gun room,' she murmured, without looking up from her book.

He wasn't. The door stood open and James was sitting at his bench alone. He looked up and smiled.

'Have you seen David?' she asked.

'He was here – he's gone upstairs to paint now.'

'Has he locked the door again?'

James pointed to a seat. 'Come and talk to me. He'll be down for lunch.'

She sat down, watching the way his fingers touched the metal barrel of a tiny pistol with the smooth caressing movements of a lover. Alongside the tools lay the broken leather dog-lead.

She leaned forward, resting her elbow on the bench. 'Do you ever miss farming, James? I mean, you used to have hundreds of sheep, didn't you?'

He shook his head with a smile. 'I don't miss all the backache, that's for sure. I'm happy with the few cows and pigs we have now. To be honest, I guess I was never really cut out to be a farmer anyway.'

'Then why did you become one?'

He shrugged. 'Hemingways have farmed Jericho for donkey's years. It was the accepted way of life.'

She was aware that it was small talk, both of them trying to avoid speaking of what really preoccupied them.

She touched a finger to the miniature pistol lying

172

in his hands. 'That's beautiful,' she murmured. 'Have you ever sold any of them?'

He shook his head as he closed his hand around her fingers. 'I only make two or three a year.'

'There must be quite a market – the Americans would love them. You could employ outworkers – make a real business of it.'

He looked deep into her eyes. 'Anna always used to say that. After she died I didn't have the heart any more.'

She withdrew her hand and picked up a piece of the dog-lead. 'Have you thought about getting another one?' she asked gently. 'A puppy?'

'No more dogs,' he said tersely. 'I don't need a dog now I'm not working the farm.'

He was aware he'd spoken too sharply, and gave a slow smile. 'Funny thing, I've taken hundreds of animals to market but somehow dogs are different. Bart was special.'

For a moment they both fell silent and then she saw his eyes flick suddenly to the doorway. When she turned David was standing there, flecks of yellow ochre on his shirt front.

'Finished for the day?' asked James.

'I think so,' David replied, 'it's nearly done. Just one or two bits still to touch up.'

'Can we see it?' Lisa asked, rising and going across to him.

'Not yet. I don't want anyone to see it until it's right.'

'You're being very secretive,' she teased.

He gave her a solemn look. 'Because it's special, that's why, and I want it to be perfect.'

David was spending more and more time painting. Lisa hated to admit, even to herself, that she was beginning to feel just a little shut out.

Even in bed he lay silent, unmoving. It felt as though he was a million miles away. Lisa touched his arm.

173

'What are you thinking?' she asked.

'Nothing. Why?'

She sighed. 'You seem so far away from me these days – it's hard to get near you.'

'I'm sorry – I'm far from everything, not just you.'

She could feel it; he'd gone away from the world already, and she felt angry. She hugged his arm tightly.

'It's not over yet, David – you said you'd fight to the end. Positive thinking – we could try that faith healer, maybe . . .'

She heard his smile in the dark. 'We might as well try Buddhism, accept what can't be changed.'

She remembered it, the poster he'd admired so much in an oriental exhibition, the serene words. *Look deep inside yourself and find peace, like the stillness of a forest pool* . . .

'You've been so well,' she argued. 'We can beat it yet, I know we can. There's James and Ellen and me—'

'There's no we about it,' he answered quietly. 'I'm on my own now.'

She rolled over on her back. Time was running out. In the darkness of the raftered ceiling she conjured up his image with his father. There would be no more Hemingways. These two were the last of the line . . .

She took a deep breath. 'David – I would like to have your child.'

She felt his body shudder. 'Oh, Lisa,' he said. 'I can't just leave you with a baby to bring up.'

'Your child,' she murmured. 'Something of you for me to love.'

'And how are you going to earn a living?'

She stroked his cheek. 'Please, it means so much to me, your flesh and blood – I'll still have something of you to cling to . . .'

'No, I can't do that to you. Oh God, why are we

174

talking like this? For Christ's sake, I can't even get an erection.'

The cry was heartbreaking. She nestled close and he buried his face in her shoulder. 'Let's get married then,' she murmured.

David's voice was muffled. 'I won't make a widow of you either. Lisa, I love you.'

She cradled him close, feeling her neck damp with his tears. 'And I love you, with all my heart.'

In the room next door Ellen was undressing, listening to the murmur of their voices. That girl angered her – why didn't she let him sleep? Anyone with half an eye could see the weariness, etching fine lines on his handsome face. It was obvious that he needed rest more than anything. That girl was sapping his strength, making thoughtless demands on him.

She was selfish and she had no right – she wasn't one of the family. Why didn't she go away and leave him to those who'd loved him all his life? With her out of the way Dad would have more of his company, and there was so little time . . .

She unfastened her bra and then, catching sight of herself in the mirror, quickly moved away. She pulled her nightdress down over her head and then peeled off her pants as though she were on some crowded beach. She knew more than the others – she'd read it up in the medical section, and when she met young Doctor Pillai on his rounds in the village she'd had a private word with him. Diffident as she'd always been with men, she found the new Malaysian Indian a gentle, unobtrusive man whenever he came up to Jericho to see David. It was almost easy to accost him.

His face showed his concern. 'I'm afraid the outlook is not too good, Miss Hemingway. Your brother's sight is very badly affected – I'd say you can count in weeks now, not months. I'm so sorry.'

She'd searched his grave young face for re-assurance. 'What will happen? Will he suffer?'

He shook his head. 'We have drugs. Sometimes these cases slip away naturally, without pain. Pressure on that part of the brain – they can just stop breathing.'

As she turned to go on she heard him murmur again. 'If there's anything I can do – don't hesitate to call me, any time . . .'

As Ellen lifted the covers to slide into bed David's voice suddenly came through the wall, raised as if in anger, and Ellen sat tense in alarm. That damn girl was upsetting him – why couldn't she leave him alone?

Tears were pricking her eyelids. We used to be so close, David and I, when we were children. Now that girl has taken my place. Ellen gripped the bedclothes tightly in both fists. Go away, Lisa – you're not wanted here – give him back to us for the last few days . . .

James went to church alone. It wasn't as though he had any deep-rooted belief. He didn't really know why he was there.

He only half listened to the vicar's sermon. In his mind's eye he was seeing images of Anna at his side, her fair head bent in prayer, her white-gloved hands turning the pages of the hymn book, and if she chanced to glance up and meet his look, her quick, bright smile which had always melted his insides . . .

The service over, he followed the others out into the grey cold of the churchyard. The Reverend Bax was, as usual, greeting his twenty or so parishioners as they came out. James was the last.

He shook his hand. 'Good to see you, James. I hear your boy's home,' he said. 'That must be very pleasant for you.'

James nodded. 'Actually, he's not been too well. He's come home to rest.'

The vicar's voice filled with concern. 'I'm sorry to hear that. I do hope he'll recover soon.'

He took James's arm and led him along the gravel path between the ornate monuments of long-dead Thaxton squires.

'You know,' he said confidentially, 'if you should be needing any help in the house I'm quite willing to let you have use of Mrs Dent's services – I can manage quite well on my own.'

James smiled. 'Thanks, vicar, but if I wanted help, Thelma would be the last person.'

The Reverend gave a slight cough. 'I know what you mean. Ah well, if you should change your mind . . .'

When he arrived home James could smell the succulent aroma of meat roasting in the oven as the girls laid the table. David wasn't with them in the kitchen.

'Is he painting?' he asked.

Lisa shook her head as she piled vegetables into a tureen. 'He's lying down. He didn't sleep very well last night.'

He saw Ellen's quick look of scorn. 'It was a bad headache,' she said. 'I called Doctor Pillai and he's given him something.'

Alarm leapt in him. 'What did the doctor say?'

'Only to let him sleep. There's nothing else we can do.'

He sat down at the table, absorbing the news. 'I think we ought to see another specialist.'

Lisa's voice came quietly. 'There's no point, James, really there isn't. We just have to face it.'

'No-one can help him now,' Ellen agreed, then added in an icy tone, 'not even your God.'

They talked little until David appeared while they were eating the rice pudding. Lisa got up and walked across to him. He looked pale but composed as he came to the table.

177

'How are you feeling now?' she asked.

'I'm fine. I was only dozing,' he said, pulling out his chair. 'You should have called me.'

'No matter,' said Ellen, fetching a covered plate from the oven, 'I've kept it hot for you.'

David lifted a brochure from the chair and glanced at it. 'What's this? A seed catalogue? Choosing your spring bulbs for the garden?'

He lay the brochure down beside his fork. Ellen laid the plate in front of him then snatched up the brochure and tossed it on the sideboard. David fixed her with a solemn look.

'It's all right, you know, talking about plans for the future. I'd much rather you all behaved naturally.'

Lisa pushed the salt cellar towards him and picked up the wine bottle. 'Do you want red wine?'

He watched the liquid filling his glass. James could see his eyes looked bemused, unfocused.

'You're all pussy-footing around,' David murmured, 'and I know it's for my sake but it won't change anything. I want you to talk just as you would if I wasn't here.'

Ellen made a choking sound and looked down at her napkin. James continued eating his pudding, seeing Lisa's lips pucker as she took another sip of red wine.

She set the glass down and leaned across to Ellen. 'Did I tell you about meeting Thelma Dent?' she said. 'She wanted to know if you needed any help here.'

Ellen took her cue. 'Thelma? Good Lord, everyone knows her house is a tip.'

James laid down his spoon and pushed his empty pudding plate away. 'The vicar was trying to push her off on to me this morning – I think he's had enough. She's a nice woman though for all that,' he said. 'Fred's always been very happy with her. It's his daughter he worries about.'

'Why?' asked Lisa.

James shrugged. 'Oh, boys always hanging around the gate, staying out half the night, that sort of thing. I suppose all fathers worry about their daughters.'

Ellen gave him a look. 'You don't have anything to worry about with me, do you?'

David stopped pushing roast beef around his plate. 'The girl in the shadows,' he murmured.

Ellen's spoon paused in mid-air. 'What?'

He looked up. 'You've still to come into bloom, Ellen. You haven't found yourself yet.'

He reached out a hand, groping for the wineglass, then covered his eyes with his hand. Lisa looked at him anxiously.

'What is it, darling? The headache again?'

He shook his head. 'I don't want to go yet,' he muttered.

Ellen threw down her napkin and stood up, her cheeks flushed. 'At least you've found yourself,' she said stiffly. 'You were lucky enough to fulfil your talent – you'll have something worthwhile to leave behind.'

'For God's sake, Ellen!' James said sharply.

'I'm sorry,' she mumbled, and as she turned and hurried from the room he looked anxiously at his son. David was shaking his head, a dazed look in his eyes.

'Girl in the shadows,' he murmured. 'Poor Ellen.'

It was a fine day in early spring and the corner of the yard where the old bench stood was a perfect sun trap. David had spent most of the afternoon sitting there with a rug over his knees, his head leaning back against the old stone of the house.

Lisa took a mug of tea out to him and seated herself beside him. He sat running his fingertips slowly along the rough wood of the bench, as though memorizing the feel of it.

'Are the crocuses out?' he asked quietly.

'Yes – there's even a clump of them growing wild outside the gate.'

A smile touched the corners of his lips. 'That'll be Mum – she was always doing things like that.' Without turning his head he waved a hand uphill. 'There'll be daffodils in the copse soon, masses of them. I love the spring, when everything comes to life again.'

For a moment she couldn't speak. The words were too pregnant with poignancy for either of them to pursue it. 'How's your painting coming along?' she asked at last.

'It's finished.' There was no pride, no exultation in his tone as there would have been in the old days.

'Can I see it?'

'Tomorrow. I'll show you all tomorrow.' He sounded dreamy, remote, and she wanted to snatch him back. But she stayed silent, watching him savour the sun on his face . . .

David lay very still in the bed, trying not to move a muscle. One misjudged move and the pain might come sweeping back, that horrible, overwhelming pain which drove all reason from the mind, locking him again into that self-centred world where nothing else existed.

They brought that young doctor sometimes, the Malaysian with the liquid eyes and gentle hands and he gave him something, but it only lasted for a while.

The whole afternoon, sitting in the sun, he'd worked consciously at relaxing every muscle to try to ease the pain away. It was so peaceful out there in the yard, soaking up the sun and the texture of Jericho's old stone, letting the mind and body drift . . .

He could afford to let go now the picture was done. He was satisfied he'd achieved what he set out to do, capturing the essence of spring, of life and hope, of resurrection. It had taken time, and patience, waiting till the futile rage had died, till calm acceptance took its place. It was Lisa who had lent him strength, the same strength which would carry her through the days ahead . . .

He moved cautiously. No pain. Thank God. Tonight he would sleep. He felt so tired. He wanted oblivion, a long, deep, untroubled sleep . . .

Lisa lay awake listening to the sound of his breathing, slow and regular. She remembered how, in the old days in the scruffy London flat, she used to try to match her breathing to his, breath for breath, but she never could keep it up for long.

After a while she heard James's measured tread as he came upstairs and went along the corridor to his room. Then she heard the creak of a spring as Ellen climbed into bed. For a long time she lay, listening to the rustle of a breeze in the old tree outside, the occasional screech of a barn owl, trying not to think of the inevitable.

Without David a vast, interminable desolation lay ahead. She mustn't think such selfish thoughts. He would be the first to say that life must go on . . .

Turn over, stop thinking, go to sleep. She lay in the dark, listening to the sound of her own breathing. And then slowly she became aware that something was missing. She listened and held her breath. The room was silent until the fear began to hammer at her temples. She was alone.

In panic, she rolled over and reached for him, put her ear to his lips. He was no longer breathing, and there was no heartbeat under her hand. A terrible cry rang out – her own voice.

'David!'

She was still shaking him, crying out his name, when dimly she heard footsteps come running and the door burst open . . .

* * *

She was only vaguely aware of Ellen telephoning for the doctor, of James bending, pale-faced, over the bed, but she registered the terrible finality of the doctor's words.

'I'm sorry, he's gone.'

The world seemed to drain away, leaving a cold, empty space inside her. She knelt by the bedside, holding David's hand while James sat beside him, holding the other. Ellen stood hesitantly in the shadow beyond the lamplight.

'Should we go downstairs?' she whispered. 'Doctor Pillai said the undertaker would come soon.'

'Not yet,' said James. 'I want to stay and keep him company a little while longer.'

Lisa understood. Somehow something had gone from the room, leaving behind this cold emptiness.

'I want to stay too,' she murmured.

Ellen crept away. For a long time they stayed together, neither of them speaking. James's hand found hers on the bedcovers and clasped it tightly. Hand in hand, all three were linked in a wordless bond.

There were no tears. They were to come later . . .

TWENTY

1940

The new year started laden with gloom; the war seemed to be developing in earnest now that young lads of nineteen were being called up for military service; the worst storms of the century swept the country, and it was so bitterly cold that for the first time in fifty years the river Thames froze over.

But spring arrived at last and the villagers in Thaxton came to life again. The ploughing had been late this year, having to wait till the ground thawed, but now tips of corn were beginning to show above the black earth. Life was getting back to normal, whatever Hitler might be up to.

True, many of their lads had gone off to war but so far none had come to any harm. Jack Tattersall, the postmaster, now wore the uniform of an Air Raid Warden and bullied them all about every little chink of light showing around their black-out curtains, in case the German bombers came their way, looking for directions to Leeds or York or Middlesbrough.

'I see they've gone and rationed meat now,' old Mrs Spivey remarked to her daughter-in-law, 'but that'll not bother us. Our Bob says they'll never miss the odd pig or two, but what's worse is the sugar. That's a blow. I do like three spoons in my tea.'

'We have to make sacrifices, Mother. Don't you know there's a war on?'

The old lady shook her head sadly. 'I know about wars, lass. Bob's dad never came home from the last one. The only lad in Thaxton he were who didn't. We

183

all thought young Hemingway had had it, but he come home in the end with a gammy leg.'

Her daughter-in-law sighed. She'd heard it all before. 'Never mind, Mother, we're going to hang out the washing on the Siegfried Line, aren't we? Now come away from that window, put your teeth back in and finish your breakfast.'

'Eeh, just look at that!' said Mrs Spivey. 'Did you ever see such a backside in your life? Doris Brook ought to be ashamed of herself, wearing trousers with a backside like that. Whatever is the world coming to, at her age and all?'

Up at Jericho Farm Doris had started on clearing out the airing cupboard. Spring-cleaning was her speciality; at home she did it all year round and it was a pleasure to have the run of Jericho to indulge her pleasure to the full. What's more it gave her the opportunity while he was out to pry freely into Mr Hemingway's things.

He kept a lot of old junk, bits of bicycles and broken vacuum flasks and roll-ends of wallpaper he'd never use. There was one pretty pink one – she could use that for lining the drawers in his dressing table – yes, she hadn't had a chance to go through that yet.

She was still on her knees when the yard door opened and he came in. She watched as he slipped off his boots and laid them on the newspaper she'd placed by the door. She gave him a big smile.

'I've got rid of a load of old rubbish from that cupboard,' she told him, 'but I couldn't get into that cupboard under the stairs.'

'You wouldn't,' he said as he limped across to his chair. 'I keep it locked.'

'Why?'

'Because my guns are in there, that's why.'

She climbed stiffly to her feet. 'There's cheese and pickles ready for you on the table. This afternoon I'll do that dressing table in your room – and put some lining paper in.'

'Don't bother.'

'Why not? It's no trouble.'

'Because that's locked and all. Private stuff.'

'Oh.' She felt disappointed. It sounded as though it might have been interesting.

'And I don't like folks rooting.' He rose and came across to the table.

She wasn't ready to give in yet. 'You've not had a proper clear-out in years, Mr Hemingway. The rubbish I've had to chuck out – why, it's unbelievable. Old scent bottles, tablecloths no more than rags—'

'It's my rubbish. I'll keep it if I want.'

'Now don't be silly – what if you was to marry again? Do you think she'd want—'

She saw at once she'd gone too far by the angry way he looked up and glowered at her. 'Marry again? Me? When I had the best wife in Christendom? Whatever gave you that idea? Nay, that'll be the day.'

Somehow for Doris the sparkle went out of the afternoon's spring-cleaning. Polishing up the old copper kettle didn't seem to have quite the same appeal any more. From the window she could see him, working with young Fred Dent, mucking out the barn, and she smiled.

He was a good man really, was Mr Hemingway, even if he was a bit rough with his tongue at times. And it was nice to have him sit beside her, a bit of male company, down at the Rose and Crown now and again even if he didn't talk much. It made a woman feel young to have a man buying her a port and lemon again, with folks like that nosey Mrs Spivey looking on . . .

He was too good to be left to fend on his own or he'd slop around in this mess for ever. Nay, somebody had to be charitable and look to his needs. She wasn't going to give up on him yet.

185

He came in as dusk was falling and Doris was lifting down her coat from the back of the door. 'You'd best be off else it'll be dark before you get home,' he commented, then added, 'Fancy a drink tonight at the Rose?'

'I wouldn't say no,' she smiled.

'You'll leave them trousers at home, won't you? You look best in a skirt.'

She bridled. 'Lots of women wear trousers nowadays – they're warm and cosy, are trousers. I thought I might as well use them – they've been hanging in my closet all these years since my husband died.'

'Best leave them there, if you ask me. Let the moths have them.'

'Moths?' she said in a scandalized tone. 'There's no moths in my house, I'll have you know. Plenty of mothballs there is.' Seeing the look on his face she softened. 'Still, if you think I look best in a skirt . . .'

'Ay, I do, and anyway the cold snap's over now.'

'Right then. Eight o'clock suit you?'

Doris hurried away down the lane. She was glad really that he'd been honest about the trousers. This freedom of movement the girls bragged about was all very well, but rough serge didn't half chafe the insides of your thighs . . .

The manageress of the Co-op café surveyed the girl critically. She was smartly dressed, wearing gloves and her stocking seams were straight. That was a good start. Now half her staff had cleared off to go and work in munitions where the money was better, it wasn't easy to come by a good class of girl.

She looked down at the paper in her hand. 'Anne Hamilton. Age twenty-one. 17 Shepley Road.' The girl stood patiently, obviously at ease with herself. 'Have you had any experience of waiting on table, Miss Hamilton?' she asked.

'No, but I learn fast. I can soon pick it up.'

She didn't talk like the locals; she said 'farst' like they did on the wireless. She was decidedly a cut above the usual kind of applicant. 'What were you doing in your last job?'

The girl smiled. 'Actually, I've just come back from America. I was a kind of nanny there.'

'So you're used to service?'

'Yes.'

The manageress nodded. It might be worth taking a chance on her – with that smile she could win over the difficult customers, and she seemed bright enough to learn quickly.

'Right. Monday morning eight-thirty sharp,' she said. 'A week's trial and we'll see how you go.'

She watched her walk out, no slumping shoulders but head held high and confident. If she turned out as good as she looked, this girl could bring back that touch of class the place sorely needed. Maybe the better-off ladies would start coming back to the Co-op for their morning coffee and pastries instead of deserting her for that smart little Mario's which had opened round the corner . . .

Anna was bursting with excitement when she met James.

'No, don't argue with me, darling – it'll be fun, wearing a black dress with a cute little cap and apron. Like Betty – remember her? Our maid at home – she let you in when you came to dinner with Daddy that time.'

'But Anna, you were trying to lie low – your father—'

'I thought of that. I gave a false name. You are looking at Anne Hamilton, waitress extraordinary, spinster of this parish.'

'Spinster?'

'I couldn't let on I was married, could I? Oh, just

187

think of it, James – we'll have money – not a lot, but we can pay the rent. Aren't you proud of me?'

He hugged her close. 'No man in the world could be prouder of his wife. I love you, Anne Hamilton – even if you lied about being a nanny.'

She gave him a mischievous look. 'I did actually take care of my little cousin Justine for a while.'

'How long?'

'Oh – while her parents played in the tennis tournament – about an hour.'

The weeks were slipping by and in the wood the pale buds of spring were fleshing out into full-grown leaves. In all this time they'd heard nothing more of Harcourt and they were beginning to breathe again. James lay with his arm under Anna's head, savouring the moment.

'I had a letter from Dorothy today,' Anna said softly.

James started. 'She knows where you are?'

'Of course. We have no secrets from each other. She won't breathe a word.'

'What does she say?'

'Myles has rejoined his old regiment. She's pleased about that – she says their social life has improved enormously. Lots of parties and things.'

He felt a twinge of guilt. Because of him there were no more parties in Anna's life.

'Do you miss the parties, going to the races, that sort of thing?' he asked.

She looked up with an expression of mock disgust. 'Me? With my aching feet? No fear. I see all the company I want in that café, believe me. Do you know, old people can be a pain in the neck, they want everything yesterday. They don't seem to know there's a war on.'

She was making light of her tiredness and he loved her for it. He'd have to stop thinking she was made of china.

'Mrs Woodcock is a real pet,' Anna went on. 'She's teaching me how to knit socks on four needles. I got some wool in town yesterday, so you know what you'll be getting for your birthday.'

He could picture her, sitting by the fire with the old lady, aching feet propped on a pouffe, her pretty face frowning in concentration as she struggled to master the intricacies of four needles and a wayward ball of wool.

He rolled over, leaning on his elbow to bend over her. 'Hand-knitted socks,' he muttered. 'It sends shivers up my spine. You really know how to get a man going.'

His hand slipped inside her jacket, feeling the rising curve of her breast, the nipple standing proud, and joy surged in him. She brought him everything a man longed for in a woman – she was beautiful, she was sexy, she was clever, she was loyal, she was strong, she was proud, she was full of life – and she wanted to knit his socks . . .

Dusty only half listened when James told him about the socks. It was clear his mind was on other matters. It didn't take long for it to come out. Dusty took a deep breath.

'Remember I told you once I used to have a girl friend?' he said, his cheeks flushing with embarrassment.

'You joined up because it went wrong, didn't you?'

Dusty nodded and pulled a dog-eared snapshot out of his wallet and handed it to James. It was a photograph of a pretty, mousy-haired girl with an impish smile swinging her legs on the railings of a seafront.

'That's Maisie, at Southend,' said Dusty. 'She left me – for my best friend, would you believe, just like in the films. Well, now that's over. She wants to meet me and talk about us getting back together again.'

'Are you going to?' James asked.

Dusty pulled a face as he tucked the snapshot away again. 'She doesn't realize I can't just up and go. I'm not due for a forty-eight till the end of the month when I finish my course. What the hell am I going to do, Jim?'

'Write to her – explain. I'm sure she can wait till then.'

Dusty's lip curled. 'Maisie wait? Not her – never was one for patience, wasn't Maisie. She led me a real dance for two years or more. She'll up and off with somebody else if I'm not there.'

It was sad to see his normally cheery young face crumpled with worry. She sounded a hardbitten little bitch this Maisie, thought James, he'd be better off without her. He was too genial, too kindly a soul to be manipulated like a puppet on a string. He didn't know whether he was coming or going, and she might not even take him back at the end of it. He deserved better.

Anna sat with her feet in a bowl of hot water and a notepad on her knees. She chewed the tip of her fountain pen as she thought what to write next to her sister.

> The party sounds as if it was fun. I wish I'd been with you, but of course that's all behind me now. Reading what you tell me makes me pine, just now and again, for the fun we used to have together in the old days, the pranks we played, the boys we teased. One day, maybe . . .

Mrs Woodcock came in from the scullery and began laying knives and forks on the table. 'Now what are you going to eat, lovey, if you don't fancy the mutton stew? I've some finny haddock – or there's a bit of cheese?'

Anna laid aside the notepad. 'I'm really not hungry, Mrs Woodcock. I've been looking at food all day.'

'You can't go on with an empty stomach. No wonder you come over faint at work,' the older woman chided. 'You must eat something.'

'It was the heat, that's all. It's very close and stuffy in the café. I'm fine now.'

Mrs Woodcock folded her hands across her thin chest and shook her head with a sigh. 'Just like my Denby, you are – he never wanted to worry me either, bless him.' She looked fondly at the picture on the mantelpiece of a young man in army uniform. 'Lovely boy he was, apple of his dad's eye. Pity he never came home. Buried in Belgium, he is, but I still go down the war memorial to see his name up there – Sergeant Denby Woodcock, killed in action 1917. I make sure the soot's cleaned off so's everyone can read it.'

'You must be very proud,' Anna murmured, stretching for the towel which was just out of reach. The landlady handed it to her.

'What I was going to say was,' Mrs Woodcock went on, 'I know the signs. Fainting, off me food – I was just the same when I was expecting him. Have you told your husband yet?'

TWENTY-ONE

1940

It was Anna's Saturday off and the late afternoon sun was warm on his back when James lifted the latch of Mrs Woodcock's gate and knocked at her front door. Anna was waiting in the hallway with her jacket over her arm.

'Let's go out for a walk,' she said urgently. 'There's something I want to tell you.'

He took her arm and led her down the street. 'There's something I want to tell you too – Dusty's gone missing.'

She stared up at him. 'Missing? Since when?'

'Since last night. It's that girl of his, I know it is. He's run off to see her.'

'Silly boy. Have you told them?'

'How could I? Anyway, I'm only guessing and I could be wrong.'

'I wouldn't worry, darling. If he does get caught they won't shoot him, will they? What will they do?'

James shook his head. 'Put him in the glasshouse, probably. Keep him locked up.'

'Which is no worse than he was,' said Anna. 'So stop worrying.'

Nearing the railway line they turned off the road and climbed the bank. For a time they sauntered, hand in hand, along the embankment. Suddenly James remembered.

'I'm sorry – I was so bothered about Dusty I interrupted you. What were you going to tell me?'

She glanced up at him under her lashes. 'I've written to Daddy,' she said.

He stopped and stared at her. 'Why – when you've been trying so hard to avoid him?'

She lowered herself on to the grass. 'To tell him I want to come home – just to see him – after all, it's nearly two years since I went to America. And to get some more of my things. I thought maybe next weekend.'

'Next weekend?' he echoed.

'The café's going to be closed till Tuesday for painting, and you can't get a pass so it seems an ideal opportunity.'

James squatted down on the grass beside her. She never failed to surprise him, but he was worried. 'You don't think he'll let you get away with that, do you? He'll try and make you stay, I know he will.'

'But he won't succeed, you know that. Besides, there's something I want to tell him – after I've told you.'

From a distance came the rumble of a train. James curled his legs round into a more comfortable position and pulled a blade of grass. 'What's that?' he asked. The grass tasted sweet between his teeth.

The train clattered past, its breath ruffling Anna's hair and whisking her words away. He saw her mouth move but made out only one word.

The blade of grass fell from his lips. The rattle of the train had died away before he could speak. 'Baby?' he said hoarsely. 'Did you say baby?'

She nodded, her eyes bright with happiness. 'In the spring, darling. By the time we see the daffodils come up again you'll be holding our baby in your arms.'

Anna felt sorry for the girl who opened the door to her. New to the job, she was evidently uncertain how to deal with the stranger who said she was the master's daughter.

'No, the master's not here, miss. He's playing golf with Mr Lawrence.'

193

Serves me right, thought Anna. He's playing hard to get. 'Is my grandmother in?' she asked.

'Oh – Mrs Harcourt? She's asleep. Shall I take your bag upstairs?'

'In a minute. Where's Betty?'

'Don't know, miss. She left before I come.'

Anna went into the drawing room. Apart from the black-out curtains draped at the windows nothing seemed to have changed. The marble clock still ticked busily on the mantelpiece, Grandmother's aspidistra still blotted out most of the light from the side window . . . She glanced back into the hall.

'Where's the Meissen bowl – the big blue one that was on that table?' she asked the girl.

The girl looked round, then back again, shaking her head. 'Don't know. There weren't no bowl there when I come.'

'Never mind. Do you think I could have a cup of tea?'

' 'Course you can.' The girl's face brightened. She could handle this. 'The master's rationed us. You can have one lump of sugar or a spoonful of honey,' she said.

Anna couldn't resist a smile. 'I'll have the sugar, please.'

The tea finished, Anna wandered about the room, fingering the familiar leather blotting pad on the writing desk, the inlay on its surface. There were cards propped up in the brass letter rack – curiosity prompted her, and she lifted them out. 'Lieutenant Colonel and Mrs Hind invite you to attend the wedding of their daughter Maria . . .'

Maria Hind, marrying? She'd been just about to leave finishing school when Anna last saw her. Imagine – Maria in a beautiful white gown, being escorted by her uniformed father down the aisle at the cathedral, the military guard of honour waiting

194

outside with raised swords. Or maybe there weren't enough young men left now with the war. In any event the Hines would make sure it was a day to remember.

What else? She picked out another printed card. '. . . to celebrate their silver wedding, a small dinner party . . .'

She'd almost forgotten that such a world existed. At one time she would have been choosing a gown, finding the right shoes and elbow-length gloves to match. Dorothy still inhabited that world, but then she was stuck with Myles. The thought made Anna feel better.

She heard the front door open, her father's cheerful voice call out as he dropped his golf bag in the hall. 'Lucy! Has my daughter arrived yet?'

'I'm here, Daddy.' Anna rose to meet him. He stopped in the doorway, his smile falling away as he caught sight of her.

'Good grief, girl – you've lost weight,' he said, coming forward and placing his hands on her shoulders. 'Dorothy told me you looked well when you got back from America.'

'She told you she saw me?'

'She didn't want to – I made her. I'm not daft, you know. You two have always been as thick as thieves.'

His hands were tight on her shoulders but he'd made no move to kiss her. Anna reached up and gave him a kiss on the cheek. He did not draw away, nor did he respond, just stood as still and unyielding as before.

'You look as if you could do with a good meal,' he said quietly, 'and your hair . . .'

'There's no money for hairdressers these days,' she said brightly. 'I cut it myself. I'd do James's too if the army didn't crop him already.'

He ignored the reference, turning away to the cocktail cabinet. 'We'll feed you up – dinner won't be long. Grandmother won't be joining us, of course –

195

she eats in her own room now she's not feeling very strong. Drink?'

'No thanks. Isn't she well?' Anna asked. 'I haven't seen her yet.'

Her father glanced up from pouring his whisky to give her a reproving look. 'Rather late in enquiring, aren't you? She's fretted a great deal about you.'

Anna hung her head. 'I'm sorry. I wouldn't for the world hurt her.'

'Only me?' Harcourt's eyebrows rose in that same cool, imperturbable way she'd often seen them rise in silent question across the bridge table to his partner. 'I had to learn you were married through a third person.'

'No, Daddy. I wouldn't deliberately hurt anyone. It's just that you wouldn't listen.'

He settled himself on the sofa and placed his glass on the side table. 'You think a parent should listen to the wilful demands of a spoilt child?' he said dryly, 'when he knows full well it is not in her interests?'

She felt her hackles rise. 'When it means her happiness, yes I do. Being with James is in my best interests, but you refused to see that.'

'And still do.' He waved his glass in her direction. 'Just look at you, thin and unkempt, wearing clothes you had before you left England – you wouldn't have dreamt of living like that once. What are you doing for money?'

'I'm working. I'm a waitress in a café.'

For a moment his poise vanished. 'Good Lord! Whatever's happened to your standards?'

She said nothing. She hadn't come to argue with him.

He seemed to take her silence for defeat. 'Never mind, we'll put it all behind us. Now you're back we'll soon sort everything out.'

'I've only come for the weekend, Daddy. I'm not staying,' she said quietly.

He waved the whisky glass in the air. 'No need to come to any decisions yet. We'll wait and see,' he said.

His confidence angered her again. 'I mean it,' she said firmly, 'I'm going back on Monday.'

The eyebrows rose again. 'Back to poverty?' he said. 'You haven't got half the sense your sister has. She has the best coiffeuse in the West End, the best tailoress in spite of the war—'

'She's welcome to them. I'm going back to James.'

He set the glass down again and leaned forward. 'Now look here, if you're going to be obstinate I shall cut off your allowance.'

'Like you cut off my letters to James?' she asked mildly.

He ignored her. 'If, on the other hand, you put all this stupid mistake of yours behind you—'

Anna stood up. 'There's something I have to tell you. It's too late to try and lure me back. I'm having James's baby.'

She couldn't see the reaction on his face; she was already out of the room and halfway up the stairs.

Grandmother sat by the bedroom window, a crocheted blanket over her knees, gazing out at the evening sunlight spreading over the garden. Anna sat on a stool at her feet, her hand clasped between her grandmother's.

The old lady looked fragile, even older than she remembered, the skin of her neck loose and puckered, but her blue eyes looked as bright and clear as ever.

'Your father does care for you for all that,' she said in her thin, flute-like voice. 'He never was able to show it, that's all. Even as a little boy . . .'

She was off again into memory, recounting in detail incidents of forty years ago as though they happened yesterday. It was odd, thought Anna, how she recalled

197

the past with such clarity when she couldn't even remember that Dorothy visited her a week ago.

Grandmother yawned. 'Turn back the coverlet for me, there's a love,' she said. 'I think I'll just have forty winks before dinner.'

Anna turned back the counterpane. The linen sheets felt soft and inviting, very different from Mrs Woodcock's stiffly starched cotton. She ran a hand over the satin cover, then saw Grandmother watching her.

The old lady cocked her head to one side. 'Do you miss the comforts of home, darling?'

Anna shrugged. 'A bit. But I've got James.' She took her grandmother's arm to help her struggle to her feet. 'And in the spring we'll have our baby too,' she said.

The old lady stopped and looked up at her, her bright blue eyes shining. 'Oh, how wonderful,' she breathed. 'I do hope I'll still be here to see the little fellow.'

'How was it?' James wanted to know. 'Did you get on all right?'

He leaned across between the teacups on the chenille-covered table to take Anna's hand. Mrs Woodcock stayed discreetly out of sight in the scullery.

Anna shook her head. 'He was as difficult as always. He made it clear I wasn't going to get a penny piece from him if I stayed with you.'

James coloured up. 'We don't want his blasted money.'

'That's what I told him. Anyway, Grandmother was sweet. She's terribly excited about the baby.'

She let go of his hand to duck down and pick up a tapestry knitting bag. 'Actually, I've started knitting a matinee jacket – let me show you.'

She pulled out a web of white wool suspended on needles, then smiled. 'I know it doesn't look anything like a jacket yet but it will be – Mrs Woodcock's helping me with the pattern. Oh – and here's your socks. I know it isn't your birthday yet but I've finished them.'

James stared at them. Hanging side by side from her hand he could see that one was clearly shorter than the other. She was still smiling at him, expectantly.

He took them from her. 'Thank you, love. They're great.'

'I know what you're thinking,' she said with a mischievous smile, 'only I couldn't wait to get started on the jacket.'

The manageress fingered her wrist-watch and looked through the glass in the kitchen door. The restaurant was starting to fill quickly. She looked back at the girl sitting, head bowed, on the stool.

'Now look here, Anne,' she said stiffly, 'any minute now we'll be starting to serve the lunches and we can't have the girls run off their feet doing your tables as well.'

Anna didn't look up. 'I'll be all right in a minute, don't worry.'

The older woman tapped her foot. 'In a minute is not good enough – I can't be doing with a girl who keeps fainting all over the place. I need staff I can rely on.'

'It's only happened once before,' Anna murmured.

'Right in the middle of the restaurant, down between the tables as if you were drunk.' The manageress sighed and shook her head. 'Honestly, if you were married I'd swear you were in the family way.' A suspicious look flickered into her eyes. 'Anne – you haven't been doing something—'

Anna looked up at her, then got slowly to her feet. 'Yes, I am pregnant,' she said quietly. 'And I am married.'

The manageress's eyes widened in horror. 'You lied to me? When you knew the rules?'

'I had to. I needed the work. I needed the money.'

The manageress's back stiffened. 'That settles it,' she said severely. 'I won't have staff who can't be trusted. Lies first, pilfering later – I know the story. Collect your cards, Miss Hamilton. You're fired – and don't come looking to me for a reference.'

Anna was just nearing the corner of the street when she saw the army truck pull up and a soldier jump out from the back. He thumped the tailboard and the truck moved on again. As he turned she saw to her delight that it was James.

He came running towards her, a big smile lighting his face. 'I was hoping I might catch you – I didn't know what time you had your break.'

'What are you doing here?' she exclaimed, hugging his arm.

'Truck had to come into town for supplies – I've got an hour before we go back. Where shall we go?'

She grabbed his hand and turned back the way she'd come 'Come on,' she said firmly. 'I'll buy you a coffee – I know just the place.'

A pretty blonde waitress came to their table, napkin over her arm and notepad at the ready. She smiled at James and as she turned to Anna, her mouth fell open.

'Two coffees,' said Anna, 'and please make certain the teaspoons are clean.'

The girl glanced back at the kitchen. 'Here, I thought—'

'And be quick about it,' Anna interrupted. 'We haven't got all day.'

The girl bobbed a mock curtsey. 'Yes, madam. Very good, madam,' she said with a mischievous smile. James could hear her sniggering as she hurried away to the kitchen.

Anna turned back to him. 'That's Ruth,' she told him. 'She's a good sport. I hope she tells the old crab I'm here.'

The manageress was scolding the vegetable cook but she stopped in mid-flow as Ruth came in. 'And what's so funny out there?' she demanded. 'Get that silly smirk off your face before you frighten the customers away.'

Ruth gave her a sly look. 'Have you seen who's on table seven?' she asked.

'No – who? Not Mr Hargreaves?'

The manageress patted her Marcelle wave into place and cleared a peephole through the misted window. 'Good grief!' she exclaimed. 'I've only just dismissed that girl and here she is back in again, large as life – and with a soldier too!'

'Fast work,' muttered Ruth.

The manageress turned on her. 'That's enough of that,' she snapped. 'I don't want the likes of her lowering the tone of my restaurant, giving the place a bad name with her fancy men. Married indeed – get her out of here.'

'I can't do that,' Ruth replied with a smile, holding up the two cups of coffee. 'She's a customer.'

As she made for the door she chanted a well-rehearsed litany. *'It behoves us at all times to spare no effort to see that the customer is happy and satisfied. The customer is always right.'*

James said little as Anna told him the story. He sat, chin cupped in his hands, watching her face closely.

Ruth reappeared and placed two cups before them. 'She's watching,' she hissed out of the corner of her mouth. 'The old cow's bloody furious. And there's nothing she can do, you being a customer and all.' She nudged Anna's arm. 'Know what? She thinks you're lowering the tone of the place.' She giggled. 'Made my day, you have.'

After she'd gone Anna turned to James. 'So what am I going to do now?' she said. 'It won't be easy getting another job without a reference.'

He straightened and took her hand in his. 'No matter. You aren't going back to work, here or anywhere. I can't risk you falling again and maybe hurting yourself.'

'But the rent – I need money—'

'Not if you have a rent-free home, you don't. I'm going to miss you like hell, but on my very next pass I'm taking you home to Jericho.'

As she opened her mouth to speak he held up a warning finger. 'Now don't argue – just for once shut up and do as you're told.'

He glanced back over his shoulder towards the kitchen. Through the misted window a face was peering angrily. He turned back to Anna. 'And since you're supposed to be lowering the tone here, how about doing it properly?'

He stretched across the table, his lips searching for hers. Just before they met she muttered round the corner of his mouth. 'I wasn't going to argue – I'd love more than anything to have the baby in the house where you were born.'

TWENTY-TWO

1940

James's father was thrilled to hear the news.

'There's never been a baby in this house since you was born. It'll be fair grand to have a little 'un running about the place again. Bring the house back to life, it will.'

He beamed as he watched Anna moving about the kitchen and his eyes grew misty. 'I can hardly believe it – another little Hemingway – me, a grandfather – would you credit it?'

But the pleasure was dispelled by the evening news. They all three gathered around the wireless set and James felt a shiver run up his spine as he listened to Alvar Liddell's sombre tones.

London was getting bombed again. When the news ended he shook his head. 'We're a damn sight better off than they are down there,' he muttered. 'Fancy hiding out in shelters every night, and coming up to find your home destroyed.'

His father's face looked grim. 'We haven't got a tube up here to hide in,' he muttered. 'Never mind, we'll beat the buggers yet. We've done it before, we can do it again.'

Anna laid a hand to her stomach. 'I hope you're right,' she said. 'It's no time to be bringing a baby into the world, is it?'

'Rubbish,' said Hemingway. 'Folks have been saying that since time began but we're here, aren't we?'

'He's right,' said James. 'You're going to be safe here. The Germans aren't interested in bombing sheep.'

The next afternoon James had to catch the train back to camp. As he kissed Anna goodbye his father turned away discreetly and pulled on his cloth cap.

'Come on, lad, I'll walk you down to the station. I've some errands to see to in the village.'

Anna was watching from the gate as they set off down the lane. For a time they walked in silence. It was curious, thought James, how his father seemed to have shrunk. He was a good four inches shorter than he was, and yet James had grown up seeing him as a tall man. Maybe it was something to do with his limp.

It was funny how going away for several months had changed his perception of things. The farm looked shabbier than he remembered, and his father distinctly older. And the air smelled sweeter. Beyond the drystone wall he could see the hay newly stacked in the meadow. He lifted his nose, catching the scent of thyme in the hedgerow.

The dusty streets of the village lay empty. As they rounded the corner by the church, past the graveyard, James nodded to the far corner, under the shade of the yews. 'Do you ever go and visit Mother's grave now?' he asked.

The older man shook his head. 'No need.' He jabbed a finger at his temple. 'Memory's here, not in a lump of stone.'

James saw that his father was looking at him from under the neb of his cap. 'Just think on,' Hemingway said gruffly, 'to drop us a line now and again. I expect you'll write to Anna anyway.'

'I'm sorry, Dad,' said James. 'I've not written as often as I should.'

'No time, eh? Well never heed, I'd no time to read 'em if you had.'

At the entrance to the station Hemingway stopped. 'I'll say goodbye to you now, lad,' he said. 'You've no need to worry about her. I'll keep an eye on the lass. You get on with what you have to do and I'll see she comes to no harm.'

'I know. Thanks, Dad.' James pulled the forage cap from his epaulette and rammed it on his head. 'Only she's not one for sitting still while there's work to be done. Just don't let her overtire herself.'

'There's no need,' his father assured him. 'Doris'll be in to see to all the housework. And there's Fred. No, the lass can take it easy.'

'Talking of Fred – how's he making out on the farm?'

Hemingway shrugged. 'Oh, he's willing enough. Problem is he's only got half his mind on the job when that young Thelma's about. She never gives him a minute's peace. It'll be milking time when I get back – I'll lay a pound to a penny she's hanging around the cowshed.'

James smiled. 'I'd have thought she could have done better than Fred Dent. She's a pretty enough lass.'

Hemingway snorted. 'Would you believe it, the lasses fight over him. He's one of the few lads left in Thaxton so he's got his pick.' Hemingway glanced back over his shoulder. 'Hey up – I can hear your train coming.'

Anna was a pleasure to have about the place, thought Hemingway a few days later as he watched her through the window pegging out the washing. She was always smiling and humming a tune, as happy as a cricket. When she wasn't working she was sitting at the table writing interminable letters to James.

She always nibbled the tip of her fountain pen while she was thinking what to write. She looked up at him, frowning.

'How many babies did that pig have today?' she asked.

He smiled. 'She's a sow – she had eight piglets.'

'Piglet,' she mused. 'I wonder why we don't have doglets and catlets too. It would make sense.'

He chuckled. He couldn't help it – she made him laugh with her comical notions. Doris didn't find it amusing at all when he told her.

'Doglets, indeed,' she grumbled. 'Silly girl. She'll be talking of horselets and cowlets next.'

'Nay, she knows about horses,' said Hemingway. 'She had horses of her own back at home.'

Doris ignored him. 'Oh, and take care when you go into your bedroom because I've shifted the tallboy – it's just inside the door now.'

'Why?'

She gave him a patient look. 'Because it makes more sense to have the dressing table where it is – by the window. The tallboy was in me way.'

She'd been doing this a lot of late, shifting the furniture around so he never knew where he was with it. And taking stuff out of their proper drawers and putting them in another. A man couldn't call his home his own any more, but you couldn't fault her cleaning. Best to stay quiet and let her have her way.

It was the day she switched the sofa and the easy chairs around that matters came to a head. Anna frowned when she came in.

'Oh – do you really like the settee over there, Dad?'

It warmed his heart, the way she called him Dad. 'No, not really,' he said.

'Right,' she said, starting to pull one of the easy chairs. 'Let's have it all back where it was.'

He could see trouble coming as he rearranged it all. Doris was going to be very put out. And she was.

'Who shifted the furniture?' she demanded next morning while she was still pulling off her coat. 'I had it all nice.'

He coughed. 'Anna liked it best the way it was,' he said.

Doris's eyebrows rose. 'Did she now? I see.'

She said no more, but her shoulders were hunched and her lips tight as she set about her work. By evening somehow the sofa was round to the side of the hearth again. Anna pushed it back.

As the weeks went by it became evident that Doris was not at all happy about Anna interfering. There's only room for one woman in any kitchen and anyone with half an eye could see that she resented having her power usurped by a much younger woman. They hardly ever spoke to each other. Hemingway tried to stay out of the way whenever the two of them were in the kitchen at the same time.

It's getting a bit tricky, (he wrote to James) *Doris's nose has been pushed out of joint, but I reckon I know who'll come off best in the end. Your little Anna's got a lot of spirit . . .*

'You know,' said Anna one morning as Hemingway was about to go out into the yard. 'I'm not so sure we need Mrs Brook coming in so often. I'm quite used to work, you know, after being at the Co-op.'

'She's been here a long time, lass.' He looked at her thickening waist. 'And we'll need her more as time goes on.'

'Hmm. Maybe.' She fingered the antimacassar on the back of the sofa. 'I've been thinking,' she said quietly, 'I'd like to do the place up a bit if you don't mind. Some new curtains there, for example, but I don't have any money.'

She gave him that sly, mischievous look he was beginning to recognize, the arch, wheedling look of a child coaxing a reluctant parent.

'So I'll do a deal with you,' she went on, coming up close. 'You pay for the material and I'll make them up. How's that?'

She was giving him a winsome smile now. He wasn't

207

going to fall prey that easy. 'Money's short,' he said slowly.

'Come on,' she cajoled. 'Money was made round so it would go round.'

'Ay,' he answered, 'and flat so it would pile up. Look, if you've got your heart set on it, Doris will get the material for you – she's a good eye for a bargain, has Doris – she got our black-out material cheap in the market.'

Anna's shoulders squared and he realized he'd made a mistake. 'No thanks,' she said coolly. 'I want to choose my own curtains.'

He'd given her the money, and oiled the old Singer sewing machine which had been lying idle under the stairs for years. She was a bit apprehensive about using it at first, but it didn't take her long to get the hang of it. She'd done well with the money he'd given her too; she'd managed to buy enough fabric not only for the curtains but for a couple of cushion covers as well. By the time James was due home on his next leave the room was looking very pretty, and Hemingway felt proud of his daughter-in-law. She'd knuckled down to their way of life very well and she had the true woman's touch.

Doris only sniffed and moved Anna's vase of wild flowers off the table and placed them on the window sill.

Hemingway stood in the bedroom doorway, watching his daughter-in-law as she plumped up the pillows and turned the counterpane back. She had quite a belly on her now, like the old mare who was due to foal about the same time, late April or early May. He couldn't use Molly for the ploughing this year; he'd have to ask Boothroyd if he could borrow his tractor again, and get Fred to drive it. He wasn't going to get on that noisy, oil-stinking thing again if he could help it.

Anna straightened and rubbed a hand down her back to ease it. Catching sight of him she smiled.

'I didn't know you were there, Dad. Did you want me?'

He dug into the pocket of his corduroys and pulled out an envelope. He checked once again that it was carefully sealed.

'I just wanted to ask a favour of you,' he muttered. 'Will you mind this till James comes home, take good care of it for me?'

'Of course I will.' She came across and took the envelope from him.

'Only it's important, do you see? And if by any mischance he shouldn't come home—'

'Of course he'll come home,' Anna interrupted. 'We've got to believe that.'

'But if he didn't, give it to the captain of the new tug-of-war team – when they set one up again.'

Anna was staring down at the white envelope. 'It's not your will then?'

Hemingway shook his head. 'Nay, it's a recipe.'

Anna stared. 'A recipe?'

'He's seen me brew it up oft enough but I want him to know the exact quantities, and how long to brew the tack. It's critical, do you see, and nobody else but me knows. If I weren't here, they'd be stuck.'

Anna looked at him blankly. Hemingway turned to go, satisfied. 'Just keep it in a safe place for the duration, then see as James gets it, there's a good lass. Now I've to go and see a man about a tractor.'

Anna watched him limp from the room and felt a stab of concern for him. He couldn't be much more than fifty yet but he was ageing fast. And he was missing James badly, much more than he'd ever let on.

She'd grown fond of the old man over the months. He was what he appeared, a straight-down-the-line, open, honest man, incapable of guile or deceit. So different from the people who used to come to dinner at Thirlbeck Manor in the old days; you couldn't trust their smiles and that effusive charm was only a mask. There was nothing sham about Hemingway. Like his son, he was solid as a rock.

She tucked the envelope away in the pocket of her thick cardigan and sat on the edge of the bed. God, but it was cold in here, just as it was everywhere else in Jericho once you got away from the heat of the kitchen. At home the maid would be banking up the fires burning in every room . . .

And yet this was what she'd wanted, this was what she'd chosen. Even so she couldn't help missing, just a little bit, those luxuries once taken for granted, and feeling a tinge of envy for the exciting life Dorothy wrote about. It was understandable – wasn't it?

But all she really wanted was here, apart from James. Every night as she lay in bed after scrubbing out the milk churns ready for morning, she made a point of reminding herself of that, ticking off her blessings on her work-roughened fingertips. Only sometimes, feeding the chickens or collecting the eggs from the muddy hay, she didn't quite believe it . . .

She used to bring the eggs in and wash them, until Doris put her right.

'Don't do that else they won't keep,' she said sharply. 'And where's that nice hot soapy water? You haven't thrown it out, have you? Eh dear, we never waste good hot water here.'

Doris was one of the problems. She was a pain in the neck. In the old days Anna would have put a woman like her in her place, but now . . . The number of times she'd gone into a room and seen what Doris was doing to it, only to bite her tongue and go out again to compose herself. It would only upset the old man and she wouldn't do that for the world.

She lay back on the bed. A hump rose up in front

of her, and she smiled and patted it. 'You're going to like your grandfather, kid,' she murmured. 'He's a lovely man.'

Doris bent over the stone sink, peeling potatoes for supper. Outside the yard was growing leaden under the darkening sky. Mr Hemingway would be on his way home soon now.

Then she'd be off home to cook her own supper. It wasn't the same, cooking for one. She'd really enjoyed doing it for the two of them, Mr Hemingway and her, before that little madam came to Jericho. She was upstairs now, having a lie-down – as well she might, her being so far gone and all.

She was young James's wife so she had some sort of right, but still it exasperated Doris the way she tried to take over, and her only a chit of a girl still, baby or not. She had no idea about running a house – how could she, coming from where they had servants and all? What would she know about baking an apple pie or a good hot-pot the way Mr Hemingway liked it?

She and Mr Hemingway had been getting along very nicely. He'd have popped the question by now, Doris was certain of it, if she hadn't come. She'd have been the one giving the orders, placing the furniture where she wanted and choosing the curtains. She'd got it all planned out, how she'd sell her little cottage at a fair price when she moved into Jericho and put the money in the bank. They'd have been comfortable, her and Mr Hemingway.

Doris carried the colander full of potato peelings out to the swill bin down by the privy. It wasn't natural, she thought as she slammed the lid down. That girl wasn't used to their way of life at all. She tried, in her dainty, ladylike way, but she wasn't born to hard work. When Doris had set her on to scouring out the sour-smelling milk churns you should

211

have seen the way her nose wrinkled in distaste.

'I could do with some hand cream,' she'd said, holding out her hands. 'Just look.'

They were a bit red, that's all. 'Bit of mutton fat,' Doris had replied tartly. 'That's what my mother used to use.'

She needed wet-nursing, that one. Mr Hemingway was forever measuring out bits of wood to make a cradle for her and fetching and carrying. As if he hadn't enough on already with the farm to run. He never had time even for a drink at the Rose and Crown these days . . .

It was decent of Boothroyd to let him have the loan of his tractor again when his own ploughing wasn't yet finished. Pity though that Fred had to go over to Otterley Hospital today of all days. Still, it hadn't been so bad. Much as Hemingway hated the bloody things, there was no doubt a tractor could get the job done in half the time.

Maybe he ought to think about getting one, if only for James's sake. He sat tense at the wheel, just as he had done all afternoon. Every muscle in his body ached. It wasn't too bad on the flat but the cumbersome thing felt decidedly top-heavy when there was a bump in the ground.

Darkness was falling as he covered the last stretch. Fred would be on his way back now in time for the milking.

Hospitals. Even if it was only for a check-up like Fred, Hemingway hated them. They all smelt the same. Always the stink of carbolic soap and disinfectant – in the field hospital in France and again in the military hospital in Surrey when they brought him home. His nostrils could smell it still . . .

Through the gate now and short-cut over the top field – that way he'd get it back to Boothroyd's yard in double-quick time.

He smiled to himself as he took the incline. He could just see James at the wheel of his own tractor, his little son on his lap, Anna waving from the gate . . .

Hell, this was more of a slope than he'd bargained for. He felt the weight of the tractor dipping on his side, the far side rising, uncontrollably, in the air. He felt himself sliding in his seat, gripped the wheel tight and tried to brace himself, felt his bad leg unable to take the strain . . .

Then somehow he was flying through the air, the world spinning around him. There was a sound of grinding, crashing metal, and then excruciating pain. He was swirling in a haze of intolerable agony, hearing the sound of far-away screaming . . .

And then the pain receded, leaving only the haze. He could see darkness closing around him, feel the world slipping away . . .

That cot – it wasn't half finished yet . . .

Doris was laying the table when she heard heavy boots on the cobbles outside, and she paused. Too many boots. They didn't come like that unless there was trouble.

She was halfway to the door before the hammering started. She wrenched the door open. Fred Dent stood there, eyes wide and his weathered young face pale.

'What is it?' Doris demanded. 'What's up?'

'Mr Hemingway,' he panted. 'He's had an accident.'

Doris pushed past him. In the gloom of the yard she could make out four of Boothroyd's men, the huddled figure lying between them on a farm gate.

'Oh my God.' She stood aside. 'Bring him in. How bad is he hurt?'

The men made no answer. They were having trouble trying to manoeuvre the gate through the doorway. Cursing under their breath and steadying the inert figure with one hand they tilted the gate with care, wriggling and easing it through.

'It were the tractor,' muttered Fred. 'Somehow he overturned it – it fell on top of him.'

The men laid the gate down gently on the table and stood back, easing their shoulders. Doris leaned over and put an ear to Hemingway's mouth.

'Is he dead?' Fred whispered.

Doris lifted her coat down off the back of the door. 'No – he's unconscious.' Her gaze travelled down to the mangled mess of his legs. 'Thank God.'

She draped the coat over the motionless body. 'Have you sent for the ambulance?' she asked.

Fred nodded, his eyes filled with tears. 'He's smashed up bad, isn't he?' he muttered. 'Is he going to be all right?'

The men began shuffling out of the door. Doris tipped the potatoes out of the bowl and filled it with fresh water. 'I'll clean him up a bit,' she said between tight lips. 'You go to the bottom of the stairs and shout Anna down.'

The two women stood in the shadows, their arms about each other in comfort. The doctor bent over the mutilated body on the table once more.

Anna broke away and turned to him. 'For God's sake, when is that bloody ambulance going to get here? Can't we do something for him? He must be suffering.'

The doctor shook his head sadly. 'Not any more, I'm afraid,' he murmured as he pulled the blanket carefully over Hemingway's face. 'He's gone.'

TWENTY-THREE

1967

Right up to the day of David's funeral Lisa felt as if she were drifting through a void of unreality where neither time nor sensation existed.

Practical matters had to be dealt with and James spent much time talking with the undertaker. Arrangements had to be made about burying David in the same grave as his mother and grandparents, about the coffin and the choice of hymns, but Lisa could see the same vacant look in his eyes and knew that he too was divorced from reality.

People came and went, Ellen made tea and small talk; everything carried on as before in a desperate attempt at normality. But Lisa had the strange feeling that they were all only filling the space left by David's going, that they were only actors walking through their parts in some surreal play. It was all hollow and meaningless without him. She felt guilty about being alive.

James had shut himself off in the gun room. 'Mind if I switch the radio on?'

There was a tentative tone in Ellen's voice. Lisa recognized the same guilt.

'Of course not.'

Ellen turned it on softly.

A distant disc jockey excitedly announced Englebert Humperdinck's lastest hit, *'There goes my everything'*. She snapped it off again quickly, but the tears had already sprung to Lisa's eyes. It was as though there was some kind of conspiracy to remind her constantly of his suffering . . .

Ellen glanced out of the window. 'Oh God, it's the vicar,' she said. 'I can't cope with him – you let him in.'

By the time Lisa had brought him into the living room Ellen had vanished. The big man turned to her with a genial smile.

'You must be Lisa,' he said softly, holding out his hand. 'I'm Reverend Bax and I wanted to express my condolences. I'm so sorry. I wanted to have a word with James. Is he in?'

Lisa felt irritated by him. His thick hand felt soft and flabby, the caressing voice felt unreal, like a stage vicar feigning concern. 'Can I help?' she said stiffly.

The vicar looked round for a chair and sat down. 'It's about my sermon, actually, what James would like me to say about his son, that sort of thing. Now,' he said, rolling his weight over on to one buttock to pull a notepad from his pocket, 'I see from our records that he was baptized here. He didn't go to church much, did he?'

'No. But he was a lovely man.'

The Reverend Bax nodded. 'I understand he painted a bit too?'

Lisa gave him an angry stare. 'He was an artist,' she said proudly, 'like his father.' It was a waste of time. This man never knew David; whatever unctuous words flowed from his lips in the pulpit he could never do justice to him.

'Ah yes,' the vicar murmured. 'I really should talk to his father. You two weren't married, were you?'

Lisa closed her eyes. We should have been, we would have been . . . 'As good as,' she murmured.

He shook his head. 'Nothing's as good as marriage, my dear. Nothing can replace the sacrament of matrimony.'

'That's right.' James's voice came quietly from the doorway. He was leaning against the doorjamb

216

and as Lisa looked round he straightened and came in. 'How's your wife, Vicar?' he asked. 'Still at her sister's is she? How long has it been now – six months?'

Bax reddened. 'I'm sorry – I didn't mean . . .'

'I know you didn't,' said James.

The vicar picked up his notepad again. 'Artist of great talent,' he murmured as he wrote. 'Man of great courage . . .' He looked up from his notes. 'Now about the hymns – might I suggest *Abide with Me?* – that's always a popular one – or perhaps—'

Lisa rose to her feet. James smiled at her. 'What do you think, Lisa? I don't want to take it out of your hands.'

'Whatever you think, James, is all right by me.'

Two letters arrived by the afternoon post, one for James and one for her, from Lazarus. She could visualize his lanky body curled over the table strewn with coffee mugs and half-sewn costumes as he penned the words:

Of course I'll make sure no harm comes to David's posters, in fact they're still upstairs. We haven't let the flat out to anyone else because we're still hoping you'll come back. It's not the same without the two of you . . .

James was sitting at his workbench. Out of habit he'd put on his apron but his files, chisels and hacksaw still lay untouched in front of him.

'I didn't much care for your Reverend Bax,' she said as James tore the envelope open. 'I can see why Ellen didn't want to talk to him.'

James gave a weary smile. 'Poor Clifford. He's got troubles of his own.' He glanced at the letter then laid it aside. 'David's Aunt Dorothy is coming for the funeral,' he said quietly. 'You'll like her.'

217

Lisa said nothing. He looked up into her eyes. 'How are you feeling, love? I've been so wrapped up in myself – I'm sorry. Grief makes you selfish.'

'David used to say that about pain. It cuts you off, he said, wraps you up in a cocoon of self.'

It was a relief to say his name without feeling it necessary to apologize. Others looked away in embarrassment . . .

James was still looking up at her thoughtfully. 'You're tough, Lisa. Like he was. I'm so proud of both of you.'

His voice was full of warmth and compassion. She felt her defences crumbling. 'I'm not,' she blurted. 'I'm lost when I think of life without him. I'm dreading the funeral . . .'

'So are we all,' he cut in quietly. 'But we'll come through it.'

For James the events of the overcast spring day were a hazy blur. He could feel only numbness still as he drove slowly with Dorothy, Ellen and Lisa down to the church, following the hearse bearing his son.

The world had gone crazy. He could remember as if it were yesterday the smile on Anna's face as they carried him down here for the first time to be christened. He should have been marrying here today, not being buried. James should have been the next to lie in the grave – David's turn shouldn't have come for another fifty years. It was all wrong.

He barely remembered taking his place at the front of the church alongside the lonely coffin. He did recall looking along the pew to where Lisa sat, her face pale, her eyes downcast as Reverend Bax spoke comforting words about David's courage and fortitude. She should have been the central figure here today, the bride aglow with happiness, eager for the future . . .

Voices began to sing – lusty voices, loud and strong. For the first time he became aware of others in the

218

little church and saw to his amazement that it was packed. Everyone was there, housewives and farm-workers, shopkeepers and schoolchildren. The whole of Thaxton must have closed down for them to be here.

'Praise my soul, the King of Heaven . . .'

He felt a warmth creep over him. They were here to celebrate David.

And then they were at the graveside, the vicar intoning yet more words and the coffin lying alongside the open grave. James looked down. Mother, Father and Anna lay waiting. David's coffin was lowered and someone offered him a handful of earth. He was aware of Dorothy to one side of him, Lisa at the other as he sprinkled the black soil and heard it patter on the wood . . .

Just like that other time . . . He could still hear Anna's voice. *'Death brings us all up short, but we've got to go on living. Your father would have been the first to say that.'*

Lisa touched his arm. He could hear the choke in her voice as she spoke. 'Come on, James. There's loads of people waiting to talk to you.'

On the homeward drive Aunt Dorothy sat silent in the front of the car while James drove. Lisa sat in the back with Ellen.

She felt choked with tangled emotions. No longer was it only the cold, unadulterated sense of loss; now she felt also a kind of wild exultation that so many people had come to express their affection and admiration, not only for David but for James too. Grief and delight mingled into a turmoil of emotion and she wanted to scream it out of her system.

'Look,' said Ellen. 'All the village shops are closed.'

Lisa nodded. A small hand stole into hers. Ellen was

looking at her shyly. 'I'm sorry,' she murmured. 'I'm so sorry. I was so wrong about you.'

Lisa squeezed the girl's hand. There was no need for words. She couldn't have spoken them anyway.

James had been surprised by Dorothy. Somehow he'd visualized her still the way she'd been that afternoon at the May Day fair when he'd first seen her with Anna, slim-hipped and dainty. He couldn't recall that she'd looked any different when she last came – when was it? Ten, eleven years ago, when Anna died.

Now, with the more deliberate movements of a mature woman well-endowed about the hips and thighs, she climbed out of the car and stood looking down at the valley.

'It's beautiful here,' she remarked. 'So tranquil.' She turned and smiled at him. 'They were very lucky.'

'Lucky?'

'Anna and David.'

He shrugged. 'It was all Anna's doing,' he replied. 'She knew just what to do with the house.'

Dorothy gave him a quizzical look. 'I didn't mean the house. I meant having you.'

He didn't want to pursue it. 'Come indoors – the girls will have the kettle on by now,' he urged her, taking her arm. She smiled before she turned to go.

'I mean it. Anna was very lucky. Now if Myles had been more like you we might have made a go of it.'

He led her into the new wing. She peeled off her gloves and strolled on into the music room. James stood in the doorway, watching her.

'Ah, I see you still have her piano,' she said, touching a finger to the polished wood. 'I'm so glad.'

He felt his stomach contract. 'I'll get rid of it now. I don't think I can stand to hear it again.'

'You said that after she died.'

'I know, but David—'

His throat closed up on him. She came nearer and

spoke softly. 'You can't shut down love and memories like shutting the piano lid,' she murmured. 'Just leave it, and wait.'

He turned and walked quickly out of the room.

Dorothy declined his invitation to stay on.

'I must get over to Harrogate today,' she explained. 'I promised Father I would. He's getting very crotchety these days, but then he is getting on for eighty now.'

'Eighty?' In his mind's eye Harcourt was a perpetual fifty-year-old, the way he'd last seen him.

'Oh yes. Fit as a fiddle. Plays golf and bridge still, but he's getting more demanding than ever. I'll see you again soon, James, I promise.'

And now she was gone. The farm lay still and quiet, Lisa and Ellen were already in bed but he couldn't sleep. He lay listening to the sound of the night breeze brushing the leaves against his window. He heard the church clock down in the village strike two.

He threw back the sheets and got out of bed. Pulling on his dressing gown he went out into the corridor. A shaft of moonlight fell on the door to the attic, lighting up the grained panels and the brass knob.

On an impulse he opened the door, clicked on the light and climbed the bare wooden steps to the top floor. David's painting room lay ahead. He wasn't ready to go in there yet; he turned away, pulling his robe closer about him. It was cold up here and the place needed tidying. Clutter everywhere. Discarded furniture, old trunks filled with paperwork over the years, the doll's house he'd built for Ellen – and the cot.

He knelt and touched its wooden bars. Dad had been building it when he died. James had completed it in time for Ellen's birth. He could see her still, the little face laughing up at him over the bars, her arms held out to him.

221

And a couple of years later it was David who'd stood there, sturdy little legs braced and a one-eyed teddy bear in his arms, refusing to go to sleep until he'd heard another story. So many memories stored away up here . . .

'You can't shut down love and memories like shutting the piano lid . . .'

James rose to his feet and turned away. At the bottom of the stairs he switched off the light and shuffled, barefoot, towards his room. Then a sound caught his ear and he stopped.

Lisa – she was crying. He paused outside her door. Through its thick wood he could hear the sound of her sobbing. He tapped and opened the door.

Moonlight fell across the bed and he could make out the shape huddled under the sheets. 'Lisa?' he whispered.

She sat up, a pale-haired figure in a thin nightdress, and seeing him, she held out her arms.

'Hold me, James!'

The words limped, broken and hoarse. He crossed the room quickly and sat on the edge of the bed, curving his arm about her shoulders. They felt soft and warm, as vulnerable as a child's.

'Hold me tight.' She buried her face against his chest. He could feel her cheeks wet with tears as he put both arms around her and held her close. She was still sobbing uncontrollably, her whole body heaving as she clung to him.

He knew it of old, this aching feeling of helplessness to ease a child's pain, wanting to draw it away into himself. All he could do was rock her gently in his arms, murmuring words in a desperate attempt to comfort.

'There, there, it's all right, I'm here. Everything's going to be all right.'

After a time the racking sobs began to slow. He heard her voice, strangled and faint, against his chest.

'I wanted so much to have his baby,' she wept. 'Now I've nothing of him, nothing at all.'

Her hair smelt sweet under his chin. James lifted a hand to stroke it. Lisa turned her tear-stained face up to him.

'It meant so much to me, but he didn't know that. I wanted so much to have a part of him, and now . . . Oh Christ!'

He saw the tears welling in her eyes again and laid a finger to her cheek. She seized the hand and held it tight.

'Don't leave me, James, don't leave me alone to-night, in this bed . . .'

'We'll move you to another room – I should have thought . . .'

'No.' She gripped his hand tighter. 'He was born here, wasn't he? I just can't bear to be alone tonight.' He pushed her gently back on the pillows, his arm still around her. 'All right, I'll stay until you fall asleep. Now close your eyes . . .'

He lay back alongside her, her head on his shoulder. She looked ethereal in the moonlight. No wonder David loved her. He could feel against his chest the warmth of her right breast through the thin nightdress, and felt a slight unease. So long ago since he'd lain like this with Anna. In the years between his life had been quietly monastic.

Was this right? For heaven's sake, of course it was – she was his daughter – more or less. Even so, the warmth of a woman's body close to his was something which had long been missing . . .

He craned his neck to look at her again. Silver hair on a silver pillow. He smiled and picked up a strand, letting it run through his fingers like fine sand.

It was a long time before the sound of her deep, regular breathing told him she was at last asleep. His arm still lay under her shoulders, and he inched away, moving it cautiously to ease the cramp. She shifted, seeming to sense what was happening.

'Don't go,' she mumbled. 'Stay with me.'

He lay still. At last she slept and he could feel sleep beginning to steal over him, scattering his thoughts.

You'd have liked this girl, Anna. And you would have been proud of our son today – the whole village turned out to see him . . .

The moonlight had gone when he awoke and the first pearl-grey streaks of dawn were filtering in the window. Lisa lay curled on her side like a child.

He bent over and touched his lips to her hair then, with the utmost care he eased himself stealthily off the bed and crept out of the room . . .

Ellen heard the muffled sound of Lisa's sobs in the room next door. She was halfway out of bed to go to her, already pulling on her dressing gown, when she heard the sound of hushed voices. She sat motionless on the edge of the bed, listening.

It must be Dad. There was no-one else in the house. Then she heard Lisa's voice, high and plaintive like a child's.

'Hold me, James – hold me tight!'

And afterwards there was a long silence. She felt ashamed of the thoughts which leapt into her mind only to be quickly discarded. Comfort, that's what Lisa needed, and she'd been ready to go herself. We all need comfort right now . . .

It was nearing dawn before she heard Lisa's bedroom door open and close softly. She felt disturbed; could she help it if she felt just a little jealous as she lay in her lonely bed?

TWENTY-FOUR

1967

'Mam!'

Kelly Dent's voice squealed down the stairs. Her mother didn't look up from the magazine she'd carefully liberated from the doctor's surgery. 'What now?'

'Where's me blue skirt?'

'How the dickens should I know? Where did you put it?'

'In the laundry basket, yesterday.'

Thelma sighed. 'That's where it is then.'

Footsteps came thundering down the stairs. Kelly stood in the doorway, the blue skirt in her hand. 'Just look at it – it's all crumpled,' she complained. 'How can I wear it tonight all screwed up like that?'

'You put it there,' said Thelma absently.

'I thought you'd wash it.' She scratched at a flaky mark with her fingernail. 'Oh I suppose it'll have to do.'

Thelma laid the magazine aside. 'Where are you off to tonight then? I thought you had homework.'

'Youth club. I promised Gary I'd be there.'

'Not in that skirt, you're not. It's indecent, split halfway up your backside. Your dad would have a fit.'

Kelly took a hairbrush out of the sideboard drawer and turned to the mirror. 'He won't see it. I'll be gone before he's back from milking.'

Thelma picked up the story again. It was a waste of time arguing with her. She had an answer to everything. 'Behave yourself then,' she muttered. 'No hanky-pankying with the lads. You don't want to end up having to get married.'

Kelly curled her lip. 'Me get married? No fear. I'm not daft. Is me tea ready?'

Thelma skimmed through the last paragraph before uncurling herself from the settee. 'What's wrong with being wed?' she asked as she put the kettle on the gas stove and struck a match. 'Your dad and me's not done so bad.'

'There's no need to these days,' Kelly replied, brushing out her long hair vigorously. 'That Lisa girl wasn't married to David Hemingway but they lived together.'

'That's different,' said Thelma sharply. 'They're from London. Folks can get away with owt down there – nobody knows if you're married or not but you wouldn't get away with it in Thaxton. Hey, did you see that suit she were wearing at the funeral? Lovely, wasn't it? She's a real smart lady, that Miss Drew.'

Kelly shrugged as she put the hairbrush away and started hunting underneath the sideboard. 'All right for a woman her age, but it's not my cup of tea. Have you seen me peep-toe sandals anywhere?'

'Oh, and while I think on,' said her mother, 'I want you to do the vicar for me tomorrow after school. I've told him you will because I can't make it, not with the doctor wanting me extra time.'

Kelly let out a wail. 'Do I have to? What about me homework you're always on about?'

'The vicar pays good money and anyway, it'll not take long if you're quick about it.'

Twice today James had found himself outside the door of the little attic room, his hand on the doorknob, and twice he'd turned away.

It hadn't seemed right somehow to intrude, not alone, at any rate, and he'd gone to work on his guns. But with Ellen back in the library and Lisa out riding, he felt restless. It was a relief when he heard the horse's hooves clopping across the yard to the stable.

From the window he watched her come back towards the house, her arms full of daffodils. With her long, easy stride she could have been taken for a boy in her jeans if it hadn't been for the long fair hair and the swing of her hips.

He hurried to meet her at the door, holding it wide. She rewarded him with a smile.

'Just look,' she said, holding out the flowers. 'The copse was absolutely full of them. David said they would be out soon.'

He watched the blonde hair spill around her shoulders as she laid the flowers on the table, and felt a swell of protective tenderness . . .

'You will take care of Lisa when I'm gone, won't you?' 'I've been thinking,' he said quietly, 'David's picture . . .'

She flicked back her hair and looked up at him soberly. 'Yes,' she said. 'I think I'm ready now.'

The spring sunshine filled the little attic room with mellow light. They stood, side by side, gazing round at the mess of dried-out paint pots and brushes, discarded sheets of sketching paper and crayons.

Lisa gave a half-smile. 'He always was a mess, even when he could see properly,' she murmured. 'He said he couldn't work tidily – it upset him.'

James was staring at the easel, which was still covered by a sheet. The last picture . . . Lisa's gaze followed his. She moved across and pulled the sheet away, then stood back.

James stood thunderstruck. There was such life, such vitality in the picture, such love in the gentle laying-on of colour.

'Springtime,' breathed Lisa, 'his favourite season.'

It was unmistakably Jericho, the farm still and tranquil under a pale sun, and in the foreground stood two figures, a man and a woman, and under the tree stood a third figure, that of a girl.

227

'I can hardly believe it,' muttered James. 'It's Jericho – look, there's the barn and the oak tree and look, he's even got the broken wall down by the pigsty.'

Lisa moved forward and touched a finger to the canvas. 'It's beautiful – it's so still, and yet so strong. He's never done anything like this before.'

Her eyes misted with tears. *Look deep inside yourself and find peace, like the stillness of a forest pool . . .*

She reached for James's hand. 'Look, there's you – he's got you to the life – and that's me—'

'And the girl in the shadows,' said James. 'I wonder what he could see in Ellen that we can't.'

Kelly let herself into the vicarage and put the key safely back in her pocket. Now if Baldy was out she could whip around in no time.

'Hello, anybody in?' she shouted.

There was no reply but her own voice echoing round the long, draughty corridors. Flinging her school blazer over the newel post she headed for the kitchen.

Kitchen floor, counter tops and any washing up that needed doing, Mam had said, then tidy the bedroom and his study. He was an untidy beggar, to say the least. Mam had a nerve telling her off for the state of her room, after she'd seen the mess he could make of a whole house.

A quick flick with the mop around the lino floor, another flick of the dishcloth along the surfaces. How the devil could he use that many pots in a couple of days? The sink was piled high with them, plates jammed together with caked-on food, pans half-filled with water under which lay a morass of something which looked like orange mash. He seemed to live on baked beans. She wondered if he farted a lot, and the thought of him letting off in the pulpit made her giggle. She must remember to tell the lads.

The bedroom wasn't as bad except for the pair of underpants on the dressing table. Picking them up between finger and thumb she dropped them in the laundry basket.

As she straightened up the bed she heard the church clock chime five-thirty. Just the study to go – there'd still be time to get out tonight once tea was over and she'd had a go at that essay for Miss Townsend. Half an hour should do it – Miss Townsend wasn't a bad sort really, whatever the others said. Bit sharp with her tongue at times, but her hair was always nice and she always had a lipstick on that went exactly right with her frock. Bet she has a boyfriend.

Kelly pushed open the study door and sighed. Books and papers everywhere, wastebasket over-flowing – where the devil did she start sorting this lot? Dust the room, Mam had said – but where? Every inch of the big desk was littered with clutter. Duster in hand she advanced on it, lifting a paper here and there to flick underneath.

'Pray for forgiveness of sin,' she read, 'for the Lord's clemency is limitless.' She yawned theatrically and replaced the sheet. On the very corner of the desk teetered a battered-looking envelope. She picked it up, thick and bulky in her hand, then gasped.

Protruding from the slit edge she could see pound notes – dozens of them, an absolute fortune. Her fingers trembled as she visualized what they could buy – a whole wardrobe full of new frocks and shoes, lipstick and nail polish to last a lifetime. All that money, just lying there – just balancing on the edge of the desk where it might easily fall into the waste-paper basket at any moment . . .

Slowly she replaced the envelope on the desk where she found it. Yes, just another inch . . . She moved it cautiously with a dusty forefinger and watched it fall into the basket . . .

*   *   *

Elsie Thewlis was on her way home from the whist drive and just saying goodnight to Freda Tattersall when they caught sight of the group of teenagers on the corner.

'Just look,' said Mrs Thewlis, lowering her voice, 'under the lamp, there's that lass of Thelma's out with the lads again.'

Mrs Tattersall gave a quick glance over her shoulder and clicked her tongue. 'This time of night she ought to be home in her bed. Whatever is Thelma thinking of, letting her stay out till this hour?'

'I don't think she has much say in the matter,' Mrs Thewlis replied with a shake of the head. 'That little madam seems to please herself. Why, a week last Tuesday – no, I tell a lie, it were Wednesday – I saw her, bold as brass, sitting on the churchyard wall, half-past ten at night, with a gang of lads round her, and her kicking her legs up for all the world to see. The Reverend would have been right upset if he'd seen her on his wall like that.'

'Disgraceful,' said Mrs Tattersall. 'She'll come to no good. What are they doing now?'

Mrs Thewlis stood on tiptoe to peer over her neighbour's shoulder. 'Well, would you believe it?' she exclaimed. 'They've set off, all four of them, down the lane to the wood.'

'What – her and three lads?'

'Ay. Mark my words, Freda, she's no better than she ought to be, that one. It's Fred I feel sorry for.'

Mrs Tattersall considered for a moment. 'Ought we to tell him and Thelma, do you think?' she ventured at last.

Mrs Thewlis shook her head firmly. 'It's no business of ours, Freda. They'll find out soon enough the way she's going on. I'm not one for making trouble.'

* * *

'Go on then, Kelly, tell us who you fancy?'

The boys clustered close to her as they walked down the lane, kicking up stones, not touching her but in easy reach if the signal came. Kelly, aware of her power, chose deliberately to misunderstand.

'Oh, I reckon maybe Mick Jagger—'

'He means us,' interrupted Gary. 'Him or Donny or me.'

She glanced back with an imperious stare. 'What makes you think I fancy any of you?'

'Come on,' said Gary persuasively. 'You know we fancy you. We been watching you.'

'So?' She tossed her head, sending the long dark hair flying across Donny's face. It gave her pleasure to see the way his eyes lit up.

'Whacko thinks you got the best legs in Thaxton,' he muttered, coming close.

'And how would he know?' she retorted.

'And the best tits,' added Gary. 'I told them.'

She turned on him with mock anxiety. 'You never!' It pleased her that he'd told them.

'Why not?' he said, preening. 'I told 'em they were bigger than Betty Elliot's. Proper Jayne Mansfield, I said.'

'You rotten bugger – you had no business telling.' She feigned shame-faced modesty but their laughter made her feel proud. In a minute they'd all want a feel.

The exchange gave Donny courage. 'What colour's your knickers?' he asked.

'What makes you think I'm wearing any?' Her answer provoked raucous laughter.

'They're blue,' said Whacko. 'I know.'

'You don't – you can't.'

'I do then – I saw 'em when you was kicking your legs up on the wall. So there.'

'Oh you.' She pushed him hard on the shoulder. From past experience she knew this usually led to a mock struggle where bodies piled on her, pushing her down, and hands groped where her mother would not like it at all. This time it didn't. Whacko turned away.

'I'm off,' he muttered, digging his hands deep in his pockets. 'I'm late enough already.'

'Suit yourself,' said Gary. 'Come on, Kelly, take your bra off.'

'Can I watch?' asked Donny eagerly.

'No, you can't,' she snapped. 'Bugger off.'

The Reverend Bax was highly agitated. He knew he'd left that envelope on his desk.

It was his fault if Thelma had succumbed to temptation – he should have locked the money safely away in the drawer. Sarah would have made certain it was locked away.

Oh dear, so many things went wrong without her guiding hand. But Thelma – it was hard to credit. In all these months she'd always been so trustworthy even if her cleaning left a lot to be desired.

Oh Sarah, you little know the harm you've done by leaving me. It wouldn't have happened if you'd stayed at your post. May you be forgiven for leading poor Thelma into mischief.

And me too. I have to confess I've had wilful thoughts in your absence, thoughts a man should only think in relation to his wife, but you failed me there too. I hope the good Lord will take this into consideration. As my sermon says, His clemency is infinite . . .

Thelma. If she returned the money intact and showed due contrition, he too could show forbearance . . .

Thelma stared at him, bewildered. 'Envelope? I never seen no envelope, Vicar. Oh, hang on – that was the day our Kelly come in – I told you, I was doing overtime at the doctor's, remember? Was it important?'

232

Of course. He'd have to have a word with the girl. The Reverend smiled.

'Would you ask your daughter to pop in and see me? No hurry – any time she's passing.'

It was some time before Lisa became aware of Ellen's coolness. Somehow the closeness they had shared on the day of the funeral had vanished.

'What are you planning to do, Lisa?' she asked casually one evening. 'Do you think you'll go back to work?'

'I don't know,' she shrugged. 'Maybe I'll do something about David's paintings. Get in touch with an art gallery or something.'

'Art gallery?' Ellen repeated.

'To try and get an exhibition, I thought. In London. Artists are always more prized when they're dead, isn't that what they say?'

James put his newspaper down. 'There's no need to make any decisions yet,' he said quietly. 'Time enough to think about it. It's early days.'

After Ellen had gone to bed Lisa turned to James.

'Ellen would be glad to see the back of me. I don't think she wants me here.'

He shook his head. 'She doesn't know what she wants yet. We're all still a little confused.'

She sat on the arm of his chair. 'She's right in a way, it might be better all round if I left. I think I've still got a job I can go back to . . .'

'You don't have to.'

'Only I feel there's something unfinished, something left in mid-air, and I can't quite put my finger—'

'I know.' He leaned forward, leaning his elbows on his knees. 'There's something I want to tell you. I found this among David's things today.' He dug in his pocket and pulled out a green notebook. 'I hope you don't mind me reading it.'

233

She touched a fingertip to the notebook. 'I remember that – he took it everywhere.'

'I'd like to read you something he wrote shortly before he died. To do with what you told me.'

'What about?'

'Listen.' James's voice was gentle as he read:

I fell in love with Lisa the first day I saw her. I've watched her unfold, but there's one thing more she needs to come to full bloom. She told me last night how much she wanted our baby, but there's nothing I can do . . . I'm impotent. I've let her down. If only I could have given her that . . .

Lisa felt the tears begin to flow. 'I wanted a part of him, another little Hemingway.'

James held the notebook out. 'Here, you take it. I just wanted you to know that he did understand how much it meant to you.'

She took the book and held it, caressing its spine. 'You keep it, James, but I'd like to read it first if you don't mind.'

He leaned back in the chair and closed his eyes. 'It's ironic,' he murmured. 'He should have been the last Hemingway, but now it will be me.'

She looked up, brushing the tears away. And then a thought sprang to her mind and, before she could stop it, it had leapt unbidden to her lips.

'Not necessarily,' she said quietly. 'There could be another. There is a way . . .'

TWENTY-FIVE
1941

James came home on compassionate leave for his father's funeral. Still numb with shock he stood with Anna at the graveside, watching the coffin being lowered gently into the muddy hole to lie with his mother's.

Lieutenant Rayne-Smith had broken the news as kindly as he could in the circumstances. 'Look here, old chap, I'm afraid I've got some rather unpleasant news for you.'

James could remember the terrible leap of anxiety – not Anna! And then the almost guilty feeling of relief when the officer went on.

'It's your father – he's had an unfortunate accident.'

Bloody tractors. He'd always hated the things. He should have waited for Fred. It wasn't time for him to die – it was too soon – he'd only just turned fifty, yet now he was joining all those other Hemingways who'd farmed Jericho, all of them here in this churchyard, Hemingways stretching back over two hundred years . . .

While the vicar droned on James stared down at his mud-caked boots, oblivious to the cold wind whipping his face. Hours he'd spent on those toe-caps, applying the polish and then heating a spoon over the billet stove to rub the polish in. Like mirrors they'd been when he left camp. Buffing and blanco-ing, drilling and learning – it surprised him how much he'd come to enjoy the life. Especially the armourer's course. Dad would never know he'd just passed it with flying colours . . .

Anna had patted his arm with a smile before they left Jericho today.

'You look terrific, darling. Dad would have been so proud of you. I only wish I could have fastened my skirt.'

He could see her now out of the corner of his eye, standing quiet beside him. No-one could tell she had a safety pin holding her skirt together across the swollen stomach. The next Hemingway – one leaves, another arrives, the next link in the continuing chain . . .

They'd agreed, Anna and he, that they didn't mind whether it was a boy or a girl – Ellen or David, they'd decided. But in his secret heart he hoped for a son. And he'd make damn sure he was kept well away from tractors. It was a terrible shame the boy would never know his grandfather now. He could see just how it would have been, the old man forking hay, a smile on his weatherbeaten face while the youngster romped around him . . .

They were going to need more help on the farm – Fred on his own wasn't going to cope. But how were they off for money? He'd have to find Dad's papers and go through his accounts to see what they could afford. Somebody had to keep Jericho going . . .

'Earth to earth, ashes to ashes . . .'

A handful of earth scattered on the coffin. It was over.

There was something macabre about hunting through a dead man's belongings. In the old days Dad always used to keep his account book in the drawer of the kitchen table but it wasn't there now, nor in the old dresser, nor in his wardrobe. Anna shook her head.

'I don't know where it is, but here's an envelope he asked me to keep for you. He said something about it being a recipe.'

James couldn't help smiling as he read, recalling an evening long ago.

'*Family secret is this, lad. Passed on from father to son. Nobody else knows it but me.*'

'*Tell me how to brew it then, Dad. I won't tell.*'

'*Nay, soon enough for you to know when I'm gone.*'

'*It'll be too late then. It'll die with you.*'

'*I'll see to it, don't you fret. You'll have it in good time to hand on to your lad.*'

Dad had kept his word. For him the secret of the resin brew for the tug-of-war team far outweighed accounts in importance. He had no doubt about where his priorities lay . . .

In bed that night he lay thoughtful, stroking the high curve of Anna's stomach. 'I want to stay here,' he muttered. 'I want to make sure you're safe – you and the baby. I'm damn well not going to lose you too.'

She touched his cheek. 'You won't. We'll be here, waiting for you.'

'Not on your own. With Dad gone, and I don't think we can afford to keep Doris – we'll need the money to hire more help.'

'She'll be very upset, James.'

'It can't be helped. We need another man on the farm. I'm going to see if I can get a discharge – I'll apply the moment I get back to camp.'

It wasn't easy telling Doris that she would have to give up working at Jericho. She'd been very subdued ever since Hemingway's death. Anna broke it to her as they carried the washing out into the yard.

'You mean you don't want me here?' she demanded, frowning as she set the laundry basket down on the cobbles. 'There isn't room enough for two of us?'

Anna shook her head. 'The truth is,' she confided, 'we don't know if we can afford it any more. James says we'll have to hire another man.'

Doris gave her a suspicious look. 'Only I had a feeling you resented me being here,' she said, jabbing a peg savagely over the corner of a tablecloth. 'Felt I was trying to push you out, happen.'

'Not at all,' Anna soothed. 'I'd have loved having you to teach me things I ought to know, how to cook, how to make lovely light pastry like yours, but I'm afraid it's impossible.'

Doris pegged the last towel in place and turned to her. 'I could come for just a few shillings,' she said slowly, 'if that would suit?'

'I'm sorry, Mrs Brook.' Anna turned away.

Doris picked up the empty washing basket and followed her back into the house. 'Then I'll pop in now and again as a friend.' She glanced down at Anna's stomach. 'You need a friend right now, and you're going to need help even more when that baby comes.'

Anna held up a hand. 'I've already explained—'

Doris ignored her. 'I'll pop in regular and do a bit – no question of money, just as a friend, you understand.'

She turned away to the sink, muttering to herself. 'Right's right. I shall keep on coming in, whether or not.' She pulled the plug out of the sink, letting the dolly-blue water run out, then suddenly she turned.

'Here – did you say you couldn't find Mr Hemingway's account book? I've just thought – there's a drawer in his dressing table he always kept locked. I've no idea where he kept the key.'

Dealing with Fred's wages was another problem for Anna. He was indispensable, and now that she was trying to tackle cooking, cleaning, washing and a thousand other household chores she'd never known existed, she couldn't possibly undertake the farm work as well. She knew nothing about milking cows, let alone ploughing a field or mending a fence. If only James were here . . .

She tackled Fred in the milking shed. The air smelled moistly sweet with the scent of hay and at the same time musty and stale with the odour of sour milk. She leaned her elbows on the stall and explained about the accounts.

'Don't you fret yourself,' he assured her. 'I'll go on same as always for a bit, while Jim's seeing if he can get out.'

'But your wages – ' she protested.

'Never bother – we'll sort summat out. I'm taking two of them sows down to the slaughterhouse in the morning – I could pay meself out of the money if that'll suit you.'

She watched his thick fingers moving rhythmically up and down the leathery teat, the milk squirting into the bucket. The old cow gave her a liquid-eyed, distrustful look.

'You'll have to teach me how to do that,' she said. 'But not right now – I've got the chickens to feed.'

Within weeks James was home.

She saw him coming, striding up the lane, for the first time in over a year not wearing khaki. She hurried to meet him as quickly as her unwieldy weight would allow.

'I've got my discharge,' he told her proudly. 'They said running the farm was essential war work, so I'm home for the duration.'

'That's wonderful,' she said delightedly. 'I was worried stiff I might be doing things all wrong, paying Fred out of the takings, but I couldn't manage without him. Now you're back . . . '

He put his arm about her shoulders and gave her an affectionate squeeze. 'You did the right thing, love. Tomorrow I'll find that key and see if Dad's accounts are in there. I need to find out about all the Ministry

239

of Food regulations too. We'll soon know exactly what's what.'

She looked up at him with an impish smile. 'I'm doing my bit for the war effort – I've learned how to milk a cow – well, Molly anyway. She's the only one who'd stand still and let me.'

James found the key, and he found the account books and papers in the dressing table drawer, and spent all evening poring over them. Father's accounts were complete up to the day he died. At least James could settle the bills up to date and afford to keep Doris.

When he yawned and put the books away, Anna told him about the letter from Dorothy. 'My sister's doing war work now, driving a mobile canteen, would you believe, delivering food to bomb victims. Funny, I never thought she would ever do anything really useful.'

James smiled. 'It does seem rather out of character. Still, war brings out the best in us – just look at you, turning your hand to anything these days.'

'It was Dunkirk that did it,' Anna went on. 'Teddy – he was a friend of ours from the old point-to-point days – he was killed at Dunkirk and it upset her badly. So she volunteered for this driving job.'

'Good for her. Talking of driving – maybe we should think about getting a van.'

She stared up at him. 'A van? Can we afford it?'

He put his arm about her shoulders and squeezed her close. 'So long as it's second-hand, reliable and reasonable – no more than twenty quid. It'll be useful around the farm – and we'll need to get you to hospital quickly when the baby comes.

There was no hiding Fred's delight when he turned up for work and saw James in the yard. 'You've timed it just right, Jim. I don't think I could have managed the lambing on me own. The pens are only half done.'

He indicated the bales of straw piled in the bottom field. 'It's getting all the ewes down from the moor on time with no-one to help that were the problem. The first'll be due any day now. You've come not a minute too soon.'

Anna was finding it hard going, scouring milk churns, seeing to the chickens, and collecting and packing eggs. Doris insisted on taking over the churning of the butter.

'We can't have you turning that heavy handle else you'll wind the cord round the baby's neck,' she scolded. 'We're not having him born strangled, not while I'm here. I'd never forgive meself.'

From the window Anna watched James driving the thick-bodied ewes down from the moor into the pens in the bottom field, and saw him and Fred disappear from sight as they bent behind the bales of straw. She carried jugs of hot tea and sandwiches out to them while they laboured to bring the lambs safely into the world.

She was fascinated. The ewes made little noise about it and the newborn lambs looked so helpless, lying limp while their mothers licked their faces and made funny chuckling sounds, yet minutes later they were stumbling clumsily to their feet and searching for the udder. Birth looked so easy, so natural . . .

By nightfall the men were still working. The air was bitterly cold as she carried lanterns down to the pens. James was on his knees, cursing softly under his breath.

'What's wrong?' she asked, setting one of the lanterns down on top of a straw bale and bending to peer into the shadow below.

'Breech,' he muttered. 'Legs are coming first – I've got to push it back.'

She watched, mesmerized, as he dipped his hand in the pail of soapy water and slid it inside the sheep's

241

body, pushing and twisting till the sweat broke out on his forehead. The ewe was making squealing sounds of distress.

'James – you're hurting her!'

He didn't seem to hear, only kept on straining and twisting, fighting against the ewe's convulsive thrusts. At length he squatted back on his haunches.

'It's no good,' he muttered. 'I can't.'

Anna saw the ewe give a mighty thrust, and the little body slid out, feet first. It lay limp on the straw. James picked it up just as Fred's head appeared over the top of the pen.

He pulled on his cap and shook his head. 'That one's had it anyway,' he murmured, 'I told you – she were one that got worried by that bloody stray dog.'

Anna turned up her coat collar. 'It isn't dead, is it?' she asked.

James got stiffly to his feet. 'I'm afraid so,' he said wearily. 'They're nearly always stillborn after a dog's been at them.' He glanced at Fred. 'How many more did it get at?'

Fred shrugged. 'Half a dozen, I reckon. I'd have shot the beast if I'd had a gun.'

'So would I,' said James. 'He's going to cost us a mint. How are you doing?'

'OK so far. Nearly lost one but she made it.'

James gave him a grateful smile. 'Another couple of days should do it. Thank God we're nearly through. You get off home now – I can manage.'

It was dark when Fred set off for home. In the kitchen doorway Anna paused and looked back towards the meadows.

James came up close behind her. 'What is it?' he asked.

She leaned back against the doorjamb, her stomach seeming more protuberant than ever. 'I've never seen

242

birth before,' she murmured. 'At first I thought it was lovely, so easy and natural.'

'So it is, most of the time.'

She straightened and looked up at him. 'What if I had a breech, James? Suppose something went wrong?'

She saw the flush which suffused his face, the way his lips tightened. 'It won't,' he said shortly. 'I shouldn't have let you come down.'

She moved close to him, as close as the bulge would allow, and rested her hands on his shoulders. 'I'm not a child any more, darling – I've grown up,' she said softly, then pointed to the cellar door behind him. 'Remember when I first came here, when I asked you if that was your wine cellar?'

Despite his weariness he smiled at the memory. 'I remember,' he said.

'I've come a long way since then,' she murmured. 'Come on, let's get you something hot to eat before you have to go out again.'

TWENTY-SIX

1941

James spent a day in York and came home driving a battered blue van bearing the inscription along its side '*K M Sadler and Sons, Purveyors of Meat, Poultry and Game*'. Anna ran her fingers over the gold lettering in delight.

'Don't worry about that,' James assured her. 'I've got some blue paint cheap so I'll soon block it out.' He patted the bonnet. 'I know the bodywork looks a bit the worse for wear but the engine's sound enough – it's only been used for local deliveries.'

He put his arm about her shoulders and they stood together, gazing at it. 'Our own transport,' she murmured. 'We're going up in the world.'

He looked down at her with a smile. He was proud of her, of the way she'd adapted to the hard life of a farmer's wife. He could see her arms folded across her stomach, the gold ring gleaming on red, chapped hands. Never once had she complained or shown any sign of regret for the old, comfortable life she'd given up for him.

He'd work his fingers to the bone to make it up to her, to make the farm pay. Once the war was over and he was no longer hog-tied by government restrictions and quotas . . . Never once would he let her know that farming was not the way of life he would have chosen . . .

James lifted his nose and sniffed as they entered the kitchen. The tantalizing aroma of freshly baked bread filled the air. Doris stood in front of the black-lead range, lifting a tray of scones out of the oven.

She turned and laid them on the table alongside the six crusty batch loaves which already lay cooling, and looked up with a smile. 'There, that should keep you going a day or two.'

As she was pulling off her oven gloves she studied Anna's face, then gave James a nudge with her elbow. 'It'll be any day now, that baby,' she said firmly. 'I've seen that look on a woman's face oft enough. It's what we call a yonderly look, and it's a sure sign, is that.'

'I was just thinking,' Anna said dreamily, 'how nice it would be if we could put *J Hemingway and Son* on the side of the van, that's all.'

James laughed. 'He won't be needing the van yet a while – but I'd better finish off that cot Dad started or the poor little devil's going to have nowhere to sleep.'

'It's a girl,' said the midwife, holding the squealing infant aloft by the ankles. 'I hope that's what you wanted, Mrs Hemingway.'

'Oh yes,' said Anna weakly. 'We didn't mind either way. She is all right, isn't she?'

'Two arms, two legs – and a good pair of lungs on her too. She's a bonny little lass and no mistake – what more could you want?'

Anna lay dozing, still half stupefied by the anaesthetic. By the light from the corridor she could make out the crib at the foot of the bed where the infant lay making guzzling noises.

Today had been unreal. From the first sensation of a trickle escaping from her body, some outer force had taken over and robbed her of herself.

'Ay, that's your waters breaking,' Doris had said. 'I'd best send Fred to let your husband know.'

The pains had started in the van on the way to the cottage hospital. They'd made James leave – he'd only

245

be in the way, they said. And then the pains started in earnest, a long, dark, seemingly endless tunnel of pain, and with them came the terrifying feeling of inevitability. For the first time in her life she felt she'd lost control; all she could do now was submit, go through with it, as in a nightmare, and hope she'd wake up to normality.

She vaguely remembered them wheeling her down to the delivery room, the mingled, unpleasant smells of rubber and ether and disinfectant. But uppermost, always, was pain . . .

Disembodied voices . . . 'Grip the bedrail, push push . . .' It was never-ending. Eternity spread around her.

And just as it seemed her body would burst apart, the pain faded . . . Now there was a stranger at the foot of her bed. They'd put a name on the end of the cot. Ellen Hemingway. Her daughter, they said. Hers and James's . . .

She half rose on her elbow to make sure. Yes, a baby lay there, eyes closed. It didn't feel like a daughter. It had nothing to do with the bulge she'd carried all these months. Oughtn't she to feel a sudden rush of mother-love for this little thing?

If she looked at it long enough, recognized some feature of James's . . . Anna gave up at last, exhausted, and lay back on the pillow. It was no use – she felt nothing. Maybe in the morning, after a good night's sleep . . .

She turned over with a groan. This damn bed – the mattress was as hard as a rock, and the rubber cover drew her legs. But at least it was warm here. If she was home in her own bed in Jericho it would be in that freezing bedroom with a bare lino floor that numbed your feet when you got up in the morning.

For a fleeting moment she yearned for the downy depths and the silky-smooth sheets of her old bed in Thirlbeck Manor, a covered hot water bottle under your feet and the maid bringing a cup of China tea in a china cup . . . What she wouldn't give to be pampered like a child again, just for a little while . . .

For ten days she remained in hospital. After a week they let her out of bed. James came daily. He was delighted with her and enraptured with the baby.

'Just look at her tiny fingers,' he kept saying in tones of wonder, over and over again, as he held the little bundle in his arms. 'Every tiny detail is perfect.'

Anna watched him fondly. He was going to be a wonderful father. He was sublimely happy; she could never spoil his happiness by letting him know that, much as she loved him, she didn't feel any more affection for the baby than she would for a new puppy.

Maybe maternal feeling would come in its own good time. If not, she'd be a devoted mother, caring and tender. She'd play the part to perfection, for his sake . . .

James was ecstatic. Now they were a family, and he and Anna were complete. Little Ellen was born when the blackthorn blossom lay over the hedges like banks of snow so there was the whole summer ahead for her and Anna to luxuriate in the sun.

'Don't you think,' said Doris, 'that maybe she has her grandfather Hemingway's eyes? They're the same dark blue – it's like having him back, looking up at you with that solemn look of his.'

Doris was enchanted with Ellen. She made certain Anna never lifted a finger now. 'You can't be too careful, not with a baby to feed. We can't have your milk drying up.'

But every second she could spare she was playing with the child, dangling keys for tiny fists to reach out for, surreptitiously dipping her finger in the honey jar and putting it in the baby's mouth when she cried. Anna felt a sense of relief. Then one day Doris brought a collection of matinée jackets, bootees and mittens.

'Hand-knitted 'em for young Louise Harper,' she told her, 'but she lost the baby at seven months, so she won't be needing them now. So I thought, waste not, want not – we can't be squanderbugs, can we?'

'I've never been asked to be a godmother before,' Doris beamed. 'Who's going to be godfather?'

'I'd have liked an old army friend of mine,' James replied, 'but I lost track of him. I thought perhaps Fred . . .'

'Whatever happened about Dusty?' Anna asked later. 'I forgot all about him, what with your father—'

James shook his head. 'They still hadn't caught up with him when I left Catterick. Shame, really. I don't suppose I'll ever hear anything of him again.'

Dorothy wrote that she couldn't get away for the christening but was thrilled to bits about the baby:

Just think of it, me an aunt! It will be wonderful, when she's older, to have Ellen here to stay, to have a child around the house. Myles and I have given up trying – we're no longer on active service, so to speak . . . I hope to be able to snatch a little time to come and see you all very soon. It's been so long . . .

She didn't mention Father, Anna noted, but she must have told him. Daily she watched for the post, but no word came.

'You could write to him,' James pointed out.

'No,' said Anna firmly. 'I don't want him interpreting it as a plea for help. We don't need his money or anything else.'

*   *   *

On a glorious morning in June James carried Ellen to Thaxton parish church to be christened. Anna loved going to church every Sunday and she would be delighted today to show off their baby daughter. Doris and Fred stood at the font close behind them, dressed in their Sunday best and highly conscious of their responsibility.

Warm sunlight fell through the stained glass window, casting a golden light over Anna's blonde head and the baby's white robe. Madonna and child, James thought proudly: they looked beautiful. He was indeed a man blessed with good fortune.

It was August when the two Land Army girls arrived to help James and Fred with the haymaking, and Thelma was not amused. She managed to catch Fred alone while he was mending the fence on the top field.

'I've seen them landgirls,' she grumbled, 'a big skinny redhead and a fat little blowsy blonde. And a right sight they look too, wearing them men's corduroys.'

'They're OK,' Fred protested, hammering in a nail. 'They do a man's job – it's hard work, is haymaking.'

'I bet it is,' she snapped, 'romping round on a haystack till all hours, long after decent folk have knocked off and had their tea.'

'We have to get it done while there's light – you know that.'

Thelma leaned her bottom against the part of the fence he'd just nailed. 'And what else do they get up to besides forking hay, I'd like to know?' she demanded. 'You can't fool me – they're away from home, with good-looking lads . . .'

Fred was enjoying her anger. It was good to feel pursued. It had never happened to him before the war . . . 'Now look,' he said quietly, 'Jim's a married man – you've no business saying such things.'

She pouted. 'And what about you?'

He put down the hammer and dug his hands deep in his pockets. 'That's different. I'm a free agent.'

He saw the worried look that crossed her pretty face. 'You was out late last night,' she muttered. 'I saw you coming home. It must have been well past ten.'

'Keeping tabs on me now are you?'

She shrugged. 'I just happened to be looking out the window. You know me mam makes me come in before black-out. Them landgirls don't have anyone to tell them.'

She looked so distressed it touched him. Time to put her out of her suffering. 'It was the rats,' he explained. 'In the rickyard – me and Jim stayed up to shoot 'em.'

Her face cleared at once. 'Oh ay – I heard the shooting. So it wasn't them girls then?'

He smiled. 'Like you said, love – one of 'em's too scrawny for me and the other's too fat. Now are you happy?'

She gave him a coquettish look. 'What are you doing tonight after work then?' she asked.

'Meeting you down by the river? Oh heck, no – I've promised Jim I'd stay on a bit late again . . .'

Thelma's expression was darkening into anger again before he could find the words to redeem himself. 'But I could make it later on – say, nine?'

She frowned as she calculated. 'Nine – that'll give us an hour before black-out – OK, the bridge at nine.'

With a swing of the hips she skipped away down the lane, humming.

Doris came in out of the yard and handed a letter to Anna. 'Postman's just brought this,' she said. 'Harrogate postmark.'

Anna took it in wonder. Daddy – after all this time? She tore it open, read a few words, then turned pale.

'Where's James?' she said quietly. 'I've got to talk to him.'

250

'Up at the pigsty last I saw.'

James looked up from pouring swill into the trough as Anna came hurrying towards him. She looked pale and agitated – trouble, he could sense it. He straightened. 'What's up, love?'

She held out a sheet of paper. 'Daddy's written – Grandmother's very ill – he thinks it's the end. Oh James, I must go to her – he's got a nanny laid on and everything. He's expecting me.'

'You want to go? Now?'

'Please.'

He took her arm. 'Right. Get your things together. I'll get the van out.'

Harcourt saw the battered blue van pull into his drive and went out to meet them. He could see Anna's smiling face through the windscreen. His daughter looked thinner than he remembered, and far from well groomed.

Young Hemingway climbed out and went round to open her door. She stepped down, carefully easing the bundle in her arms round the edge of the door. That print dress she was wearing – it looked as if she'd run it up herself.

'Your granddaughter, Daddy,' she said. He looked down at the minute shapeless face and smiled. He felt he was expected to touch it, but he didn't quite know how.

'Funny little things, aren't they?' He held out his arms to Anna. 'And how are you?' he asked.

She came close and leaned over the bundle to kiss his cheek. 'I'm fine,' she said.

'You've lost weight,' he remarked. 'Not eating enough?'

She shook her head firmly. 'I eat like a horse. I'm healthier than I've ever been.'

He grunted and turned to James, but did not hold

251

out his hand. 'I was sorry to hear about your father,' he said brusquely. 'I admired him even if we were on opposite sides of the fence. He was a tough old bird.'

'He could be if he was pushed.' James turned away to pull a bag out of the van. Anna waited, then put her face up for a farewell kiss. Harcourt turned away until he saw Anna going carefully up the steps into the house and then turned to James.

'You've no need to worry about Anna and the child,' he said brightly. 'I intend to spoil her for a while – some new clothes, perhaps – she's the sort who needs a bit of spoiling now and again. She doesn't get the chance very often.'

James gave him a sober look as he handed him the bag. 'She's happy, Mr Harcourt, and that's what matters. And she's welcome to come and see you whenever she wants – I won't get in the way. I'll never come between you and your daughter.'

Harcourt drew himself up. 'I'm glad to hear it.'

'But if you ever try to come between Anna and me,' James went on quietly, 'I'll break every bone in your body.'

Harcourt swallowed as he watched the younger man climb back into the van. 'You mean that, don't you?'

James looked down at him from the driving seat. 'Yes I do,' he said. 'I mean every word.'

Somehow, despite the heat of the afternoon, Harcourt felt a sudden chill in the air. He watched as the battered old van roared noisily into life and jolted away down the drive.

He was his father's son and no mistake. Whether you liked him or not, he was a man you had to respect.

TWENTY-SEVEN

1967

Lisa felt overcome with embarrassment. What on earth had possessed her, telling James that it wasn't yet too late for another Hemingway to be born?

'There is a way . . .'

For God's sake, she'd gone on long enough about wanting David's child, hadn't she? It didn't require an Einstein of a brain to realize what she had implied. She hadn't even thought it out – inept words had just sprung mindlessly to her lips.

James had made no reply. She couldn't even be sure that he'd heard her. He'd changed the subject, suggested that she slept in another room.

She shook her head. 'I don't mind, James. That bed has happy memories for me.'

'And for me,' he smiled. 'He was conceived and born there.'

They were beginning to talk of him more naturally now, not in the desperate way of the first days, trying to dredge for happy memories to ease the pain. But it was curious how memory was starting to blur his features in her mind, leaving only the atmosphere of love which was the essence of David.

New patterns were forming and life was beginning to revert to normal. Even the furniture seemed to relax its stiff formality and sag back into its scruffy old comfort. Surely this was right and proper, the way it ought to be. Surely she should not be feeling this twinge of guilt, as if it were somehow disloyal.

Grief might continue, but the period of mourning must come to an end sooner or later – that was how he would want it to be. She could almost hear him saying it.

'Cast the widow's weeds aside, Lisa, and put on your glad rags – get on with living.'

Right, she decided. I have to start making plans . . .

Kelly Dent sat on the top deck of the number twenty-three bus watching the branches of the trees brushing the windowpanes. Once the last of the other passengers clambered down the stairs she was able to have a proper look at the gorgeous orange sweater in the carrier bag she clutched on her lap.

One of those trendy skinny-rib sweaters, it was, one that stuck close to your skin and showed up your nipples. It would go perfectly with the flared emerald trousers. Just wait till the lads at the youth club saw her . . .

There was a problem, however – how to keep them secret from Mam. She nosed everywhere – nothing was private. If she spotted a bag with Fulcrum's name on it . . . She could get rid of the bag, but what about the clothes? Two items weren't too bad, but next Saturday she wanted to go back and get that lovely fluorescent pink plastic mac and boots as well. Mam would want to know where the money came from . . .

A hiding place. There must be somewhere Mam wouldn't look. The garden shed? No, Dad would find them when he got the lawnmower out. There must be somewhere . . .

'Rose and Crown.' The conductor's voice roused her from her reverie and, clutching the carrier bag tightly, she scrambled down the stairs.

Dusk was beginning to creep in from the fields as she turned the corner by the church. A bulky figure emerged from under the lych gate as she passed, and she recognized the vicar.

'Ah, Kelly,' he boomed. 'I've been wanting a word with you – didn't your mother tell you?'

At once she was on the defensive. 'What about?' she asked, edging past him.

He turned and fell in step beside her, the sleeve of his sports jacket brushing her hand. It felt all hairy and horrid. 'About you coming round to my place to work,' he said, and she could see a smile on his pudgy face. At the vicarage gate he paused. 'Come in, we'll have a cup of coffee while we talk.'

She hesitated. 'Mam'll be expecting me . . .'

'It's important, Kelly.' His voice was stern. Obediently she followed him up the path.

He watched her closely. Her face was a picture of innocence.

'Envelope? No, I never saw no envelope.'

'You're sure? On my desk?'

She shook her head, the pretty hair swinging slowly from side to side. 'I took good care not to touch owt on your desk,' she said quietly. 'I only dusted the bookshelves in here – oh, and I emptied the waste basket.'

He sighed. There was an outside chance she was telling the truth – if so there was only one other explanation for it – the envelope and all that money must have been inadvertently thrown out into the dustbin. It was his job to be charitable, but it was hard at times.

'A great pity,' he murmured. 'That money was for the children's seaside outing – more than a hundred pounds, there was. Ah well, I suppose it can't be helped.'

She was still sitting, mug clasped between her hands and her eyes downcast. No blush, no fidgeting, nothing to indicate she had anything to hide.

'Well now,' he went on, leaning forward over his desk and arching his fingertips together, 'there was another matter I wanted to talk to you about. I believe you'll be looking for a job shortly. I was thinking –

255

how would you like to come here to clean regularly?'

She looked up sharply. 'Regular? Like every day, do you mean?'

'I know your mother has enough work on, and I'd like to have you,' he said smoothly. 'In fact you could start coming in for a while every day now, after school, if you like. Talk it over with her and let me know.'

She set the mug down on his desk and stood up. 'I'll take it,' she said. 'How much?'

Kelly felt very pleased with herself as she walked down the lane towards home. Like Mam had said, the vicar paid good money, and not only that but he'd given her the solution to her problem.

She was proud of the idea which suddenly came to her.

'Do you mind if I just pop up to the toilet before I go, vicar? And don't worry, I can let myself out.'

So now the Fulcrum bag lay cosily tucked into a corner of Mrs Bax's wardrobe where she knew for a fact he never went. And next week the plastic mac and boots would lie there too . . .

What a wicked old devil he was, trying to con her there was over a hundred pounds in that envelope. That was a downright lie. There was only eighty-seven . . .

'I was so sorry to hear about your brother, Ellen . . . It must be awful for you, so young . . . it's tragic . . .'

Ellen tossed about in bed. Why the devil did they have to keep reminding her every time she stamped a book? They meant well, but it hurt like hell. Her nerves were raw, jangled by the slightest thing.

Still, it helped to be at work. Dad had spent all day alone with Lisa again. You couldn't dislike Lisa – she was quite nice, really – lovable, even. She and Dad seemed to be enjoying themselves, acting as if everything was normal – they were actually laughing together tonight. How could they, so soon . . . ?

All night together, alone in Lisa's room the night of the funeral . . . Oh God, all this anger bubbling up again. She's done nothing wrong. How can you resent somebody you really like? She couldn't help it. Go away, Lisa, go away, you bitch, and leave us alone! No-one can hear me shout – it's all staying trapped inside my head.

Oh, if only this jangle of thoughts swirling in my brain would stop! They keep playing over and over, relentless, monotonous, like a gramophone record.

Sleep – block out the hurt. There's another one of those vicious headaches coming on, just like they used to do all those years ago . . . There's no-one to talk to . . . Who can you talk to when there are things you never allow yourself to think about, let alone tell, things you thought you'd blotted out, things that sneak up on you again at night when you're unprepared and invade you . . . No-one knew, not even Dad knows the half of it . . .

Oh God, if only there was some way to escape this turmoil of seething thoughts, and feelings swishing back and forth like bilge in a ship's hold.

Medicine, or pills – there must be something which might help. Doctor Pillai looks approachable. But he might suggest an examination – I don't want that . . .

On the other hand, perhaps he could prescribe some magic potion which would block out the tumble of thoughts and bring sleep. Escape into the dark oblivion of sleep . . .

Ravi Pillai watched his patient leave then picked up the next record card. Ellen Hemingway. He remembered seeing her up at Jericho Farm – the sister of the young man who died recently of a brain tumour. Quiet girl, beautiful dark eyes.

257

He scanned quickly down the notes before pressing the buzzer. Septic finger two years ago, tonsillitis – nothing serious since a bout of migraines in her teens which had resolved itself spontaneously in the end. That was long before he'd come to take up the junior partnership here. He buzzed for the receptionist to send her in.

There was a delicate tap at the door, so light he might not have heard if he hadn't been expecting it. She walked well as she crossed the room, head erect, like the women at home in Kuala Lumpur. He appraised her clinically as she sat on the chair beside his desk, pale face which could indicate anaemia, tension in the way she sat on the edge of the chair, clasping her handbag tightly on her lap.

The dark eyes looked troubled. Not surprising in view of her recent bereavement. She sat looking down at her shoes, waiting for him to speak.

'How are you, Miss Hemingway?' he asked.

She gave a slight shrug. 'Not too bad really, I suppose. It's not been long . . . We're still all a bit confused.'

'Of course. That's perfectly natural. These things take a little time.'

She nodded dumbly, her fingers weaving in and out of the straps of her handbag. He could wait. He wouldn't hurry her.

For a few moments she sat in silence. He heard another car pull up in the car park. She wasn't finding this easy.

'Is something troubling you?' he prompted gently. 'Is there some way I can help you?'

She took a deep breath before answering but still her gaze did not meet his. 'I don't know – maybe it's just me. I'm all mixed up.'

She paused, turning her gaze to the window. 'I can't eat, I can't sleep,' she said in a flat monotone. 'And sometimes I get these dreadful headaches. I can't think properly any more. It's affecting my work.'

The classic symptoms of stress. He put down his pen and sat back thoughtfully. She was very tense. It would seem her problem was more emotional than physical. She needed to talk – but in her own good time, and patients were waiting . . .

'I could give you something to help you sleep,' he murmured, 'but would that really answer your problem?'

She looked up, startled, and he could see the depths of anxiety there, then she regained her composure. 'It would help,' she said. 'If I can sleep, then maybe I can think more clearly than I can right now.'

'Think about what?'

She looked away again. 'Oh, I don't know. Just horrible thoughts that keep whirling in my head, negative things.'

'Like guilt?'

She nodded, screwing up the straps on her lap. 'And anger, and envy. Things I'm ashamed of.'

He smiled gravely. 'There's no need for shame. It's human – we all have it.'

She stood up abruptly. 'I've taken up enough of your time. I'd be glad of some sleeping pills, doctor.'

He picked up his pen and began to write. 'A few days' holiday wouldn't do you any harm,' he murmured. 'And maybe another time we can talk more—'

'You've been very kind. Thank you.'

The signal was clear. She wasn't ready to lower the drawbridge – not yet, anyway. He smiled as he handed her the prescription.

'Well, if you should change your mind, remember I'm here. Whatever you want to tell me will go no further than this room.'

Liza gazed at the painting. She was alone in the house and had time to examine it at her leisure. Surprisingly, it didn't hurt any more.

There was little doubt it was the best thing David had ever done, so different from all his other work. Love showed in every stroke, such delicacy of colour and touch, yet there was strength in it, and a hint of mystery . . .

It was the girl under the tree, her expression shaded from sight. The girl in the shadows, he'd called her. What was it David had seen? He was right – there was something strange about Ellen, the way she could change so suddenly and inexplicably. One moment she was warm and affectionate, the next remote and unapproachable. She made it very hard for anyone to get to know her . . .

Lisa moved to the far side of the room and surveyed the painting again from that angle. It was still beautiful. It deserved to be shown to a larger audience – maybe she should try to find out if it could be accepted for inclusion in an exhibition somewhere . . .

Voices drifted up the stairs. She hurried out on to the landing. She could make out James's resonant tone, and felt glad. She always looked forward to his coming home.

'It's your Aunt Dorothy,' James said, turning with the telephone in his hand as Ellen came in at the front door. 'She's coming up to Harrogate to see your grandfather again – she wonders if you'd like to go back with her for a break.'

Ellen was shrugging off her jacket and she hesitated. He covered the mouthpiece with his hand. 'You don't have to if you don't want to,' he whispered. 'Have a word with her.'

She threw the jacket over the banister rail and took the 'phone from his outstretched hand. 'Hello, Aunt Dorothy.'

'Ellen, my dear – I was just saying to your father that you might like to come south for a while, just for a change. I'm sure you could arrange time off from the library, and I'd love to have you for company. It would be a good opportunity for us to get to know each other better.'

Ellen listened to the lively voice rattling on. 'It's something of a chore for me, visiting your grandfather, I can tell you,' Dorothy said. 'He's such a demanding old devil. He's got a nurse looking after him now and she's giving him hell. Serves him right, the old buzzard. I hand-picked her myself specially. I thought he deserved an ogre.'

Ellen couldn't resist a smile. Aunt Dorothy was refreshing. 'Well,' she said hesitantly, 'I have got a couple of weeks due to me—'

'That's wonderful,' Aunt Dorothy cut in. 'I've got quite a library here – probably bigger than the one you work in – you could sort it out for me if you feel like it. When we're not shopping or driving out into the country, that is. I'll come and pick you up next Saturday when I leave Harrogate.'

Ellen stood alongside the gleaming car parked outside the farm gate while Aunt Dorothy put her bag into the boot and climbed into the driving seat. Across the car's roof she could see the late afternoon sunlight lying flat over the cobbled yard, the two figures standing close together as they waved.

Together on the doorstep, like a couple. She was leaving them alone together. Now they would have each other, undisturbed, for two whole weeks . . . Together . . . together . . .

For God's sake, it's me leaving them, not them shutting me out . . . But it's like the night of the funeral all over again . . . Stop thinking like this – it's unworthy of you!

Summoning up a smile she gave one last wave and bent to climb into the car alongside her aunt. She didn't look back as the car slid away downhill.

* * *

Lisa was humming softly to herself as she closed her bedroom door and walked along the corridor towards the shower room.

There was something different in the air, a kind of ease about the house, as if a shadow had lifted. Perhaps it was the sun streaming in through the windows, or maybe Ellen's absence, but whatever it was, she felt sunnier than she could remember for a long time.

James was so easy to be with. They'd both sat at table in their dressing gowns, relaxed, completely at ease, as they chatted over bacon and eggs. It was just like the old days with David. Now James was going over to see someone up at the nearby farm while she went down into the village.

She pushed open the shower room door, then stopped. She could hear the rush of water and through the opaque glass of the shower cubicle she could see a figure moving. A man's body, naked, tall and dark-haired, whistling softly as he lathered. Her hand flew to her mouth – David!

She stood transfixed, unable to take her eyes from him. She could make out the movements, the hands soaping vigorously up and down his body while he whistled.

The ache came flooding back. She moved forward, longing to rush to him, cling to the naked, slippery skin, hold him close . . .

Don't be stupid – it's James – David is dead. She backed away carefully towards the door, shame reddening her cheeks as she remembered . . . *'There is a way . . .'*

It was time she left . . .

'I honestly didn't think Ellen would go,' said James that evening over dinner. 'It'll do her a world of good, being with Dorothy.'

'Yes, she seems nice,' Lisa said absently.

'She knows how to enjoy herself, just what Ellen needs. She was always the same, and now she's a merry widow, so to speak – she's divorced from Myles – he was an army officer – and she's pretty well off. She'll make sure Ellen has a good time.'

He stopped, aware that Lisa wasn't really listening. 'What's up, love? You're very quiet.'

She put down the dessert fork and leaned her elbow on the table. 'It's time I left, James. I ought to go back to London.'

He stared at her. 'What on earth for?'

She looked away. 'There could be talk in the village – you and me alone together.'

He smiled. 'I doubt it. Would it bother you?'

She shrugged. 'I'm a scarlet woman, remember. It's your good name, James.'

'That's rubbish,' he said firmly. 'If they don't know me by now—'

'And I've got to get back to work – I've a living to earn,' she went on. 'I can't stay here idle for ever.'

She was tracing patterns on the tablecloth with her fork. He eyed her thoughtfully. 'What's the real reason, Lisa?' he asked quietly. 'You're not telling me everything.'

She put down the fork, sat back in her chair and took a deep breath. 'I don't feel comfortable here now.'

He leaned forward anxiously. 'It isn't me – I haven't made you feel uncomfortable, have I?'

She gave a half-smile. 'It's not you, it's me. I said something idiotic to you. I made a fool of myself.'

'No you didn't,' he said, shaking his head, but she wasn't listening.

'It was only because David was the most wonderful man I ever met. It was stupid of me. I wish I'd kept my mouth shut.'

He understood. He remembered. *'There is a way . . .'* He wanted to lean across the table and touch her

263

hand but she was out of reach. 'We all say things we don't mean in the heat of the moment—' he began.

'But I did mean it – at the time.' She pushed her chair back and stood up. 'I can't stay here any longer. I'm going back to London.'

There was a sinking feeling in his stomach. She paused beside his chair and he looked up at her. 'There's no need,' he said quietly, 'but if that's what you really want, I won't argue.'

For a brief second her hand touched his shoulder as she passed. He turned to watch her leave the room, and it came to him with a start that his whole world was walking out with her.

TWENTY-EIGHT

1967

Lisa watched as James placed her bag in the boot of his car.

'You will take care of Gladys for me, won't you?' she said, nodding towards the Mini parked in a corner of the yard. 'The old girl's given us sterling service.'

'Of course I will.'

She stood by the drystone wall, looking down over the broad sweep of the valley. 'I love this place,' she breathed as he came to stand beside her. 'It's so beautiful. I shall always think of it as home.'

'It is your home,' he muttered. 'Whenever you want to come back . . .'

She squeezed his arm. 'Thanks, I know. We'd better be on our way now or I'll miss my train.'

He opened the car door for her. 'What do you want me to do with David's painting?' he asked as she climbed in. 'Send it on, after I've had it framed?'

She hesitated. 'I don't want to rob you of it, James, but I would like to try and find someone who might be able to get it exhibited. It'll come back to Jericho.'

'I'll see to it. Once you're settled.'

He went round to the driver's seat and sat silent for a moment. 'You know I'd drive you to London—' he began.

'No.' She shook her head firmly. 'I've got to start anew, on my own. The journey on the train will give me time to ease my way back in.'

Maybe she was too sharp. She glanced up at his

profile, compelling and sober against the grey stone of the farm. 'I'm going to miss you,' she said quietly. 'You won't feel lonely, will you?'

He turned and gave her a smile. 'I'll have Ellen back next week. What about you?'

She laughed. 'Oh – I'll have Lazarus.'

There was a reassuring sense of familiarity the moment she walked into Lazarus's tiny flat and dropped her bag. The old familiar smell of greasepaint hung in the air, mingled with the savoury garlic scent of his supper, the old ironing board still standing by the cooker with its brown scorch marks on the cover, the old wooden clothes horse laden with half-sewn costumes . . .

He was overjoyed to see her. He jumped up from behind the old sewing machine on the table and came hurrying across the room, bending his lanky height to embrace her, then held her at arm's length to inspect her anxiously.

He clicked his tongue. 'Oh love, I do wish I could help – you don't look yourself at all.'

'Nonsense,' she smiled. 'Good bracing Yorkshire air – it's done me a world of good. I'm fighting fit and anxious to get back to work – if they'll still have me.'

He shook his head gravely. 'I think you're very brave, love.'

'Bollocks,' she said, picking up her bag and heading for the door. 'Have you aired the bed for me?'

As she turned the key in the lock and walked in it was like taking a step back in time. Memories flooding over her as she looked around – the old kettle drum still bore the rings of their coffee mugs, the door to the bathroom stood half open . . .

'Yes, I've been sick again . . .'

It was hard to look at the bed and not recall all those nights of long, sensual love-making, and later the nights they'd tried to comfort each other when they both knew it was too late . . .

The curtains still trailed across the floor as she drew them together. In the dusk she could just make out the factory across the way, the flat roof he'd told her had a dip in the middle – the first sign . . .

And his posters – banks of them, ranged along the far wall still. At any moment he might come into the room and pick up his brush – no, she must stop all this make-believe.

David was dead. He would never come back. She must come to terms with the fact and go on. Yes. Tomorrow she would ring Martin Lewis.

She pulled out the contents of her bag and strewed them on the bed, then sorted them out and turned to hang a blouse in the wardrobe. His clothes still hung there.

She touched his old denim jacket and saw him again in her mind's eye, running between the traffic that day, across to the specialist while she waited in the coffee bar. Her fingers remembered the feel of his body beneath the fabric . . . She buried her face in the jacket, smelt the warm, intimate smell of him, and the tears broke free . . .

'Lisa, my dear.'

Down the phone Martin Lewis's cool, practical voice took on a gratifyingly warmer tone when he recognized her. Behind her she could hear Lazarus singing with shrill enthusiasm in his room.

She stuffed her finger in her ear to shut out the sound.

'How are things?' Martin asked. 'About your young man, I mean?'

She told him. 'So I'm looking for work now,' she concluded. 'You did say if I wanted to come back . . .'

'You couldn't have timed it better,' he cut in smoothly. 'That's all I needed to know.'

'You mean—'

'I mean I can sack your replacement now. And guess who rang last week asking if you'd be available when they come down? The Braithwaites – remember them? Harold and Cynthia, from Lancashire.'

'Of course I remember – a lovely couple. When are they coming?'

'Next week. So if you could come in tomorrow morning we'll go through the schedule.'

Lazarus crouched on Cinderella's little three-legged stool, nursing a coffee mug between long, slender hands. 'My, but you've been busy since you got back,' he remarked. 'I've hardly seen anything of you this past week.'

'Best thing for me,' said Lisa. 'Keeps me from fretting.'

He looked around the room, cluttered with props and scenery mixed up with Lisa's belongings. 'It can't be easy for you here, with all this bringing back memories,' he murmured.

'I'll get used to it,' she replied. 'Every day it hurts less and anyway, there's so much to occupy me now. What time is it?'

'Nearly six.' He drained off the last of his coffee. 'I'd better go down – I've got one of the cast coming for a fitting any minute. Beautiful Edwardian costume, pale blue with tiny appliqué flowers at the neck and on her hat. She's going to look absolutely divine.'

'Who is?' Lisa asked as he crossed to the door.

He paused, his hand on the doorknob. 'Melanie – she's playing Gwendolen – we decided on Oscar Wilde again this time. You know Melanie, don't you?'

'The elegant, dark-haired woman? I've spoken to her once or twice, that's all.'

'Oh – she thought a lot about David. She was asking after him when he was ill. Pretty name, Melanie.'

Lisa held up a finger. 'Tell me something, Lazarus,'

she said. 'I've often wondered – why did your parents give you that name?'

He grinned. 'They didn't. I nearly died when I was fourteen – ruptured appendix, you know – and when I recovered they said it was like Lazarus. I thought it was a lovely name, far better than mine, so I stuck to it.'

Curiosity aroused, Lisa followed him as he opened the door and went out to the stairs. 'What's your real name then?' she called after him.

'Keith,' he shouted over his shoulder. 'But don't you dare tell a soul.'

James was looking forward to seeing Ellen again – Jericho had been an empty place since Lisa left.

There ought not to be this vacuum in his life. He had too little to occupy his mind, that was the problem. He had only played at being a farmer since he'd sold off those pockets of land for development; he'd had no serious interest in anything since Anna died, and with David's death there seemed even less point to it. He had money enough and to spare.

What a futile way to exist! He was still a comparatively young man – not yet fifty – he couldn't spend the rest of his days pointlessly meandering through life. He had to make something of himself; Lisa had the right attitude: *I can't stay here idle for ever. I've got to get on with my life.*

She was dead right. That's what he had to do. Set a goal, make some plans.

He saw her coming down the platform, her hair for once swinging loose on her shoulders and a bounce in her step. As she held out her hand to seize his there was a light in her eye.

He took her suitcase and squeezed her hand affectionately. 'Had a good time, love?'

She smiled. 'It was wonderful. Aunt Dorothy was so

269

kind. She helped me choose some new clothes, took me to her hairdresser—' She swung round. 'Do you like it?'

He touched a finger to the nut-brown silk of her hair and smiled. 'It suits you. You will keep it that way, won't you?'

'It won't be very practical for work – but I think I might, for a while anyway.'

He was gripped by a sense of excitement as he guided her out of the station to where the car lay waiting. His daughter looked better than she'd looked in months, and he felt a new urgency in his stride, as if he was going somewhere at last. Perhaps they could go there together.

The car turned off the main road and headed down the country lanes towards Thaxton. Ellen leaned back in her seat.

'When did Lisa leave?' she asked casually.

'A day or two after you. She rang to tell me she's settled down into the old flat and got her old job back. She's got a very busy timetable ahead.'

Ellen nodded. 'And what have you been doing?'

Now was his chance. 'I've been making plans,' he said proudly. 'To start up a business – with my guns.'

She looked at him dubiously. 'You talked about that before . . .'

'But this time I mean it. I've checked it out – there's a gap in the specialist market for miniature reproductions, and I'm going to fill it. I've got to find the clients – go to Sotheby's and other places where the sales take place, see who the buyers are.'

Ellen was staring at the road ahead. 'And when did you decide this?' she asked quietly.

'After Lisa left I had time to think about it. I'm going to make a success of it if it kills me.'

She turned her head to him and smiled. 'Best of British luck, Dad.'

*   *   *

As the taxi ploughed through the busy teatime traffic Lisa watched London's skyline. Harold Braithwaite leaned back beside her, exhaling clouds of smoke from an expensive-smelling cigar. He pulled it from his mouth and patted his knee in satisfaction.

'Not a bad exhibition, that,' he remarked. 'Mind you, Hargreaves Textiles could have given any of 'em a run for their money. There weren't a fabric there that's a patch on ours.'

She turned her head to smile at him. 'Why bother going then, if you know you're the best?'

His chubby face registered surprise. 'Got to keep an eye on the opposition, lass. That's what business is about.'

He waved his cigar towards the window. 'See that building over there – the big one with the smoked glass windows?'

She could see it, towering above its neighbours. 'Yes?'

'I bought it last time I were down here.' He beamed and began puffing on his cigar again. 'Diversification, that's what they're all on about these days. I were doing it before most of 'em were born. It's no use having brass if you don't make it work for you. Invest, that's my motto. Shares, antiques, racing cars – I've got a garage full of them.'

Lisa shook her head. 'I'd no idea your interests were so wide – I only knew about the textiles.'

Braithwaite chuckled. 'Why should you? Your firm only deals with the Hargreaves end. Nobody knows the half of it. I've always played my cards close to my chest.'

'Odd,' Lisa murmured, 'you don't seem hard enough to be a tough business man.'

Again he chuckled. 'Oh, I'm very hard, love – when I have to be.'

271

For a moment he fell silent, gazing out of the window at the shops sliding by. 'It's taken some getting, has my brass,' he muttered, as if talking to himself. 'I've had to work for it, all I inherited from my dad was a pile of bills. Most of it's in Cynthia's name now. She's a very rich woman, is my Cynthia – only for God's sake don't tell her.'

The taxi drew up at the hotel. The commissionaire stepped forward to open the door for Braithwaite to alight. He turned to Lisa.

'Are you coming in to have dinner with us, Lisa love?' he asked. 'Cynthia and me'd be glad of a chance to spoil you a bit.'

She shook her head with a smile. 'Thanks – another time, perhaps. I've promised to be at a dress rehearsal tonight.'

Lazarus's fair hair was dark with perspiration by the time the rehearsal ended. He sank on the bench in the dressing room with a sigh.

'Oh, love, I don't know how I'd have managed without you,' he said wearily. 'They're always the same – it's too tight here, a flowerbud's fallen off there – as if I haven't enough on with the props and everything.'

'You did wonders,' Lisa assured him. 'The costumes look fantastic, especially Gwendolen's.'

He beamed. 'I told you, didn't I? She looked a real treat.'

Once again Lisa found herself wondering about this woman Melanie. Why had she asked after David when he was ill – they hardly knew her?

The dressing room door opened and, as if conjured up by her thoughts, Melanie walked in. She looked incredibly expensive with her cashmere coat and a silk scarf draped about her neck.

Lazarus held out his hands to her. 'Darling – we were just talking about you – how divine you look in the blue dress,' he enthused. She smiled, and her pretty face became beautiful.

'I just came back for my gloves – have you seen them?'

He snatched them up off the bench and handed them to her. She turned to Lisa. 'Hello,' she said softly. 'I think we've met once or twice, haven't we?'

The voice matched her face, sultry and warm. Lisa nodded. 'I think you knew David better,' she said.

'Of course she knew him,' Lazarus said. 'She twisted my arm to get the flat for him, didn't you, sweetie? And I've never been able to refuse you anything, have I my love?'

The flat? Lisa could hear David's voice now, the night he told her. *'I heard about it from these friends of mine, this accountant and his wife – I met them at a student do, a long time ago, and they just happened to hear of it. The rent's next to nothing – we just have to keep an eye on the place . . .'*

Lazarus was still chattering on. 'If it hadn't been for Melanie the other couple would have moved in. As it was, I had to put them off and give them their deposit back. Still, I wouldn't have got to know you, would I, love?'

Melanie was looking at her closely with those deep violet eyes. 'Well, we thought him a delightful young man, my husband and I.'

Lisa sensed that the emphasis on the last phrase was a tinge too heavy.

'We must get to know one another better,' Melanie added.

In that second Lisa had a sudden feeling she'd never known before, a kind of blinding flash of intuition. There was neither rhyme nor reason to it, but she knew beyond a shadow of doubt. *'You slept with this woman, didn't you, David?'*

'Yes,' said Lisa quietly. 'I think perhaps we should.'

*   *   *

After Melanie had gone Lisa went back upstairs to the flat, leaving Lazarus to lock up for the night. For several minutes she paced up and down between the kettle drum and the window, hugging her arms close to her chest.

'So there were things you didn't tell me, David,' she muttered. 'And I thought I knew you so well. You didn't tell me about the sick headaches for long enough, did you, or the funny vision? And you certainly didn't tell me about her.'

She stopped and glared at the bed. 'You did sleep with her, didn't you?'

The accusing words fell into the silence of the night. She grabbed her jacket from the chair and jerked open the wardrobe door.

His denim jacket, his second-best pair of jeans, hanging alongside her coat and blouses. Fury erupted and before she could think she snatched his clothes off the rail and flung them on the floor.

'You bastard!' she raged. 'You utter bastard!'

Turning, she caught sight of the posters against the far wall. The first one was in her hands, raised high above her head, before reason returned. She lowered her arms and stared at the vibrant colours. She couldn't do it. He had so little to show for his life.

She put it down, but the anger refused to die. Flinging herself on the bed she sobbed, unrestrainedly, and between gasping gulps for air she cried out savage words.

'You bastard – why can't you be here now? I hate you!'

At last she lay quiet, exhausted. The tears dried hard on her cheeks. She stared up the cracked ceiling.

'Why can't I hate you?' she whispered. 'I want to hate you. For God's sake, tell me she meant nothing to you.'

274

She rolled over and stroked his pillow. 'I never thought I could be jealous. We had something special, you and I. When we made love, it was love. I know that. Your precious Melanie was only a bit on the side – wasn't she?'

TWENTY-NINE

1941

Anna and Dorothy, still dressed in funeral black, sat in the drawing room at Thirlbeck Manor. Dorothy broke the intense silence with a sigh.

'Well, she had a good send-off,' she murmured. 'Daddy did well by her.'

'I thought there'd be more people at the church,' Anna replied. 'She used to have so many friends.'

'They're all dead,' Dorothy said. 'That's what happens when you get to her age.'

Anna sighed. 'Poor Grandmother – she looked so pitiful at the end – I think she was almost glad to go.'

Dorothy nodded. 'I would be too, in her shoes. Still, you'll be able to take baby Ellen home now, be with James again – every cloud has a silver lining. I wish I could say the same for Myles.'

'Things still not so good between you?' Anna asked.

Her sister shrugged. 'Thankfully he's away most of the time – he got posted to Intelligence headquarters. Myles in Intelligence – I ask you! I thought we were trying to win this war.'

Anna smiled and stood up to look out of the window. 'James should be here soon,' she said. At that moment the door opened and a nanny came in carrying the baby. Anna took her. 'I'm going to miss you,' she said to the nanny. 'It's been wonderful not having to deal with dirty nappies these past few weeks.'

James drove with care. Ellen lay sleeping on Anna's lap beside him and Anna seemed lost in thought. She looked delectable in black, her blonde hair newly washed and set and a gleaming necklace at her throat. He glanced away from the road frequently to watch the emotions chasing across her pretty face. He didn't speak; he didn't want to intrude on her thoughts.

'I couldn't have stayed any longer,' she murmured at last. 'It was good seeing Dorothy again but the house is so sad – Grandmother looked awfully fragile. She couldn't talk – she just seemed to be lying there, waiting for the end. It was awful not knowing if she could hear me or not.'

James nodded. 'At least she'd know you were there, I'm sure.'

Anna sighed. 'Daddy was cheerful enough. He wanted me to stay for the will-reading, but I couldn't. I don't think he understood – he's been spoiling me rotten with a nanny for Ellen and this crystal necklace and everything. He thought I ought to stay.'

'Never mind,' said James. 'So long as you did what you think right.'

She nestled her face against the baby's head and he could see her eyes were moist. 'She was a lovely old lady,' she murmured. 'I did love her, James.'

He patted her knee. 'She knew that, sweetheart, don't worry.'

It was never easy, he mused, choosing between what you wanted and what you ought to do. More than anything he wanted to be with his wife and child, but that meant giving up his guns for farming. How he'd love to have done for ever with muck-spreading and the stench of branding, to be able to absorb himself entirely in the intricacies of steel and spring.

The others on his course would have been posted now. Some of them were already in the front line of battle. He ought to be there with them. He was missing out on the action. The war was passing him by . . .

* * *

277

They reached Garthdale and he swung the van to follow the river downstream towards Thaxton. Anna gazed out of the window at the bronzing woods and the purple hills beyond.

'I love the rusty colours of autumn,' she murmured. 'Isn't it peaceful here? It's always the same. You could go to sleep for a hundred years like Rip Van Winkle and wake up and find the valley hasn't changed a bit. We're awfully lucky, aren't we – not being bombed or anything? Apart from black-out and rationing we wouldn't know there was a war on.'

She was right, he thought as he nursed the van round the twisting lanes. Short of a disaster his loved ones would be safe for the duration. He should count his blessings.

Doris looked up from washing dishes in the kitchen sink. Out of the window she could see Anna sitting on the yard wall, soaking up the late autumn sun.

A basket of blackberries lay on the draining board. Doris turned to James.

'Have you seen this lot she's gathered?' she asked. 'There must be five or six pounds.'

He didn't look up from the accounts spread before him on the deal table.

'Her arms are covered with scratches,' Doris went on. 'She's done well, has yon lass – she wasn't born to it. She'll turn her hand to anything, no matter how mucky.'

'Yes,' James murmured absently, shuffling the papers around. 'All credit to her.'

'I wouldn't have believed it possible,' muttered Doris, 'but she's a real trier and no mistake. She says she's going to take them berries down to the WI's jam-making at Mrs Drake's this aft.'

Doris shook the soapsuds off her hands. 'Hey up,' she said, reaching for the tea towel, 'the postman's brought summat – she's opening it.'

For a few moments she watched, then turned away from the window. 'Nay, it can't be nowt important,' she muttered. 'She's sat down on the wall again. She'll get her death of cold sitting on that damp stone – I'd best call her in for her dinner.'

Recognizing the implicit suggestion that she wanted to lay the table, James gathered his papers together and stowed them away in the sideboard drawer. 'I'll fetch her,' he said.

She hardly seemed to notice as he came up close. She was staring into the middle distance, the letter in her lap. James slid an arm around her waist and she started.

'What is it, love?' he asked.

She turned to him, her eyes wide. 'I'm rich, James. I can't believe it.' She held the letter out to him. 'Tell me I'm not dreaming,' she said faintly. 'I thought she might leave me a hundred or two, but this—'

The letter was from a firm of Harrogate solicitors, couched in legal words but the content was clear. After certain bequests Grandmother had left the bulk of her estate to Anna. The total figure astounded him, a sum way above his comprehension. She was right – she was a very rich woman.

She sat staring over the valley. 'I can buy anything I want,' she murmured. 'Silk stockings – perfume – we could have a new house even.' She looked up at him, bewilderment in her eyes turning to delight. 'We can do anything we want now. Oh James!'

He watched her expression with pleasure. The money would mean she wouldn't have to worry any more, but for him the greater satisfaction lay in watching her delight. She was looking at the letter again, her blue-stained fingertips trembling as she read.

'She's left me Grandfather's guns too,' she said. 'I remember the Purdey – Grandmother used to tell me about the palaver they made about measuring him up for it – and it says there's a Holland and Holland as well. You'll have those, darling.'

He could already feel the Purdey's stock cradled in his elbow, its warm wood nestling against his cheek, just like the one the Brigadier had loaned him once.

She jumped up from the wall and seized his arm. 'We can make all kinds of plans now,' she said excitedly. 'We'll have the money to do everything we've ever wanted.'

Her eyes sparkled with anticipation, like a child who's just opened the very Christmas present she'd been hoping for. James's hand closed over hers.

'I'm delighted for you, love, I really am.'

Doris called from the doorway. 'Dinner's on the table – come and eat it while it's hot.'

He steered Anna towards the door. She jerked her arm free and danced up and down on the cobblestones. 'Just think – we could get you a tractor or – I know, we could go on a real holiday, anywhere you want.'

'Dinner,' he said firmly. 'And don't let's say anything in front of Doris. We can talk about plans tonight when she's gone.'

Near the doorway he pulled her close. 'Just one thing,' he whispered. 'Promise me you'll never change.'

She looked up at him soberly. 'I won't,' she said. 'I never have.' She looked down at the scratches on her coarsened palms. 'Only I want to be comfortable.' She smiled. 'I think I'll bathe in asses' milk tonight to celebrate.'

'We haven't got any asses.'

'The Boothroyds have got a donkey.'

'I'll go and fetch it when we've had something to eat.'

*   *   *

280

At the end of the afternoon he stood with Fred on the edge of Gorsey Field watching the smoke rise from the burning stubble. Fred coughed and cleared his throat.

'Is it all right if I get off sharp as soon as milking's done, Jim?' he asked, pulling off his cap to wipe the sweat from his forehead, 'only I want to go to the pictures in Otterley, first house.'

James leaned his pitchfork against the drystone wall and smiled. 'You seem to be always at the pictures – is it young Thelma again?'

Fred turned away to hide the sheepish look on his face. 'She asked me to take her – she's nervous about coming home alone in the black-out, she says, and anyway I want to see the film meself.'

James smiled. Thelma had made good headway since the landgirls had left. 'It's OK,' he said. 'I can manage the pigs on my own.'

Anna wasn't back from the jam-making session when the milking was finished and Fred went home. Doris was unconcerned.

'She'll be enjoying herself in company for a change,' she remarked. 'And anyway I've given baby her bottle and put her to bed.'

James went down to the pigsty. He sat on a bale of straw, watching the porkers snuffling in the trough. Ellen had only been on the bottle since Anna came back from Harrogate. Before then it had afforded him infinite pleasure to watch the baby's tiny eager mouth pulling on the breast, to see Anna's tender look as she gazed down at the little one. It was silly to feel sad. All things change and move on . . .

Anna's money, for instance. She was a wealthy woman now in her own right, financially independent of him, and he felt awkward. It wasn't the way things ought to be. He should be the breadwinner. That was what husband meant, providing and nurturing. Anna

281

would be eager to lavish gifts on him, but it wasn't going to be easy. It just wasn't natural for a man to take from his wife.

The fat-bellied sow lifted her head from the trough and gave him a lugubrious look. James shook his head. 'I don't know, Peg,' he muttered. 'What difference is this money going to make to us? I've always dreamed of having a Purdey of my own, but what price am I going to have to pay for it?'

An enthusiastic letter arrived from Dorothy a few days later:

> I'm so glad Grandmother left most of her money to you. She left quite a decent bequest to Daddy and me, and she's also left me her favourite pearl necklace with the matching earrings. She must have known I always craved that set – she never missed a thing – and she had the sense to realize I have money enough already. I just hope you start spending it soon on the things that really matter – like getting a telephone put in so we can talk!

'Good idea,' said Anna as she put the letter down. 'She seems terribly busy organizing hospitality for overseas troops. London's full of them, she says, Canadian and French and Polish. She'll love playing hostess.'

James stood at the window, watching the smoke still drifting over Boothroyd's fields. 'I noticed fresh flowers on Dad's grave when we were at church this morning,' he said. 'Did you put them there?'

She nodded. 'Well, not exactly. I gave the green-grocer orders to put fresh ones there every Friday from now on. I thought it would please you.'

'It does. That was very kind of you.' From upstairs came a thin cry. 'Ellen's awake,' he said. 'Are you going to bring her down?'

'She's teething, that's all. Doris will bring her down as soon as she gets here.'

She was opening a second envelope. 'What's that?' he asked.

'It's a catalogue I sent for from Selfridges. I want to see what make of pianos they have. Oh, and by the way, I had an idea – it might be nice if we went to the horse sales and got ourselves a couple of hacks – what do you think?'

He hesitated before he answered. 'Look, it's your money, sweetheart, and I'm not going to tell you how to spend it, but let's just ease ourselves into this gently, eh?'

He saw the smile slip away in disappointment. 'But it's a lovely idea,' he went on, taking his jacket from the hook. 'And I reckon there's just about enough room in the stable . . .'

She waved a hand airily. 'We can always extend the stable – if we're staying here, that is.'

He glanced back sharply. This was a matter they hadn't discussed. 'We have to stay here,' he said quietly. 'At least until the end of the war.'

'I suppose so. That's why they let you out of the army, isn't it, to run the farm?' He was standing by the door, the jacket half pulled on. She came up close. 'I'm not serious. I wouldn't want to leave Jericho any more than you do. But we'll do things to it – extend it.'

It was a thought. He buttoned the jacket before he spoke. 'Would you like me to have a go at extending it for you? There's plenty of stone up at the quarry.'

She hurried across to the sideboard and took some sheets of paper from the drawer. 'I was thinking – the barn's attached to the house and it's got a high roof – we could convert that. I've done some sketches.'

He smiled. She always took him by surprise with her ideas. 'But we need the barn for the hay—'

'Not if you build a wooden one – on the far end.'

He spread patient hands. 'We have enough work on as it is, trying to meet our quotas, and we're short-handed now the girls have gone—'

She brushed his protests aside. 'We can get workmen in to do it – we can well afford it. Please, James.'

She was gazing up at him with that pleading look he knew so well. It was more than time he started the milking. The cows were lowing impatiently in the byre. He patted her arm as he opened the door and a chill breeze swept a handful of leaves into the kitchen. 'We'll talk about it later,' he promised. 'Are you going to bring Ellen down?'

'In a minute.'

As he crossed the cobbled yard he saw Doris lumbering uphill towards the farm. Behind him he could still hear the faint wail from an upstairs room.

There was hardly room for the grand piano in the parlour. Anna had the sofa and chairs moved around three times before she was satisfied. James stood looking doubtfully at the cramped arrangement.

'It's only until we convert the barn,' Anna reassured him. 'I'll have a music room all of my own then.'

He could hear her playing wherever he went, in the bedroom, in the kitchen, even in the pigsty. Beautiful, melodious music it was, and every now and again he would hear her hit a wrong note and stop, only to start again and repeat it until she got it right.

She emerged from the parlour at last, flexing her fingers. 'I'm dreadfully rusty,' she said with a rueful smile. 'I'll have to practise a lot to get my fingers working again.'

Anna handed him a letter. 'For you,' she said briefly. 'Smells of cheap scent.'

It bore a London postmark and was addressed in a childish hand to 'Mr Jim Hemingway, a farm near Otterley, Garthdale, Yorkshire'.

He was aware that Anna was pretending not to be concerned as he opened the letter and scanned the contents.

Being as you was a good friend of Dusty's I thought as you might like to know that he been killed in action in North Africa. I know he would like to know that you been told. He always talked a lot about you and him in the army together, and he was very sad when they took him back to Catterick and you wasn't there any more. He missed you something cronic. Yours faithfully, Maisie Dooley.

James sat down sharply. Anna looked up. 'What's the matter, darling?'

'Dusty,' James grunted. 'He's been killed in action. I should have been there too.'

In the next weeks Anna spent as much time as she could at the keyboard and the sound of lyrical music filled the house. James was glad. She was happy, and that was all that mattered.

It was just after Christmas when the bombshell dropped. Doris had gone home and they sat alone together by the fireside. The news ended and James reached over and switched off the radio.

'That's it, love,' he said quietly. 'Now the Japanese and the Americans are in the war too.'

She looked up at him questioningly. 'I've never heard of Pearl Harbor. Will the war be over quicker now?'

He shook his head. 'Who can say? It means more people are involved now, more casualties, more poor innocent sods like Dusty getting slaughtered.'

She stared into the fire. 'I don't want the war to go on longer. It's been over two years now – I want it over and done with.'

'So do we all, love.'

She pulled the cushion out from behind her. He could see the glitter of tears in her eyes as she punched it angrily. 'But I've got a very special reason,' she muttered. 'We're going to have another baby.'

THIRTY

1968

Lisa stood by the window in the dimming light of evening. It was curious how David's presence was fading. Only a few months ago it had seemed as if he would never leave here; the essence of him had soaked, deep and ineradicably, into the very fabric of the place, and she would catch a whiff of him exuding from everything she touched, and yet now . . .

Even the painful business of taking his clothes to the charity shop and giving his painting materials to Lazarus had not dissipated his presence in the early days.

But now he was dissolving fast. It was inevitable, she supposed, and yet somehow she felt disloyal. Now she could even take out the photograph of the two of them together on the beach at St Ives, his arm about her shoulders and his hair blown back by the wind. It had lain hidden in the drawer long enough. Now she could look at it without the gut-rending pain it used to bring, like jagged glass ripping through her flesh. Now it brought only a wave of infinite sadness.

It had taken time, but now she recognized that he was gone, life would go on.

'It won't be easy,' she mused aloud. 'I've lost touch with all my friends – we found all we wanted in each other.'

They'd locked themselves away together, so tightly it left no room for others. There were colleagues at work of course, but there'd been no social life apart from when he played the piano in the pub. Even then there were only the punters ordering pints while she sat alone, watching his fingers fly over the keys as he immersed himself in Scott Joplin. She had no friends, not even a girl friend she could talk to. She'd never realized just how narrow their life had been.

And now she was alone. Through no will of her own, she was a free woman again . . .

'If you're going down to the shops I'd wrap up well,' James warned his daughter. 'It's bitter out today.'

Ellen smiled as she coiled a thick red scarf about her neck. 'Look who's talking – you've been up on the moor all morning with only that thin jacket on. Even Fred's got the sense to wear his duffle coat.'

'I'm all right – I'm used to it after all this time.'

She picked up her shopping bag, then paused. 'You were talking of selling Jericho a while back – the vicar seems to have told everybody. Are you still?'

James shook his head firmly. 'That was last year. Things are different now. I've got other plans.'

She had a way of smiling with her eyes lately, and there was an elasticity in her step as he watched her set off down the lane. That holiday with Dorothy had done her a world of good. He must see to it that she took a break more often.

He stood on the crest of the hill looking down over Thaxton, the cold wind biting his cheeks, but he was suffused with an inner warmth. Ellen was more relaxed and at ease with herself than he had ever known her, and Lisa's phone calls made it clear she too was making her way. And his new business was growing, slowly but surely. It afforded him great satisfaction to be able not only to make his beloved guns, but to find appreciative customers for them too. The response to his advertisement in the *Shooting Times* had been gratifying and it was clear that there was a hole in the market for replica firearms – how big was another question.

A fine mist hung over the valley but he could make out thin grey wisps of smoke spiralling from grey chimneys. People were down there, his people, living out their simple lives just as their forebears had done for centuries. All manner of life was going on, a microcosm of the greater world outside, the village seething with events he knew nothing about. A thousand dramas were probably being acted out this very moment . . .

Thelma Dent dipped into the chocolate box for the last coffee cream. She nibbled it slowly while she pored over the brochure.

Fred caught sight of her as he turned the page of his newspaper to the racing tips. 'What's that you got?' he asked.

'Terry's All Gold,' she murmured absently.

'I mean the magazine – not another holiday brochure, is it? Summer's months away yet.'

'Butlin's sounds nice,' said Thelma, breaking off to scan the list of remaining chocolates. 'Do you like praline?'

'Never heard of it,' said Fred. 'Why not stick to Morecambe like we always do?'

'We ought to have a change now and again. There's lots going on at Butlin's – our Kelly would like all that dancing and coffee bars. She could meet some nice folk.'

Fred grunted. 'Better than that blooming Gary, you mean.'

Thelma offered him the last chocolate. 'She deserves it, love. She's doing right well at work. The vicar's real pleased the house always looks so nice, and she's up at the vicarage all hours and never a grumble out of her. I'm right proud of her, the way she's set to. I'd like to give her a treat.'

Fred put the paper aside, rose from his chair and took the chocolate. 'Ay well,' he said, popping it in

Thelma's mouth, 'we shall see. Now I'm off back to my work.'

'Miss Hemingway – what a nice surprise.'

Dr Pillai held out a hand, his open face reflecting his pleasure. Ellen transferred the bag of green-groceries to the other hand and held out gloved fingertips.

'Hello,' she said, feeling a rush of uncomfortable shyness. 'On your rounds?'

He smiled and shook his head. 'My afternoon off. Tell me, I haven't seen you lately – how have you been?'

He didn't want a medical report, not on his day off, she thought. 'Much better after a holiday and a change of scenery,' she replied. 'I went mad – bought a lot of new clothes.'

She didn't know how to handle this; a doctor in a surgery was one thing, but to meet him on the street . . . She made to pass him. He turned and fell in step beside her.

'May I carry your bag for you?' he asked.

She jerked it away. 'No, it's all right – it's not heavy.'

She felt clumsy and awkward. A few minutes ago she had felt like a new woman, now she was behaving like a gawky schoolgirl.

But he didn't seem to notice as they walked to-gether along the frost-whitened pavement. 'So you're feeling happier now?' he asked.

She nodded. 'Yes thanks. It's surprising how problems can seem smaller from a distance.'

He gave a soft laugh, and it was a pleasing sound. 'New interests can often put old problems into pers-pective,' he said. 'Art, knitting, dancing – whatever takes your fancy. I'm thinking of going to that new sculpture exhibition in Bradford – I thought I might try my hand at it.'

Ellen looked up quickly. 'I read about it in the *Yorkshire Post* – it sounds very good.'

Doctor Pillai gave her a sidelong glance. 'Why not come with me and see for yourself? You just name a day, any day so long as it's Thursday.'

She felt her cheeks redden. 'No thanks – I mean, thanks all the same, but I'm terribly busy.' Why did she say that? It wasn't true.

He shrugged. 'Well, it's on for another month, so if you want to change your mind . . .'

She left him at the corner, and all the way up the hill she felt his eyes upon her back. It was odd how the burning sensation of embarrassment mingled with the most unaccustomed glow of excitement.

Kelly Dent let herself quietly into the vicarage. Even if the Reverend Bax was in he would take no notice of her. He would remain in his study, preferring the cleaning to get itself done without disturbing his concentration.

Tonight was going to be something special, what with the dance at the youth club and the hot-pot supper thrown in, and what with Gary being allowed to borrow his dad's car now he'd passed his driving test, so there'd be excitement still to come after the dance was over . . . Something special to wear, something that would knock his eyes out . . . maybe the blue blouse you could just about see through . . .

She closed the door of Mrs Bax's bedroom softly behind her and opened the wardrobe, trying not to let it creak. She held the blouse up to the light. Yes, perfect.

Slipping off her green jumper, she slid the blouse up over her shoulders and fastened it. It felt gorgeously expensive – as it should, seeing what she'd paid for it. She twisted in front of the mirror. Yes, in the right light you could just about make out the lacy bra beneath. Now for the navy mini skirt and the glitter tights . . . then the nice new make-up . . .

As she let herself out of the back door again she paused. The Reverend was alone in his study but his deep voice was booming out. He must be rehearsing his sermon again. With a smile she closed the door and locked it.

The Reverend Bax's stomach started to rumble as he was about to read the sermon aloud for the second time. He put the sheaf of paper down and glanced at his watch. That time already? No wonder his stomach was complaining.

At least there was no problem about what to eat for his evening meal tonight – those salmon fish cakes Mrs Tattersall had recommended from the Co-op would be easy to grill and they'd go down nicely with a tin of butter beans and some of that tasty picalilli. He was rather enjoying the jar Miss Walker had presented to him on behalf of the Church Wives at the Harvest Festival. Which was more than he could say for the leaden lardy cake.

He'd just removed the fish cakes from the packet and placed them under the grill when the telephone rang in the hall. Wiping greasy fingers on his cassock he picked up the receiver.

'Hello?'

The voice made him start. 'Clifford – it's me. Sarah. Now don't get excited—'

'You've thought it over,' he cut in eagerly.

'I'm ringing because I want my winter things, that's all. I'd like you to get my blue coat and my boots out of the wardrobe for me.'

He thought quickly. At least she'd made contact again – all was not lost. If he had the opportunity to talk to her, face to face . . . 'When do you want to collect them?' he asked. 'Or shall I bring them to you?'

'That won't be necessary. My brother-in-law will be

going to York on business on Monday. He'll pick them up on his way back. All right? Oh, and there's a plastic bag of my jumpers on the top shelf. Thank you, Clifford.'

And she was gone. Disappointed, the Reverend returned to the kitchen. A powerful smell of fish filled the air and blue smoke was wreathing up from under the grill.

A glass of red wine and two Rennies later he was beginning to feel better. The heartburn was subsiding at last and he could turn his attention to the sermon once more.

On the way to his study he paused. What was it Sarah had asked for? The blue coat – or did she say grey? He ought to have made a note straight away. Tomorrow would be a busy day with morning and evening service, and the Confirmation class in the afternoon – maybe he should sort out the clothes now ready for Monday.

It took a little time to heave his weight up the double flight of stairs. By the time he reached the top landing he was breathing deeply and as he made his way along the corridor to Sarah's room he could feel the fish cakes still lying heavy on his stomach.

He went in and switched on the light. It seemed odd, being in her room again. He hadn't been there since she'd left. There was a nice clean smell about the place – Kelly must have been polishing. He lifted his nose and sniffed appreciatively. It was a sweet, almost exotic scent like perfume, but not the lavendery perfume Sarah used to wear on Sundays.

The wardrobe door groaned as he pulled it open. He ran his fingers along the row of garments on the rail – only one coat, a blue one – he pulled it out and laid it carefully on the bed.

What else was it now? A plastic bag of jumpers –

there, on the top shelf. He took it down and placed it beside the coat. Boots now – they'd be on the floor of the wardrobe.

Pulling the dresses aside he bent to peer into the shadow below. Alongside the boots and her old bedroom slippers lay a cardboard box, a tall bottle protruding and several smaller jars and bottles beside it. As he bent closer he could smell the sweet scent, stronger and more cloying now. Kneeling, he pulled the box out and placed it on the bed.

Make-up, masses of it. He frowned. Odd – Sarah only occasionally put the merest touch of colour on her thin lips. This lot couldn't be hers. Whose then? The only other female who ever came in here was Kelly. She wore make-up, lots of it.

But why would she put her things here? He stared up at the row of clothes and another thought which had been nibbling at his subconscious sprang to the surface. There was something odd. Sarah's habitual grey and beige tones were mingled with vivid red and startling emerald green. Sarah would never wear such dramatic colours. He raised a hand to touch a strange orange thing, and pulled it out. A plastic macintosh. Rising to his feet, he lifted the gauzy red garment from the rail.

It wasn't a blouse as he thought at first; it was a frock, a skimpy little thing which would hardly cover a woman's modesty – a mini, he believed the modern girls called them. And the emerald green was another. There was no doubt of it – only Kelly would wear outrageous things like this.

But why should she hang them here, and not in her own wardrobe at home? Of course, she didn't want her mother to see them. Thelma would be horrified. He looked back at the rail. So many of them – if the girl had bought them secretly, how on earth had she managed to afford them?

Suddenly a thought came to him – the missing

money in the envelope. There had never been a satisfactory explanation. Kelly's face had been the very picture of injured innocence when he'd tackled her.

Perhaps it would be a good idea to keep an eye on her for a time . . .

THIRTY-ONE

1968

Lazarus emerged from his room just as Lisa let herself in through the stage door.

'Darling,' he squealed, 'I've hardly seen you all week. You've been dashing up and down like a yo-yo.'

She sank down on the stairs and kicked off her shoes. 'Rushed off my feet, Lazarus. Those damn women this morning – I'm glad that shoot's over.'

Lazarus smiled benignly. 'Oh come on, it can't be that bad – surely you can get perks?'

She pulled a face. 'Not unless you're in the market for foundation garments for the larger lady – it was for a catalogue. Honestly, they made such a fuss about their hair and make-up – you wouldn't believe most of them were only being photographed from the waist down.'

Lazarus squeezed his bottom into the gap beside her. 'What's on tomorrow?'

She started to pull on her shoes. 'I'm going to meet this soap manufacturer – we're shooting a series of ads for him, starting first thing.'

Lazarus peeled himself off the stairs. 'So you're finished for the day? Come in and I'll make us a nice cup of tea.'

She rose to her feet and began to climb the stairs. 'Sorry – got to arrange things with the film director this afternoon, make sure everything's ready for morning.' Halfway up the stairs she stopped and turned. 'Oh Lazarus – you wouldn't do me a favour, would you? Take my stuff to the launderette for me?'

He stared up at her with mock horror. 'What, again? I took them last week – and the week before.'

She gave him her sweetest smile. 'I won't have time – I haven't got a clean pair of pants to my name.'

'I don't know,' he said reproachfully, reluctant to forsake his role. 'Don't they allow you time off to see to your own chores these days? Do I have to be everyone's dogsbody?'

'Please, Lazarus – for me?'

He hunched thin shoulders, folding his arms across his chest like the proverbial pantomime dame, and made to go back into his room. 'Serve you right if you had to go out without your pretty undies on,' he grumbled. 'Too busy hob-nobbing with film stars.'

Lisa put on a severe tone. 'You're not going to let me down, are you – Keith?'

Lazarus turned in the doorway and gave her a mortified look. 'Oh, all right then – if you put it like that.'

The director sat behind his desk and told her of his plans. Lisa listened, then leaned her elbows on the desk.

'Sounds good,' she said, 'but Martin Lewis says Mr Owen is a pretty obstinate sort of man. He'll want to keep interfering, so I suggest the best thing we can do is flatter him – make him think everything's his idea.'

The director tapped his pencil thoughtfully on the wooden surface. 'He's already approved the scripts, hasn't he?'

'On paper, yes, but Martin says he can be a bit of a bastard, so watch out.'

The director pushed the pencil into his top pocket. 'OK, we soft-soap the soap man. Anything else?'

'The locations – you weren't happy with the last one we chose, the shop.'

He shook his head. 'Too clinical. I visualized something more welcoming, the old-fashioned kind with lots of mahogany and funny-shaped bottles.'

'Have you seen anywhere that would fill the bill?'

'Not yet – but we've time enough before the end of the week. By then we'll be sick of the sight of Amorelle. I ask you – what a damn stupid name for a bar of soap. You can tell what kind of man your Mr Owen is.'

Lisa smiled as she rose to leave. 'You can't blame him for that – our firm suggested it.'

She didn't like the feel of Vincent Owen from the moment she laid eyes on him. When she arrived at the studio, the bathroom scene was already set up and he was standing talking to the director, waving his hands in elaborate gesticulation.

He was tall, and some women would no doubt say he was good-looking in a craggy sort of way, with reddish hair and a freckled face which seemed to be creased into a permanent smile. But it wasn't a genuine smile – it had a greasy, ingratiating flavour about it, as if he expected people to fall prey instantly to its Celtic charm.

'Well, hello,' he said, turning away from the director and spreading the smile wide as he advanced with outstretched hand. 'My, my, I didn't expect the agency to give me such a beauty to look after me.'

His voice was as oily and ingratiating as the smile, deep and rich with the lilt of the Welsh valleys, but there was little sincerity in its effusiveness.

She gave him the briefest of handshakes. 'It's my job, Mr Owen. I'm liaising here so if you have any problems, refer them to me.'

The smile didn't slip as he stood close to her, too close for comfort. 'You ought to be under the bubbles,' he said affably. 'With a face and figure like yours we couldn't go wrong.'

Over his shoulder she saw the director's eyes roll

ceilingwards. She took a seat on a side bench, well out of camera-shot. Mr Owen watched appreciatively as she crossed her legs.

'Nice legs too,' he murmured, and came to sit beside her.

Slimeball. She was going to have trouble with this one. Determining to ignore him, she turned her attention to the set. It looked good – a pale, opalescent bath with gold-plated taps mounted on red velvet-covered steps where thick towels lay strewn, and behind hung red velvet drapes. With the strong arc lights playing on the rich colours it looked luxurious and strangely incongruous in its surroundings. The camera would not expose the cracked white-tiled wall behind the drapes, nor the dusty floor with its litter of trailing cables and cigarette ends. A thick layer of bubbles glistened on the surface of the water. All that was missing was the girl.

To the uninitiated eye the scene looked chaotic, with technicians standing around, hands deep in pockets or puffing on fag-ends while they waited for the order to begin. The director glanced at his watch. On the far side of the room a young man was setting up a tripod. Lisa looked again, and cried out.

'Chris – I don't believe it – Chris!'

She was halfway across the room already. The young man looked up, then his face split into a grin. 'Lisa – my God!'

His arms were round her and he was hugging her close. At last he held her at arm's length. 'You look great – you haven't changed a bit since St Ives.'

She laughed. 'You have – last time I saw you, you had hair down your back and wore Jesus sandals – walking along the beach, taking snaps of anyone who'd buy them.'

She looked him up and down, the well-cut black hair, the open-necked shirt and jeans. 'Whoever would have dreamed you'd ever become respectable?' she teased. 'When they said someone called Winterton was doing the stills I never dreamt it was you.'

He laughed, a deep, throaty laugh. 'It took me a second to recognize you without the caftan and love beads.' He broke off and looked around. 'And David – is he here? How is the old rogue?'

Lisa's smile fell away. 'He's dead, Chris. Died last spring. Brain tumour.'

The director's voice cut in. 'If everyone's finally ready, we'll get started, OK? Tell Fiona we're ready to shoot.'

Chris touched her arm. 'I'm so sorry. Look – I'll see you when we break.'

Lisa returned to her seat on the bench. She was aware that Mr Owen was watching her closely.

'About lunch,' he began, 'I've found a nice little place near here—'

'Sorry, Mr Owen, I've already arranged lunch.'

'Oh please, call me Vincent. Everyone does. What about dinner then? My hotel – we can talk over how the shooting's going.'

She gave him a thin smile. 'Let's see how it goes first, shall we?'

'Oh.' She saw the disappointed look as he turned away, and then the sudden gleam of interest which leapt into his eyes. She followed his gaze. Fiona had arrived on the set and was slithering out of her macintosh.

She stood by the side of the bath in bra and panties, dipping her toe into the bubbles. Without a trace of embarrassment she slipped out of the bra and into the water. Lisa heard Owen's quick intake of breath.

'Wow!' he murmured. 'Now she's something else.'

When lunchtime came Mr Owen disappeared with Fiona. Lisa and Chris ate sandwiches in a nearby coffee bar.

'Fiona's expensive,' Chris remarked. 'It'll cost him if he's going to get anywhere with her.'

'Oh?' said Lisa, swallowing a mouthful of egg and cress. 'And how would you know?'

'She's my landlady.'

'Nothing else?'

Chris looked horrified. 'Good Lord no! I couldn't afford Fiona – she likes the heady life. I've seen the Bentleys and Rolls that come for her. But she's OK. We often work together – actually, she put in a word for me and got me this Amorelle job.'

Lisa regarded him thoughtfully over her coffee cup. 'Don't you have a girlfriend then?' she asked. 'I'd have thought you'd have settled down by now.'

He shook his head. 'I'm still footloose and fancy-free. I like it that way. Means I can concentrate on my work.'

She nodded. She shared the feeling. He had changed to some extent from the Chris of the old days who didn't give a damn about the future, but he still had the same old easygoing attitude towards women. Sunny and light-hearted, he'd never had to make the effort to pursue them – they'd chased him.

She felt easy in his company, she thought as they made their way along the street to the studio for the afternoon's shooting. He was sauntering along, hands deep in pockets and whistling. Suddenly he stopped.

'Fancy going to the pictures tonight?' he asked.

'I'd love to.'

As they turned the corner she almost collided with the director, his face flushed with pleasure. 'Lisa,' he said breathlessly, grabbing her arm, 'I've found it – the perfect shop for the last ad and it's just round the corner – come and see.'

Chris smiled and went on his way. Lisa let the director lead her on along the crowded pavements, threading their way between lunchtime shoppers. It wasn't just round the corner but three streets away.

He pointed to a tall building on the far side of the road, and Lisa recognized it as the one Harold Braithwaite had pointed out with pride.

'What about that then?' said the director eagerly. 'Bullseye windows, brass poles, the lot. Absolutely perfect. Do you think you could find out who owns it?'

Lisa smiled. 'Well, I think I could do even better. I know who owns the building.'

Vincent Owen's face was aglow when he returned, late, with Fiona on his arm. He sat, enraptured, while the afternoon's shooting went on. Lisa watched as Fiona exerted her power to the full.

'My hair's getting wet at the back,' she said wistfully.

The director sighed. 'Someone tuck the ends up for her,' he said wearily.

'And the water's getting cold,' she complained. 'I can't afford to catch my death.'

The director tried to sound patient. 'Oh, come on, love. Only a few minutes more – you can manage.'

She turned huge eyes on the soap manufacturer. 'Vincent?'

He stood up. 'Change the water,' he ordered. 'We can't have her catching pneumonia.'

She rewarded him with a sultry smile and he sat down to watch her step out of the water. His eyes gleamed as someone draped a towel around her glistening body. Lisa caught Chris's eye and they smiled.

Mr Owen turned to Lisa. 'She's good, isn't she? I've been thinking – why don't we shoot the whole series round her? There's no need to use the other models.'

Lisa took a deep breath. 'I don't think that's a good idea, Mr Owen. You've talked this over at length with our people, I'm sure, and they've gone to a lot of trouble to see your ideas carried out. The whole strategy is to show the universal appeal of Amorelle – that was your idea, that's why we've engaged the others.'

He rubbed his freckled nose for a moment. 'I guess you're right – I should stick to my first instinct. It's stood me in good stead so far.'

Ten minutes later Fiona dipped her toe into the fresh water. Her lips rounded into a pout and for a second Lisa thought she was going to wail that it was too hot, but she lowered herself gingerly under the bubbles. Mr Owen sat entranced.

'Right then, Fiona,' said the director, 'once more. Lay the bar of soap against your cheek.'

'The Amorelle,' muttered Mr Owen. 'Always refer to the product by name.'

Fiona wrinkled her little nose. 'Do I have to? I never let soap near my face – my skin's getting dried out.'

'A dry bar of soap,' said the director patiently.

'It's not now – it's all wet,' Fiona pouted.

Lisa felt the bench jerk as Mr Owen sprang to his feet and hurried across to the bath. He knelt on the steps and murmured to Fiona, so softly Lisa could hardly hear the words. 'It's Amorelle, love – made from a secret recipe with exotic oils which emulsify the skin – it can't harm your pretty face, I swear.'

Oh boy, thought Lisa. He was believing his own blurb now. Fiona gave him a mischievous look and dabbed a sudsy finger on his nose.

'Oh, all right then – for you.'

For the rest of the week Owen appeared only briefly at the shooting sessions. Lisa could see the crew's secret smiles as soon as he turned to leave.

'Well she got him hooked and no mistake.'

At least they could proceed unhampered. In every free moment Chris sought her out, and Lisa found herself enjoying his easy company. They laughed at

303

the cinema together, strolled in the park together, and then one night she took him back to the flat for coffee.

'This is terrific,' he remarked as he steered a careful path between the kettle drum and a plaster cast of Venus de Milo. 'I thought Fiona's place was exotic.'

He took the coffee mug from her and nodded towards the canvases in the corner. 'Are those David's?' he asked. 'They're really good. You ought to do something with them.'

'I know. I plan to, one day. It's knowing how, and who to get in touch with.'

'I could talk to a friend of mine – he works in an art gallery.'

She looked up eagerly. 'Could you? I'd be so grateful.'

He gave a warm smile. 'No trouble. Remind me tomorrow.'

She leaned back in her chair, relaxed and content. She liked being with him, he was good company. Perhaps life could begin again after all.

As he was leaving he turned in the doorway. 'By the way, we're having a bit of a party tomorrow night to celebrate wrapping it all up. My place as I'm the new boy on the team. It's a tradition they've just thought up. You will come, won't you?'

She hesitated before answering. It was a long time since she'd been to a party, and never alone since her student days.

'Thanks, Chris – I'd like that.'

She heard the stage door close behind him. She stood by the rain-spattered window and watched as he emerged into the street, pausing under the lamp to turn up his collar against the drizzle. He was good to look at with his wide-set shoulders and blond hair. She remembered teasing David in the old days.

'If ever I fancied any other man in St Ives, it would be Chris Winterton.'

She watched his long stride as he moved away up the street. Why shouldn't she go to the party? After all, it would do her good to socialize.

As she turned she caught sight of the canvases arrayed in a row like accusing faces, and she flushed.

'I'm only going to a party, dammit,' she snapped. 'I'm not going to try and seduce him.'

Turning her back on the canvases she peeled off her clothes and dropped them on the bed. Come on now, don't be a slut – she slipped the dark grey suit on to a hanger and found another for the simple white shirt. She replaced them in the wardrobe and ran a finger along the rail.

All her working clothes were citified and sober, not a single item of spicy nonsense amongst them. Nothing she could wear to a party.

'Right,' she said defiantly, 'tomorrow I'm off to Carnaby Street. I'm going to get something that will really knock their eyes out.'

As she climbed into bed she cast one last rebellious glance at the silent row of posters. 'And don't you look at me like that,' she ordered. 'You weren't even faithful to me while you were alive.'

She searched the length of Carnaby Street and the King's Road before she found it. The air was filled with the noise of excited shoppers and tinny pop music blaring from busy record shops. She riffled through row upon row of rails on the pavements, fingering multitudes of wild fabrics and psychedelic colours until she came across the very thing, a froth of sea-green chiffon shot with a fine gold thread and with the hemline dipping into handkerchief points. It was frivolous, it was wispy to the point of being daring, and she felt guiltily excited at the thought of wearing it.

Clutching her trophy she pushed her way along the crowded street towards home. She'd just reached the corner when the poster caught her eye. It stood cock-eyed in the shop window: *Melanie*.

She screwed up her eyes against the sunlight to see it better. It was her name, but not her face. The poster proclaimed a wellknown American folksinger's latest record.

For a moment she stared. The name alone was enough to stir up ungovernable anger. She swung the carrier bag high in the air and shook it at the smiling face.

'I'll show you, Melanie,' she vowed. 'Just you watch me.'

THIRTY-TWO

1968

James came across Fred sitting on the wall edging Gorsey Field, his cap pulled well down over his eyes and a blade of grass between his teeth.

'Hey up, Fred,' he said cheerily. 'Still debating whether or not to go to Butlin's?'

Fred shook his head and removed the blade of grass. 'If that's what Thelma wants I reckon we shall go. Nay, I were watching that lot down there – them hippies in caravans.'

James climbed on the wall beside him. From here he could see them, three dilapidated caravans towed by battered lorries. A half-dozen or so figures moved about them, a couple of children and a yapping dog. One of the figures was a girl in a loose-fitting Indian dress which floated about her ankles. She looked like Lisa, the first time David brought her home.

'They're hippies all right,' said Fred. 'Remember when your lad wore beads like that? He were always on about peace, and making love not war. It were all peace and flowers, weren't it?'

'How long have they been there?' James asked.

'Just pulled up this aft,' said Fred. 'Have I to tell 'em to shift? They've no right to be there.'

'No, leave them,' said James. 'They're doing no harm. They'll probably be on their way again in the morning.'

Fred shook his head and sighed. 'Things haven't half changed since I were a lad. Your father'd have chased them off like a shot and no mistake.'

James smiled. 'Dad had to make that field work for

him, we don't. Things have changed a lot since his day.'

Fred pushed back the neb of his cap. 'Ay,' he murmured. 'Remember them big longhorns we used to have – pulled the plough for us? I can still recall their names.'

'Damsel and Carnation. Do you remember old Rufus?'

Fred chuckled. 'How could I forget? The old sod led me one hell of a dance. Many's the time I threatened to cut him into rashers.'

Those were the days, thought James affectionately, when the farm teemed with cattle and goats and sheep, and the pigs roamed free outdoors, scratching around the orchard for windfall apples and farrowing under sheets of tin. He remembered how Dad used to grumble.

'Funny how they always choose to do it just at supper time. It's as if they know, the little buggers.'

It was all very well to be nostalgic about the past, but those hectic days had been filled with back-breaking grind and there'd been little time even to think. Thanks to Anna that world had given way to an easier life; now it had shrunk to what he wanted – peace, and his guns. The business was doing well. The waiting list was growing, and now there was the antique sale to look forward to and the chance to see Lisa again . . .

A movement down the field caught his eye. The girl in the Indian frock was running across the grass and a burly man with dark hair flowing from under a headband was chasing her. James watched as he closed in on her, the girl darting this way and that in an effort to elude him, hampered by her long skirt. And then he saw the big man raise his arm and give her a hefty crack across the cheek.

Before the girl's cry reached him he was running downhill towards them. The girl was cowering, her arms above her head to ward off further attack. The man grabbed a handful of her long hair.

'You get back there this instant or I'll flay the hide off you,' he shouted. Then he looked up as he saw James come running.

'Let her go,' James ordered. 'And don't you touch her again.'

The man drew himself up, his dark eyes level with James's. 'Oh yes?' he mocked. 'And what gives you the right to interfere? She's my missus and she'll do as she's told.'

'You won't hit her,' said James firmly. 'Not unless you want the same treatment. And you'll get off this land this minute.'

The girl circled warily out of reach as the big man put his hands on his hips and laughed. 'Oh – who says? It's common land—'

'It's my land. Pack your things and get on your way.'

The man took a stride forward. 'And who's going to make me?' he sneered.

Without a word James grabbed his arm and swung him about, wrenching it halfway up his back. As the big man squealed he pushed him towards the parked caravans.

'Leave off – you're breaking my arm!'

'That's nothing to what I'll break if I see you touch her again,' muttered James. He was aware of the little knot of people clustered around the lorries, watching in silence.

'Which is his?' he demanded of a faded-looking youth with spectacles. The youth pointed to the lead lorry. James yanked open the door and, letting go of his arm, shoved the big man's behind. 'Get in. And don't let me see you here again.'

The man sat muttering and rubbing his arm. The girl slammed the caravan door shut and climbed in the lorry's passenger seat. The others trickled away to their own vehicles.

309

One of the children was staring up at James. He turned and ran to his mother. 'Was that man going to hit Dave?' he asked.

'Never mind that – shut up and get in,' his mother replied, and James fancied he saw her lips flicker as she tried not to smile.

The lorries lumbered away at last, leaving the gate open. James closed it and retraced his steps to where Fred still sat on the wall.

'Well that's got shot of them,' Fred murmured round the blade of grass in his mouth.

'Yes,' said James. 'Thanks for your help.'

'Don't mention it. It's a good job he were more frightened than you were.'

James smiled. 'It's a good job he didn't realize it. See you in the morning.'

As he set off down the lane he heard Fred's voice call after him. 'If I'm honest with mesen, Jim, I was a bit impressed with all that. Well done, lad.'

James felt light-headed. What on earth had possessed him to wade in like that? It was a damn stupid thing to do, take on a burly fellow twenty years his junior. Was it because that girl reminded him of Lisa?

To be honest, he missed Lisa. Perhaps missed her more than he ought . . .

Lisa could hear the party was in full swing before Chris opened the door to her. The sound of laughter and loud pop music wafted from the windows and down the length of the mews.

'Come on in,' said Chris, holding the door wide. 'You're late – you've already missed out on the first five drinks.'

Lisa slipped out of her coat and turned to him eagerly. 'Did you talk to your friend today?'

His eyes looked already misty with wine as he frowned. 'What friend?'

'At the art gallery – remember? You said you'd have a word with him about David's posters.'

He screwed up his face. 'Oh shit – I forgot. Never mind, I'll get round to it, I promise. First thing Monday. Now come on in and get some vino down you.'

She watched as he poured the red liquid into a glass, then she looked around the room. The director lolled on a settee, deep in conversation with a brunette wearing a microscopic mini dress. The rest of the team were there, and several other faces she didn't recognize.

'Beautiful house,' she said. 'It's fabulous.'

Chris smiled. 'Fiona's made a lot of money and she believes in spending it on comfort. I'm not complaining. She said we can use the whole house for the party, not just my bit.'

'Is she here?'

'She's out with your soap man again. She'll be along later. Here, let me top you up.'

As he tilted the bottle over her glass his gaze rested on her cleavage. 'Wow – some dress,' he murmured. 'You look like a mermaid. Terrific. You can swim into my pool any time.'

Putting down the bottle he slipped his arm about her waist and drew her towards the circle by the fire. Lisa felt good. The director looked up, then his face broke into a smile.

'Lisa – I didn't recognize you at first,' he confessed. 'You look completely different without the suit and briefcase.'

'That's the working me,' she laughed. 'Tonight I'm off duty and free as a bird.'

Yes, I am, she thought. Free to be whatever I want to be. I'm going to enjoy this.

Someone passed round the pot. Out of curiosity she took the cigarette Chris offered and put it between

311

her lips. Maybe it was because she wasn't used to smoking, but it tasted pretty awful. Maybe it was the wine, but she felt more relaxed, more at ease with herself than she had for ages. So relaxed time seemed to fade into insignificance, and it came as a surprise to realize at last that everyone had gone. She and Chris were alone.

Soft music was still playing somewhere, and a thin haze of cigarette smoke hung under the low beams. Chris was sitting beside her, his arm thrown along the back of the settee behind her head, a lazy smile on his lips.

'Penny for your thoughts,' he murmured.

'I haven't any. I'm too sleepy.'

'Shall I tell you mine?'

'Are they repeatable?'

'No.'

'Tell me.'

His arm slipped down around her shoulders. He pressed his nose into her hair, close to her ear. She listened to his whispered words, spoken in snatches between gentle kisses on her ear lobe, conjuring up liquid images of undulating waves and slippery, elusive creatures. There was magic in his words, in his touch as persuasive as his tongue. She bathed in the warm, languorous headiness of being admired and desired. It was intoxicating, wonderful . . .

At last he rose and held out his hand. Was it he who was unsteady on his feet, or was it her? What the hell did it matter?

'Coming, little mermaid?' he said.

She smiled as she stood up, wavering a little, and took his hand. It felt warm and kind as she followed him into the bedroom . . .

Lisa awoke suddenly to the crash of a milk crate in the street. She yawned and stretched leisurely, her whole body suffused with warmth and the pleasantly satiated sensation of a cat who has dined on cream.

The pale grey light of dawn filtered in around the edge of the curtains, and it seemed to her hazy mind that something was odd.

The curtains – they weren't trailing clumsily on the floor, the thick drapes hung straight, with ornate swagging at the top. And the sheets felt sensuously smooth and satiny. She looked around the room in the half-light. It definitely wasn't her room. And then she became aware of the warmth next to her – another body in the bed.

She rolled over on her elbow. A tousled fair head lay on the pillow, and below it the sleeping face of Chris. Of course. She remembered now, and felt a faint touch of embarrassment. She'd been making love with this man who for years had been nothing more than a friend.

But it had been good, even if she wasn't in love with him. Lying skin to skin, feeling herself respond to gentle persuasion. It had been a wonderful night, given over to the wild impulse of instinct, and she'd savoured every moment.

He had been a caring lover, anxious to pleasure her rather than seek his own gratification. She looked down at the sleeping face with affection.

He moved and she saw the smile curving his lips. He was nice, she thought – forgetful, unreliable maybe, but he was kind and he meant well.

Without warning the bedroom door suddenly opened. A woman's figure stood in the doorway, framed against the light in the corridor. For a moment she stood silent. Chris stirred and opened his eyes.

'Oh, I'm sorry, Chris,' the girl said. 'I thought you'd be up and about by now.'

Lisa recognized the sultry tone. It was Fiona. Chris half sat up. Fiona caught sight of Lisa. 'Oh no,' she said, a pained tone in her voice. 'Who have you got this time?'

313

Chris fell back on the pillow. 'I'm sorry,' he mumbled, 'only your bed's bigger than mine.'

Fiona took a step forward, peering round the covers. 'It's the girl from the last shoot, isn't it? Lisa?' She moved back towards the door. 'Well, I'll just go and have a shower and maybe I'll join you later. See you.'

The door closed. Lisa sat stunned, staring down at Chris. 'What did she mean, join us?' she whispered. 'Did she mean the three of us – in bed together?'

He made no answer, only smiled. Suspicion began to grow. 'She did, didn't she?' Lisa demanded. 'You know her better than you led me to believe. How often have you done this before?'

He rolled over and buried his smile in the pillow. Lisa felt suddenly sick. 'Oh my God,' she moaned, and leapt out of bed, turning over trailing sheets to find her clothes. She snatched up the green frock from the floor and pulled it over her head, but nowhere could she see her underwear. She ran a hand under the bed, but found only an empty wine bottle lying on its side.

'Oh sod it,' she muttered. *Forget it. Get out of here. Suddenly I feel sick.*

Chris sat up as she wrenched the door open. 'Wait a minute – Lisa – where are you going?' he called, but she ran away down the corridor and into the living room. It looked chaotic with cushions strewn on the floor, cigarette ends piled in ashtrays and dregs of wine, and the stink of stale smoke still lingering under the low ceiling. The place looked sordid in the cold morning light. She wanted to be out of here, be back home again in the quiet of the flat.

The morning air struck chill through the flimsy green frock but she ran on, heedless, along London's deserted streets with tears of vexation stinging her eyes. She was barely aware of the rain starting to splash.

314

*   *   *

Lazarus wasn't about yet when she let herself in at the stage door. If she moved quietly she could reach the stairs and he'd never know she'd been out all night.

But for some reason her feet took her past the stairs and along the corridor to the stage. As she pushed the door open and stepped into the wings she could smell the auditorium, a mingled scent of dust and fusty old upholstery. Switching on one of the lights she wandered on to the stage.

The set lay ready for the night's performance, a kitchen table and chairs and an old settee. Another kitchen sink drama they were so fond of, she thought, raging husbands and beaten-down wives, the opportunity to stamp and rage and act their hearts out. As if life wasn't full enough of real drama.

She slumped miserably on the settee and gazed out over the black emptiness of the auditorium. She felt cheap, stale with last night's make-up still crusting her face, like a whore just risen from bed after satisfying her latest customer. And her body felt cold beneath the damp frock.

She felt cheated. Last night had seemed so wonderful – until Fiona had burst in. *'Don't mind me – maybe I'll join you later.'*

She'd said it with easy comfort, like a woman who expected it to be accepted. As if she was already on intimate terms with Chris. And he hadn't denied it. Lisa buried her fingers in the green chiffon folds of her skirt. It clung wetly to her thighs.

'Let's face it, you're no better than a whore,' she groaned. 'Wearing this thing, getting drunk and letting him take me to bed.'

No, that wasn't fair. She'd wanted to go to bed with him. It had all been what she wanted, until that blasted woman came in and spoilt everything. It was her own fault if she felt cheap and dirty.

She looked up. On the far flat there was a window, and through it she could see a view of rolling fields and trees. They'd hung a landscape beyond the window to simulate distance, and the view was – surely – one of David's paintings?

She crossed the set to see it better. Yes, it was his work, and she felt the tears pricking her eyes. It was a scene near Jericho. Jericho – how she ached for the peace of the place, far from sleazy London – if only she could be there now . . .

Lazarus was yawning noisily as he fetched the milk in off the doorstep. As he was about to turn into his room he caught sight of the open door to the stage. Funny – he could swear he'd closed it last night before Robin came to call for him.

Putting the milk bottles down on the table he went back to check. There was a solitary light on stage – and someone sitting there on the set. A girl – it was Lisa. What was she doing up so early, and on stage too?

She looked up as he came close. 'Hello, Lazarus.' Her eyes looked red, as if she'd been crying.

'Hello, love. You all right?' He perched himself on the arm of the settee.

She gave him a thin smile, but it held none of its usual warmth. 'I'm fine,' she said. 'Went to an all-night party.'

'Nice,' he said doubtfully, 'but you don't look like you enjoyed it much.'

'I did – up to a point. What have you been doing?'

He spread long fingers and smiled as he inspected his nails. 'Robin came for me – he took me out for my birthday.'

'That's good. Did he buy you a nice present?'

Lazarus smiled. 'Melanie's latest record. It's lovely.'

'Melanie?' She looked up at him sharply.

'The pop singer – she writes all her own songs.'

Lisa nodded. 'Oh yes. I saw an ad in a shop window.'

'You can borrow it if you like.' Lazarus stood up. As he did so his hand brushed her hair. 'Gracious me, you're soaking,' he exclaimed. 'You'd better go and get changed before you catch your death.'

As she rose to leave he watched her go. 'I don't know,' he said sadly, shaking his head, 'I thought you were joking when you said you hadn't any undies left. I didn't think you meant it.'

Half an hour later she emerged from the bathroom. The green dress still lay on the floor where she'd stepped out of it. She kicked it aside as Lazarus tapped at the door and came in. He held out the record.

'Just brought you this to listen to – you'll love it,' he said.

He put it down on the bed and scuttled away. She pulled the cord of her robe tighter and picked it up curiously. *Melanie*, it shrieked on the sleeve, and under it the title, *Leftover Wine*.

She sat on the edge of the bed, turning it over on her lap. Ironic, she thought. That's just how I feel, like dregs slopping around in the bottom of a bottle. She turned the sleeve over.

Once again Melanie's familiar themes – of the stifling nature of city life which brings sadness, of the need to return to the simplicity of country life in order to survive spiritually . . .

Downstairs the telephone rang. She heard footsteps and then Lazarus called up the stairs. 'Lisa – it's your friend with the lovely voice.'

It was James. 'Lisa? Just wanted to tell you I'm coming down to an antiques sale next Thursday – any chance we could meet?'

At the sound of his warm, enthusiastic tone, the world suddenly seemed a cleaner, saner place. For a second she was tempted to tell him that more than anything in the world she wanted to go back with him to Jericho, but she held her tongue.

He was talking eagerly. 'And I'll bring David's picture down for you – I've had it framed now.'

'No – keep it,' she cut in. 'It belongs in Jericho.'

'I'm looking forward to seeing you again, love,' he said softly. 'There's so much I want to tell you.'

THIRTY-THREE

1968

James perched on a high stool at the corner of the bar so that he could see her the moment she came through the door. Around him lunchtime drinkers eddied, jostling to catch the barman's attention and calling out in over-loud voices. It wasn't like this in the Rose and Crown.

He sipped his drink, seeing in his mind's eye how she would look when she came in, anticipating the slightly bewildered expression on her pretty face as she searched for him among the drinkers, and then her quick smile of recognition. But the minutes were ticking by. She was a quarter of an hour late already, and he'd arranged to meet O'Hara at the sale room at two.

Someone reached past him to get a glass from the bar. He craned his head so as not to lose his view of the door, and felt a sudden leap of pleasure. She stood in the doorway, shaking her long hair back as she looked around the room. Then he saw her eyes light up as she caught sight of him and walked quickly across.

'James – oh, it's lovely to see you.'

She was holding out her arms, her hands sliding around his neck and her face upturned. He bent his head and touched a kiss to her lips, warm and soft.

Her hands fell away and she stood back. Suddenly he felt awkward. He shouldn't have kissed her like that – he'd embarrassed her. They'd only ever kissed on the cheek before, warmly but briefly, like father and child. He searched her face. It didn't seem to have ruffled her. He breathed a sigh of relief. She seemed so poised here in the city.

'It's wonderful to see you again, love,' he said gently. 'You look great.'

The generous mouth curved in a way he remembered well. 'You too,' she said, taking a seat on the stool he'd vacated. 'Sorry I'm late – the appointment I made for Mr Braithwaite ran over. By the way, I asked him to join us – you don't mind, do you?'

'Of course not.' It was good just to look at her, be aware that others in the room couldn't help looking with appreciation at this pretty girl with swinging blonde hair and slim legs. There was a glow about her.

'How's business?' she asked as he signalled to the barman.

He smiled. 'I put an ad in a gun magazine and I got enquiries from as far away as America. What would you like to drink?'

'Lime and lemon, please.' She crossed her legs and leaned back against the bar. 'If your guns are so sought after maybe you should take on some extra staff.'

He spoke a few words to the barman and turned back to her. 'It's not that easy, finding people with the right skills. It takes years to become a real craftsman. I don't want to settle for the second-rate – I want only the best. So I have to build slowly.'

He became aware that she was watching him closely, a faint smile touching the corners of her lips. 'I'm sorry,' he said. 'I'm riding my hobby horse again, aren't I?'

The hint of a smile broke out into a full-blooded beam. 'I love your enthusiasm, James,' she said. 'I wouldn't change you for the world.'

He smiled and glanced at his watch. 'Look, love, I haven't got a lot of time – I'll have to leave in half an hour for an appointment in St James. Shall we grab a sandwich and maybe you'll let me take you out to dinner to make up for it?'

'Fine. Mr Braithwaite won't be needing me tonight.'

They had almost finished eating when Lisa suddenly looked up. 'Ah, here he is now.'

She waved her glass towards the door. Turning, he saw a tall, broad figure coming towards them. He looked a typical prosperous businessman with his well-cut suit, well-groomed grey hair and confident manner. Lisa's smile of welcome proved how much she liked him.

'Mr Braithwaite, I'd like you to meet a friend of mine – James Hemingway,' she said.

'Harold Braithwaite,' the man boomed, offering a firm handshake. 'I'm delighted to meet any friend of Lisa's. Mind if I join you?'

He was already pulling up a chair. 'You're very welcome,' said James. 'But I'm afraid I've got to be at Christie's by two.'

'Business or pleasure?' asked Braithwaite.

'I'm meeting this American chap at the auction. He's interested in one of my guns.'

'Guns?' echoed Braithwaite. 'Nasty things. I never shoot 'em myself, just collect 'em, specially copies of antiques.'

James saw Lisa's look of surprise. 'Do you?' she said. 'I didn't know that.'

'Anything mechanical, I collect – like my racing cars,' said Braithwaite proudly. 'Anything mechanical fascinates me. Dates from my apprentice days in the mill, I reckon.' He turned to James. 'I didn't inherit my brass, you know. I came up the hard way – made every penny of it myself. I'm what they call a self-made man.'

'Well done,' said James.

'This sale at Christie's you talk about – is it guns then?'

'Yes – antique copies, actually – miniatures.' James

321

bent to pick up his briefcase, opened it, and took out the velvet-wrapped bundle. Unrolling it, he laid the miniature gun on the table.

Braithwaite's eyes rounded. 'That's beautiful,' he said, laying a reverent finger on the stock. 'German, fifteenth century, isn't it?'

James felt a glow of pleasure. Here was a man who knew what he was talking about. 'Sixteenth, actually,' he said, 'but the features are the same.'

'Ivory inlay – stained green just like the originals,' murmured Braithwaite. 'It's a real beauty – it must have cost you a pretty penny. How did you come by it?'

'I made it,' said James.

When he had gone Braithwaite still sat marvelling. 'I find it hard to believe,' he said to Lisa. 'He says it were only a hobby, yet he produces a scale copy like that. He's a ruddy genius.'

Lisa smiled. 'He was an armourer, you know. He learned his craft the hard way too.'

'Even so, craftsmanship like that, perfect in every detail – I've never seen anything like it. Did you see the carving he's done on the ivory, that hunting scene? It's exactly like the originals. He must have the patience of Job, that man. He'll go far. He's a true artist.'

'Yes,' Lisa agreed. 'It runs in the family.'

Braithwaite rubbed his chin thoughtfully. 'Does he have many contacts in the States, do you know?' he asked.

'I don't think so. Only this one today.'

'Ay, well, I think I might be able to help him there. I've got a lot of respect for him – I feel he's a man you can trust.'

'Absolutely,' said Lisa. 'With your life.'

'I want to meet him again,' said Braithwaite, pushing his chair back. 'I like him.'

Lisa held up her glass to the light. 'And so say all

of us,' she said fervently, and tossed back the last of her drink.

The Reverend Bax laid aside the newspaper, drained the last of his dry sherry and nerved himself to head for the kitchen. At least Kelly had taken to peeling a few potatoes for him each day so dinner had become a relatively easy matter. The only problem was what was to go with the chips.

A fried egg, perhaps, or maybe a bit of that cold ham. Or he could even spoil himself and have both – why not? Washed down with a glass of red wine and finished off with a nice crisp apple for dessert, he'd be fortified enough to return to his paperwork for another couple of hours.

As he was crossing the hallway he heard a creak upstairs. What was that? He stopped and listened. Surely Kelly had gone home ages ago. There it was again – the creak of a floorboard. Could someone have got into the house while he'd been immersed in his work?

He tiptoed cautiously up the stairs and crept along the landing. Stupid – he should have remembered to pick up his heavy blackthorn walking stick from the umbrella stand. Listen – there it was again – a groaning sound, coming from Sarah's room.

He was about to grab hold of the doorknob and march in, but then he saw the crack of light down the edge of the door where it was not quite closed. He moved nearer, and put his eye to the crack. As he did so he heard the sound of someone humming softly.

It was a girl's voice, and the next moment his eyeballs almost started from their sockets as a girl's naked back came into view. It was Kelly, stripped to the waist and wearing only the tiniest pair of pants. She was reaching up into the wardrobe, unaware of him.

He stood, transfixed and breathless, taking guilty

delight in the slim suppleness of her, the downy texture of her skin. It looked firm, not like Sarah's sagging flesh, and the sight brought back a leaping sensation he'd almost forgotten.

She took down something vivid blue and slid her arms into it, then turned, buttoning it at the neck. He felt a keen stab of disappointment. The lovely little body was hidden from view now by a hip-length blouse; in a moment she'd put on her skirt. He pushed the door open and went in. He heard her gasp, saw her fingers fly to her mouth.

'Well, well,' he said softly. 'Be sure your sins will find you out.'

'Oh Vicar – I didn't hear you coming,' she said in a whisper, her eyes wide in alarm. Then he saw the eyes narrow again as she added, 'What do you mean – sins?'

He crossed to the wardrobe. As he passed her she snatched up a skirt and held it in front of her. 'This,' he said dramatically, pointing to the array of violent colours on the rail. 'All these clothes – they're yours, aren't they?'

'Some of them,' she admitted. 'They're mostly Mrs Bax's.'

'This? And this? And what about these?' He held up a pair of orange boots. 'You're not trying to tell me Mrs Bax ever wore anything so indescribable, surely?'

Kelly gave him a surly look. 'And what if they are mine? I'm not doing any harm.'

He planted the boots on the bed. 'You couldn't afford all these, Kelly – not on what you earn. So where did the money come from?'

'It's none of your business,' she snapped.

He faced her squarely. The buttons of the blouse were still not fastened and he could glimpse the hint of a curve. He licked his lips. 'It is my business,' he said quietly. 'It was the church's money – in that envelope. More than a hundred pounds.'

'It never was,' Kelly blurted, 'there was only eighty—' He saw her colour up violently. Now she'd done it. He touched a trembling finger to her cheek, tracing the curve to her neck. He felt her shiver, but she made no move. Encouraged, he let his hand slip gently down to her breast. It felt firm and warm beneath the cotton. She stood unmoving, looking down at the floor.

'I've seen you down in the wood with your boy-friend,' he murmured.

'What of it?' she muttered.

'He's not the only one, is he?'

She looked up now, and he saw the fear in her eyes. 'What do you mean by that?'

He smiled, remembering his schooldays. She was like the red admiral butterfly he'd chased all afternoon before he scooped it at last in his net.

'I think you know,' he said softly, taking hold of her shoulders and pushing her gently towards the bed. The fearful look in her eyes changed suddenly to terror.

'No,' she whispered, then louder, No!'

He pushed her down, clawing at the blouse, eager to savour the firm, warm body beneath. Her finger-nails clawed at his hands.

'Get off,' she shouted. 'I'll scream for help.'

'I wouldn't if I were you,' he panted, ducking to avoid her nails. 'It isn't as if you haven't done it before – everyone knows your reputation.'

'I'm not a tart – let go of me! I'll tell everybody!'

'Who would believe your word against mine? And what if I told about the money, eh? It would mean a court case, and how would your parents feel about you in prison?'

A button fell to the floor. Kelly stopped flailing her arms and stared at him. 'You wouldn't,' she said faintly. 'You wouldn't do that.'

'Wouldn't I?' said the vicar, wrenching the blouse

325

off her shoulders with fevered fingers. 'Wouldn't I?'

Soft music was playing somewhere in the dark recesses of the restaurant as they finished dessert and the waiter brought coffee. Lisa leaned across to James.

'Mr Braithwaite was terribly impressed with your gun, James. You never told me how you learned to do all that intricate inlaying and engraving. Did you have to study it?'

James stirred his coffee and leaned back. 'I started with plain guns, but even that's tricky work, setting the lock and the other metal parts into the wood of the stock so there's no gap between them. It has to be a perfect fit, so in time I decided to inlay precious metals the same way. Fruit woods and ivory too. It was just a matter of practice.'

She sipped her coffee thoughtfully. 'I don't approve of elephants being killed,' she murmured.

He laughed. 'This one died at least a hundred years ago. I saw this gong set in an antique shop in York, a gong suspended between a pair of tusks. There was enough ivory there to last me a lifetime.'

Lisa nodded. 'With all that elaborate engraving too, those guns are works of art.'

James raised a finger. 'That reminds me – Ellen told me Dorothy took her to an art gallery, someone she knew. It occurred to me that perhaps if she has contacts in the art world—'

'David's pictures?' Lisa interrupted.

'It might be worth ringing her. She only lives an hour away from London.'

'Hello,' a husky voice suddenly cut in. Lisa looked up and recognized with a start the smiling face of Melanie. James put down his napkin and rose from his chair. It was strange how the woman had materialized just as they mentioned David's name.

'Hello,' Lisa said dubiously. Melanie indicated the

326

rangy, bespectacled man behind her. 'My husband and I were just leaving – I felt I couldn't go without having a word with you. How are you getting on?'

She was smiling broadly at James. Lisa felt obliged to be polite. 'James – this is Melanie.'

He took her hand. 'Delighted to meet you,' he said. Lisa felt irritated. It seemed as if Melanie let her hand rest in his just a moment too long before she turned to Lisa.

'It's nice to see you out enjoying yourself,' she said softly. 'I do hope all goes well for you. Goodnight.'

James watched her take her husband's arm and let him lead her away. He sat down again. Lisa toyed with the coffee spoon.

'Beautiful woman,' he murmured.

'Yes,' Lisa said dully.

'But you don't like her very much.'

'No I don't.'

'Why?'

Lisa bit her lip, trying to hold back the tears of vexation. 'That woman slept with David,' she muttered, 'I know she did.'

There, she'd said it. James simply nodded.

'I didn't think you knew.'

She brushed an escaping tear away and stared. 'You knew about it? How could you?'

James's voice was low and reasoned. 'David told me, not long before he died.'

'Oh God!' So it was true. The tears were running free now. James reached across and covered her hand with his.

'It's not that important, you know. He hated himself for it. He never stopped loving you more than anyone else in the world.'

She heard her own sob. James stood up. 'Come on, love, let me take you home.'

As he paid the bill Lisa pulled her coat on and stood waiting by the door. As he joined her he put his arm around her shoulders and drew her out into the street.

They stood on the darkened pavement. James held up his hand to call a taxi, then turned to her. His voice sounded warm, so close to her ear.

'He wanted to tell you but I stopped him. When two people have something as special as you had together – nothing should be allowed to spoil it. Believe me, I know . . .'

THIRTY-FOUR

1942

The war news was far from good. James switched the wireless off and picked up his newspaper again. Doris slapped cutlery down noisily on the table.

'I don't think it's right,' she muttered, 'taking it out on the Prime Minister just because we've lost Tobruk. What do they want with a vote of no confidence – it's not his fault.'

James smiled. 'You always stick up for Winnie, don't you, Doris?'

'Well, he's not the sort to give in, no matter what. He's what we need right now. We ought to be backing him same as he always backs us.'

James glanced at the clock on the mantelshelf. 'Where's Anna?' he asked.

Doris jerked her head towards the stairs. 'Having a lay-down after she put Ellen to bed. This heat's getting to her, poor little love.'

'I know,' said James. 'She'll be glad when it's all over.'

Anna lay on the big bed, her frock unbuttoned to the waist. She felt huge and heavy. It would be a relief when the baby was born. Even with the window wide open there was no breath of air to cool her.

At the beginning she hadn't wanted this baby at all. The memory of labour was still too fresh in her mind. It was a horrible, painful business, and now she couldn't avoid going through it again.

She'd felt cheated when she was caught out – she'd been told it couldn't possibly happen while a woman was breast-feeding. She'd felt angry and let down. The one small consolation was that James was so overjoyed.

It had taken time to think of Ellen as hers. At first she'd seemed just an alien being, depending on her for life, clinging like a leech to her breast. It was odd how, gradually, the baby had taken on an individual personality all of her own, and now she was really quite fond of her. If only she could feel as besotted as all those other mothers in the ward. At least she had hidden her true feelings from James. He must never know.

As it was, she had grown to welcome those smiles and chuckles and those chubby arms around her neck and she would content herself with that.

This time it would be much easier – not the birth itself, perhaps, but she tried to push that from her mind. Coping would be far simpler with the luxuries Grandmother's money had bought – the new telephone put in ready to call the doctor when the moment came, a shining new coach-built pram in the hall with bundles of thick terry towel nappies inside and the baby clothes she'd sewn with the new Frister and Rossman sewing machine. There had even been talk of a nanny.

'I can't for the life of me see why you need one of them,' Doris had grumbled, 'when there's me here and you pay me good wages. Two women – two babies. That's more than enough, I'd have thought.'

It had only been a fleeting idea anyway, soon lost in the joy of being able to buy for James what she knew he needed. It had been hard to persuade him to choose the tractor, and even harder to get him to help her select a couple of riding horses, but she'd won him over in the end. He'd drawn the line at a new car but she was working on that. Dear James – he never looked for anything for himself. It was in his nature to give and it came hard to be on the receiving end. She was a lucky woman.

She heard his voice call up the stairs. 'Anna – supper's ready.'

She levered her weight off the bed, fastened the buttons of her frock and made her way out to the landing. Through the banister rails she could see him waiting for her on the stairs.

Doris watched as James rooted through the contents of the sideboard drawer. 'What's up?' she asked. 'Lost summat?'

'Keys for the van,' said James. 'I've to pick Dorothy up at the station in five minutes.'

Doris growled as she turned her attention back to folding mashed potato into the fish cakes. 'Don't know what she's coming for,' she muttered. 'We could manage quite well without another mouth to feed.'

James pounced on the key. 'You've said yourself there's enough work for two women in this house. She'll be a great help while Anna's in bed.'

As he reached his jacket down off the peg Doris scowled at him. 'Ay, well that's as may be. How long's she stopping?'

James opened the door, then turned. 'As long as she likes. She'll always be welcome here. Now you put the kettle on and we'll have a nice hot cup of tea ready for her the minute she comes in.'

He was aware of the scent of freesias surrounding her the moment he embraced Dorothy outside the ticket office. As they came into the kitchen at Jericho he saw Doris lift her nose and give a disapproving sniff before slapping the big brown earthenware teapot in the middle of the table.

'Tea's just mashed,' she said curtly. 'Anna's waiting for me to bath Ellen so if you don't mind . . .'

She bustled out of the room. Dorothy smiled at

331

James as she peeled off her kid gloves, finger by finger. 'I have the distinct impression I'm intruding,' she said softly. 'Your housekeeper's face spoke volumes.'

'Don't mind her,' said James, taking her coat. 'Doris has a heart of gold. She worships Anna and the baby and she's very possessive about them, that's all.'

Dorothy seated herself on a fireside chair, took off her chic little hat and put it down beside her, then looked about the room. 'It's very cosy here,' she remarked.

James smiled and picked up the teapot. 'Not as grand as your place, but Anna's done wonders. She's a natural home-maker.'

'Yes,' Dorothy agreed, 'I'll give her that. Even if everything doesn't come naturally.'

He stopped pouring and gave her a quick look. 'Meaning?'

She leaned back comfortably. 'Come on, James, you know her as well as I do. Her letters are always full of little Ellen, her first baby words, how quickly she learned to walk and all that, but I can read between the lines.'

He handed her the cup. 'She's very proud of Ellen,' he said. 'We both are.'

Dorothy searched his eyes as she took the tea from him. 'You know what I mean, don't you?' she said quietly.

He turned away, his back towards her as he poured the second cup. 'I had a lamb this spring whose mother wouldn't accept her,' he said, so softly she could hardly hear. 'She was fostered by another ewe – her lamb had been stillborn. She's the best of the bunch now.'

Dorothy leaned forward and touched his arm. 'So leave Ellen to me, James. I'll take care of her while I'm here and that will leave your housekeeper free to see to Anna and the new baby.'

'She's hard work, Dorothy—'

'And I'm not used to it?' she chuckled. 'Don't you believe it – now America's in the war London's full of GIs – I have to entertain them, and if I can do that I can look after a toddler. At least I won't have to worry about her making a pass at me.'

He turned to her with a smile. 'OK – but wait till you meet her and then decide.'

Dorothy could smell the soapy scent of lavender and talcum powder as Doris carried Ellen in.

'There we are,' said Doris, holding the child out to Anna, 'all spanking clean and ready for bed, aren't we, lovey?'

Anna levered herself upright, trying to make space on her lap. Doris placed the little one in front of the bulge and stood back, hands on hips. 'And don't you go filling your nappy again like you did last night, miss, or I'll have something to say,' she scolded, but the light in her eyes was pure love.

Anna took hold of the baby's hand. 'Wave to your Auntie Dorothy,' she said, flapping the little hand. There was no response. 'Then go and give her a kiss,' said Anna. 'Kiss for Auntie.'

She set the child down on the floor. Ellen stood, wavering a little, one hand on her mother's knee, the other rammed in her mouth. Dorothy saw the child's eyes fasten on her, round and speculative. They were the eyes of an adult, assessing whether or not to trust her. Dorothy blinked. There was something so direct, so probing about that gaze. After a moment the little one turned her head away and buried her face in her mother's lap.

'Come on now, don't be silly. You're not usually shy.' Anna's tone was irritable. James bent to take the child from her.

'Isn't she beautiful?' Dorothy murmured. 'So wise-looking.'

'She's cute all right,' Anna agreed wearily. 'She knows how to twist you round her little finger. She's got Doris right where she wants her.'

Ellen's fingers squelched out of her mouth. 'Doggy,' she pronounced. Doris smiled proudly.

'Doggy – that's in her picture book. She wants me to read it to her.'

'I'll do it – where's the book?' Dorothy was startled to hear herself saying. She saw Doris's smile fade.

'There's no need – I'll do it.'

'No, it's all right – you get supper ready,' said Anna. 'Dorothy can read to her in bed. She'll soon settle down.'

Four days later Anna went into labour. James and Doris helped her upstairs to bed, and then James telephoned the doctor.

Anna was in pain and he felt powerless to help. It was ridiculous – in lambing time or when the sows farrowed he knew exactly what to do, he was in control – but now . . .

When he hurried back up to the bedroom Anna was holding her breath and grimacing. Doris was bending over her, pressing a hot water bottle to her back.

'Dr Melrose is out on his rounds,' James said, 'but the midwife will be here directly.'

Anna's contorted face smoothed out. Doris straightened. 'Betty Ullathorne do you mean?' she demanded. 'If it's her, then I'm staying put. I'm not leaving her on her own with Anna.'

'She'll want us out of the room,' James said. 'We'd only be in the way.'

'She won't want you here, that's for sure, but I know Betty Ullathorne, have done since she were a kid. I remember her picking her nose once till it bled and crying when I put iodine on for her. I'm not leaving her alone with you.'

James stared. 'Because she picked her nose?'

Doris shot him a scornful look. 'Because she drinks a bit on the side since her husband left her. Shame, that – but I'm not risking Anna on her own – I'm staying whether or not. Now you'd best be off and get the kettle on. First thing she'll ask for is plenty of hot water.'

They'd left James pacing up and down in agitation in the house. Dorothy sat on the grass in the orchard watching Ellen staggering around under the trees, squealing in pleasure as she tried to catch the birds. Out here the little one would be unaware of the tension in the house.

They'd read the story book four times. They'd shared the bag of sweets and made a long daisy chain, shreds of which still dangled from Ellen's neck and speckled Dorothy's hair. Ellen's vocabulary seemed to consist of the same question over and over again.

'What's that? What's that?'

It surprised Dorothy just how much patience she could find for this enchanting child. 'That's a bird – say bird, Ellen.'

But she only chuckled and scuttled away after the scruffy little sparrow. Long shadows were beginning to slant across the grass but Dorothy was reluctant to go back to the house. She couldn't handle suffering and there had been no message yet – nothing could have happened. And the little one was such a joy to have all to herself.

But as it began to grow cool Ellen started to yawn. She flopped down beside her aunt and laid her head on her lap. Dorothy touched a finger to the baby-soft hair and felt a swell of tenderness.

This was the child she'd wanted so much, the child she'd failed to conceive. And now it seemed she never would. Myles never commented, but his attitude made it clear that he considered it her fault. He hardly ever came home from Intelligence headquarters even on his weekend passes, and truth to tell, she didn't want him to. The distance between them had grown too wide now. They shared little these days but a common name. Some day, when the war was over perhaps, there would probably be a quiet divorce. Daddy wouldn't like it, but then he didn't know what a stuffy old bore Myles was.

Ellen's eyes were drooping. She couldn't stay out here – the child needed her supper and bed. She gathered the little one up in her arms and headed back towards the house. The chubby little body lay quiet and trusting in her arms. Dorothy felt weighed down with an unfamiliar ache. *If only you were mine, I'd love you to bits. I'd spoil you rotten.*

As they neared the farm gate the toddler lifted her head. 'What's that?' she asked sleepily.

A slant-eyed tom cat stood on the wall, stretching itself luxuriously. It gave them an imperious stare before jumping down and heading for the barn. Dorothy smiled.

'That's a pussy cat,' she said. 'Like the one in your story book.'

The farmhouse door suddenly jerked open. James stood there, his face aglow with delight.

'It's a boy,' he cried. 'They're both fine. A little boy.' He took the toddler from Dorothy's arms and buried his face in the silky hair. 'You've got a little brother, Ellen,' he murmured softly. 'A baby brother for you to love.'

For the next ten days while Anna was lying in, James walked on air. Not only was his family now complete with both a son and a daughter, but Anna seemed to have taken to the new baby from the start.

She crooned to him as she held him to her breast, planting many little kisses on the downy head, and the sight delighted him. She'd never spoken of it, but he'd been aware how hard she'd tried for his sake to

336

feel maternal towards Ellen. But she clearly hadn't fooled Dorothy.

And the curious thing was, she kept asking for Ellen to be brought to her, to sit on the bed with her and talk to the baby. She didn't seem to be feigning any more, and he felt he could sing out for pure joy.

Dorothy and Ellen seemed to have struck up a loving partnership too – Dorothy, the elegant socialite, ignoring baby fingermarks on her frock while she nursed the child and sang to her. Wonders would never cease. Jericho seemed charged with love, everyone bathing in its glorious glow – all, that is, except for Doris who would only be happy when Dorothy had gone.

'I'd love to have her come to stay with me,' Dorothy said one evening as Ellen played on the hearth.

James heard Doris's quick intake of breath. 'She's too young to be away from her folks yet,' she muttered.

'Not right now – sometime,' said Dorothy.

'What with them German bombers down south too – it doesn't bear thinking about,' Doris went on.

Dorothy half turned to her. 'You get them up here too – I heard them the other night.'

'Only now and again, not regular,' retorted Doris. 'They never drop bombs here anyway – they're on the way to Middlesbrough.'

Dorothy sighed. 'I meant when she was older – the war will be over by then.'

Doris had had more than enough of that woman, pushing her nose in where it wasn't wanted, taking things for granted without so much as a by-your-leave to anybody. The day couldn't come fast enough when she'd be on her way and Doris could get her family back to herself.

And it was her family, whatever folks might think. If Fate had played fair she'd have been Mrs

Hemingway senior, young James would be her stepson and the little ones her grandchildren. She wasn't having any lah-di-dah southerner telling her what was best for her family. The sooner she got off home back to her own kind, the better.

James finally told her what she wanted to hear.

'Dorothy will be leaving in the morning, Doris. Just make sure she packs everything, will you? I'll take her to the station at ten.'

So it was with a cheerful face that Doris prepared supper that night. James was still out in the milking shed. Ellen sat on the hearth tracing a finger over the pictures in her story book, looking like a little angel in her clean nightdress. Anna sat watching her, the baby in her arms.

Dorothy slid off her chair and sank down behind the child. 'What's that?' she asked, pointing to the sheepdog.

'Doggy,' said Ellen.

'Good girl. And what's that?'

'Doggy,' said Ellen again.

'No, it isn't a doggy – what is it?'

Doris looked over her shoulder. 'She can't say cat,' she muttered. 'She hasn't learned it yet.'

Ellen took her finger out of her mouth. 'Pussy,' she said quietly, and turned the page.

Her aunt kissed the back of her head in silent delight.

338

THIRTY-FIVE

1969

Thelma Dent placed her husband's tea in front of him the moment he got home from the farm. Fred stared at the steaming plate and then up at her in surprise.

'You're sharp off the mark tonight, love,' he said. 'Something good coming up on telly?'

She threw the oven glove aside and sat down opposite him. 'I'm off down to the WI, that's why. Our Kelly's had her tea early and gone out. She says she wants to do a few of the brasses down at the vicarage.'

'What you going to the WI for?' asked Fred round a mouthful of scalding hot stew. 'You always said jam and Jerusalem wasn't your cup of tea.'

Thelma gave him a scathing look. 'I know, but if I want to find out what's going off in Thaxton, the WI's the place to get to hear all the gossip. I keep getting it second-hand off Mrs Thewlis.'

Fred smiled. 'There's nowt worth gossiping about ever happens in Thaxton.' He wagged his fork at her. 'If it's scandal you're after, you stick to your *News of the World*.'

The front door slammed. 'Hey up,' said Thelma, 'she's back already.' She turned in her seat to watch the door, then turned back as footsteps faded away. 'She's gone up to her room. Getting ready to go down the club, most likely.'

'Very likely,' agreed Fred.

Thelma leaned her elbows on the table. 'Have you noticed owt different about her?' she said in a whisper.

'Who?'

'Our Kelly. She seems to have gone all quiet of late – do you think there could be summat up?'

Fred looked bewildered. 'How would I know? I hardly ever see her.'

'Would you have a word with her? She might tell you.'

Fred looked confused. 'Oh Thelma, I wouldn't know what to say. She'd rather tell you, I'm sure, being her mother.'

Thelma clicked her tongue. 'Not when they're teenagers, they won't. They go all moody and funny on you.' She straightened up. 'Ah well, it'll be summat and nowt, I expect. A tiff with Gary, it wouldn't surprise me. Be all over in a day or two.'

Fred mopped up the last of his gravy with a piece of fresh bread. 'Is she coming with us to Butlin's – has she said?'

Thelma shrugged. 'I still haven't got a straight answer out of her.'

'Best find out soon so we know whether to cancel her chalet or not – it's the week after next, isn't it?'

'That's right – oh heck, just look at the time!'

'Ay, if you don't make a shift you'll miss the start.'

'Start be blowed. I shall miss hearing all about Sadie Forster's operation – I still don't know what she went in for.'

James turned off the road along the path to the river meadow, the clatter of the horse's hooves on the tarmac softening to a dull thud on the grass. The weather was tired and damp even for this time of year, but the air was soft and warm down here in the shelter of the valley; up on the moor it had been exhilaratingly nippy.

Starlings chattered in the trees above him but as he reached the pool the world seemed to fall silent. Dismounting, he stood on the reedy bank while the horse cropped quietly nearby. He gazed down at his reflection, barely moving in the still air.

The world was good. Ellen was coming to life again, taking an interest in village affairs. She'd only let it slip out by accident last night that she'd been to the sculpture exhibition in Bradford.

'Dr Pillai knew I wanted to see it,' she'd said shyly, 'so when he offered to take me . . .'

They'd had tea and cakes together afterwards in a little café, Ravi and she. Several times she called him Ravi, and each time her voice lingered self-consciously over the name, and there was a gentle glow in her eyes. James was glad for her. She needed a friend. Her world was opening up again.

And Lisa had looked well and happy, the way she used to be when she first came to Jericho, alive with youth and vitality. She'd get over Melanie. People did; it had taken him a little time to recognize Anna's needs. And their love had stayed impregnable, always, right up to the end . . .

He looked down into the dark depths of the water, trying to recapture Anna's face that night they swam here together, all those years ago, before they were married. He could remember her laughing, the wet camiknickers moulding themselves to her slim body, the trailing fair hair. He could see below him the trees mirrored in the still surface, his own face – and then a woman's shimmered into view, and he started.

As he sat down abruptly on the bank his fingers touched a stone. He seized it and hurled it into the pool, watching the shadowy reflections in the water, shadows shuddering as they fragmented and broke apart.

It wasn't Anna's face – it was Lisa's.

He was still in contemplative mood when he reached the farm. He reined in at the gate and looked at the old grey stone of the building, its shadows purpling in the evening dusk.

He loved this place. It was as much a part of him as he was of it. In the shadows he fancied he could almost see the generations of Hemingways stretching back over the years. Dismounting, he laid a hand on the drystone wall.

'If only the stone could soak me up,' he thought, 'so that long after I'm gone there will still be a trace of me left. Something of Dad, something of David, something of me . . .'

Kelly shook the chip pan vigorously, droplets of fat flying everywhere. Her mother gave a critical look.

'Watch it, love – don't go making a mess of our new electric cooker. Your dad worked overtime to get that.'

Kelly only grunted. Thelma came up close. 'What's up, love? You've not been yourself – is summat wrong?'

'No,' growled Kelly.

'Only I was wondering if it was Gary – has he upset you?'

'Gary? That's all over – he's history.'

'You mean you don't go out with him any more? I didn't know – you still go out most nights. To the club, is it?'

Kelly tossed chips in the air. 'Why are you asking? I'm sixteen, you know, not a kid any more.'

'Oh I know, love. It's not that I don't trust you – I'm just worried. If there's summat on your mind—'

'There isn't.'

'Only you'd tell me, wouldn't you?'

Kelly made no answer. Another thought struck her and Thelma tried again. 'It's not the job then – you're happy there, aren't you?'

'It's OK.'

'The vicar's not finding fault, is he?'

Kelly swung round, waving the dripping chip

basket. 'For Christ's sake, Mum, leave off, will you? Just leave it alone.'

'Kelly – watch out – the chip fat!'

Behind the girl a sheet of flame seared up the wall. Mother and daughter stared in horror as the net curtains at the window began to blaze. Kelly let the chip basket fall and grabbed up a cushion from the chair. Thelma dived for the bowl of washing-up water in the sink but Kelly pushed her aside and shoved the cushion over the burning fat.

The flames vanished. The little kitchen was thick with smoke, the net curtains melted into a flaky mess on the window sill. For a few moments they both stood in silence.

'I'm sorry,' Kelly muttered. 'I'll make it up to you.'

Thelma gave a thin smile as she surveyed the smoke-blackened wall. 'Never mind, love. Your dad's been saying the kitchen could do with decorating anyway. Only now he'll have to get round to it sooner than he thought.'

She picked up the dishcloth and began cleaning the sill. 'Know what, love?' she said. 'I think we need that holiday. How about we start packing our things for Butlin's?'

'Yes – great,' said Kelly. To Thelma's surprise her voice was almost eager.

'You know, Dad,' said Ellen after supper, 'it mightn't be a bad idea to get another dog. You used to talk to Bart.'

James looked up from his book. 'Am I being quiet? Sorry, love – I was just thinking, that's all.'

'About the trip to the States?' She sat down at the table and rested her chin on her hands. 'It'll be the first time you've ever been abroad – looking forward to it?'

'It'll be a new experience.'

'It'll do you good. Mind you, the place won't be the

343

same without you – you're almost a fixture in Jericho.'

He laughed. 'Time I changed things then before I take root. Will you be OK on your own?'

She smiled. 'I'll be fine – plenty to do. I'll hardly notice you're gone. But about that dog—'

'No,' he cut in sharply, then added apologetically, 'I'm sorry. I know you mean well, but the trouble is they're not like other farm animals – you grow fond of them. I've had enough of losing those I'm fond of. I don't want to go through that again.'

Kelly made her way up the garden path and sidled round to the back, peering in at the windows. There was no light to be seen. With luck, he was out and she'd be safe.

Letting herself in quietly at the back door she tiptoed across the hall to the study and put her ear to the door. No sound, not even a snore. He must have been called out. Thank heaven.

She ran up the stairs, two at a time, and went into Mrs Bax's room. Taking a yellow frock out of the wardrobe she laid it on the bed, then slipped out of her blouse and skirt. Please don't let him get back before I've changed.

Turning, she caught sight of the frock lying limp and pale against the dark maroon of the counterpane. For all the world like a girl lying on her back. For a moment Kelly paused, staring down at it, feeling a knot of revulsion in her throat. It was her lying there, prone, defenceless, the way he saw her as he lowered his great fat, greasy body on to hers.

She turned away with a shudder. She had awful dreams about it, that heavy weight pressing down on her, the skin flabby and puckered like a plucked chicken. He was ancient, at least three times as old as her – what right had he to be still doing things like that at his age?

Mercifully the whole rotten business only lasted a

minute or two, but it was horrible not being able to
breathe properly, seeing that wrinkly old face coming
down, trying to find her mouth, and all the time
contorting as if he was in pain. Why the hell did she
put up with it?

But what other choice was there? She didn't want
the world to know about the money. She couldn't take
all the new clothes home or that would mean having
to explain them away. She could tell on him, but like
he said, who'd believe her word against a vicar's?

Time was ticking by – if she didn't get a move on
he'd be back and catch her again. She pulled the
yellow frock on and gathered up the blouse and skirt.
For the time being she'd have to put up with it. Much
as she loathed him, what else could she do?

One day, somehow, she'd get even with the old
bastard . . .

Lisa had just kicked off her shoes when she heard the
telephone ring. Lazarus called up the stairs.

'It's him again, love.'

Still shoeless she ran down the stairs. 'James? How
lovely to hear your voice. I've had a pig of a week.'

She heard his chuckle. 'Still busy then? I don't
suppose you've had time to get in touch with Dorothy
yet?' he asked. 'She'd cheer you up.'

'Funny you should say that – I rang yesterday. I'm
going down to stay with her at the weekend.'

'Did you find out if she has any contacts in the art
galleries or mention David's pictures?'

'I thought I'd do that when we meet. Is that why
you rang me?'

'No. To tell you I'm going to America next week.
Somebody in New York wants to see my miniatures.
I thought I'd stay for a couple of weeks or so, give
me chance to look for more business, have a bit of a
holiday.'

'Oh.' Lisa could not explain why she felt

disappointed. She hardly ever saw him away up in Yorkshire.

'And I thought maybe we could meet on my way to or from the airport. If only just for a meal.'

'I'd never forgive you if you didn't.'

She was going to miss him, Lisa thought as she lay in the bath. Silly. What difference did it make whether he was in Yorkshire or America? Two hundred miles or three thousand?

But it did make a difference. For the two or three weeks he'd be travelling around, inaccessible. At home, at the other end of the telephone line, he seemed close, available.

Slithering down under the water she scooped up a spongeful of bubbles and let them dribble on to her breasts. David used to sit on the edge of the bath and lather her body with bubbles then blow them away, laughing as he kissed her. She closed her eyes, savouring the trickling water running down her body, and replayed the scene in her head just as she'd done a thousand times before.

But David's face wouldn't come. However hard she tried, the figure on the edge of the bath remained a hazy, faceless blur . . .

THIRTY-SIX

1969

Lisa sat on the floor of Dorothy's elegant sitting room, arms hunched around her knees and laughing. Dorothy reached for her drink and cocked her head to one side.

'You know,' she said thoughtfully, 'it's almost like old times. Anna and I used to have fun together like this. I've missed her dreadfully since she died.'

'Did she come and stay with you often?'

Dorothy nodded. 'Quite often, specially after the war when James gave up farming and sold off some of the land. She wasn't so tied then. She spent a lot of time planning and building the extension – she loved that. And having fun. Anna threw herself into everything she did.'

Dorothy's eyes grew misty with reminiscence and her voice fell to a soft whisper. 'It was a terrible shock when she died so suddenly. It must have been far worse for James.' With a start she recollected herself. 'Oh my dear, I'm so sorry—'

Lisa smiled. 'It's all right. It doesn't hurt so much any more.'

Dorothy sat forward on the edge of her seat. 'Talking of David, why don't you send some of his pictures on to me? I think I know the very person – not promising anything but I'll see what I can do.'

'I'll send them as soon as I get back. The best one is his last one, and James has got that.'

'No hurry. Send me what you have – that'll do to start with.'

*   *   *

Thelma's pretty face was creased into a worried frown as she unpacked her suitcase. 'I've never known her be like that before, Fred. Our Kelly's always been the life and soul of anything but she hardly ever went out of the chalet all week.'

Fred nodded as he untangled the pile of socks in his case. 'I thought it were just summat she ate at first but if it were it didn't affect us.'

'Nay love, she looked sick as a dog all week. In fact I reckon she were really sick and didn't let on. I'm sure I could smell it when I went in to waken her this morning. I'm going to get her to see Doctor Pillai before she goes back to work.'

'Some good the holiday did her,' growled Fred. Thelma straightened, a flimsy black item in her hand.

'But you enjoyed it, didn't you, love? I know I did.'

He looked down at her with a broad smile. 'Ay, I did and all. Proper second honeymoon, were that.'

She dimpled proudly. 'I told you it'd be worth our while going to that lingerie place even if it was a bit on the dear side. Now do you believe me?'

'When are you going to the airport?' said Lisa, holding the telephone close.

'Tuesday,' James replied. 'Are you free?'

'Dammit, I'll be in Nottingham and I'm staying overnight.'

'Never mind. I'll make it up to you when I get back,' he promised. 'You choose where you'd like to go – the best restaurant in town for the prettiest girl in town.'

She made a mock yawn. 'Ho-hum. I bet you say that to all the girls.'

'And it gets me precisely nowhere.'

A week later a small package arrived from Dorothy.

I found this in a sketchbook among the paintings you sent me and I don't think you knew it was there.

It seems to be the rough draft of a letter to you, and I won't pretend I didn't read it. Other people's private papers are always a great temptation and few of us can resist, though we usually deny it like mad. With you, however, I can't be less than honest. It moved me deeply.

I assume you must have known about – Melissa, was it? I can only admire you for being such a generous, warm-hearted girl to be so forgiving. You and James have a lot in common. No wonder you get on so well.

Lisa stared at the sheet of paper. James – what did she mean? Had he learned that Anna had been unfaithful too? And then she remembered his words: '*It's not important, love. Believe me, I know . . .*'

It seemed strange to read David's handwriting again after nearly two years, but now it brought only a painful sense of loss, no longer the searing agony of the early days. There were also notes from the time he'd learnt about the tumour, describing the turmoil of his feelings, the anger and frustration of being forced to leave those he loved, the sense of betrayal and helplessness.

She read of his turning to Melanie, of being unable to explain to her, and the tears stung her eyelids. Oh David, if only I'd known . . . But it was clear Melanie was a kindly port in the storm of his anguish, no more. By rights she ought to feel grateful to this woman who had comforted him without demanding anything in return.

Towards the end he seemed to have achieved some degree of calm and acceptance. He wrote of his last painting with tenderness:

This picture needs a border round it to contain in isolation all the things I love most. The world is always too busy, but now I've found stillness where I can forget the bustle outside. I can slip through into my walled garden, my haven, like the boy in the story who could slip into his secret, magic garden.

That's how it is for me in Jericho. There's a timelessness about the place. I'll paint my loved ones there, relating them to a larger whole – they will grow old, have children and die, but I'll capture this moment where life still lies before them.

Dr Pillai laid the stethoscope on his desk and leaned his forearms across the polished surface. The girl was staring down sullenly at her knees, fidgeting with the hem of her mini-skirt.

'You'll have to tell your parents, Kelly,' he said quietly.

'No,' she muttered defiantly. 'I can't – they'll go mad.'

'You're going to need their help. They'll have to know sooner or later.'

'You heard me – no!' She gave him a sharp look. 'You won't tell, will you?'

He sighed. It was always a tough problem getting girls in her situation to see sense. Shock, fear, shame – she couldn't think rationally yet. 'You're sixteen, Kelly, old enough to marry. Have you thought of that – talked it over with the father?'

She hung her head again. 'No.'

'Why not? He has a responsibility in this too.'

'I can't,' she blurted. 'I wouldn't want him, and anyway it isn't possible.'

Dr Pillai raised his eyebrows. A married man? No wonder the girl was so surly and uncommunicative.

He spoke gently. 'Are you going to tell me who the father is, Kelly?'

'What good would that do?' she muttered truculently. 'I'm up the creek, aren't I, and that's the point. Can I get rid of it?'

He shook his head slowly. 'I'm afraid not. You're a healthy girl – there's no question of an abortion.' He saw the look of utter misery cloud her pretty young face. 'Look, you're not the first girl this has happened to,' he said gently. 'You'd be surprised how well parents can react once they've got over the shock. I'd tell them if I were you.'

'They'll have a fit. They'll throw me out, and then what'll I do?'

'Not if I know them. They'll want to stand by you, see you and the baby well cared for.'

She glared at him. 'How would you know? You Indians have loads of wives and beat them up all the time. I should have gone to Dr Whitaker.'

He could see the tears glinting in her eyes as she chewed her fingernail. 'Me dad'll want to find out who it was and murder him,' she grunted, 'and I've half a mind to let him. Serve the bastard bloody well right.'

Ellen was pleased and at the same time felt awkward when Ravi accepted her invitation to come in for a cup of coffee. She shouldn't be doing this, asking a man into the house at this time of night, and with Dad away too. But Ravi had been so gentlemanly and attentive on their visit to the cinema, it seemed discourteous not to ask him in when he brought her home.

He sat at ease in the armchair sipping coffee from Mother's treasured Royal Albert china. She sat on the edge of the sofa, legs neatly crossed, and made a mental note to buy herself a pair of stiletto-heeled shoes next weekend. Country brogues did nothing for a girl's femininity.

'Thanks for bringing me home,' she said softly. 'I did enjoy tonight.'

Ravi smiled. 'I couldn't let you come back alone,

351

and no-one here to keep you company. Are you sure you'll be all right on your own?'

'I'm fine. Dad will be home at the end of the week.'

'And Lisa – is she still in London?'

'Yes.'

'A dangerous place, the city. It's a good job they've jailed the Kray twins now – at least she'll be a lot safer.'

When the church clock struck eleven he glanced at his watch. 'I'd better be going,' he said, laying his cup aside and rising. Ellen walked with him to the door. 'How would you like to show me around York on my next day off?' he asked as she held the door open for him.

'I'd like that,' she answered shyly. 'I love York.'

'I'd be most grateful.' He bent and touched his lips lightly to her cheek. Ellen shuddered and pulled away.

His dark eyes were immediately filled with concern. 'I'm sorry,' he said brusquely. 'I shouldn't have done that.'

'No, it's me,' she murmured. 'I was just taken by surprise. Good night, Ravi.'

He opened his mouth to speak but she closed the door, then turned and leaned against it. You stupid woman, she scolded herself, gathering up the coffee cups and taking them through to the kitchen. It was clumsy of her – she'd hurt his feelings, but she couldn't help it.

Picking up the tea towel she turned and looked back towards the living room. Until a few moments ago the atmosphere between them had been so warm and comfortable, and now she'd spoilt it and all because of a peck on the cheek.

From here she could see the chair where he had been sitting, the coffee colour of his skin glowing in the firelight. Oh Lord – maybe he thought she'd recoiled because of his colour.

She flung the tea towel angrily across the room. 'Oh God!' she muttered to herself, 'now you've done it. And I liked him. It's no good, my girl, you've just got to face it – you're a mess. And I liked him so much.'

James looked down at the pretty blonde girl standing beside him in the airport departure lounge.

'Thanks for driving me here,' he said. 'It was kind of your boss to arrange everything for me.'

She smiled engagingly. 'Well, I must say, Mr Hemingway,' she drawled in a deep southern accent, 'looking after you has sure been the best assignment he's given me this year. Hope you'll get in touch when you're in New York again. I'd really like to see you.'

Lively blue eyes challenged his. James smiled. 'With luck, Shelley, your boss's next client will be twenty years younger than me.'

She shrugged and looked up at him from under her lashes. 'I hope not – I get on best with mature men – I can relate to them.'

He liked the open friendly way Americans talked – so different from the folk at home. Yorkshire people were direct to the point of bluntness, but here people said what they thought you wanted to hear. Often he couldn't work out what they really meant, but it amused him.

A tinny voice spoke over the tannoy. Shelley lifted a red-nailed finger. 'Oh listen – that's your call now. I'll walk with you to the gate.'

Her high heels clicked along beside him. At the gate he offered his boarding card and Shelley reached up to kiss his cheek. 'Don't forget now,' she drawled casually, 'next time you're Stateside, be sure and call me.'

As he crossed the tarmac he turned and waved. She blew him another kiss.

*   *   *

James was smiling as he boarded the plane and settled in his seat. He'd enjoyed the trip more than he'd expected. Jericho seemed a million miles away from the bustle and noise of New York with its enormous skyscrapers and frenetic way of life, and the people had been so welcoming and helpful. It was the first time he'd ventured out of England, but if this was what travelling was like, he reckoned he could develop a taste for it.

Harold Braithwaite had done him a great favour, introducing him to Max, and Max had been more than generous, arranging meetings with other potential clients and lending him his car and secretary. James smiled again as he thought of Shelley. Was he mistaken, or had he really been chatted up by a pretty young girl in her twenties? With her long fair hair, slim body and shapely legs she was very much like Lisa, just about her age and just as confident. But she didn't have Lisa's unique mercurial quality, her unpredictability, and the intense way she felt about things.

With a start he realized that for the first time in his life he wasn't comparing other women with Anna. Up till now she'd always been the yardstick by which they were measured – and fell short. All, that was, except Lisa.

He was eager to see her again. That was why he'd caught an earlier flight home . . .

Lisa was sleepily trying to come to terms with the morning when she heard the doorbell downstairs ring hollowly along the corridor. As she swung her legs out of bed she heard voices, Lazarus talking to someone. Probably the milkman.

Shivering in the cold morning air she went into the bathroom. This shortie nightie was useless for the winter, she thought as she cleaned her teeth – she'd have to get something warmer before long. There was a tap at the door. She put down the toothbrush and went to answer.

She opened the door a few inches and an icy draught whipped around her bare legs. A tall figure blocked the light.

'It's me, Lisa.'

Her lips parted in surprise and she opened the door wide, holding out her arms to him. 'James – I wasn't expecting you until tonight!'

He gathered her up in a hug, holding her close. Involuntarily she turned her face up to his and kissed him. For a second he returned her kiss, and she realized with a start that it gave her a strange sensation, the way she used to feel with David.

Abruptly he let go of her. 'I got through the business early,' he murmured, 'so I caught the night plane home. I hoped I'd catch you before you left for work.'

For a moment she stood just looking at him, the touch of grey at his temples, the fine network of laughter lines edging the corners of his eyes. He looked tired, and he was fidgeting from foot to foot. Oh Lord, she'd embarrassed him. Suddenly she was acutely conscious of the thin shortie nightie. She turned away towards the bathroom, trying to sound casual.

'You must be dying for a coffee – put the kettle on while I have a wash,' she said, and pulled the door closed.

The bathroom mirror reflected a cloud of dishevelled hair and the faint blush of skin through flimsy cotton. Oh God, he'd caught her completely unawares and only half awake; like a child she'd acted on impulse, hurling herself into his arms like that – now he'd think she had a schoolgirl crush on him.

Act normal now, casual and easy so he'd forget. 'Guess what?' she called out. 'I saw Mr Braithwaite again the other day. I happened to mention Anna's name was Harcourt and he said he once did business with your father-in-law.'

'Really?' she heard James say.

'He said he was a cold devil.'

'Yes,' came a muffled reply. 'He was.'

She pulled on her skirt and blouse and came out. The fragrant scent of coffee filled the air and James was filling two mugs.

'You must be tired after travelling all night,' she said. 'Why don't you have a good sleep while I'm at work?'

He handed her a steaming mug. 'You know what – I'd like that. Then tonight I'll take you out for that dinner I promised.'

She took a hasty swig. 'And it's going to cost you – I've booked the most expensive place I know. Look, I've got to fly – see you at six.'

James lay naked in bed in the hollow where she had lain, still warm from her body. He could smell the fragrance of her skin in the pillow, touched with the fresh, piquant scent of her perfume.

He shouldn't be here, invading her privacy, lying in her bed, unable to control the wild thoughts scuttling through his brain. It was damn near incestuous. For God's sake, she was his daughter-in-law, near enough.

But he couldn't control the images racing in his head. He'd been so glad to see her. The sight of her was like a draught of water to a thirsty man. He curled his fingers round the edge of the pillow and drew it close to his face. Sleep, dammit – you're dead-beat. Forget how you felt when she kissed you like that. Banish the memory of her in that tiny nightie, the glimpse of warm flesh . . .

It took a long time before he finally fell asleep.

Over dinner he watched her animated face as she talked. She looked relaxed and confident, her skin

356

glowing pearl-white in the candlelight against the deep green of her dress.

She broke off. 'What is it?' she asked.

He laid his napkin aside. 'I've just remembered. I slept so long I forgot to book a hotel for tonight.'

She waved a hand. 'Forget it. You're in luck – they've just brought back the settee they were using in the last play. You can sleep on that if you like. I'll wake you in time to get your train.'

He hesitated only a second. 'Well, if you're sure—'

She leaned her elbows on the table and smiled at him. 'Of course, and you can start spending the money you're saving on another bottle of wine. You promised you'd spare no expense.'

'And I meant it.' He held up a hand. 'Waiter!'

Lisa was swaying slightly as he helped her up the stairs to the flat. Her face wore a bemused smile as she fished in her bag for the key. At last she found it and held it up triumphantly.

'I knew it was here somewhere. Lurking under my make-up and purse, the sly little devil.'

She gave a wicked smile, like a child who'd been cribbing in the end-of-term exams and got away with it. James took the key from her and unlocked the door, watching as she walked carefully in, trying hard to keep a straight line.

'Shall I make some coffee?' he asked.

She shook her head and let her coat fall from her shoulders. 'I've drunk enough. I just want to go to bed.' She waved one arm in the general direction of the sofa. 'There's your bed. You'll find some blankets in the airing cupboard.'

'Don't worry about me – you just see to yourself.'

She swayed into the bathroom. James peeled off his jacket and shirt then sat down on the sofa to take off his shoes and socks. Now what? He didn't possess a pair of pyjamas. He'd wait until she was in bed.

She came out at last in the tiny nightie and he watched as she slithered under the sheets.

'James,' she murmured sleepily.

'Yes?'

He moved over to the bed, feeling the linoleum icy under his bare feet.

'It's a cold flat – will you be warm enough?'

'Of course I will.' He sat on the edge of the bed and looked down at her, her fists curled alongside her face on the pillow. She was so much a woman and at the same time as vulnerable as a child. She gave him a drowsy smile.

'I wish you weren't my father-in-law.'

'I'm not your father-in-law.'

'That's true.' The words were slightly slurred. 'We could have an affair, couldn't we?'

James felt a sudden lurch in his chest. 'You've had too much to drink.'

She propped herself up on one elbow. 'We could have a cuddle anyway. That's not against the law.'

For a long moment a silence hung between them and when Lisa spoke again her husky voice had sobered and there was a question in her eyes. 'I've thought about it often enough – haven't you?'

'Yes.' James heard himself saying the word but it was as though it had been spoken by someone else. 'I'm too old for you,' he muttered.

'Who says?'

James closed his eyes. What on earth was he talking about? It didn't matter a damn how old he was; what really mattered was that she had been his son's wife, in all but name, and he wanted her so much.

Lisa gazed at him, unblinking. Such wisdom lay behind those earnest young eyes. 'James,' she said, 'he isn't here any more.'

'Isn't he?'

'No. There was a time when he was everywhere, surrounded me. But now he's let me go.'

She covered his hand with hers. 'You're shivering,' she said, and then, throwing back the bedcovers, she moved to one side. 'Come on.'

She looked so beautiful lying there, waiting for him. He could have cried at the sight of her and he wanted so much to be with her, not just for tonight but for always.

'I should have booked into a hotel,' he said as he slid down by her side.

'Of course you should,' she murmured.

He pressed his forehead close against hers. 'I did mean to,' he whispered.

'I know – and I'm so glad you didn't.'

THIRTY-SEVEN

1969

It was growing late when James neared Thaxton. He loved this time of year, when heather and ling splashed the landscape with royal colour but now, with misty night drawing on, the very moor seemed to exhale darkness.

He still couldn't believe it. Less than twenty-four hours ago . . . Last night had been completely unplanned, yet it devastated his mind. In all these years he'd almost forgotten the blinding heat of passion and the tender closeness between a man and a woman which defied words. The closeness of two people in love . . . It was still hard to believe, impossible to contemplate.

As he drove along the familiar lane towards Jericho he could see lights glowing in the house.

He put the car away in the garage, then lifted his case from the boot. Turning, he saw the dusty Mini lying quiet against the wall.

'What the hell am I to do, Gladys, old girl?' he murmured. 'Keep it to myself, or shout it from the rooftops?'

'Dad – is that you?' Ellen's voice called from the house.

'Coming.' He patted the Mini's bonnet and smiled. 'One more secret, I guess. It won't be the first.'

'Had a good time, love? You look great.'
Anna's face shone with excitement as she hurled herself into his arms and he could see her hands were

360

white and her nails manicured and red-tipped as she touched his cheek.

'It was wonderful,' she breathed.

He smiled as he led her indoors. 'Maybe you should take these breaks more often.'

Anna turned her face up to his. 'I'd like that. You're a good man, James. You never complain.'

'What is there to complain about? I love to see my wife come home looking lovelier than ever. I'm a lucky man.'

Her expression grew serious. 'I just needed to go, have a taste of the old way of life, just to see if I was missing anything, that's all.'

'And were you?'

'Not much – all I want is here in Jericho. Oh – I brought a present for you – a pair of miniature pistols.' She gave him a mischievous smile. 'I had to pull a few strings, mind you, on the black market.'

He couldn't believe his eyes when he saw the puppy lying asleep in the basket by the fire. Ellen was watching his expression.

'Listen,' he said, 'I told you I didn't want another dog. I appreciate the thought—'

Ellen cut in quietly. 'He's not yours – he's mine.'

He smiled as he sat down to supper. 'That was very clever of you,' he said.

Ellen beamed. 'I shan't mind if you pat him now and again. You might even like to take him for a walk.'

James shook his head. 'It looks like I've got a dog whether I wanted one or not.'

When she'd dried the last of the supper dishes Ellen came to sit by the fire. 'Look, I hope you don't mind, Dad, but while you were away I cleared out a lot of David's things – his clothes and so on. I felt it was high time . . .'

He nodded. 'Yes, love. You did right. Thanks.'

She'd done it to spare him pain, he knew. The job had been put off for far too long.

'And I came across this,' she said gently. 'I hadn't the heart to throw it out yet.' Bending, she picked up something lying under her seat. He recognized it at once. The toy gun he'd made all those years ago out of the handle of an old hoover.

'I remember you making it,' Ellen said quietly. 'I remember Mother asking you to make it for him.'

'Why won't you let me buy you a lathe, James?' Anna asked. 'I could buy it for your birthday.'

James shook his head. 'You've bought me enough. I'll get more tools in time.'

'How?'

He shrugged. 'I could sell some of the land – not yet, with our barley quotas to fill, but after the war . . .'

She smiled and picked up his catalogue, flicking the pages over. 'Is this it? A Myford?' she asked.

It was no use arguing once her mind was made up. The lathe arrived just in time for his birthday.

'Maybe now you'll find time to make that gun for David,' she said. 'He's been badgering for one of his own for ages.'

'You can remember that?' James said. 'You'd only be about five then.'

Ellen nodded. 'I was jealous – I wanted one. Then you made my doll's house, and I was happy.' She gave him a smile. 'You didn't know I could be jealous, did you?'

The telephone rang. Ellen made to rise. 'I'll go,' James said, and went quickly out into the hall. With luck it could be Lisa.

'Mr Hemingway? It's Ravi Pillai. Could I have a word with Ellen, please?'

*　　*　　*

'I'm afraid I embarrassed you the other evening, Ellen. I'm so sorry.'

She could feel herself blushing. 'No, Ravi – it's the other way around. I feel I embarrassed you, and I'm sorry.'

There was a silence for a moment before he spoke again. 'Look, I hope this won't spoil our friendship. You will meet me again, won't you? We have to talk.'

She hesitated. 'About what?'

'Many things. You, mostly.'

She felt her defences go up, heard her own abashed laugh. 'There's nothing much to say about me that you don't know already. There must be more interesting things—'

'Not for me. There's so much more under the skin, so much I want to learn. Say you'll meet me tomorrow . . .'

James was aware of her lighter mood when she came back. He watched her sit and lean forward to stroke the puppy's sleeping head. Her hair swung free and it looked longer and silkier, and wasn't that a new dress she was wearing? It was shorter than usual, and her legs looked good – it must be the shoes, high heels and pointed toes – he hadn't seen those before either. He'd been too absorbed in his own thoughts to notice until now.

'You going out with him again?' he enquired.

'Yes,' she said shyly. 'We're going to York tomorrow.' She sat back. 'Did you see Lisa while you were in London?'

'Yes – I took her out to dinner last night.' Dinner? That was only the start, but how could he tell her?

'Nice girl,' Ellen murmured. 'I quite grew to like her.'

He felt his throat tighten. 'She gets on well with Dorothy – she'd just been to stay with her.'

Ellen looked up. 'That reminds me – Aunt Dorothy

363

rang. She wants you to send on David's last picture. Something to do with an exhibition a friend of hers might be able to arrange. I told her I've still got a few days' leave due to me and she suggested I might come and stay with her.'

'Good idea. You'll enjoy that.'

The puppy's legs twitched in his sleep. Ellen bent to stroke him again. James watched the long, sensitive fingers, recalling Lisa's hands caressing his body . . .

'Do you ever get lonely, Dad?' Ellen's voice made him start guiltily.

'Why do you ask?'

She shrugged. 'I know we've got each other, but don't you ever feel you'd like someone really close, a partner of your own, I mean? Someone who is like the other half of you?'

She was talking of herself, not him. James leaned forward. 'We all need that, sweetheart. Sometimes it just takes a long time to find the right person.'

She gave a quiet sigh. 'Even then, how can you be sure if it is the right one?'

He smiled. 'You'll know, believe me. You just know.'

Grey eyes swung up to meet his. 'You did with Mother, didn't you? You just knew there'd be no-one else?'

He couldn't help the lunge of disappointment. There was no chance he could ever talk to her about Lisa . . . He couldn't expect anyone else to understand either . . .

What a confusion of thoughts tumbling in his brain – should he feel ashamed of the way he felt? He didn't. Should he put all thoughts of Lisa from his head? He couldn't. Was it shameful?

He needed to talk to someone, look for guidance to sort out this muddle in his mind . . .

Lisa felt exhilarated. She loved James, and she knew he loved her, and throughout the day this one blinding fact dazzled her so that everything else was blotted out.

But now, sitting in the half-light of evening in the cluttered flat with a packet of fish and chips on the table, the cold voice of reason was beginning to take over.

He was David's father; he was twenty-odd years older than she was; Ellen would never accept her as James's wife – even if he asked her to marry him. The question had never arisen last night.

It had been wonderful, and it hadn't been a casual thing, she knew that for sure. More than anything she longed to be with him, at least to hear his voice.

She unwrapped the packet on the table. Greasy chips were congealed to the fish. She looked towards the door, fancying again the sound of his voice, tender and gentle over the telephone.

She couldn't ring. He too needed time . . .

Clifford Bax held out a warm hand to his visitor. 'James – how nice to see you again – do sit down. Is everything well with you?'

James sat on the edge of the uncomfortable horse-hair seat while the vicar told him about the vandals who had been despoiling his graveyard. 'Not local boys, I'm glad to say – youths on motor bikes, with studded leather jackets. They just rode into the grave-yard in the middle of the night. Such a mess they left. Tyre-tracks, beer cans, graffiti – it was a dreadful expense to clean it up.'

'I'm sure,' said James. 'Perhaps I can help.'

The vicar raised plump hands. 'I wasn't asking for money, my dear fellow, truly I wasn't. But if you feel inclined . . . And of course I shall be making an appeal for the orphanage again as usual before long. Sarah used to handle all that, but now . . .'

He gave a deep sigh. James felt sorry for him. 'She's definitely not coming back then?' he asked.

Bax shook his head. 'Highly unlikely after all this time, I fear. But if it's the will of God I have to come to terms with it. The Lord moves in mysterious ways.'

'Yes,' James murmured. 'That's why I wanted to see you.'

Bax's normally ruddy face paled. 'I don't believe I'm hearing this – and from you of all people, James! You can't, you simply can't!'

'Why not?' James asked. 'Is it against the law?'

'For a man to marry his daughter-in-law is strictly against canon law, but I'm shocked you should even think of it. It's a wicked thought.'

'They never married – she isn't my daughter-in-law,' James said quietly.

Bax spread thick fingers. 'To all intents and purposes she is – your son had carnal knowledge of this woman. Often.'

James's fingers were tightly interlocked as he listened, clenched knuckles gleaming. Bax stood watching him, then patted his shoulder. 'Put these sinful thoughts from your mind, James – that's my advice. It's out of the question.'

As he accompanied his visitor to the door the vicar murmured words of comfort. 'It is only human to give way to wicked thoughts now and again. The real victory lies in overcoming them. We must seek the Lord's help in the battle to be strong.'

James made a grunting sound. In the doorway Bax took his hand. 'Look, I know you're always ready to dip your hand into your pocket for the church but why not come along to Sunday service? It could help you to pray, and we will pray for you.'

James's face reddened and he drew his hand away sharply. 'You've already got my mother and father, my wife and son here,' he blurted. 'You're not getting me yet.'

Before the vicar could recover his breath James was already striding away down the laurel-bordered drive.

Kelly slouched in a chair, staring sullenly at the cartoon on the television set in the corner. Thelma looked up sharply as she heard the door open.

'Hey up, there's your dad now. Best let me break it to him.'

She turned back to the pan simmering on the stove. Fred came in, hung his jacket on the back of the door, then reached for the newspaper on the sideboard.

He glanced across at his wife. 'Summat smells good, love,' he remarked. 'I'm hungry as a hunter.'

Her eyes looked funny, as if she'd been weeping. Puzzled, he looked to his daughter. 'You been up-setting your mother again?' he asked. Kelly gave him a surly glance and ran from the room. He stared at Thelma, bewildered.

'What's going on?' he said. 'You two been having words again? What is it this time?'

Thelma shook her head and bent over the pan. 'Sit down, love,' she said in a strangled voice. 'You're not going to like this . . . '

'In the family way? Our Kelly? No, I don't believe it.'

Fred sat stunned, the unopened newspaper on his lap, his kindly features blurred into disbelieving pain. 'Not our Kelly.'

Thelma came to sit down opposite him, drawing a hanky from her pocket. 'It's right enough, I'm afraid. Dr Pillai told her this morning. Three months gone, she is.'

'Our Kelly – why, she's nobbut a child herself.'

Thelma sniffed. 'Not so much a child as we thought, evidently. Six months, and she'll have a child of her own.' She looked up suddenly, eyes wide. 'Just think, we'll be grandparents, Fred.'

His face grew dark. 'Who is it? Who did this to her?

367

Was it that Gary lad?' The newspaper slid to the floor as he leapt up from his chair. 'I'll take a horsewhip to the little bugger, that I will.'

'Sit you down, love – she swears it wasn't Gary.'

'Then who was it?'

'She won't say who, but she's definite it's not him.'

Fred sat down again slowly. 'Three months ago, you say?'

Thelma blew her nose noisily. 'I've thought about that. We were at Butlin's that month.'

Fred stared. 'Are you saying it could be anybody – a complete stranger?'

'I'm not saying nowt of the kind. I don't know what to think. Oh Fred, what are we to do?'

His expression grew serious. 'Make her tell. The lad's got to face his responsibility.'

'Easier said than done – I've tried and better tried. You know our Kelly when she's made her mind up – she can be that stubborn.'

Fred stared around the room helplessly. 'I don't know what to do, love. I'm forced to admit, I'm fair flummoxed. Who'd have thought it . . . ?'

Thelma pocketed the handkerchief. 'We'll stand by her though, won't we, whatever folk might say?'

'No two ways about it. She's our lass.'

Thelma gave a thin smile. 'You're a good man, Fred. I'll ask the vicar what we should do – he'll be sure to know.'

Thelma sat twisting her gloves between numb fingers. The Reverend Bax sat silent at his desk, curling the edge of a sheet of paper while she talked. She finished the tale, then sat waiting for his reply. Moments passed, and still he said nothing.

'I just don't know what to do, Vicar,' she muttered. 'Fred and me thought as how you might have some word of advice.'

'She won't tell you who the father is, you say?'

'No – we've tried to get it out of her till we're blue in the face. We've coaxed her and threatened her – Fred even said he'd throw her out. He wouldn't, of course, but it was no use. She says it's nobody's business but hers.'

The vicar sighed deeply. 'Well, I suppose you might have expected it, Thelma. You know what kind of girl Kelly is.'

Thelma frowned. 'How do you mean, what kind of girl?'

He spread his hands. 'We all knew what she was like, my dear – always with the boys. I've seen her myself, going off down into the wood with them. You ask any of the villagers – they've all seen her.'

Thelma hung her head miserably. 'I didn't know – I trusted her. I never thought she'd let us down like this.'

Reverend Bax shook his head. 'Children can be very ungrateful, I'm afraid, but despite that it's our duty to show Christian charity. You must put your hurt feelings aside, Thelma, and help her all you can.'

'But if she won't tell us who done it we can't get her married. She'll be an unmarried mother – what's to become of her then?'

The vicar smiled. 'She's a capable girl – she'll manage, with your help. And I know you'll stand by her, you and Fred. Remember that the child is innocent – it may have no father, but it will be fortunate in having a good family none the less. Whatever wagging tongues might say, they'll soon stop and this child may bring you great joy.'

He stood up and closed the book on his desk. 'Dry your tears, my dear. In time you may come to recognize that this apparent blow was in fact a blessing in disguise. You know what they say – every cloud has a silver lining.'

Thelma gathered up her bag and gloves and stood up. 'Thank you, vicar,' she said, summoning up a brave smile. 'You've been a great help. You're a good man.'

With Ellen away at her aunt's James felt an emptiness in the house. He desperately wanted to talk to Lisa; it was a great temptation to lift up the telephone, just to hear her voice, but the vicar's warning still rang in his ears. He tried to busy himself with his guns, taking infinite care to perfect every piece.

That was what he always aimed for, perfection in every detail of lock and stock, of knuckle and barrel, of lever and striker. So many intricate pieces to assemble into an object of mathematical precision, an object of beauty he'd never have known about if it hadn't been for the army. Before then a gun had been only a necessary tool for getting rid of marauding rabbits and barnyard rats.

The telephone rang. He put down the chisel and went to answer, trying to ignore the leap of hope. It wouldn't be her – more likely it would be Ellen.

'James? It's me.'

'Lisa?' He couldn't hide the delight in his tone.

'I'm sorry I haven't rung before. I've been so busy . . .'

'I know. Don't worry. How are you, love?'

'Fine. And you?' Her voice sounded small and tentative. Was it because she felt apologetic, or was she feeling strained and unnatural too? Where was that wonderful closeness they shared that night?

'I've been up to my ears in work,' she said, then abruptly she went on. 'Oh, for God's sake, this is stupid. James, we can't go on like this.'

'No,' he said quietly. 'We can't. I've been thinking about it a lot.'

'Have you? And what conclusion have you come to?'

'Like you said, we can't go on like this. It's got to stop.'

There was a silence at the other end, and then he

heard her sigh. 'Yes,' she said softly, 'it's got to stop. It's out of the question.'

He felt hollow inside, but they had to be sensible. 'It won't alter the way I feel about you,' he murmured. 'Nothing can do that.'

He heard a sound like a gulp before she answered. 'James,' she said urgently, 'I'm coming up. I'm not going to let it end like this. I want to see you, face to face . . .'

THIRTY-EIGHT

1969

Ellen lay back in the sunken bath, revelling in the silky fragrance of the water. Bottles with Harrods and Fortnum and Mason labels stood ranged along the ledge, and a pile of thick, fluffy towels lay waiting. Aunt Dorothy certainly knew how to pamper herself.

Ellen slipped into one of the silk robes hanging behind the door and felt the sheer sensuous delight of its delicate fabric against her skin. Barefoot, she wandered back to where her aunt sat reading by the fire.

Dorothy took off her spectacles and looked up. 'I forgot to tell you – Antonia liked David's work – she's agreed to hang one or two in an exhibition of new artists.'

'That's great,' said Ellen. 'Lisa will be delighted and Dad will be ever so proud.' She paused for a moment, then added casually, 'Mind if I use the phone?'

Her aunt smiled. 'Your father – or your doctor friend?'

Ellen's eyebrows rose. 'What makes you say that?'

'Only because his name's cropped up at least five times today. Ravi said he likes me in blue, Ravi took me for a Chinese meal in York . . . He seems to loom large in your thoughts.'

Ellen felt the colour tinge her cheeks. She curled herself on the floor at her aunt's feet. 'He's different, that's all. Everybody in Thaxton likes him.'

'I see. And how is he different – something other than the colour of his skin, I presume?'

Ellen curled her fingers round her bare toes. 'He's

a quiet man, he's gentle, he's a good listener . . . I don't know, there's just something distinctive about him, a kind of integrity you can feel.'

Dorothy gave her a knowing smile. 'Rather like your father, in fact. Funny how girls often admire replicas of their fathers.'

Ellen's fingers stopped moving. She hadn't thought of that, but Ravi did have some of Dad's characteristics.

'I didn't, of course,' Dorothy went on. 'My father was so overbearing I wanted a man who was completely the opposite. I couldn't have the one I fancied, so stupidly I settled for another I thought would let me have my own way. It was doomed to failure. Myles bored me to death. He's probably done the same to his second wife by now.'

Ellen looked up curiously. 'What happened to the man you really wanted then?'

Her aunt smiled down at her and patted her hand. 'I let someone else get in first – don't you make the same mistake, my girl, or you too could wind up staring every morning at a face covered with bits of tissue paper stuck to his shaving cuts and wondering why the hell you let it happen. Get in there fast, before it's too late.'

Ellen hunched up her knees and stared into the fire. 'He's from a different background, a different culture—'

'That's of no great importance when you're in love.'

'And we hardly know each other – deep down, I mean. There are things he ought to know about me—'

'He'll find out what he wants to know.'

'—things I've never told anyone.'

Dorothy shrugged. 'Tell him what you want, forget the rest.'

Ellen looked up sharply. 'But it wouldn't be honest.'

'Too much honesty can be a bad thing. It depends on the circumstances, of course, but I've no time for those who are too darn scrupulous for their own good.'

Ellen frowned. 'I don't know that I agree with you. A couple shouldn't have any secrets from each other.'

Her aunt stroked the silk shoulder. 'Don't you believe it, love. It's selfish to unload your mind if it makes someone else feel bad. Believe me, some things are best left unsaid . . .'

Dorothy sat watching James thoughtfully. His fingers lay calmly intertwined on his lap as he gazed into the fire but his voice still sounded strained whenever he spoke of Anna. It was last spring when her body had been laid to rest in the quiet of the churchyard, and now a scattering of the autumn leaves she loved so much fluttered over her grave. James was still finding it hard to come to terms with her death.

'It was so sudden, Dorothy. One minute she was playing the piano, happy as anything, then suddenly I heard her play a wrong chord, as I thought. I found her slumped over the keys. She wasn't ready to die.'

Dorothy shook her head sadly. 'Strokes happen like that. She wouldn't have known.'

'I miss her so much.'

'I know, but you can't go on grieving for ever, James. Life has to go on. She would want you to get on with living, you know she would.'

'She was so full of life, so eager and curious about everything.'

She touched his shoulder gently. 'Don't idealize her, my dear. She was only human like the rest of us.'

For the first time she could remember Dorothy saw anger in his eyes. 'She was wonderful – she loved me.'

Dorothy drew her hand away. 'Oh yes, there was never any doubt of that, but she was no angel.'

James glared at her. 'Just what do you mean by that?'

Dorothy shrugged. 'Only that she had feet of clay just

like anyone else – that's what made her rounded and human. She wasn't perfect.'

'Don't say that – to me she was.' He stood up sharply and was about to turn away. 'If you're referring to her trips to London, forget it,' he muttered. 'I know about them. I always knew.'

Dorothy stared up at him. 'You knew? Did she tell you?'

He turned away. 'She didn't need to. Anna was transparent to me.'

He stared out of the window. 'Whatever she did, she always came back to me. She knew she could be sure of my love. Anna was mine, and she loved me. I'll never marry again.'

'I wouldn't dismiss it too lightly,' Dorothy said softly. 'You're young still.'

He shook his head. 'There'll never be anyone else.'

Dorothy's voice was no more than a whisper. 'Anna and I were very close, you know. We were very much alike.' James stood silent. Dorothy took a breath and went on. 'James, I could never say anything while she was alive – I loved her too much – but now—' She hesitated a moment. 'I know I couldn't replace her but perhaps in time you could let me into your life a little.'

He came quickly back across the room and put a hand on her shoulder. 'Don't say any more, Dorothy, please. You'll only get hurt.'

She hung her head. 'I think perhaps it might be best if I left,' she murmured at last.

'I think perhaps it might.'

'But you see,' Ellen murmured, rubbing her chin on her knees, 'nowadays there's so much more openness about things; we're more liberated, people can talk about anything.'

Dorothy smiled. 'And you think we didn't? Look, why don't you talk to Lisa – she's your age, and she's a good listener.'

375

'I'm going to,' Ellen replied. 'Mother was lucky – she had Dad – they were very close.'

Dorothy looked down at the girl's tousled head. 'You missed her very badly, didn't you? We all saw the change in you.'

Ellen's voice was barely audible as she sat with her forehead pressed against her knees. 'It wasn't only Mother's death. It was a bad time. I thought my life was over.'

'Such a tragedy,' Dorothy sighed, 'just when she had everything to live for. I used to be so envious . . .'

'You envied her?' said Ellen. 'You were well-off – she had to struggle for a long time.'

'But she was rich in other ways – she had two beautiful children and a husband who adored her. I'd have given my right arm . . .' Dorothy's voice tailed away, then she sat upright. 'But what about that phone call – if you leave it much longer it will be too late.'

James could see her fair head bobbing along the platform towards him and at once he felt as clumsy as a schoolboy on his first date.

As she came to the barrier, a smile on her face, he still didn't know whether he ought to give her a fatherly peck on the cheek or gather her up in his arms like a lover.

Lisa resolved the problem. She took his arm and handed over her case. 'Hello,' she smiled. 'Boy, am I glad to get off that blessed train. It was packed.'

The suitcase was light – she evidently wasn't planning to stay long. He looked down at the bouncing hair, blown about by the breeze, feeling the warmth of her arm against his chest as she walked close beside him. Outside on the street she paused.

'Let's not go up to the house yet,' she said. 'I'm not ready to face Ellen – not till we've talked.'

'She isn't there,' James replied. 'She's not coming home from Dorothy's until tomorrow.'

She nodded. 'All the same, let's talk out here.'

Letting go of his arm she swung off into the lane towards the wood and he followed, down among the trees until the village was lost to sight. In a moment he knew she'd turn and speak. He steeled himself.

They reached the clearing. The pool lay dark and inscrutable under a leaden sky, its surface rippling in the breeze. Lisa stopped on the bank. James put down the suitcase.

She was looking down into the murky depths. Her words came out clipped and precise. 'We can't go on like this, James. We have to make a decision, one way or the other.'

'Yes,' he said gravely. He wouldn't prompt her; the choice must be hers.

Squatting, she pulled at a reed. 'The way I see it, we have two choices. Either I fetch Gladys now and get out of your life . . .'

There was an alternative? Hope leapt in him. 'Or?'

She straightened and looked him squarely in the eyes. 'Oh for God's sake – you know what the alternative is. If you want me I stay and we face it out, together.'

He could feel his body tremble. 'And which do you want?'

She planted her hands on her hips. 'Do you have to ask? More than anything I want to stay with you. I love you.'

He felt he could explode with joy. 'The point is,' she murmured, 'do you want us to go on?'

For a moment he couldn't speak, he put his arms around her and held her close. 'I want you,' he said gruffly. 'I love you.'

Her kiss was warm with the tenderness of a child mingled with the passion of a woman. Happiness invaded every pore of him as they stood close in the shadow of the trees, their fused reflection breaking up and spreading over the pool.

She lay warm and trusting against his chest. 'You have to be sure, James,' she murmured. 'You're the one who'll have to put up with the gossip in the village. It's you they'll point the finger at.'

'I don't give a damn,' he muttered. 'If they don't know me by now . . . There's only one person who matters. If Ellen understands . . .'

Lisa broke away and looked up at him, an earnest look in her eyes. 'Let me talk to her, James, please. I want so much for everything to be right between us.'

'It won't be easy.'

'I know, but let me try.'

He picked up the suitcase. 'OK. Now let's go home. There's someone I want you to meet . . .'

She frowned. 'I thought there was no-one at Jericho but us?'

He smiled and drew her arm through his. 'I don't think you'll find he's any trouble. All he'll want is a cuddle and a biscuit.'

When Lisa awoke early morning sunlight was filtering into the room, giving promise of a fine day. The hollow where James had lain was still warm. Nearby she could hear the sound of running water.

Swinging her legs out of bed she padded, naked, to the shower room and stood leaning against the door-frame. Through the glass she could see him, his head thrown back as the water splashed down his body. She felt so full of love for him she could burst.

'James.'

He stepped out, rivulets of water running down his body, his hair darkly plastered to his forehead. 'Lisa, love.'

He pulled her close, kissing her with the ardour of a lover who'd been long away. His skin was warm and wet against hers, trickles of water dripping down on her breast. At last he straightened.

'Promise me you'll always say good morning like

that,' he said with a smile. 'I can take any amount of it.'

He reached for a towel. Lisa leaned against the doorframe again and folded her arms. 'You know, I watched you shower once before,' she said softly. 'A long time ago. You never knew.'

He grinned. 'There's probably a lot I don't know.'

'I remember thinking how like your son you were.'

He stopped towelling and looked at her. 'Like David?'

'Do I ever remind you of Anna?'

'No.' He came close and held her by the shoulders. 'You mustn't ever think I love you because of Anna. Yes, there's something in common – guts, a positive attitude – but you're very different. I love you for what you are, Lisa.'

She smiled, reaching up to kiss the tip of his nose. 'And I you. Now what are we going to do on our last morning alone together?'

He threw the towel on the laundry basket. 'What would you like to do?'

'I must move my stuff to another room until we've talked to Ellen.'

'Right. What then? Go for a ride on the moor? The horses could do with some exercise.'

Smiling mischievously, she tugged him firmly by the arm. 'Blow them – turn them loose and let them exercise by themselves. I've got a better idea . . .'

Ellen sat on the edge of the bed, her eyes glittering and her voice brittle with anger. 'You're in love with my father?' she echoed in disbelief. 'You can't be – you're my age – it's unthinkable!'

'Look,' said Lisa gently, 'I know it's hard to understand and I don't blame you for feeling shocked – a lot of people will be – but we love each other. It would make us so happy if you—'

Ellen leapt to her feet. 'If I gave you my blessing?

379

How could you? It's unnatural, a man his age, and a girl who was living with his son. What on earth is he thinking of?'

She was staring out of the window. Lisa could see her fingers twisting the necklace at her throat. 'He's been a long time on his own,' she murmured. 'He deserves to be happy.'

Ellen swung round, anger burning in her eyes. 'But not with you – for heaven's sake, it's damn near incest!'

'I know,' Lisa said shortly, 'but what are we going to do about it?'

'What do you mean, we? It's got nothing to do with me!'

'It's got everything to do with you!'

Ellen threw her hands up in the air. 'What are people going to think? A girl half his age—'

'I know, but it's a fact – you can't just tidy it away in a drawer because it's inconvenient.'

'Why not? Other people have to. You're stubborn – you're wilfully setting out to ruin things!'

'I have to be stubborn. When you want something this much you've got to fight for it.'

'I don't want to hear about it! It's abnormal – the very thought of it disgusts me.'

'I know, I agree it's ridiculous, but what can we do? I love him, and he loves me. We'd like to be married.'

'He was married.'

'I'm not asking you to see me as your stepmother, Ellen. I'd like us to be friends.'

Ellen buried her face between her hands. 'I don't want any part of this,' she said thickly. 'Please go away and leave me alone.'

'It won't change things,' Lisa said quietly. 'There's no other way out. I love him.'

Ellen turned suddenly and flung her arms around Lisa. 'I love him too!' she cried. 'And I wanted to love you!'

For a moment Lisa stood dumbfounded. Ellen's face was buried in her neck. 'Don't do it, please, Lisa,' she sobbed. 'I don't want a mother – I wanted a sister. I needed you – I needed you so much . . .'

Lisa was getting supper ready in the kitchen when James found Ellen sitting alone in the dark of the music room. She sat on the stool, her back to the piano, looking like a silver-grey wraith in the half-light.

'Don't put the light on,' she muttered as he reached for the switch. He could tell by her muffled tone that she'd been crying. He stayed, motionless, by the door.

'Ellen—'

'Don't talk to me,' she said. 'I can't bear it.'

'I have to. Lisa wanted to explain first, because she cared—'

'Cared?' There was bitterness in her tone. 'For herself, that's all. So long as she got what she wanted.'

'It's what I want too, love,' he said gently. 'The last thing in the world I want to do is hurt you, but I love her.'

Ellen's voice came small and strangled in the darkness. 'I can't bear the thought of you and her together. I keep getting this horrible image in my head . . .'

'You like her, don't you? You said so yourself.'

'That was before I knew.' Ellen's voice grew hard. 'You kept that dark, the two of you.'

'We didn't plan to fall in love – it just happened. It just sort of grew. I hoped you'd understand. You and she have so much in common.'

'I thought we had – I was beginning to think of her as my sister – you've robbed me of that! I feel so alone, shut out . . .'

James came a step closer. The piano stood between them. 'Nothing will ever change how I feel about you, love. You ought to know that.'

'You love her!'

'Love isn't a finite quantity to be shared out, Ellen.' His fingers strayed along the surface of the piano. 'I loved your mother too, and always will. Lisa understands.'

Ellen stood up abruptly. 'How can you talk about Mother and her in the same breath?'

'Ellen, please try to understand.'

'I can't! I won't!'

James sighed. 'She means so much to me, but she won't have me if you're dead set against it—'

She turned and blazed at him. 'I don't want her putting the responsibility on me! If you do this thing, on your own heads be it, not mine!'

James made a move towards her, but she backed away. 'It's been a shock to you, I know,' he murmured. 'Let's leave it for now – we'll talk about it in the morning.'

Ellen took her belongings and the puppy over to the new wing. She couldn't bear to sleep in the old part of the house where the two of them had gone to bed. In separate rooms, but even so . . .

She was angry with herself. She'd made a fool of herself, pouring out her news the minute she arrived home, with all the excitement of a child who'd been away on holiday. With hindsight now she could see they'd only feigned interest. She ought to have been aware of the artificial atmosphere, the electric charge in the air which should have given her a clue. Dad and Lisa had spoken little to each other, and kept a distance between them. She ought to have sensed that something was odd.

She heard the church clock strike two and still sleep refused to come. The puppy scrambled on to the bed and nuzzled a cold nose against her cheek. Ellen threw back the covers and let him snuggle down beside her. The little body quivered in delight as she stroked the velvet of his back.

'She's with him, and it's all wrong,' she told the puppy. 'I was so glad to see her. Now it's all spoilt.'

She buried her face in the soft fur, unable to stem the tears. 'What am I going to do? I've made a complete fool of myself, pouring out everything like that. I'd started to trust people again – but now she's let me down. How long will it be before Ravi does the same?

'Oh God, I'm all mixed up, I'm angry and disappointed and hurt – I'll explode if I don't pour it out to someone.'

The puppy looked up, a forlorn expression in his brown eyes, as she slithered out of bed and knelt by the side, her hands clasped and tears still trickling from under closed eyes. 'Dear God,' she prayed, 'help me to sort out this confusion in my head before I go mad.'

The puppy whimpered and staggered across the bed to lick the salt tears running down her cheek. She curled her arms about him. 'Why the hell am I praying to Him?' she wept. 'He never listens. He doesn't exist. A real God would never have let David die or let this happen.

'Or that night . . .'

THIRTY-NINE

1969

Morning came at last with bright, cold clearness but still the angry words of last night kept on playing over and over in Ellen's head, and she saw again the frustration in Lisa's eyes. *'I know, I know, but it happened and there's nothing I can do about it, can't you see?'*

'You can – you could get out of his life!'

'Do you think I haven't thought about it? Don't you think he has too, knowing how hard it would be for you, whoever he brought home?'

'But you – of all people!'

'Look, I'm not going to try and persuade you – I'm just telling you how it is.'

And then Dad, his eyes all tender and full of pain. This morning their off-hand manner made it only too agonizingly obvious that they were trying hard, behaving with an air of forced casualness to one another, and the tension in the air was almost tangible. They were picking their way with care in her presence, like children venturing on to a half-frozen pond. The atmosphere was electric. At any moment she would crack under the strain and cry out.

The kettle was humming to a crescendo. Lisa stood at the sink, drying dishes. 'How about a coffee?' she suggested. 'The kettle's boiling.'

'Here, let me,' said James as she reached for the coffee jar. Ellen saw his hand momentarily touch Lisa's, saw the girl's quick upward glance at him before she moved her fingers away.

Ellen's chair scraped the floor noisily as she jumped

up and headed for the door. She couldn't bear to be in the house with them any longer.

Thelma twisted her head this way and that in front of the mirror, readjusting the net veiling on the little blue hat. She turned to her husband.

'What do you think, Fred?'

He lowered the *Reynolds News* an inch or two. 'What about?'

'Me new hat – do you like it?'

He retreated behind the sports page. 'Nay, don't ask me, lass. I know nowt about these things. See what our Kelly says.'

Thelma clicked her tongue. 'I'm asking you – do you think it really suits me? Does this blue go with my hair?'

Fred lowered the newspaper again. 'It's fine. Where is she?'

Thelma pulled the veiling further down. 'Upstairs last I saw.' She turned to her husband. 'I tried again this morning but she still won't tell who the lad is. I doubt we'll ever find out. You know her – once she's made up her mind there's no shifting her. She's every bit as stubborn as you.'

Fred ignored the jibe. 'You're going to be late – it's a quarter to already.'

Thelma threw an anxious glance back over her shoulder at the clock on the mantelshelf. 'It never is! Good Lord – Kelly!'

At that moment the door opened and her daughter shuffled in, still wearing the threadbare dressing gown and pink fluffy slippers she'd worn at breakfast. Her mother gave her an anxious shove.

'Come on, love, be sharp or we shall be late. I hate having to slip in at the back once the vicar's started.'

Kelly picked up a magazine and slumped on to the settee. 'I'm not going to church,' she muttered.

Her mother stared. 'Why ever not?'

'They'll only stare at me.'

Thelma touched the girl's shoulder. 'Come on, don't be daft. You've got to hold your head up, stop folks talking.'

The girl thrust out a sullen lip. 'They're talking already.'

'How do you know?'

'They all stop talking the minute I come in, that's how.'

Thelma's tone grew exasperated. 'You just get ready and come with me – put that nice red jacket on you bought out of your wages last week – it's lovely, and you haven't worn it yet.'

Fred laid the newspaper aside. 'Go on, do like your mam says. Best to put the lie to any gossip.'

'I don't want,' growled Kelly.

Her father stood up and pulled on his jacket. 'You heard me – get yourself dressed and back down here sharp. We're all going to church together.'

'Do I have to?' Kelly grumbled, but she got slowly to her feet.

'You heard me,' her father said sternly, and the girl slouched out of the room.

Thelma stared admiringly at her husband. 'You're never going to church?' she murmured. 'You've not been in years.'

'Ah well, this is different,' he said.

She snatched up the clothes brush from the sideboard. 'Well you're not going looking like that,' she admonished him affectionately, flicking the brush across his shoulder. 'I'll not have you letting the side down. You just hold still while I shift that dandruff off your collar.'

'I hope you don't mind me just turning up like this,' Ellen said huskily, 'but I had to see you.'

Ravi stood on the doorstep of the cottage, looking down into her troubled eyes. She was clearly upset about something. 'Come in,' he said gently, holding the door wide. 'I am always happy to see you.'

She stood hesitantly in the little hallway as he hung her coat over the newel post. 'You're not on call, are you?' she asked.

'I am – Dr Whitaker's away in the Lakes for the weekend, but it's all right. Come inside.'

He led the way into the living room. She stood uncertainly in front of the fire. 'I don't want to be in the way—'

'You're not,' he assured her. 'On Sundays it's almost always quiet. Please, sit down.'

She smoothed her skirt behind her knees and sat, her back straight but her gaze not meeting his. She was a graceful woman, he thought once again, with the lithe, easy movements of the women back home. If it wasn't for the pain in her eyes, the suspicion of tears . . .

'Coffee?' he said softly. She shook her head. She needed time; he would not hurry her. For a few moments she gazed into the fire, her fingers twisting folds in her skirt.

'I feel ashamed to tell you what's on my mind,' she said in a low voice.

He wanted to reach out and touch her hand by way of reassurance, but she would flinch. Instead he spoke encouraging words. 'I have heard many things in my job, Ellen. Nothing will surprise me. Pretend you are talking to yourself.'

She closed her eyes and took a deep breath. 'It's about my father – and Lisa.'

'Yes?'

She shook her head, as if trying to shake into some kind of order the confused thoughts tumbling inside. 'I don't know – just when I was looking forward to coming home and seeing her again—'

'Lisa?'

'I didn't like her much at first, when David was

387

alive, but I spent all week at my aunt's thinking about the two of us and finally came to terms with all the bad vibes between her and me . . .'

'That's good.'

'Maybe it was selfish of me but I needed someone – I thought she would be my sister. I lost my mother, and I'd almost come to love her like a sister, but now . . .'

She buried her face in her hands and fell silent. Ravi leaned close. 'What is it, Ellen? What has happened?'

Her head jerked up. 'She comes home and flings this in my face – she wants to marry my father!'

'I see.'

'He's too old for her! She was his son's lover! What are people going to think?'

Ravi spread his hands. 'My father married a much younger woman – my mother – after his first wife died. They were very happy.'

'That was different,' Ellen muttered.

'Why different?'

He saw the flicker of embarrassment in her eyes. 'You have different customs. My father will be a laughing-stock.'

Ravi shook his head. 'If they truly love each other you must admit he is very brave to fly in the face of custom.'

Ellen's lips tightened. 'That's as maybe. Anyway, she won't have him if I don't agree – it's damned unfair to put the responsibility on me.'

'If they were selfish they'd just go ahead and do what they wanted. You have the opportunity to show how unselfish you can be . . .'

Ellen chewed her lip. The way she looked caught at his heart, so small and defenceless. He could hear the tremor in her voice. 'It's not that easy,' she murmured. 'You think I'm being petty, don't you?'

'If your father's happiness matters to you . . .'

Her eyes darkened. 'He ought to be ashamed of himself,' she muttered.

'For being human?'

She gave him a quick, angry look. 'For being so stupid. You're missing the point, Ravi – she and David were lovers, dammit – how could he even think of marrying her? It's as good as incest!'

Ravi leaned his elbows on his knees. Now she was coming to it. 'Is that how it seems to you?' he asked. 'Tell me.'

Her eyes were fixed on him. 'Yes I'm afraid it is,' she said quietly, rising to her feet, 'I can't help the way I feel. The very idea is loathsome, it repels me, and I'm going to tell them so.'

He was helping her on with her coat, then suddenly he let his hands fall on her shoulders, and she did not shrink away. 'Look,' he said urgently, 'it's been a shock – why not wait a while, give yourself time to consider. Why not stay and have lunch with me?'

She turned and looked up at him. 'To be honest,' she said slowly, 'I'm in no hurry to go back into that house, not yet.'

'Then stay. You're very welcome here.'

She gave a slow smile and shrugged the coat off her shoulders. 'Why not? Tell you what,' she added eagerly, 'let me cook for you.'

He took the coat and slung it over the banister. 'I've got a better idea. Why don't we do it together?'

Outside the village church a young woman lifted her baby from the pram while Mrs Tattersall prattled on.

'I thought happen you hadn't heard yet. Mrs Spivey overheard young Kelly talking to the receptionist in the surgery, so we know it's a fact.'

Mrs Roberts bunched the baby under her arm and rooted around in the pram for his dummy. 'I never hear owt, out in Barnbeck,' she murmured. 'Still, I'm not surprised, the way she was going on.'

'Only thing is,' Mrs Tattersall went on eagerly, following the younger woman into the porch, 'I haven't found out yet who the lad is.'

Mrs Roberts shook her head. 'The way she hung about with them lads from the youth club it could be anybody.'

'I reckon so,' muttered Mrs Tattersall, disappointed. 'I just thought as how you going to Mothers and Toddlers club, you might have heard summat.'

The young woman pushed the door open and went in. Mrs Tattersall followed glumly. 'I fancy it's that young Gary meself. Funny how he suddenly shot off to work in Leeds like that.'

The Dent family sat near the back of the church on purpose.

'That way,' Thelma had said, 'not so many folk can stare without turning round and drawing attention to themselves. Mind you, I had intended to sit down at the front so as everybody could see my new hat.'

'Told you you should have come on your own,' muttered Kelly. 'Anyway, it looks daft.'

Her mother's mouth fell open. 'It does not – it matches my bag and shoes a treat.'

Kelly gave a grunt. 'It doesn't go with your hair with that red in it.'

'You should have told me at home.'

'You should have asked.'

Fred nudged his daughter as the vicar emerged from the vestry. 'Shut up, the service is starting.'

Dorothy's voice was trembling with excitement. James held the telephone close to his ear, at the same time watching Lisa through the window as she emerged from the stables, duster in hand.

'Antonia will be thrilled to bits,' Dorothy was enthusing. 'I'm going to ring her in a moment.'

James tapped on the window and beckoned. Lisa

390

came in through the kitchen and stood, puzzled, in the doorway. He held out his free arm and she came to him, nestling under his shoulder.

'I've just been cleaning Gladys up,' she murmured.

'Are you still there?' Dorothy queried.

'I'm here,' said James. 'Just tell Lisa, will you?'

Lisa took the phone. 'It's in the paper,' Dorothy said excitedly, 'a review of the exhibition – you know, the one David's pictures are in. In a national paper too!'

'Yes?' said Lisa, catching the urgency in her tone. 'What does it say?'

'Listen, I'll read some of it. "In this exhibition of young British talent the most eye-catching work is without doubt the *Girl in the Shadows*, by David Hemingway."'

Lisa caught her breath. 'How did you know the title?'

'There was nothing on it,' Dorothy replied, 'so Antonia chose it, for the sake of the catalogue. Rather apt, I thought. Anyway, listen, it goes on: "This work has a quality rarely seen in a painter so young, a sense of stillness and peace, and at the same time the shadowy figure under the tree endows the work with mystery and magic. It is as though the artist were gifted with a glimpse of another reality, another level of perception granted only to the few. Perhaps it was the artist's impending death which lent him this heightened vision. It is a tragic loss to the world of art that Hemingway should die before he could reach his full potential."'

James's arm tightened about her. 'That's wonderful,' breathed Lisa. 'Just what he deserved.'

Fred sang the hymn with deliberate gusto.

> *'Breathe on me, breath of God,*
> *Fill me with life anew . . .'*

He glanced down at the tight-lipped girl seated between him and Thelma and stopped singing. It wasn't God's breath which had filled her, and he wished like hell he knew who it was. He'd beat the living daylights out of the young swine.

The organ droned to a halt. The vicar climbed ponderously up the steps of the pulpit, opened the book on the lectern and took his time arranging meticulously the sleeves of his surplice.

'Dearly beloved brethren,' he intoned when he was finally satisfied, 'it gives me great pleasure to see so many of our faithful flock here today despite the inclemency of the weather . . .'

Thelma wasn't listening as he launched into his sermon. She felt regretful that, sitting where she was, no-one could appreciate the dainty blue hat. She'd make a point of stopping to chat on the way out, never mind the chilly breeze.

'Lust.'

She pricked up her ears at the one word which filtered through her consciousness. The vicar was leaning on the pulpit rail, waving a plump arm.

'Thou shalt not covet thy neighbour's wife,' he declaimed. 'The sins of the flesh are to be abhorred, my children. Adultery and fornication reduce man to the level of beasts.'

Kelly watched the plump fingers curled around the edges of the Bible. Those were the fat fingers which held out the pound notes to her yesterday. '*Your wages, my dear.*' They were moving slowly up and down the spine of the Bible, just like he stroked me, she thought angrily, slavering like a bloody animal while he did it.

'We must be strong,' the Reverend Bax went on smoothly, 'fighting off temptation whenever it presents its evil face.'

That intrusive fat finger wagged. Kelly fidgeted and snorted.

'Only by show of that strength,' said the vicar, 'does man distinguish himself from the animals.'

Kelly wriggled from buttock to buttock. Those ugly fingers again, like slimy, fat slugs which had squirmed so often between her thighs as he lowered his horrible greasy weight over her . . . She felt sick and swore under her breath.

Her mother gave her a sharp glance and frowned. 'What's up with you?' she whispered crossly. 'You should have paid heed to this before.'

Kelly scowled. 'I can't stand any more. I'm off.'

She made to move. Her mother grabbed her arm. 'Just you sit still – whatever's the matter with you?'

The girl's face grew scarlet. 'It's not what's wrong with me,' she snapped. 'It's him!' She leapt to her feet, pointing at the figure in the pulpit. 'It's him,' she cried out, 'telling folk what to do, after what he done to me!'

Bodies shifted uncomfortably. Faces turned to stare, puzzled and annoyed. Reverend Bax hesitated only a second before going on.

Fred laid an anxious hand on his daughter's arm. The girl shook him off.

'Who does he think he is,' she yelled, 'him a vicar and doing things to me he never ought? He's the animal!'

'Kelly!' Fred's voice was alarmed and fearful. 'What the devil do you think you're playing at? Sit down and shut up!'

Kelly turned a fierce look on him. 'Ask him,' she cried, pointing towards the pulpit, 'ask him what he's playing at, interfering with young girls like me? Go on, ask him!'

The vicar stood transfixed, his ruddy face paling. 'Please sit down,' he said with an air of calm authority, but the pudgy fingers shook. 'We'll forget all about this outburst if you will sit down quietly, and I will announce the next hymn.'

Scenting his fear, Kelly pushed past her father and

out into the aisle. 'You haven't denied it,' she shouted, waving her fist at the vicar as she marched towards him. 'Cos you can't, can you? How you have the nerve to say all that stuff, knowing what you done – it's all your fault – you're the one who got me into trouble!'

Bewildered faces looked from the girl standing defiantly in front of the pulpit to the vicar. His plump features reddened. 'What utter nonsense,' he said quietly, but there was alarm in his eyes. 'How could you tell such a wicked untruth?' He straightened up and squared his shoulders. 'However, let us continue. Turn to page sixty-seven of your hymnal . . .'

Fred hurried down the aisle, seized his daughter's arm and began to hustle her out. She struggled to get free.

'He makes me feel sick with his great fat belly!' she screamed.

The organ began to wheeze. Pages fluttered and voices began to sing uncertainly. Thelma, an embarrassed smile of apology touching her lips, pushed past the others in the pew. Above the music Kelly's receding voice could be heard sobbing as her father dragged her out.

'It is true – he kept on doing it, he wouldn't stop! He's the one who put me in the family way! He's a horrible, dirty old man and I hate, I hate, I hate him!'

FORTY

1969

Kelly was still screaming and crying hysterically when they reached home. Thelma too was in floods of tears.

'I'll bloody well never go back there again, bugger the wages!' howled Kelly. 'I can't tell you all the horrible things he did – or the things he made me do to him!'

'That's not true!' her mother exploded. 'How can you say such wicked things when he's been so good to you?'

'Good to me? You're joking!'

'He gave you a good job, didn't he? Paid you good wages? Where else would a girl your age get that much? I can't believe you could be that ungrateful and tell such awful lies.'

'I'm not telling lies, Mam – honest! It's been going on ever since I started there.'

'Then why did you never say nowt? Why did you go on working there?' Thelma demanded. 'If he was really doing what you said, why did you let him go on?'

'He threatened me – what choice did I have, for God's sake? Who'd have believed me?'

'You'd have told us,' Thelma sobbed into her hand-kerchief. 'You're not telling the truth, are you?'

Kelly wept loudly. 'You see, even you don't believe me! Dad – you know I'm not lying, don't you? Tell her she's wrong!'

Fred spread his hands helplessly. He could under-stand Thelma's suspicions but it was difficult to believe Kelly was lying. Lazy, mischievous she might be, but she never told any proper lies, and hazy doubts were beginning to simmer in his brain.

'I don't know what to think, love,' he said quietly. 'Only if you are lying, it's very wicked of you. The reverend's a man of the cloth, think on, and he's supposed to set an example to us all.'

'Why the hell should I make it up?' screamed Kelly.

'Cos you don't want to let on who the lad is,' raged Thelma. 'But blaming it on Reverend Bax – that's scandalous!'

Kelly began to howl even more loudly, beating the cushions with her fists. Fred stood impotent. He couldn't bear to watch the two of them with their ravaged, accusing faces, screaming abuse at each other, and it hurt not to be able to help either of them. Hysteria was something new to him and he couldn't cope.

He headed out of the door and up the street towards the doctor's house.

It was cosy, thought Ellen, sitting with Ravi at the small table, finishing off the last of the saffron rice and succulent, subtly flavoured vegetables. He too looked at ease in shirt sleeves, not the formal grey suit she'd always seen him wear before.

Unusual food with an unusual man. He'd seemed just as much at home in the kitchen. Never since Doris Brook's days at Jericho had she watched anyone cook so confidently and with such deftness.

'Like it?' he asked as she put down her fork.

'I could easily get used to it,' she smiled. 'It's very different from roast beef and Yorkshire pudding.'

He laid his napkin aside and rose to his feet. 'Speaking of pudding, I'll just go and put the apple pie in the oven.'

She looked up in surprise. He smiled. 'Not my work, I'm afraid – a gift from a patient. It won't take long to heat.'

She could hear him in the kitchen rattling a baking tray, opening the oven door. Suddenly the doorbell rang, and she heard Ravi go to answer. Voices murmured indistinct words, and a moment later he came back into the room, pulling on his jacket.

'I'm sorry – I have to go out, but I'll be back as soon as I can,' he said. 'Don't go – just stay and make yourself at home.'

She smiled up at him. 'I'll keep an eye on the pudding for you till you get back.'

This is what being a doctor's wife would be like, she thought as she heard the door close behind him, never knowing when he'd be called away, being prepared to delay meals and postpone social arrangements. No more the dull inevitability of an orderly, planned life where nothing exciting ever happened.

She carried the empty plates out into the scullery and ran the hot tap. She might as well do the washing-up while she waited. A wide, shallow pan lay half submerged under the water in the sink, the one he'd called a wok which he'd used to cook the rice. Alongside the gas cooker stood a row of spice jars with strange, fascinating smells. There would be so much for a European wife to learn . . .

The water in the tap ran cold. She found the immersion heater in the airing cupboard and switched it on, then went back to the living room.

She could remember this room from her childhood days when ancient Mrs Thewlis used to live here and Mother would bring her goodies at Christmas and harvest time. The low ceiling with its blackened beams, the small window with its tiny panes of glass – it couldn't have changed much since the old lady's days. It still wore its benign air of peace and warmth. Mrs Thewlis wouldn't recognize the television set or the electric fire glowing in the opening where her coal fire once burned but otherwise little had changed.

Ravi had evidently chosen to maintain the olde-worlde character of the place.

She ran a finger along the rows of books on his shelves, a varied collection of medical text books and astronomy, of psychology and philosophy. It pleased her to see how they were grouped according to subject, but her librarian fingers itched to arrange them in alphabetical order.

It was a comfortable room, but it still had a bachelor-bare feel about it. It needed more ornament to give it a homely touch. That small jade figurine on the end of the mantel was pretty. She moved it to the middle and stood back. It needed another piece alongside for balance, a vase of flowers, perhaps, or that pair of brass candlesticks at home they never displayed.

The carved wooden elephant on the bookshelves balanced the figurine beautifully. Standing back to admire it, she suddenly felt alarmed. She had no right to be doing this – it was intrusive of her. Hurriedly she replaced the elephant in front of the books.

Sinking into the armchair she leaned back and closed her eyes. The cottage had a wonderful atmosphere, wrapping its serenity and warmth about her like a cloak, soothing and healing. She'd almost forgotten the hurt which had driven her to come here today. This was what she wanted more than anything – a haven, and Ravi.

She could see him now, his slow way of smiling and cocking his head to one side as he listened, his manner as comforting as a caress, and there was a depth of wisdom in those dark eyes of his, as though they knew an inner peace. He was like a cool, clear fountain where she could drink and be for ever cleansed and renewed. If it hadn't meant it would probably drive him out of her life she almost felt she could have told him what she'd never spoken of to anyone . . .

The parish church clock struck half-past two and Ravi still wasn't back. The oven had long ago been turned off and Ellen sat by the fire with a book lying open on her lap but her mind was drifting.

It was odd, she thought, how being left alone in someone else's house made one curious, tempting one to explore, and the lure was even greater when the owner was as intriguing as Ravi. And he had invited her to make herself at home. He wouldn't mind if she had a quick peek upstairs.

She felt excited as she opened the bedroom door. It wasn't the snowy whiteness of the sheets or the subtle scent of jasmine in the air which made her shiver. Nor was it the neatness of the room with its oriental wall-hanging over the bed and the brush and comb lying on the dressing table. It was the thrill of being in his private room, where he slept and dreamed, where he lay thinking his innermost thoughts, inaccessible and alone. She was like a peeping Tom, playing the voyeur where she had no right to be.

There was a shameful thrill in opening the top drawer of the dressing table and touching a finger to the crisp white shirt. She remembered how, down in the kitchen, she'd watched him in his shirt sleeves while he cooked, the white of his sleeve gleaming against the coffee of his skin, and she'd longed to reach out and caress the hollow of his spine.

Images sprang to mind, a mental picture of him peeling off this shirt, amber skin glowing in the evening dusk, and she trembled. Then he would lie here, on this bed . . .

She kicked off her shoes and lay back, her head on his pillows, and closed her eyes. This was where she would lie if she were mistress here; this was where she would wait for him to come to her, arms outstretched . . .

She could feel his body lying close against hers, his lips on hers, and then they would make love . . .

Making love. Noises in the next room, animal noise, David and Lisa. Ellen caught her breath. Another image had thundered in, shattering her dream. Lisa and Dad. She'd almost forgotten them. They were probably at it right now, and the thought sickened her.

She struggled to push the fantasy away, to recapture the idyllic dream, but the horrible picture kept thrusting itself back into her mind again like the wrong channel on a television set.

It was no use. The images refused to leave. She curled herself up into a tight ball and began punching the pillows with her fist.

'It's all your fault, you bastard!' she moaned. 'You wrecked my life – if only you'd left me alone!'

Clifford Bax paced up and down his study, his brain racing and his knees still feeling rubbery. What on earth had possessed that stupid girl, coming out with it like that, in front of everyone? God, how the tongues must have babbled outside in the churchyard after he'd managed to get through to the end of the service.

He hadn't gone out to shake his parishioners by the hand afterwards the way he always did, or dared to come out to walk back to the vicarage while they were still around. He'd waited alone in the vestry, until the last knot of villagers had given up and disappeared, most of them probably to the pub where they'd carry on with their excited speculation.

Sweat began to break out on his forehead. He'd have to deny it, of course. He should have done so straightaway instead of saying they'd simply overlook the interruption and carry on. What a damn fool he was, letting a chit of a girl throw him into confusion like that.

Oh Christ, what were they all going to think, the

bishop and the landed worthies of his congregation? A hideous thought hit him in the pit of the stomach – he might not be collecting money from his wealthy parishioners any more . . . Unfrocked, sent away in disgrace . . . Just because he'd been so damnably careless!

He could kick himself. She was too tempting a sight, that was why, lying there on Sarah's bed, her naked little body all firm and pink and tight like a sucking pig, not Sarah's loose, pallid, plucked-chicken flesh. It was her fault, the juicy little temptress, a Jezebel sent to try him. He was only human, like other men.

God, if it reached the bishop's ears . . . He groaned and, wrenching open the cupboard, poured himself a stiff whisky and tossed back a mouthful. He stared unseeingly at the gilt tooling on his books. She'd done it on purpose, of course, the malicious little bitch, but why the hell should he let the whore rob him of a good living? She hadn't been a virgin when he took her – in all probability all the lads in the village had straddled her before he'd succumbed to her wiles.

An image sprang into his head – Kelly lying in the long grass, skimpy skirt hoisted around her waist, a queue of youths waiting, all hot and eager . . . Bax felt the icy panic in his guts beginning to transmute to a hardening glow . . .

He swallowed another mouthful of whisky and welcomed its comforting warmth. *Come on, you stupid fellow*, he scolded himself. *No need to panic – the game's not over yet. You're too bright to be brought down by a spiteful little tart. You can manufacture a convincing story – clear your good name, at the same time gently show her up as the desperate, malicious little slut she is.*

It wouldn't be too hard – would it? He could feel his new-found courage beginning to ebb. He drained the glass and peered through its base at the distorted room beyond.

Come on, of course you can do it.

I can't – I can still feel her solid little body wriggling under me.

Then put it from your mind, you fool – it's your living at stake. It never happened. Act like you've never acted before.

He squared his shoulders. He could do it. Acting was part of his job, and he hadn't been a leading member of the university drama society for nothing. He would simulate an air of compassion and hurt innocence as movingly as any Gielgud.

Oh yes, he told himself, refilling his glass to the brim, it shouldn't prove too difficult to win public sympathy. And rather than wait to be questioned, it would be far wiser to take the initiative.

Sitting down at his desk he pulled the telephone to him and dialled a number. It would pay to reach the most influential people in the parish before the tittle-tattle spread any further – the churchwardens, of course, Charles Hanson, the Brigadier, Mrs Calverley-Hines . . .

A voice answered. 'Ah Charles,' said Reverend Bax smoothly, 'about that little incident in church this morning – it's of no real consequence, of course, but I thought I'd just like to put your mind at rest. If you've a free half-hour this afternoon, I'd like you to come round for a glass of sherry – say about four? Fine. I'll look forward to seeing you then.'

All the six he rang were free that afternoon, as it turned out – or eager to learn more. Bax smiled as he pulled forward a sheet of paper and took out his fountain pen.

Just a few notes of the most telling phrases he would use. He could wriggle out of this yet.

* * *

Ravi let himself into the cottage, hoping she'd still be there. He found her in the living room, dozing in the chair by the fire.

'Sorry I took so long,' he murmured. 'I thought I'd be back ages ago.'

She gave him a warm smile. 'Was it serious?' she asked.

He gave her a long, searching look before he answered. It couldn't do any harm . . . 'Well, I suppose it'll be all over the village by morning – I might as well tell you.'

She listened intently while he told her, and he saw her eyes round like a child's. 'I've had to sedate both mother and daughter,' he concluded. 'They were both hysterical.'

Ellen was frowning. 'I'm not surprised,' she said quietly.

He nodded. 'No-one believes her, it seems – I'm not sure even her parents do.'

Ellen sat still, chin cupped in her hands. 'Poor Kelly,' she murmured. 'Oh, the poor girl.'

'Poor Vicar too if she's lying,' said Ravi. 'This could ruin his whole life.'

He went on talking, his eyes never leaving the bent figure before the fire, the smooth shine of her hair, the neat fingers curled across her cheek, like a child listening to a story. Only she wasn't listening. He was aware that his voice was settling softly over the room like dust, unnoticed.

Suddenly Ellen stood up and made for the door. 'I've got to go,' she said.

He followed her out into the hallway and held her coat while she slid her arms into the sleeves. 'Shall I walk with you?' he asked.

'Not this time, thanks,' she said with a firm shake of the head. 'I need to be on my own.'

*   *   *

Lunch lay only half eaten on the kitchen table in Jericho. Lisa watched James's tall figure silhouetted against the window as he stood looking out at the lead-grey sky.

'I wonder where the devil she's got to,' he muttered. 'She never stays out this long. It's not like her.'

Lisa tried to make soothing sounds. 'She'll be all right, love. She just needs time.'

He turned away from the window and came to sit beside her on the sofa. 'We were never able to talk, Ellen and me,' he said moodily. 'Talk properly, I mean. Ever since Anna died we've been distant, kind of locked in on ourselves.' He gave a short grunt. 'And they say grief brings a family closer.'

Lisa lay a hand over his and felt his fingers lock between hers. 'David brought you and me close,' she murmured.

His fingers tightened around hers. 'And I'm not going to let you go,' he said savagely. 'I lost Anna and David but I'm damned if I'll lose you.'

'You won't,' she said with an air of false brightness, 'not unless you kick me out.'

She heard the intensity in his tone in the dimming light. 'And I don't want to lose Ellen either.'

'I know.'

He reached up his free hand to lift her chin, gazing deep into her eyes. 'If only she were more like you – and Anna. I wish I could help her come out of her shell and take life by the throat.'

Lisa shook her head. 'Maybe you can – but the first move will have to come from her.'

Fred lumbered on, unaware of the brambles catching at his trousers or the chilly breeze whipping his cheeks to crimson. He only knew he'd had to get out into the fresh air, away from the venomous heat and accusation in the air at home. The women were quieter now, not screaming and carrying on any more once the doctor had seen to them, but Fred's brain was still reeling in confusion.

It was going to be a long time before the rift between mother and daughter could heal. He couldn't bring himself to believe Kelly any more than Thelma could, but he loved her too much to want to think she could be a liar. And why should she lie? She could have named any other man in the village and he'd have known exactly what to do – but Reverend Bax? He was a middle-aged man of God – could he really have laid hands on his sixteen-year-old daughter, his baby – Fred's brain veered away in revulsion from the idea.

But if it were true, how could a simple man like him take on the massive power of the church? He felt giddy and utterly confused, nausea clawing at his stomach. If only he'd been a clever man like Jim. Maybe he should have asked Dr Pillai to give him some of them tablets. Maybe then he'd be able to think more clearly . . .

He became aware that he was stumbling through the muddy ruts of a ploughed field – Top Field, Jim's land. Out of years of habit his steps had unwittingly led him towards Jericho and the one friend he knew he could trust. He had to talk to Jim before he went crazy . . .

FORTY-ONE

1969

Dusk was already stealing down from the hilltop to settle over the cottages as Ellen made her way through the village. No-one seemed to notice her as she passed, preoccupied as they were with the business of dragging indoors their prams and bicycles, drawing the curtains and switching on the lights.

She could imagine the gossip behind those curtains. Those who hadn't heard the latest titbit of news already would certainly have learnt of it by the time evensong was over. Poor Kelly Dent – pregnant at her age, suffering the ignomiy of being disbelieved, even by her own parents, alone and defenceless, and called a liar into the bargain . . .

The lights glimmering in cottage windows fell away behind her. Ellen walked on with purposeful step. She felt good. For the first time in years her mind was crystal clear, as though she'd bathed in a mountain torrent and washed away all the doubts and fears and morbid internalizing which had clouded it for so long. She'd come to a decision; life had a purpose.

As she rounded the corner of the churchyard she could see in the gloom between the trees the tall outline of the old vicarage and the light gleaming in a downstairs room. The Reverend Bax was at home, probably eating his Sunday tea alone before getting ready to conduct evensong.

A man's figure hurried along the street in the other direction and turned in at the vicarage gate. He was short and slight, clearly not the Reverend Bax. She saw him disappear up the path and let himself in at the door.

She paused at the gate, fingering the rusty spike on the iron rail, and looked up at the thin trail of smoke spiralling upwards from the chimney like a pious prayer. But a prayer for what? Silence and hypocrisy, or courage and the truth?

The Reverend Bax could feel his confidence growing. He'd taken pains to put his half-dozen visitors at their ease in his drawing room, each ensconced in a comfortable chair with a glass of his best sherry in hand. The worried, slightly sceptical look on their faces was starting to give way to perplexity and the occasional nod of understanding.

He put on his most genial, compassionate tone. 'I feel very sorry for poor Kelly, of course,' he murmured, waving an expansive hand. 'We must pray for her. She's not a bad girl.'

Mrs Calverley-Hines laid aside her glass. 'The whole village knows how loose she is,' she said. 'Her parents seem quite unable to control her.'

'Indeed,' agreed Forbes, the churchwarden, who'd been the last to arrive. 'It was only a matter of time before this happened.'

The Brigadier frowned. 'But why accuse the vicar – I mean, dammit, she must have some basis for such an accusation.'

'The ravings of a girl half out of her mind with worry,' said Bax smoothly. 'The child is more to be pitied than reviled.'

'It's slanderous,' said Mrs Calverley-Hines. 'You could sue.'

The Brigadier snorted. 'She'll maybe sue him for paternity. Still, she'll hardly be able to produce witnesses.'

This had gone far enough, thought Bax. But for the Brigadier things were going his way. 'To tell the truth,' he said hesitantly, 'I don't think the girl really knows what's going on – I think she lives in a fantasy world of her own.'

Charles Hanson came out of his reverie and looked up at the vicar. 'I must say, her story does sound rather far-fetched . . .'

'Of course it is.' Bax wagged a plump finger. 'And you know what, I think it may go even deeper than we realize.'

He paused for a moment, aware of the air of expectancy in the room, then put his empty glass down. 'There's something I'd like to show you,' he said quietly, hoping his tone would excite the right air of mystery. 'Please come with me.'

He took his time climbing the stairs with slow deliberation, knowing they were trooping behind like sheep. At the door of Sarah's room he paused.

'I think this is going to surprise you,' he said. 'It certainly shook me.'

He could feel the throb of curiosity behind him as he went into the room and crossed to the wardrobe. The others eased themselves, rather self-consciously, into the room.

'Look,' said Bax, flinging the wardrobe door wide. 'This is my wife's wardrobe.'

They all stared at the rail of multi-coloured dresses and skirts, blouses and jackets, the lime-greens and oranges, the royal blues and purples.

'Goodness gracious!' exclaimed Mrs Calverley-Hines, elegant fingertips to her mouth. 'What appalling colours!'

'These are not Sarah's clothes,' said Bax. 'And look here.'

He lifted the box from the bottom shelf and laid it on the bed. The men stared at the bottles and jars.

'What is all that stuff?' asked the Brigadier.

Mrs Calverley-Hines picked up one of the bottles and inspected the label. 'Make-up,' she said in wonder. 'Woolworth's.' She looked back at the vicar. 'Are these Kelly's things?'

He gave a grave smile. 'I fear so. I only discovered them today.'

'But why?' asked Hanson. 'Why would she put them here? I don't understand.'

The vicar shook his head. 'Who can explain the workings of a simple mind under stress? The only conclusion I can come to is that in some strange way she wanted to move in. Come and look at this.'

He led the group along the corridor to the bathroom, pulled open the linen cupboard and took out a plastic bag. 'I found this stuffed behind the water tank. It contains some of Sarah's clothes.'

Forbes's watery eyes stared wide. 'You mean – Kelly took them out of the wardrobe – and put her own clothes in?'

'So it would seem,' replied Bax. 'She had every opportunity, working here. And in hindsight I realize other things – the way she took to coming round to clean far more often than was necessary – she even used to come back at night, letting herself in without my knowing. Now I discover all this . . .'

He waved a bewildered arm. 'The girl's crazy,' muttered the Brigadier. 'Why the devil should she do a thing like that?'

The vicar gave a sad shake of the head. 'I've come to the sad conclusion that she wanted to get rid of Sarah – and did so, in her head. She knew Sarah had gone away and I believe the poor, deluded girl actually imagined herself taking Sarah's place as my wife.'

There was a gasp from his audience which gratified the vicar. He moved around the group towards the stairs. 'Yes, it's very disturbing,' he said smoothly. 'Let us go down and talk about it over another drink.'

In the drawing room they regrouped in silence while he poured more sherry. Hanson nodded his thanks as he took the glass from him.

'But even if what you say is true, Vicar,' he said dubiously, 'surely the girl couldn't imagine you responsible for her condition. Why didn't she name the real father?'

Mrs Calverley-Hines cut in. 'Maybe she was trying to protect one of the village boys, divert attention from him,' she suggested.

The Brigadier nodded. 'Diversionary tactics – good thinking.'

Bax gave a considering shrug. 'Perhaps, but it seems to me far more likely she truly believes it was me, poor child. She'd put herself into Sarah's shoes.'

'She needs her head examined,' snapped the Brigadier. 'Professional help – that's what she needs.'

'She certainly does,' agreed Hanson. 'Otherwise she could cause a lot more harm with her lies.'

Bax felt elation beginning to stir. He'd got them right where he wanted them. Everyone was sitting comfortably now and had a full glass. Now for the clincher, the final, mortal blow he'd been saving to the last, just in case any tiny flicker of doubt remained.

'I'd like to tell you all something,' he said quietly, laying his glass aside, 'something I've never told a soul, not even my best friend.'

Glasses paused halfway to lips. Faces focused on him expectantly. Bax bowed his head and took a deep breath. 'You all know my wife went away, to visit her sister you were told. But I don't think you were taken in – anyone with any sense knows she wouldn't stay away this long, however ill her sister, without good reason. The truth is, my wife left me.'

He paused for dramatic effect, his head still bowed. He could feel the stir in the room, saw the quick exchange of glances. Adopting just the right degree of hoarseness he went on. 'Maybe I should have told you before, but I hadn't the heart. You all know we never had children, Sarah and I. It was by no

410

choice of our own, I assure you. We would have loved a family, but it was impossible. This is why my wife left me.'

Head on chest, he could still feel their eyes fixed on him. He heard Hanson's disbelieving whisper.

'Mrs Bax left – because you didn't have children?'

'Our marriage was one of companionship only,' said the vicar in broken tones. 'My fault. I have a disability which has resulted in impotence.'

He heard the Brigadier's horrified gasp, heard a glass clatter on the table. He did his best to conjure tears to his eyes, to repress a sob.

Mrs Calverley-Hines laid a gentle hand on his sleeve. 'You didn't have to tell us this, vicar. We know how much it must hurt.'

'You had to know,' he moaned. 'I owed you that much.'

Hanson cleared his throat. 'Terribly sorry about this, Reverend, but we're very honoured by your confidence.'

The Brigadier growled agreement. 'Indeed, we feel privileged. Hell of a thing for a man to admit – can't help admiring the way you've handled it.'

Bax turned his face to the wall, trying to hide the smile of triumph. He'd got them now. Their sympathy was almost embarrassing. By morning Mrs Calverley-Hines would have spread this tantalizing secret all round Thaxton. He'd got these yokels in the palm of his hand.

Pulling himself together he took out his handkerchief and blew his nose. 'So you see,' he said with an air of deep sadness, 'poor Kelly picked on the wrong person to accuse. It couldn't be true of an impotent man.'

'Liar,' cut in a cool voice from the doorway. 'You loathsome, hypocritical liar. You raped me.'

Bax turned, bereft of words, to see the Hemingway girl standing in the doorway. He almost choked.

411

'What are you doing here?' he demanded, trying to keep the panic from his voice . . .

She came forward into the middle of the room and he could see the faces turned, the wide eyes watching her. 'I came to see you, vicar,' she said, 'but I'm glad you're here, Brigadier, and you, Mrs Calverley-Hines and Mr Hanson. What I have to say concerns you all. Everyone should know what kind of man they have as their spiritual mentor.'

Bax rose to his feet, towering above her but his guts reeling in panic. 'Now look here, I think you should leave,' he said severely. 'This is a private meeting. You have no business here.'

Her eyes looked up at him coolly. 'Oh yes I have,' she countered quietly. 'It's my business if you call Kelly a liar. You're the one who's lying. I know she's telling the truth because you did the same to me. Remember?'

'Rubbish,' exclaimed Bax. 'You're talking utter nonsense.'

'At just the same age,' the girl went on. 'I was sixteen too. I know how she's feeling – dirty and slimy, no self-respect left. She'll hate herself for ever, and all because of you.'

Faces were turning from the girl to him and back. He was unable to keep his voice from trembling. 'You don't know what you're talking about,' he said. 'Please leave at once.'

'That's what you did to me,' she went on, the calm in her eyes giving way to venom. 'You ruined my life. And now it's Kelly, and who knows, maybe we aren't the only ones. Maybe there are other young girls you've fouled.'

Panic exploded in his head like a sunburst. 'No, no, that's not true!' he said sharply. 'Get out!'

She gave a sly smile. 'You mean there were no others – only Kelly and me? Isn't that enough?'

He tried to protest but the words only spluttered in

412

his throat. She turned away from him, smiling at his guests. 'I'm glad to have had the opportunity to show you your vicar in his true light,' she said confidently, 'for the scheming, hypocritical lecher that he is. Now I've said my piece I'll be happy to get out of this place.'

As she made for the door she looked back over her shoulder at Bax.

'You disgusting little toad, you make me feel sick,' she hissed, and walked out.

The night air felt cool and fresh and clean on her face and her step was buoyant as she walked up the rutted lane towards Jericho.

Maybe she'd burnt her boats now as far as Ravi was concerned. Maybe he wouldn't want to know a woman who was shop-soiled, but Clifford Bax had been exposed at last for what he was and soon the whole village would know, and there was bitter triumph in the thought.

But the real triumph lay in having spoken of the rape at last. After all this time she'd got it out of her system, and the relief was incredible, like drawing a splinter out of a festering wound. Now the pain was eased, the poison dissolving away. She felt cleansed and renewed. She was strong now; she had been honest with herself and was a whole woman again.

She closed her eyes and thought of Ravi. Now she could imagine lying with him, without shame or disgust. If he still wanted to know her . . .

She pushed the thought aside as the familiar long, low lines of the farmhouse loomed out of the darkness. Rain was beginning to fall. She laid a hand on the familiar rough, wet wood of the gate and lifted the latch eagerly. Dad would be anxious. This was where love always lay waiting.

*　　*　　*

The vicar sat slumped in a chair, his heart thundering. They'd all gone and left him alone, leaving behind them a vapour of disbelief and scorn.

That damn girl – she couldn't have come at a worse moment, just as he'd got it all sewn up. She was a respectable young woman, they'd said, well-educated, a librarian. James Hemingway's daughter was no village chit like Kelly Dent. They'd clearly believed her.

She was evil, that one – she'd been the cause of the trouble between him and Sarah, the reason why Sarah had gone cold on him all those years ago. Between her and that little bitch they had him cornered. She-devils, the pair of them, that's what they were – sent to lure him from the path of righteousness and bring about his destruction.

So what the devil was he to do now? Sick anxiety gnawed at his guts. What would the bishop do once he got to hear – as he undoubtedly would now?

The villagers would hear of it first – and the Dents – oh God! What of them? What if Fred Dent came round? Everyone knew him as a quiet, gentle fellow but he was built like an ox and in a towering rage he might not be so gentle . . .

Bax shivered. Tonight he'd be safer out of Thaxton. He must get away from here – a hotel, anywhere, away from the danger. He leapt up and made for the door. An empty wineglass rolled off the side table to the floor as he lumbered up the stairs and into Sarah's room where the suitcases were kept on top of the wardrobe.

The wardrobe. That little tart's kaleidoscope of brash colours. He scooped up an armful, wrenched them off the rail and flung them on to the bed . . .

Fred sat hunched by the fire while James poured whisky into a glass.

'I just don't know what to make of it, Jim,' he

muttered. 'Our Kelly's not a bad lass as a rule, but this tale of hers has me beat. They're both in a bad way, Thelma and her.'

Lisa came to sit by him. 'You did the right thing, calling the doctor,' she said. 'You'll all be able to think better in the morning.'

Fred groaned. 'Ay, and then it'll start. They'll all be talking – soon there'll be a trail of folk calling round.' He took a sip of the whisky. 'Oh hell, I wish I knew if she's telling the truth or not. I'd kill the bugger.'

James put a hand on his shoulder. 'I know how you must feel – I'd feel the same if it was my daughter. She wouldn't lie to you over something as big as this, would she?'

Fred hugged the glass between chapped hands. 'But the vicar, dammit – he's old enough to be her father.'

Lisa glanced up at James just as the door opened and Ellen came in. Her cheeks were flushed and her eyes glowing. James went to her, holding out his arms.

'Ellen, love – where have you been?'

She peeled off her coat and flung it over the back of a chair. 'I've been to the vicarage,' she announced. 'To prove that Kelly was telling the truth. I told them all how he raped me too.'

James gasped. Lisa saw his knuckles whiten as he gripped the back of a chair. 'Raped you?' he echoed. 'When?'

'When I was sixteen.' Ellen perched herself on the edge of the table. 'I should have told you years ago, Dad. He kept me back one day after Sunday School. Mrs Bax came in and caught him. It was horrible. I hated him, the way Kelly must be hating him now.'

James stared at her, her head held defiantly high.

'He made me feel dirty,' she muttered. 'I hated him so much I had the most evil thoughts. I cursed him to Hell, I wished him dead. Then Mother died and my whole world collapsed around me.'

'Why didn't you tell me?' James's voice was a hoarse whisper. Ellen shrugged.

'I don't know – I was going to but, well, Mother died suddenly just two days after. I felt somehow it was my fault, my curse on him had backfired on me. You looked so ill – I'd done that to you. I couldn't tell anybody then.'

For long seconds there was silence except for the crackle of the fire and the sleeping puppy snuffling in his basket. 'Now they all know,' Ellen muttered, 'Hanson, the Brigadier, the Hines woman – they were all there.'

Lisa came close and touched Ellen's arm. 'That took some doing,' she murmured, 'coming out with it now. Well done.'

She turned to James. He was sitting, head bowed, his shoulders heaving. Suddenly he rose and left the room. Lisa gave Ellen an anxious look. 'I think one of us ought to go after him.'

'I don't know what else to say,' Ellen said quietly.

Footsteps rang along the corridor. James came back into the room carrying the Purdey. He sat down in silence at the kitchen table, his face grim, and, breaking open the breech, he began to load it.

Ellen came close. 'What are you going to do, Dad?'

He made no answer, just carried on loading.

'Why the gun?' Ellen persisted. 'You never use guns.'

His voice was thick with suppressed fury. 'I only use them for vermin.'

'No,' cried Lisa. 'You can't – I won't let you!'

The breech clicked shut. He stood up, kicking the chair away. 'Out of my way, Lisa. Don't interfere.'

Ellen made no move to stop him as he crossed to the back door. Lisa flung herself in front of him. 'No, James – don't do it! He's not worth it!'

She stumbled as he pushed her aside and hurried out into the night.

'Tell him, Fred—' She turned to appeal to the farmhand – but he was no longer there.

The girls rushed out into the yard. In the darkness rain spattered their faces as they heard his car rev up and speed away down the lane.

'We've got to stop him – he'll kill the bastard!' Lisa cried. She raced back into the house, snatched up the car keys from the shelf, and ran to where the barn door stood open. She leapt into the Mini's driving seat and switched on the ignition. Ellen scrambled in beside her. Nothing happened.

'Oh for God's sake, Gladys,' Lisa exclaimed, 'come on, don't let me down now.'

Again and again she tried, swearing under her breath, but the car refused to start.

'It's no use,' said Ellen. 'It's as dead as a dodo. He'll be there by now.'

Lisa clambered out. 'Come on, we don't want him in jail for the rest of his life – we've got to try and stop him before it's too late!'

Ellen hurried out into the yard after her. 'Listen, I'll ring Ravi – maybe he can get there in time . . .'

She raced back into the house and Lisa began to run down the narrow lane towards the village, oblivious of the rain and the mud sucking greedily at her thin shoes . . .

FORTY-TWO

1969

James drove like a man pursued by all the furies of hell. Black hatred was eating at his heart, a dense, unreasoning hatred.

'He raped me . . . he raped me.' Over and over the words thundered in his head. The bastard had laid his foul hands on Ellen, forced his vile body on hers – God, how she must have suffered all these years – in silence – and the swine had got away with it. Vermin, that's what he was, no better than the rats plundering the rickyard.

And all the while parading under a guise of goodness and piety. To think of the times he'd sat in Jericho, taking James's whisky and money, that unctuous smile on his flabby face – sat at his ease in Jericho, sleek and untroubled by what he'd done. James had a sudden vision of Ellen at maybe twelve or thirteen, scrubbed and scented for Sunday morning service, a picture of purity and innocence, standing at her mother's side outside the church door while the new vicar patted the child on the head and smiled.

James's stomach heaved into his throat. The slimy, despicable hypocrite! And to think he had believed she'd lost her faith because Anna died. He took one hand from the wheel and laid it on the Purdey at his side. A twelve-bore shotgun was hardly the weapon to kill a man neatly, but what the hell? Anna's gun to avenge Anna's child. There was a kind of poetic justice in it, and the rat deserved everything that was coming to him.

The car skidded on the wet leaves as it lurched round the corner by the church and slithered to a halt in the gutter. Lights were burning in the vicarage, one of them in an upstairs room. For a moment James sat staring up at it. Was it in that room Bax had laid his loathsome hands on the virgin Ellen? And maybe Kelly too? Was the rat still in there, skulking in his sewer?

He snatched up the Purdey and walked purposefully up the path to the front door and tried the handle. It opened, and he went inside.

There was no-one about. Then from upstairs he heard a scuffling and muffled shrieks and the sound of something heavy falling to the floor. Fred, dammit – he'd got here first.

He climbed the stairs and flung open a door. Beyond a garish heap of rags on a bed he saw Fred's broad back towards him, raindrops glistening in his hair. One brawny arm pinned the vicar to the far wall by his throat while the other punched him rhythmically in the face. The vicar's eyes were bulging in their sockets, blood was running from his nose, and his pudgy hands flapped helplessly.

'Stop, Fred!' James cried. 'Leave him to me!'

'He deserves it after what he done!' Fred gasped as he stood back, wiping his bloodied knuckles down his trousers. He jerked a thumb towards the bed. 'And just look what he done to them clothes – they must be Kelly's – cut 'em to shreds.'

He glared at the shaking Bax. 'There you are, Jim, you finish him off.'

James nodded. 'Ay, if anyone's going to swing for him, it's me.'

He raised the gun. He could see the blood oozing from the pulp of Bax's mouth, the terror-stricken eyes staring at him. Bax's hands rose to cover his face. Those hands, those thick, revolting hands on

Ellen's young body – Black hate enveloped him once again.

He heard Fred's startled voice at his elbow. 'For Christ's sake, what the devil are you doing with that? I mean, I know I've made a bit of a mess of him, but you'll splatter him all over the place. He's not worth it.'

Bax had slithered down the wall and was grovelling on the floor now, slobbering and whining like a whipped dog. What a miserable wretch he was, thought James, a pathetic apology for a man. Despite the fleshy body there was no substance. Slowly he lowered the gun.

'You're right,' he said quietly. 'He's not worth it. We don't need to kill him – he's dead already.'

Lisa splashed through the puddles as she raced up the path and into the vicarage. James and Fred were just coming down the stairs. There was blood on Fred's hands and James was carrying the gun. She stared up at him questioningly.

'It's all right,' he assured her. 'Bax is upstairs. He knows now how we feel.'

'What have you done to him?' she asked breathlessly.

James gave a wry smile. 'A bit cut up, but he'll live.' He touched a hand to her sodden hair. 'But you're wringing wet, love. Let's get you home, away out of this rat-hole.'

Lisa knelt by the fire, towelling her hair. The puppy crouched eagerly, waiting to tug at the towel each time it swung within reach of his jaws. Ellen sat tensely on the edge of the sofa.

'Stop it, monster,' she warned, then added to Lisa in a casual tone, 'So Ravi hadn't arrived when you left? It took me ages to get through to him – he'd been out on another call.'

'Did you tell him what happened?' Lisa asked.

Ellen shook her head. 'There wasn't time to go into explanations,' she said quietly. 'I just said I was afraid there might be violence and get there quickly. I thought we might have heard from him by now.'

She squared her shoulders and forced a smile. 'Still, he'll ring when he's ready. I'll give Dad a call.'

James was quiet over supper. He was only toying with his meal. Lisa eyed him thoughtfully.

'What are you thinking about, love?'

He shrugged. 'Oh, things.'

'Like what?'

He looked up at Ellen who was feeding titbits to the puppy on her lap. 'Bax,' he murmured. 'I nearly killed him.'

'Thank heaven you didn't, much as he deserved it.'

James laid his spoon down. 'The man's crazy,' he said wonderingly. 'Do you know, he'd cut Kelly's clothes into ribbons. They were all over the bed.'

Ellen put the puppy down on the floor and shooed him away. 'Well, I'm glad you didn't kill him,' she said. 'He's got to live with the consequences.'

'True,' said Lisa. 'Everyone will know what he's done.'

'So let him live with that if he can,' said Ellen.

Lisa laid a hand over hers. 'And what about you? It was very brave of you, speaking up like that.'

'What choice did I have? I had to be honest, even if belatedly, for Kelly's sake.'

James smiled at his daughter. 'More important, you've been honest with yourself.'

'At last. It took me long enough. All those years I let him damn near ruin my life. I couldn't let him do it to Kelly too.'

James pushed back his chair and stood up. 'Where are you going?' Lisa asked.

'To the gun room – make sure everything's locked away.'

As he passed behind Ellen's chair he laid a hand gently on her shoulder. 'You've been very brave, love,' he said quietly. 'I'm proud of you.'

James left the door open. The puppy raced out into the corridor after him and came back with a furry pink slipper in his mouth and carried it into his basket.

Lisa searched Ellen's face. She showed no outward sign of disquiet over what had happened. Maybe Bax's beating had somehow helped to atone for what he'd done, been some measure of expiation . . .

Ellen looked thoughtful. 'You know, I'd never been with anyone. It ruined it for me.'

'I'm sure it did.'

'I couldn't bear to think of lovemaking without feeling sick. I'm sorry.'

Lisa looked at her in surprise. 'What for?'

'Things I used to think about you and David. I could hear you in the next room. I was jealous too, because I had no-one.'

Lisa spread her hands. 'Well, that's understandable.'

Ellen's voice was low. 'I couldn't even bear to think of anyone making love to me. Now I think I can learn. I'm healed, I'm whole again.'

Lisa rose and came round the table, laying a hand on her shoulder. 'You've come a long way, love. Your father has every reason to be proud of you.'

Ellen turned in her chair and hugged Lisa to her. 'I'm going out after what I want now, if he'll still have me,' she said. 'I'm going to fight, live my life to the full.'

Lisa gave her a squeeze. Ellen looked up at her, her eyes warm. 'I won't blame you for doing the same,' she added quietly.

Lisa held her breath. Was she saying what they wanted so much for her to say? Ellen nodded.

'Make my father happy,' she murmured. 'He deserves that. I don't want him to live with guilt the way I had to.'

The phone rang just as James came back along the corridor. Ellen waited, fingers crossed, watching Lisa's vain attempts to make the puppy obey her.

'Sit, you monster,' she was saying, pressing the wriggling little haunches down. 'You heard me, sit!'

The puppy leapt away, panting and eager to continue the wrestling. In the hall the telephone tinged as it was replaced. James came into the kitchen.

'Ellen,' he said softly, putting his hands on his daughter's shoulders, 'it's Ravi. He's seen to Bax. He wants to see you.'

She looked at him anxiously. 'Did he say anything?'

'Only that he's coming round.'

Alarm leapt in her eyes, then she tried to cover it with a smile. 'Right,' she said brightly. 'I'll put the fire on in the music room.' As she turned to leave she whispered to Lisa, 'Is my hair tidy? Do I look all right?'

'How did he find out?' Lisa asked.

James sprawled on the sofa beside her, his arm lying along the back. 'It'll be all over the village by now. There wouldn't be any shortage of people wanting to tell him.'

Lisa snuggled up close. 'Well, he hasn't rushed off again. They've been together down there for ages now.'

He stroked her arm. 'I'm glad you two managed to talk together,' he murmured. 'I think we're going to be all right.'

'Let's hope the rest of the world sees it that way,' she said.

'If they don't, to hell with them.'

She looked up with a mischievous smile. 'It's almost midnight – don't you think it's about time we found out what your daughter's up to?'

'You mind your own business.'

'I just want to know if it's working out for her. Maybe if I go and polish that doorknob . . .'

She wriggled out of his arms and tiptoed to the door, putting her ear close to the panel . . .

'It's a lovely room, isn't it?' said Ellen. 'Mother built it years ago. It's got a sort of melodic air about it, don't you think, as if chords of music have been sort of caught up and held in abeyance for a while.'

'It's a lovely idea,' said Ravi with a smile. 'You're a strange girl.'

She turned away, touching a finger to the wood of the piano. 'I used to think lots of thoughts like that,' she murmured, 'like thinking that buildings could soak up voices from the past, soak up vibrations into the crevices of the stone.'

'Held in abeyance too?' he asked.

'Yes – waiting to come back in another embodiment. Why not? We wouldn't have believed in tape recorders a few years ago.'

She turned to him, searching his face. She couldn't dodge the issue with small talk any longer. 'You've heard, haven't you?' she asked quietly.

'Yes.'

'And?'

'And I think I love you very much.'

Relief poured through every vein. 'Oh thank God!' She sank on to the piano stool. Ravi came close and kissed her on the forehead. She closed her eyes, savouring his gentleness.

'I lay on your bed today,' she murmured.

'Did you?'

'I pulled open a drawer and touched your shirts. Do you mind?'

'Not at all – I'm glad.'

'I just want everything between us to be out in the open.'

He stroked the back of her head. 'You'll never need to worry about what I think. You're safe with me.'

She lifted the piano lid and played an arpeggio. It rang false as she struck a wrong note. She looked up at him with a wry smile. 'I'll have to start practising again,' she murmured. 'There's so much I have to re-learn . . .'

'Come away from that door – she'll catch you,' James warned.

'Shush! I just want to be sure she and Ravi are getting on. I can't wait.'

Lisa was still half bending to listen. She held up a finger. 'She's playing the piano now,' she whispered. 'You said she hasn't done that for years.'

James patted the cushion beside him. 'For goodness sake, woman,' he smiled, 'come and sit down before she catches you.'

She shook her head. 'She sounds happy enough anyway – she's laughing.'

A blur of brown fur shot past her, a yard of nylon trailing behind it. 'Oh no!' she cried. 'You little sod – those are my new tights!'

James scrambled under the coffee table, trying to grab the elusive little body. The puppy darted out and cannoned, yelping into the door, catching Lisa off balance.

She dropped on him and held the squirming body tight.

'Got you, you little swine. Just look what you've done to my tights.'

He stared up at her, bewildered innocence in his eyes, one ear flattened to his head by the length of nylon still firmly tangled around his chest. She scooped him up and was reaching for the door handle to pull herself up, but the door moved away out of grasp. Ellen stood there with Ravi close behind her.

'What's going on?'

Lisa held out the length of laddered nylon. 'I'm sorry – I wasn't listening, honestly,' she stammered. 'It was him—' Then she caught sight of James, shaking his head with a mocking smile. 'Oh dammit, yes I was listening,' she admitted. 'I couldn't help myself. I just wanted to know how you two were getting on.'

Ravi laughed. 'It's a day for confessions, isn't it?' Ellen looked up at him. He touched her cheek. 'I've just told her I love her.'

'Join the club,' said James.

Ellen had gone out into the yard to see Ravi off. On the sofa James bent his head to kiss the tip of Lisa's nose.

'What a strange day it's been,' he said softly. 'It's incredible – this afternoon I could have been a murderer yet now I've never been happier.'

She leaned her head on his shoulder. 'David's girl in the shadows seems to have stepped out into the sunlight at last,' she mused.

He gave a deep sigh of contentment. 'Jericho's seen its share of troubles over the years, but somehow they always seem to work out in the end.'

'I know,' she whispered. 'I've always loved it here.'

He leaned back, folding his hands behind his head. Lisa sat forward, chin cupped in her hands, gazing thoughtfully into the dying embers of the fire. The puppy lay asleep in his basket, one stumpy back leg dangling out over the edge. A pair of torn tights and a chewed-up furry slipper lay alongside, forgotten.

'James?'
'What is it?'
She nodded towards the basket. 'Him,' she said. 'Who's going to get custody of him, I wonder?'

THE END

A DURABLE FIRE
by Brenda Clarke

Imogen and Anne Seymour had known the Haldane boys all their lives. Sons of a distinguished knighted actor, Christopher and Timothy were as handsome, as charming, and nearly as talented as their brilliant father. Imogen and Anne, especially when they were young, were quite dazzled by them. As they grew older, Imogen's childish passion turned into deep and obsessive love. There would never be anyone for her but Timothy Haldane, even though he seemed to have turned into a self-centred and neurotic young man, consumed with envy over his brother's success both in his career and with the one woman Timothy wanted.

But Anne, as she became more thoughtful and perceptive, found the charm of the two older Haldane boys fading. It was Richard, the youngest son, who suddenly became the impressive man of the family, quietly turning his back on the theatrical world in order to become a veterinary surgeon. He was to prove the abiding strength of both the Seymours and the Haldanes as one emotional conflict after another threatened to tear the families apart.

0 552 13952 1

PROUD HARVEST
by Janet Haslam

Hannah Critchlow, orphaned after a storm which carried away her beloved father and destroyed her home, was given refuge by the notorious Bunting family at their remote hilltop farm, Bunting's Tor. The three men of the family were feared and hated in the area: George, the autocratic and brutal patriarch; Jed, his profligate and much-favoured elder son; and Sam, the best and most steadfast of the three, who had to grow up believing that he was tainted because of his deformed hand – a deformity which had cruelly led the locals to rename the farm Bunting's Claw.

Sam had come to believe that no woman would ever want his love, and that no children would ever be born to inherit the great farmhouse and rolling acres. Only Hannah, proud and self-willed, could see the real Sam beneath his imperfect body, and only she could bring new love and hope to the doomed family.

0 552 14138 0

ANNIE
by Valerie Wood

Annie Swinburn had killed a man – the killing was timely and well-deserved, for Francis Morton had been evil in every possible way. But Annie knew that however justified her crime, only the rope and the gibbet awaited her if she remained in the slums of Hull. And so she ran – up river, along the wild and secretive paths of the great Humber – a new and unfamiliar territory which was to lead her into a new and unfamiliar life.

Her first refuge was with Toby Linton, well born, estranged from his father, and – with his brother Matt – earning a dangerous living as a smuggler. Annie led a double life, as smuggler, and as a pedlar roaming the remote countryside of the Wolds. It was this new existence which led her, once more, into allowing herself to love, in spite of all the things that had gone before.

But even as a newer, richer world began to overtake her, she could never forget the shadow of the man she had killed, and the family she had been forced to abandon.

0 552 14263 8

WITH LOVE FROM MA MAGUIRE
by Ruth Hamilton

From the very first meeting of Philly Maguire and Richard Swainbank, a pattern of overpowering love, conflict, hatred, and secrecy was born. For although Philly and Richard were on opposite sides of the mill floor, they recognized – both of them – that they were equally matched in strength of character and the capacity for overwhelming sexual passion.

Thus began the forty years of conflict between the two families – the Swainbanks, cushioned by wealth but tearing each other to pieces with the violence of their emotions – and the Maguires, proud, betrayed, and led by the vibrant and magnificent Philly.

A major saga of the Lancashire cotton mills – of the strong, violent, real people who both owned them, and worked in them – and of the dangerous things that love can do to families throughout the generations.

0 552 13616 6

A SELECTED LIST OF FINE NOVELS
AVAILABLE FROM CORGI BOOKS

THE PRICES SHOWN BELOW WERE CORRECT AT THE TIME OF GOING TO PRESS.
HOWEVER TRANSWORLD PUBLISHERS RESERVE THE RIGHT TO SHOW NEW
RETAIL PRICES ON COVERS WHICH MAY DIFFER FROM THOSE PREVIOUSLY
ADVERTISED IN THE TEXT OR ELSEWHERE.

☐ 14036 8	MAGGIE MAY	Lyn Andrews	£4.99
☐ 13718 9	LIVERPOOL LOU	Lyn Andrews	£4.99
☐ 13992 0	LIGHT ME THE MOON	Angela Arney	£4.99
☐ 14044 9	STARLIGHT	Louise Brindley	£4.99
☐ 13952 1	A DURABLE FIRE	Brenda Clarke	£4.99
☐ 13685 9	THE GOLDEN STRAW	Catherine Cookson	£5.99
☐ 13576 3	THE BLACK CANDLE	Catherine Cookson	£4.99
☐ 13688 3	THE OYSTER CATCHERS	Iris Gower	£4.99
☐ 13687 5	HONEY'S FARM	Iris Gower	£4.99
☐ 13897 5	BILLY LONDON'S GIRLS	Ruth Hamilton	£4.99
☐ 13616 6	WITH LOVE FROM MA MAGUIRE	Ruth Hamilton	£4.99
☐ 13872 X	LEGACY OF LOVE	Caroline Harvey	£4.99
☐ 13917 3	A SECOND LEGACY	Caroline Harvey	£4.99
☐ 14138 0	PROUD HARVEST	Janet Haslam	£4.99
☐ 14262 X	MARIANA	Susanna Kearsley	£4.99
☐ 14045 7	THE SUGAR PAVILION	Rosalind Laker	£4.99
☐ 13910 6	BLUEBIRDS	Margaret Mayhew	£4.99
☐ 13904 1	VOICES OF SUMMER	Diane Pearson	£4.99
☐ 10375 6	CSARDAS	Diane Pearson	£5.99
☐ 13987 4	ZADRUGA	Margaret Pemberton	£4.99
☐ 13636 0	CARA'S LAND	Elvi Rhodes	£4.99
☐ 13870 3	THE RAINBOW THROUGH THE RAIN	Elvi Rhodes	£4.99
☐ 13346 9	SUMMER VISITORS	Susan Sallis	£4.99
☐ 13545 3	BY SUN AND CANDLELIGHT	Susan Sallis	£4.99
☐ 14154 2	A FAMILY AFFAIR	Mary Jane Staples	£4.99
☐ 14230 1	MISSING PERSON	Mary Jane Staples	£4.99
☐ 14118 6	THE HUNGRY TIDE	Valerie Wood	£4.99
☐ 14263 8	ANNIE	Valerie Wood	£4.99